ANGELIQUE

Book Two

THE ROAD TO VERSAILLES

Seventeenth-century Paris—for the green-eyed, golden-haired Angélique, a city of terror and despair.

Penniless and deprived of title, sworn to kill the men who had caused her husband's death, Angélique plunges into the underworld—to the squalid Court of Miracles, home of the villainous, the degraded and the deformed—a world of violence and lust. Spurred by a relentless ambition, her only weapons her beauty and her courage, Angélique begins the slow climb back to wealth and power; and always before her the glittering court of the Sun King himself. . . .

SERGEANNE GOLON is a composite name for the two authors of ANGELIQUE—Anne and Serge Golon.

ANGELIQUE

(The Road to Versailles)

SERGEANNE GOLON

UNABRIDGED

Book Two

PAN BOOKS LTD : LONDON

By arrangement with

WILLIAM HEINEMANN LTD
LONDON

First published 1959 by Wm. Heinemann Ltd.
This edition published 1961 by Pan Books Ltd.,
33 Tothill Street, London, S.W.1

330 30052 0

2nd Printing 1962
3rd Printing 1962
4th Printing 1962
5th Printing 1963
6th Printing 1964
7th Printing 1964
8th Printing 1965
9th Printing 1966
10th Printing 1968

TRANSLATED BY
RITA BARISSE

Printed in Great Britain by Richard Clay (The Chaucer Press), Ltd.,
Bungay, Suffolk

CONTENTS

CHAPTER 51

ANGÉLIQUE looked at the face of the monk Bécher through the window. Indifferent to the thawing snow that was dripping from the roof on to her shoulders, she remained standing in the darkness outside the inn of 'The Green Trellis'.

The monk was sitting before a tin pitcher and drinking with a fixed stare. Angélique could see him quite distinctly, despite the thick window pane. The inside of the tavern was not very smoky. The monks and clerics who made up the bulk of the patronage of 'The Green Trellis' did not care much for the pipe. They came here to drink and, above all, to play draughts and dice.

"Hey, sister, you oughtn't to be outside on a night like this. Haven't you anything to toss into the pot?"

Angélique turned round to see who was addressing her in such a strange language, but she could not see anyone. Suddenly the moon emerged between two clouds and disclosed at her feet the squat shape of a dwarf. He was raising two fingers crossed in a peculiar way. She remembered the gesture the Moor Kouassi-Ba had shown her one day, saying: "Cross your fingers like this and my friends say: 'It's all right, you're one of ours.'"

Mechanically she made Kouassi-Ba's sign. A wide grin split the midget's face.

"You're one of the gang, I thought as much. But I can't place you. Do you belong to Rodogone the Egyptian, Toothless Jean, Blue Jacket or The Raven?"

Without answering him, Angélique turned away and began to stare at Friar Bécher again through the window. With a leap the dwarf jumped on to the window sill. The light from the inn lit his big face, above which sat a dirty felt hat. He had plump, round hands and tiny feet in canvas shoes.

"Where's the customer you can't take your eyes off?"

"Over there, the one sitting in the corner."

"Do you think that squint-eyed old sack of bones will pay you much for your trouble?"

Angélique took a deep breath. Life suddenly began to course in her veins again. At last she knew what she had to do.

"That's the man I must kill," she said.

The dwarf quickly passed a deft hand around her waist.

"You haven't even got a knife. How will you manage?"

For the first time, Angélique gazed attentively at this weird creature who had popped out of the pavement like a rat, like one of the loathsome animals of the night that invaded Paris with the gathering darkness.

She had been roaming aimlessly, wildly, in the night for hours. What instinct of hate, what hunter's flair, had led her to 'The Green Trellis', where she had recognised the monk Bécher?

"Come with me, Marquise," the dwarf said suddenly, jumping down to the ground. "Let's go to the Saints-Innocents. You can arrange with the fellows there how to bounce your pigeon."

She followed him unhesitatingly. The dwarf walked ahead of her with a rolling gait.

"My name is Barcarole," he said after a while. "Isn't it a pretty name, as pretty as me? Hoo! Hoo!"

He gave a sort of joyous whoop, cut a caper, then kneaded a ball of snow and mud, which he flung at the window of a house.

"Let's go, my pet," he went on, quickening his step, "or the chamberpots of these good burghers whom we've kept from snoring will come pouring down on our heads."

No sooner had he spoken than a shutter slammed and Angélique had to leap aside to avoid the shower he had foretold.

The dwarf had vanished. Angélique went on walking. Her feet got bogged in the mud. Her clothes were damp, but she did not feel the cold. A low whistle drew her attention to the mouth of a sewer. Out of its opening appeared the dwarf Barcarole.

"Forgive me for giving you the slip, Marquise, but I went to fetch my pal, Wood-Bottom Janir."

Behind him, a second squat figure extricated itself from the sewer-hole. He was not a dwarf but a legless cripple, a trunk of a man sitting in an enormous wooden bowl. In his knobby hands were two wooden handles by which he propelled himself from one paving-stone to another.

8

The monster scrutinised Angélique. He had a bestial face, sprouting with pimples. His sparse hair was carefully combed back over his shiny skull. His only garment consisted of a sort of blue cloth tunic with goldbraided buttonholes and lapels which must have belonged to a noble officer. Wearing a high collar with an impeccable stock, he was an extraordinary sight. After peering at the young woman for a long time, he cleared his throat and spat at her revoltingly. She stared at him in amazement, then wiped herself with a handful of snow.

"It's all right," said the cripple, satisfied. "She's respectful. She realises whom she's talking to."

"Talking! Hm! That's one way of putting it!" exclaimed Barcarole. He burst into his whooping laughter. "Hoo! Hoo! Aren't I witty?"

"Give me my hat," said Wood-Bottom.

He put on a felt hat adorned with a handsome plume. Then, gripping his wooden handles, he started off.

"What does she want?" he inquired after a moment.

"Someone to help her bounce an enemy."

"That might be arranged. Who does she belong to?"

"Can't find out. . . ."

Gradually, as they proceeded through the streets, other figures joined them. First she heard whistles coming from dark recesses, rising from the riverbanks or from the depth of courtyards. Then beggars would appear, with long beards, barefoot, in wide, tattered capes, old hags who were mere bundles of rags tied with string and big rosaries, blind men and cripples who would swing their crutches over their shoulders to walk faster, hunchbacks who had had no time to remove their humps. Genuine paupers and invalids mingled with the bogus beggars.

Angélique found it hard to understand their thieves' talk studded with quaint terms. At a crossroads a group of armed killers with swaggering moustaches came up to them. She thought they were soldiers or perhaps even watchmen, but she quickly realised that they were just bandits in disguise.

Recoiling at the sight of the newcomers' wolf eyes, she glanced backward and saw herself encircled by these hideous shapes.

"Afraid, my pretty one?" said one of the bandits, putting an arm around her waist.

9

She slapped his arm down and said no. And as he per-severed, she slapped his face. This produced a commotion during which Angélique wondered what would happen to her. But she was not afraid. For too long, hatred and revolt had been smouldering in her heart, were concentrating in an over-whelming urge to bite, claw, scratch eyes out. Thus hurled into the bottom of the abyss, she found herself in natural harmony with the wild beasts that surrounded her.

The queer Wood-Bottom was the one who eventually re-stored order with his authority and his frantic bellowing. This truncated man possessed a booming, sepulchral voice which sent a shudder through those around him whenever he used it, and he finally prevailed.

His vehement words quashed the quarrel. Looking at the killer who had started it, Angélique saw that his face was furrowed with rivulets of blood and that he was holding a hand over his eyes. But the others were laughing.

"Oho! She's settled your account, the wench!"

Angélique heard herself laughing too, with an unfamiliar, provocative laughter. So it was no harder than that to tread the depths of hell? Fear? What was fear? A non-existent feel-ing. It was all right for those Paris burghers who trembled as they heard the beggars of the underworld pass beneath their windows on their way to the Churchyard of the Saints-Innocents to see their prince, the Great Coesre.

"Who does she belong to?" someone asked again.

"To us!" roared Wood-Bottom. "And let everyone take notice!"

He was allowed to take the lead. None of the beggars, not even those with a nimble pair of legs, tried to overtake the human trunk. As they approached a steeply mounting street, two of the bogus soldiers, called *drilles*, rushed forward to lift the cripple's bucket-base and carry him up.

The stench of the district became all-pervading and horrible. Meat and cheese and rotting vegetables in the gutters, and over all the reek of putrefaction; it was the district of the Halles, the central market, sealed by that dreadful flesh-eater, the grave-yard of the Saints-Innocents.

Angélique had never been to the Saints-Innocents although this gruesome place was one of the most popular rendezvous in Paris. One even met great ladies there, who came to choose their books or lingerie among the shops set up under the charnel-houses. It was a familiar sight in daytime to see elegant noblemen and their mistresses strolling from arcade to arcade, carelessly pushing aside stray bones or skulls with the tips of their canes, while chanting funeral processions passed by.

At night this privileged spot, where, traditionally, no one could be arrested, served as a refuge for rogues and ruffians, and libertines came here to choose their partners in debauchery among the bawds.

As they were approaching the precincts, whose crumbling wall gave access to the interior at several spots, a crier of the dead came out of the main gate, dressed in his long black gown embroidered with skulls and crossed bones and silver tear-drops. On seeing the group, he said placidly:

"I can inform you that there is a dead man in the rue de la Ferronnerie. Some poor are wanted for the procession to-morrow. Everyone will get ten *sols* and a black smock or coat."

"We'll go, we'll go," cried some toothless old hags.

They were on the point of proceeding forthwith to the given address, but the others berated them and Wood-Bottom roared once again and abused them copiously:

"Damnation! Who in hell's name do you think you are to pursue your bloody business while the Great Coesre is waiting? What the devil am I doing with such a miserable bunch of hags? What are manners coming to? . . ."

Shamefaced, the harridans hung their heads and their chins quivered. Then they all slipped into the graveyard through one hole or another.

The crier of the dead walked away, shaking his little bell. At the crossroads he stopped, raised his face towards the moon, and chanted mournfully:

> "Hark all ye who're asleep in bed,
> Pray God for the dead. . . ."

Angélique walked, wide-eyed, through the vast area with its centuries-old throng of corpses. Here and there wide common graves gaped, already half full with corpses sewn into their shrouds, and waiting for a new contingent of bodies before being closed. Stone slabs placed directly on the ground marked the graves of the more well-to-do families. But this was the graveyard of the poor. The nobility were buried at Saint Paul's.

11

The moon, which had at last decided to rule over a cloudless sky, now illuminated the thin film of snow which covered the roofs of the church and the surrounding buildings. The Croix des Bureaux, a tall metal crucifix, standing near the Preacher's Pulpit in the centre of the yard, gleamed softly.

The cold mitigated the nauseous stench. Anyhow, nobody seemed to attach any important to it, and Angélique herself breathed with indifference the decay-saturated air.

What drew Angélique's gaze and dumbfounded her to such a degree that she felt she was the prey of a nightmare were the four galleries radiating from the church, which formed the enclosure of the graveyard. These constructions dating from the Middle Ages rose above a basement formed by a cloister with vaulted arcades where the merchants set up their stalls in the daytime. But above the cloister were garrets covered with tiled roofs and resting, on the graveyard side, on wooden piles, thus leaving open bays between the roofs and the vaults. All these bays were crammed with bones. Thousands and thousands of skulls and pieces of skeletons were piled up there. Lofts of death, gorged with their gruesome harvest, they exposed to the eyes and meditation of the living an unbelievable stack of skulls; the air dried them and time reduced them to dust, but a new supply extracted from the soil of the graveyard ceaselessly replaced them.

All over the place, near the graves, she could see piles of skeletons arranged in bundles, or the sinister white balls of skulls, carefully stacked by the grave-digger, which tomorrow would be stored in the lofts.

"What . . . what is this?" stammered Angélique, to whom such a sight seemed incredible, afraid she might have gone out of her mind.

Perched on the tablet of a tombstone, the dwarf Barcarole eyed her quizzically.

"The boneyard," he replied, "the boneyard of the Innocents, the finest in Paris."

He added after a moment's silence:

"Where have you sprung from, girl? Never seen this before?"

She went and sat down beside him.

Ever since she had, almost unwittingly, belaboured the *drille*'s face with her nails, they had all left her in peace and did not speak to her. Whenever curious or lewd glances strayed towards her, there was always someone to offer a warning:

"Wood-Bottom says she is ours. Hands off, boys."

Angélique did not notice that the area all around her, which had been almost deserted when they arrived, was gradually filling up with a formidable, tatterdemalion crowd.

The sight of the boneyard held her spellbound. She did not know that this macabre taste for piling up skeletons was peculiar to Paris. All the big churches of the capital strove to compete with the Innocents. Angélique thought it was horrible and the dwarf Barcarole thought it was marvellous . He murmured:

> ". . . death at last before them rose.
> Oh! the pain of departing this world
> And knowing not whither one goes."

Angélique slowly turned towards him.

"You are a poet?"

"That's not me talking, but the little Gutter-Poet."

The flame flared up in her and revived her.

"You know him?"

"Do I! He is the poet of the Pont-Neuf."

"Him, too, I want to kill."

The dwarf leaped up like a toad.

"Hey! Easy there! He's my pal."

He looked around, taking the others to witness, and tapped his forehead.

"She's mad! She wants to bounce everybody!"

There was a sudden clamour, and the crowd opened to make way for a weird procession.

In the lead walked a very long, lean individual, whose bare feet trod the slushy snow. An abundant white mane hung to his shoulders, but his face was hairless. One could have taken him for an old woman, and perhaps he wasn't a man, despite his hose and ragged tunic. With his jutting cheekbones, lustreless, glaucous eyes deep-set in their hollow sockets, he was as sexless as a skeleton and very much in keeping with this lugubrious setting. He was carrying a long pike from which dangled the impaled body of a dead dog.

Next to him a fat little man, also beardless, was brandishing a broom.

After these two strange standard-bearers came a hurdy-gurdy grinder, who was busily turning the handle of his instrument. The musician's originality consisted in an enormous straw hat which reached down almost to his shoulders. But he had cut a hole in the front part of the brim and his mocking eyes could be seen gleaming through it. He was followed by a child who was lustily drumming on the bottom of a copper basin.

"Would you like me to tell you the names of these very famous gentlemen?" the dwarf asked Angélique.

He added with a wink:

"You know the sign, but I can see you aren't one of us. The ones you see out in front are the Big Eunuch and the Little Eunuch. The Big Eunuch has been at death's door for years, but he never dies. The Little Eunuch is the keeper of the Great Coesre's women. He is carrying the emblem of the king of the underworld."

"A broom?"

"Hush! Don't make fun of it. That broom can do a thorough house-cleaning. Behind them are Thibault the hurdy-gurdy man and his page, Linot. And here come the king of the underworld's ladies."

Under their grimy bonnets the women he pointed out showed the bloated faces and deep-ringed eyes of prostitutes. Some were still good-looking and they all cast insolent glances around them, but only the first one, an adolescent, almost a child, had some freshness. Despite the cold, her bosom was bared and she proudly exhibited her young, full-blown breasts.

There followed the torch-bearers, the sword-wearing musketeers, the beggars and bogus pilgrims of Saint-Jacques, and then, with creaking axles, there appeared a heavy wheelbarrow which was pushed by a giant with vacant eyes and a prominent lower lip.

"That's Bavottant, the Great Coesre's idiot," the dwarf announced.

Behind the idiot a white-bearded personage closed the procession, clad in a black gown whose pockets bulged with parchment scrolls. From his girdle hung three rods, an ink-horn and some goose-quills.

"That's Jean the Greybeard, the Great Coesre's archhenchman, the one who lays down the law of the kingdom of the underworld."

"And where is the Great Coesre himself?"

"In the wheelbarrow."

"In the barrow?" repeated Angélique, flabbergasted.

She hoisted herself up a little to get a better view. The wheelbarrow had come to a stop before the Preacher's Pulpit which was in the centre of the graveyard, raised by a few steps and sheltered by a conical roof.

The idiot Bavottant stooped and picked something up from the wheelbarrow, then sat down at the top of the dais and placed the thing on his lap.

"Good God!" sighed Angélique.

She was seeing the Great Coesre. He was a creature with a monstrous torso which ended in the scrawny white legs of a child of two. The powerful head was adorned with a hirsute black mane around which a dirty towel was wrapped which hid his scurvy scalp. The deep-set eyes under the bushy brows had a hard glint. He wore a thick black moustache, its tips raised like fangs.

"Hee! Hee!" Barcarole jeered, savouring Angélique's surprise. "You'll learn, my lass, that here, with us, the little ones rule over the big ones. Do you know who may become Great Coesre when Squat Rolin croaks?"

He whispered into her ear:

"Wood-Bottom."

Then, nodding his big head:

"It's a law of nature. It takes brains to rule over the rabble. And that's what is amiss when one has too much leg. What do you think, Lightfoot?"

The man called Lightfoot smiled. He had just sat down on the edge of the grave and he was putting his hand over his chest as if he were in pain. He was a very young man, with a gentle, simple look. He said in a breathless voice:

"You are right, Barcarole. Its better to have a head than a pair of legs. For when your legs give out, there's nothing left."

Angélique looked with surprise as the young man's legs, which were long and sinewy.

He smiled sadly.

"Oh! I've still got them but I can hardly move them any more. I was a runner for Monsieur de La Sablière; and then, one day, when I had covered almost twenty leagues, my heart gave out. And since then I can no longer walk."

"You can't walk any more because you've run too much!" cried the dwarf, cutting a caper. "Ho! Ho!"

"Shut up, Barco," growled a voice, "you're a pain in the neck."

A powerful fist grabbed the dwarf by his tunic and sent him rolling among a heap of bones.

"That misbegotten squirt is an awful bore, isn't he, my beauty?"

The man who had just stepped in bent over Angélique. Oppressed by so much deformity and horror, she found a kind of relief in the newcomer's handsomeness. She could not very well make out his face, which was hidden by the shadow of a wide-brimmed hat on which a meagre plume was stuck. She could guess, however, that he had regular features, big eyes, a well-shaped mouth. He was in the full flush of youth. His brown hand rested on the hilt of a short dagger fastened to his belt.

"Whom do you belong to, pretty wench?" he asked in an ingratiating voice, in which a faint foreign accent rang.

She did not reply and looked away disdainfully.

On the steps of the pulpit, in front of the Great Coesre and his giant idiot, someone had just placed the copper basin which had previously served the child as a drum. And the people of the *gueuserie* came forward, one after the other, to throw into the copper the levy exacted by their prince.

Everyone was taxed according to his speciality. The dwarf, who had moved close to Angélique again, informed her in an undertone of the ranking of all these beggar-folk which, ever since Paris had existed, had codified the exploitation of public charity.

He pointed out the *riodés*, who were respectably dressed and affected a shamefaced air as they held out their hands. They would tell passers-by that they used to be honourable folk whose houses had been burned down and whose property had been plundered in the war. The *mercandiers* pretended that they were former merchants stripped by highway robbers, and the *convertis* would confess that they had been smitten by divine grace and were going to become Catholics. After pocketing their premium, they would go and get converted all over again in another parish.

The *drilles* and the *barquois*, who were former soldiers, exacted alms with their swords, threatened and frightened peaceful burghers, while the 'orphans', small children who held each other by the hand and wept from hunger, sought to soften the citizens' hearts.

All these beggar-folk paid homage to the Great Coesre, who maintained order among the rival bands. *Sols*, *écus* and even gold pieces fell into the copper basin.

The dark-skinned man did not take his eyes off Angélique. He drew close to her, touched her shoulder lightly with his hand and, as she was about to shrink back, said quickly:

"I am Rodogone the Egyptian. I have four thousand people under me in Paris. All the passing gipsies pay me a levy, and so do the dark women who read the future in people's hands. Do you want to be one of my women?"

She did not answer. The moon was moving above the spire of the church and the boneyard. Before the Preacher's Pulpit the procession of real and false invalids was now passing, those who had crippled themselves deliberately in order to attract compassion and those who, when evening fell, could throw away their crutches and bandages. That was why their lair had been nicknamed the Court of Miracles.

They had come from the rue de la Truanderie, from the Passage du Caire, from the suburbs of Saint Denis, Saint-Martin and Saint-Marcel, from the rue de la Jussienne and Sainte-Marie-l'Egyptienne, all these bogus sick: the scrofulous, the ailing, the lame, the misshapen, the outcasts and, finally, the *frances-mitous* who, twenty times a day, collapsed dying at the foot of a boundary-post after tying their arm with a string to stop the beating of their pulse; and, one after the other, they tossed their dues before the hideous little idol whose sceptre they had accepted.

Rodogone the Egyptian put his hand once again on Angélique's shoulder. This time she did not draw away. His hand was warm and alive, and she felt so cold! The man was strong, and she was weak. She turned her eyes towards him and sought, in the shadow of his hat, the features of this face which did not inspire her with horror. She saw the gipsy's long eyes gleam like white enamel. He uttered a curse between his teeth and leaned heavily towards her.

"Do you want to be a 'marquise'? Yes, I believe I'd go as far as that!"

"Would you help me to kill someone?" she asked.

The bandit threw his head back in a fearful, soundless laugh.

"Ten, twenty, if you like. You have but to point him out and I swear to you that before dawn he'll have spilled his guts on the pavement."

He spat into his hand and held it out to her.

"Shake! It's a deal."

But she put her hands behind her back, shaking her head.

"Not yet."

The other swore again, then stepped away but without taking his eyes off her.

"You're stubborn. But I want you. I'll have you."

Angélique passed her hand over her brow. Who was it who had said the same nasty, greedy words? She could not remember.

A brawl broke out among two soldiers. The beggars' parade being over, it was now the turn of the rogues. There appeared on the scene the worst bandits of the capital, not only cutpurses and coat-snatchers, but murderers for hire, thieves and pick-locks, and, mingling with them, profligate students, valets, former galley-slaves and a vast assortment of foreigners cast up by the hazards of war: Spaniards, Irishmen, Germans, Swiss, and gipsies too.

Suddenly, the principal henchmen of the Great Coesre cut a path through the crowd by lashing out with their rods and made their way towards the tomb against which Angélique was leaning. Only when she saw these ill-shaven men loom before her did she realise that they had come for *her*. The old man called Jean the Greybeard was leading them.

"The king of the underworld asks who this wench is," he said, pointing to her.

Rodogone passed his arm peremptorily round the young woman's waist.

"Don't move," he whispered. "I'll deal with this."

He pulled her towards the Preacher's Pulpit, holding her tightly all the while. He cast arrogant and yet suspicious glances at the crowd all around them, as if he feared that an enemy might appear and wrest his prey from him.

His boots were of fine leather and the cloth of his tunic had no patches. Angélique's mind recorded these details without her being aware of it. The man did not frighten her. He was used to force and fighting. She submitted to his hold like a vanquished woman who needs a master.

When he arrived before the Great Coesre, the Egyptian craned his neck forward, spat and said:

"I, Duc d'Egypte, take this woman for my marquise."

"No you don't," said a quiet, brutal voice behind them.

Rodogone wheeled round.

"Calembredaine!"

A few steps away in the moonlight stood the man with the violet wen who twice before had risen with a jeer in Angélique's path.

He was as tall as Rodogone and broader. His tattered clothes showed his sinewy arms and hairy chest. Well set-up, his legs wide apart, his thumbs stuck in his leather belt, he stared at the gipsy insolently. His athletic body was younger than his hideous face under its bushy grey shock of hair. Through the dirty strands gleamed his single eye. The other was hidden by a black patch. The moon shone full on him and behind him the snow glistened on the roofs of the charnel-houses.

'Oh! the horror of this place!' Angélique thought. 'The horror of this place!'

She shrank back towards Rodogone. The Duc d'Egypte was busily reeling off a string of abuse against his impassive adversary.

"Cur, son of a bitch, devil's scamp, carrion, this will finish badly . . . there is one too many here. . . ."

"Shut your trap," retorted Calembredaine.

Then he spat in the direction of the Great Coesre, which seemed to be the traditional mark of homage, and flung into the copper basin a heavier purse than Rodogone's.

A sudden burst of laughter shook the dreadful runt of a man sitting on the idiot's knees.

"I have a good mind to put this beauty up for auction," he cried in a rasping croak. "Let her be stripped so that the lads can judge the merchandise. For the time being Calembredaine is one up. Your turn, Rodogone."

The beggars yelled with delight. Hideous hands were reaching out towards Angélique. The Egyptian pushed her behind him and drew his dagger. At that moment, Calembredaine stooped and flung a round, white projectile which hit his foe on the wrist. The projectile rolled away. Horrified, Angélique saw that it was a skull.

The Egyptian's weapon had fallen to the ground. Calembredaine had him by the middle. The two bandits grappled so violently that their bones cracked. They rolled in the mud.

This touched off a frightful battle. The representatives of five or six rival bands of Paris hurled themselves upon one another. Those who had swords or daggers struck wildly and blood spurted. The others, imitating Calembredaine, picked up skulls and threw them like cannon-balls.

Angélique tried to flee, but forceful hands gripped her and brought her back to the pulpit, where the arch-henchmen of the Great Coesre held her tightly. The Great Coesre himself surveyed the battle, twirling his moustache.

Jean the Greybeard had seized the copper basin. The idiot Bavottant and the Big Eunuch were laughing in such a way as to make one's flesh creep. Thibault the hurdy-gurdy grinder turned his handle and sang as loud as he could. The old beggar women, who got jostled and trampled on, screamed like harpies.

Angélique saw a crippled old man with only one leg hitting Wood-Bottom's head with his crutch as hard as he could, as if he were trying to hammer nails into it. A rapier pierced his belly and he collapsed over the legless cripple.

Barcarole and the Great Coesre's women had taken refuge on the roof of a charnel-house and there helped themselves to the plentiful reserve of skulls to bombard the battlefield.

With all these strident screams, shrieks, groans, there now mingled the cries of the inhabitants of the rue des Fers and the rue de la Lingerie, who, leaning out of their windows, above this witches' cauldron, appealed to the Holy Virgin and clamoured for the men of the watch.

The moon was slowly moving down over the horizon.

Rodogone and Calembredaine were still fighting like mad dogs. Blow followed upon blow. They were of even strength. Suddenly there was a cry of amazement which spread in widening ripples. Rodogone had vanished as if by magic. Panic and the fear of a miracle gripped these unbelievers. But he could be heard to shout. A blow of Calembredaine's fist had hurled him to the bottom of a common pit in the grave-yard. Recovering his wits among the dead, he was begging to be pulled out.

A gale of laughter shook the closest bystanders and spread to the other spectators. The craftsmen and workmen in the neighbouring streets listened, with sweating brows, to this thunderburst of laughter that succeeded the cries of murder. The women at the windows crossed themselves.

Suddenly a silvery bell tinkled, announcing the Angelus. A stream of blasphemies and obscenities rose from the church-yard into the grey night. But the other churches replied.

It was time to flee. Like owls or demons fearing the light, the people of the underworld left the graveyard of the Saints-Innocents.

In the grimy dawn, with its faint rosy tint like pale blood, Calembredaine stood before Angélique and looked at her, laughing.

"She is yours," said the Great Coesre.

Once again Angélique ran towards the fencing. But the same brutal hands caught and paralysed her. A gag of rags choked her. She went on struggling, then lost consciousness.

CHAPTER 52

"Don't be afraid," said Calembredaine.

He was sitting on a stool before her. His enormous hands were propped on his knees. A candle in a beautiful silver candlestick on the ground struggled against the wan daylight.

Angélique moved and saw that she was lying on a litter on which an impressive quantity of cloaks of all kinds and colours were heaped. There were sumptuous velvet cloaks with gold braid, such as young noblemen wear when they go to play the guitar under windows of their mistresses, and others in rough fustian—travellers' and merchants' comfortable coats.

"Don't be afraid . . . Angélique," the bandit repeated.

She stared at him wide-eyed. Her mind was unhinged. For he had spoken in the dialect of Poitou and she had understood him.

He raised his hand to his face and at one stroke tore the fleshy protuberance from his cheek. She could not help uttering a nervous cry. But he was now tossing back his dirty hat which took with it a wig of bushy hair. Then he untied the black patch he wore over his eye.

Angélique now had before her a young man with rough features, whose short black hair curled over his square forehead. Deep-set brown eyes under bushy brows were gazing at her. She put her hand to her throat; she was choking. Her cry was stillborn. At last she mumbled like a deaf-mute who moves her lips and does not know the sound of her own voice:

"Ni . . . cho . . . las."

A grin broadened the man's lips.

"Yes, it's me. You've recognised me?"

She glanced at the awful disguise that lay scattered on the ground by the stool: the wig, the black eye-patch. . . .

"And it's . . . you who are called Calembredaine?"

He stood up and fiercely struck his fist against his chest.

"That's me, Calembredaine, the Illustrious Scamp of the Pont-Neuf. I have made my way, haven't I, since we last saw each other?"

She looked at him hard. She was still stretched out on the litter of old coats, unable to move. Through the barred loophole a fog thick as smoke was penetrating into the room in slow wreaths. Perhaps that was why this tattered personage, this Hercules in rags and a black beard, who was striking his chest saying "I am Nicholas. . . . I am Calembredaine," seemed to her like an unreal phantasy.

He began to walk up and down without taking his eyes off her.

"The forests are all right when it's warm," he said. "I worked with the salt-smugglers. And afterwards I found a band of men in the forest of Mercoeur: former mercenaries, peasants down from the north, escaped galley-slaves. They were well organised. I got in with them. We held up travellers for ransom on the road from Paris to Nantes. But the woods are all right only when it's warm. When winter comes, you've got to make for the towns. Which isn't so easy. We did Tours, Chateaudun. That's how we got to Paris. Oh, we had the devil's own time with all those beggar- and rogue-chasers at our heels! Those who got nabbed at the gates had their eyebrows and half their beards shaved off and—hop, back to the country, back to your smoked-out farmstead, your plundered lands and your battlefield. Or else off you went to the General Hospital or even to the Châtelet, if you happened to have a piece of bread in your pocket which the baker's wife gave you because she couldn't do otherwise. But I discovered good spots for slipping through cellars that communicate from one house to another, the sewer holes that end in the ditches, and, as it was winter, the ice-bound barges all along the Seine from Saint-Cloud. Skipping from one barge to the next, believe it or not, we all sneaked into Paris one night, like rats. . . ."

She said listlessly:

"How could you fall so low?"

22

He winced, then bent over her, his face contracted with rage.

"And what about you?"

Angélique gazed at her torn dress. Her untied, dishevelled hair was escaping from her linen bonnet.

"It's not the same thing," she said.

Nicholas's teeth gritted and he snarled like a savage dog.

"Oh yes, it is! Almost the same thing . . . now. D'you hear me . . . slut?"

Angélique stared at him vaguely with a sort of distant smile. . . . It was he all right. She could see him again as he used to be—Nicholas upright in the sunshine, with his big hands full of wild strawberries. And the same nasty, vengeful expression on his face. . . . It all came back to her mind, gradually. He would bend over like this. . . . A more awkward, rustic Nicholas then, but already out of place in the warmth of the little wood in springtime. . . . Passionate as a quivering animal and yet putting his arm behind his back in order not to be tempted to seize and abuse her: "I want to tell you . . . there was never anyone but you in my life . . . I'm like something that doesn't belong and that keeps wandering here and there without knowing why. . . . The only place I belong is with you. . . ." Not too bad for a peasant's proposal. But in fact his real place was where he stood now, terrifying, insolent: a robber chief in the capital. . . . The place of good-for-nothings who'd rather take from others than trouble to work for themselves. That was already evident when he deserted his herd of cows to go and steal the snacks of the other little cowherds. And Angélique had been his accomplice.

She sat up with a sudden jerk and looked at him with her green eyes.

"I forbid you to insult me. I've never been a slut with you. And now give me something to eat. I'm hungry."

In truth, the hunger that gripped her was churning her stomach to the point of nausea.

Nicholas Calembredaine seemed stunned by her attack.

"Don't move," he said. "I'll take care of that."

Seizing a metal bar, he struck on a copper gong that gleamed on the wall. Immediately there resounded in the staircase a gallop of clogs, and a man with a half-witted look appeared in the doorway. Nicholas turned to Angélique, motioning towards the newcomer:

23

"Let me introduce Jactance. One of my cut-purses. But above all an outsize imbecile who found a way of getting himself put in the stocks last month. So I'm keeping him here to do the cooking until the customers of the market forget the shape of his nose a little. After that we'll put a wig on his head, and out with the scissors: look to your purses! What's cooking today, good-for-nothing?"

Jactance sniffed and passed his sleeve under his wet nose.

"Pig's feet, chief, with cabbage."

"Pig yourself!" Nicholas bawled. "Is that suitable food for a lady?"

"I don't know, chief!"

"It'll do," said Angélique impatiently.

The smell of food made her almost faint. It was really very humiliating, her feeling so ravenous at the most important and dramatic moments of her life. And the more dramatic they were, the more hungry she felt!

When Jactance returned, carrying a wooden bowl brimming over with cabbage and jellied giblets, he was preceded by the dwarf Barcarole. The latter cut a caper, then addressed a courtly salute to Angélique. His tiny plump legs and enormous hat rendered the gesture grotesque. His monstrous head was not lacking a certain handsomeness. Perhaps that was why, despite his deformity, he had immediately struck Angélique as likeable.

"I have the impression that you are not displeased with your new conquest, Calembredaine," he said, casting a wink at Nicholas, "but what will the Marquise of the Polacks think of it?"

"Shut up, louse," growled the chief. "What right have you to come into my den?"

"The right of the faithful servant who deserves a reward! Don't forget that I was the one who brought you this pretty piece whom you've been ogling for ages in every part of Paris."

"Bringing her to the Innocents! That was a bright idea. It was by sheer luck that the Great Coesre didn't appropriate her and that Rodogone the Egyptian didn't filch her from me."

"It's only right that you had to win her," said the minute Barcarole, who had to throw his head back to look up at Nicholas. "What kind of a chief wouldn't fight for his marquise? And don't forget, you haven't yet paid the whole dowry. Has he, my pretty one?"

Angélique had not listened, for she was eating greedily. The dwarf gazed at her tender-eyed.

"The best part of the pig's feet are the little bones," he said amiably, "it's good to suck them and fun spitting them out. To my mind, apart from the little bones, you can have the rest."

"What do you mean, the dowry hasn't been paid?" inquired Calembredaine with a frown.

"Faith! What about the fellow she wants put out of the way? The cross-eyed monk. . . ."

The chief turned towards Angélique.

"Is that true? Is that what you want?"

She had eaten too quickly. Sated and filled with a dull apathy, she was stretched out on the coats again. To Nicholas's question she replied with closed eyes:

"Yes, it must be done."

"It's only right!" roared the dwarf. "Blood must sprinkle the paupers' wedding. Ho! Ho! The blood of a monk. . . ."

He uttered horrible blasphemies, then, at a threatening gesture from his chief, fled down the stairs. Calembredaine slammed the badly-joined door shut with a kick. Standing at the foot of the strange litter on which the young woman was reclining, he gazed at her for a long while, with his fists on his hips. She opened her eyes.

"Is it true that you've had your eye on me in Paris for a long time?"

"I spotted you at once. With my men all over the place, you can imagine I am quickly informed of all newcomers, and I know better than they do themselves how many jewels they have and how one can get into their homes when midnight strikes from the belfry of the Place de Grève. But you saw me at 'The Trois Maillets'. . . ."

"How loathsome!" she murmured, with a shudder. "Oh! why did you laugh as you looked at me?"

"Because I was beginning to realise that you would soon be mine."

She looked at him coldly, then shrugged her shoulders and yawned. She was not afraid of Nicholas as she had been afraid of Calembredaine. She had always dominated Nicholas. You don't fear a man whom you have known as a child. She felt increasingly drowsy. She put one more question, vaguely:

"But why . . . why did you leave Monteloup?"

"Now, there's a question!" he cried, folding his arms over

25

his chest. "Why? Do you think I felt like having old Guillaume impale me on his pike . . . after what happened with you? I left Monteloup on your wedding night . . . had you forgotten about that, too?"

Yes, that, too, she had forgotten. Under her lowered eyelids, the memory of it came back with the smell of straw and wine, the weight of Nicholas's firm body upon her and the unpleasant sensation of hurry and anger and of something left unfinished.

"Oh!" he said bitterly, "it certainly looks as if I did not take up much space in your life. And, naturally, you have never thought of me during all these years?"

"Naturally," she confirmed casually. "I had better things to do than to think of a menial."

"Slut!" he shouted, beside himself. "Be careful what you say. The menial is your master now. You are mine. . . ."

He was still shouting when she fell asleep. Far from upsetting her, this voice filled her with the sensation of a brutal but benevolent protection. He stopped short.

"And there we are," he said in an undertone, "just as in the old days . . . when you used to fall asleep on the moss half way through our squabbles. Ah well, sleep, my sweet. You are mine, anyhow. Are you cold? Do you want me to cover you up?"

She gave an imperceptible nod with her eyelids. He went to fetch a luxurious cloth coat and threw it over her. Then, very gently, he passed his hand over her forehead, with a kind of awe.

This room was really a very strange place. Built of enormous stones like the ancient dungeons, it was round and gloomily lit by a barred loop-hole. It was filled with an array of multifarious objects, from dainty mirrors mounted in ebony and ivory to old iron scrap, work-tools such as hammers and picks, and weapons. . . .

Angélique stretched herself. Only half awake, she gazed around with astonishment, got up and went to look in one of the mirrors. Its reflection showed an unknown face: that of a pale girl with wild, staring eyes, like those of a ferocious cat watching its prey. The evening light added a sulphurous glint to her tousled hair. She threw the mirror away, frightened. This woman with the hunted face of an outcast could surely

26

not be she . . .! What was happening? Why were there so many things in this circular room? Swords, pots, caskets filled with baubles, sashes, fans, gloves, jewels, canes, musical instruments, a warming-pan, piles of hats—above all, coats, which, thrown one on top of another, composed the bed on which she had slept. A single piece of furniture, a dainty chest of drawers with inlaid wood from the West Indies, seemed quite out of place within these damp walls.

Inside her belt she felt something hard. She pulled at the leather hilt and withdrew a long, tapering dagger. Where had she seen that dagger? It had been in some deep, distressing nightmare, during which the moon had juggled with skulls. The man with the swarthy skin had held it in his hand. Then the dagger fell and Angélique had picked it up in the mud while the two men had wrestled and rolled on the ground. That's how she came to hold in her hands the dagger of Rodogone the Egyptian. She slipped it back into her bodice. Her mind assembled confused images.

Nicholas. . . . Where is Nicholas?

She ran towards the window. Between the bars she caught a glimpse of the Seine, rolling its slow, wormwood-coloured waters and its incessant traffic of boats and barges under the cloudy sky. On the other bank, already swathed in dusk, she recognised the Tuileries and the Louvre.

This vision of her former life gave her a shock and convinced her that she was mad. Nicholas! Where was Nicholas?

She rushed towards the door and, finding it closed and double-locked, she hammered on it wildly, screaming, calling for Nicholas, tearing her nails against the rotten wood.

A key creaked, and the red-nosed man appeared.

"What in hell are you bawling for, Marquise?" inquired Jactance.

"Why was this door locked?"

"I don't know."

"Where is Nicholas?"

"I don't know."

He gazed at her, then made up his mind:

"Come down and have a look at the fellows, that'll cheer you up."

She followed him down a winding stone staircase which was damp and dark. She was greeted by an increasing din of shouts, rôars of laughter and children's cries.

She emerged into a large vaulted hall filled with sundry characters. She caught sight of Wood-Bottom placed on the big table like a piece of beef on a dish. At the far end of the hall a fire was glowing, and Lightfoot was seated on the hearthstone watching the pot boil. A big woman was plucking a duck. Another younger woman was holding a half-naked child between her knees engaged in the unsavoury occupation of delousing him. Lolling all over the place on the straw thrown on the flat-stones there were old men and women, covered in rags, and dirty, tattered children fighting for food scraps with the dogs. Some men were sitting around the table on old barrels, playing cards or smoking as they drank.

At Angélique's entrance all eyes turned towards her and a comparative silence fell over the wretched gathering.

"Come forward, my girl," said Wood-Bottom with a solemn gesture. "You are our chief Calembredaine's woman. We owe you consideration. Come on, move aside, boys, and make room for the Marquise!"

One of the pipe-smokers nudged his neighbour with his elbow.

"Nice bit, she is. Calembredaine for once has picked almost as well as you."

The other walked up to Angélique, and raised her chin with a gesture that was at once friendly and peremptory.

"I'm Pretty Boy," he said.

She slapped down his hand with ill-temper.

"That's a matter of taste."

A roar of laughter shook the entire audience.

"That's got nothing to do with it," said Wood-Bottom, hiccuping with laughter, "it's his name, Pretty Boy, that's what he's called. Here, Jactance, give the wench something to drink. I like her."

Someone placed before her a long-stemmed glass which bore the crest of a Marquis whose house must have been visited by Calembredaine's gang on some moonless night. Jactance filled it to the brim with red wine and made the round of the other goblets.

"Your health, Marquise! . . . What's your name?"

"Angélique."

The coarse, foul laughter of the bandits broke out afresh under the vaulted roof.

"Why, that tops it all! Angélique! . . . Ha! Ha! Ha! An

angel, fancy! There's never been anything like it here. . . . But why not? After all, why shouldn't we all be angels too! Since she's our Marquise. . . . Your health, Marquise of the Angels!"

They roared, slapped their thighs; the din resounded like a baneful, whirling roll of drums around her.

"Your health, Marquise! Go on . . . drink!"

But she remained motionless, gazing at the bibulous, bearded and ill-shaven faces all around.

"Drink, slut!" yelled Wood-Bottom, with his terrifying voice.

She faced the monster without answering. There was a threatening silence, then Wood-Bottom sighed and looked at the others with a dismal air.

"She don't want to drink! What's the matter with her?"

"What's the matter with her?" came the chorus of the others. "Pretty Boy, you know all about women, try and do something."

Pretty Boy shrugged his shoulders.

"Bunch of rats," he said scornfully, "are you too blind to see that you can't tame this one by yelling at her?"

He sat down next to Angélique and stroked her shoulder softly.

"Don't be afraid. They aren't bad, you know. It's just an air they put on to frighten the burghers. But not you: we already like you. You are our Marquise. The Marquise of the Angels! Don't you like that? The Marquise of the Angels! It's a pretty name, though. And it suits you, with your beautiful eyes. Come on, drink, little one, it's good wine. Comes out of a barrel from the port of the Grève; it has come waddling on its own feet right to the Tower of Nesle. That's how things happen here. It's the Court of Miracles."

He raised the glass close to her lips. She responded to the sound of this caressing, male voice. She drank. The wine *was* good. It suffused her frozen body with a cosy warmth and suddenly everything became simpler and less terrible. She drank a second glass, then propped her elbows on the table and began to look around her. The stunted cripple gazed at her dismally like some monster of the watery depths. Was he instructed to watch over her? She felt no desire to run away, though. Where could she go to anyway?

Nightfall brought back to their lair the beggar-men and -women who lived under Calembredaine's rule. Among them were many women who were carrying in their arms invalid children or babies wrapped in rags, whose shrill cries never ceased. One of them, whose face was covered with purulent pimples, was handed to the woman sitting by the hearth. The latter, with a deft hand, tore all the crusts off the baby's face, passed a towel over it, and the little face was smooth and sound again. Then she put the child to her breast.

Angélique had been unable to suppress a shudder. Wood-Bottom grinned and commented in his raucous voice:

"You see, with us people get cured quickly. No need to go in processions to see miracles. Here they happen every day. At this very moment there may be some lady devoted to good works, as they say, who is telling a friend: 'Oh, my dear! I saw a child on the Pont-Neuf today, so wretched! Covered with blisters. . . . Of course I gave its mother some alms . . .' And they are quite pleased with themselves, the smug old cows. And yet it was nothing more than a few pellets of dried bread smeared with a little honey to attract the flies. Why, here's Rat-Poison coming in. You'll be able to leave. . . ."

Angélique gave him a questioning, surprised look.

"Never mind trying to figure it out," he grumbled. "Everything's been arranged with Calembredaine."

The man called Rat-Poison was an emaciated Spaniard, so skinny that his pointed knees and elbows had pierced his garments. A sorry survivor of the battlefields of Flanders, he none the less affected swashbuckling airs, with his long black moustache, his plumed hat and, over his shoulder, a rapier on whose blade the corpses of five or six big rats were impaled. In the day-time the Spaniard wandered through the streets, selling products to kill these rodents. At night he supplemented his meagre income by hiring out his talents as a 'duellist' to Calembredaine.

With much dignity, he accepted a goblet of wine, gnawed a turnip which he pulled out of his pocket, while some old harridans wrangled over the spoils of his hunt; he sold a rat for two *sols*. After pocketing the money, Rat-Poison gave a salute with his rapier and put it back in its sheath.

"I am ready," he declared pompously.

"Go!" Wood-Bottom said to Angélique.

On the defensive, she was on the point of asking a question, then thought better of it. Other men had risen, the *drilles* or *narquois*, one time soldiers with a taste for pillage and battles whom peace-time had reduced to idleness. She saw herself surrounded by their gallows-birds' figures. They wore battered uniforms from which there still dangled the trimmings and gold braids of some princely regiment.

Angélique raised her hand to her side, under her bodice, to feel the Egyptian's dagger. She was determined, if necessary, to sell her life dearly.

But the dagger had disappeared.

Rage overcame Angélique, whom the wine had excited and pulled out of her lethargy. Forgetting all prudence, she yelled:

"Who has taken my knife?"

"Here it is," Jactance said at once in his drawling tone of voice.

He handed her the weapon with an innocent look. She was dumbfounded. How had he been able to remove this dagger from under her bodice without her realising it?

Meanwhile, the same uproarious laughter, the horrible laughter of the beggars and bandits, burst out again—a laughter that would haunt Angélique for the rest of her life.

"A good lesson, my pretty one," Wood-Bottom exclaimed. "You'll get to know Jactance's hands. Each one of his fingers is more skilful than a magician. Go and ask the housewives in the market square what they think of them."

"Nice blade, this is," remarked one of the *narquois*, grasping it.

After examining it closely, he flung it back on the table, visibly scared.

"Hey! It's the knife of Rodogone the Egyptian!"

With a mixture of respect and alarm they all gazed at the dagger, which gleamed in the candlelight. Angélique picked it up and slipped it into her belt. She had the impression that this gesture established her in the eyes of these wretches. They did not know in what circumstances she had got hold of this trophy of one of the gang's most formidable enemies. A mystery hovered about it, surrounded her with a slightly perturbing halo.

Wood-Bottom whistled:

"Hey, hey! She's smarter than she looks, the Marquis of the Angels."

CHAPTER 53

OUTSIDE, Angélique could see the dilapidated shadow of the Tower of Nesle outlined against the almost complete darkness. She realised that the room where Nicholas had taken her must be situated at the top of the tower. One of the *narquois* explained to her obligingly that it had been Calembredaine's idea to lodge the men of his gang in the old, medieval stronghold of Paris. It was in fact an ideal brigands' lair. Half-ruined halls, crumbling ramparts, tumbling turrets, offered hiding-places which the other gangs, in the faubourgs, did not possess.

The washerwoman who, for a long time, had been putting her laundry out to dry on the battlements of the Tower of Nesle had fled before the terrifying invasion. Nobody had come to dislodge the rogues who made a practice of lying in wait for the carriages of the Faubourg Saint-Germain, hiding under the small, hump-backed bridge that spanned the ancient moats.

People confined themselves to whispering that this passageway by the Tower of Nesle in the heart of Paris had become a real cut-throat alley. And the sounds of the violins in the Tuileries, on the other bank of the Seine, would sometimes mingle with the fiddling of Father Hurlurot or the refrains of Thibault the hurdy-gurdy grinder, playing for the beggars' dances on a night of revelry.

The bargemen of the small timber port, not far away, lowered their voices as they saw the fear-inspiring figures approach the banks. The place was becoming impossible, they would say. When would the city aldermen at last decide to dismantle those old ramparts and chase all these vermin away?

"Gentlemen, I greet you," said Rat-Poison, approaching them. "Would you be good enough to conduct us to the Quai de Gesvres?"

"You've got money?"

"We have this," said the Spaniard, placing the tip of his sword against the other's belly.

The man shrugged his shoulders resignedly. Every day they were up against these rogues, who would hide in the barges, steal the merchandise, and get themselves ferried, like lords, from one bank to the other for nothing. When the boatmen were there in strength, it would usually end in bloody fights with knives, for the rivermen's guild was not of a particularly patient disposition.

That night, however, the three men who had just lit their fire to watch near their barges gathered that it was to their interest not to seek an argument. A youngster rose at the sign of his chief and, not very reassured, untied his boat, in which Angélique and her infamous companions had taken their seats.

The boat passed under the arches of the Pont-Neuf and, close to the Bridge of Notre Dame, it drew alongside the foundations of the Quai de Gesvres.

"That will do nicely, my lad," said Rat-Poison to the young ferryman; "not only do we thank you but we'll let you go back safe and sound. Just lend us your lantern. We'll let you have it back when we think of it. . . ."

The immense arch that supported the quite recently constructed Quai de Gesvres was a gigantic piece of work, a masterpiece of weight-pulling and stone-cutting.

As she stepped on to it, Angélique heard the roar of the river, which, as it flowed by in torrents, reminded her by its thunderous echo of the great voice of the ocean. The noise of the carriages rolling over the vault with a sound of distant rumbling added to this impression. Inside, it was icy cold and damp. This grandiose cavern, isolated in the heart of Paris, seemed to have been created for the express purpose of providing a refuge for all the rogues of the great city.

The bandits followed her through to the end of the vault. Three or four dark passages, which served as sewers for the butchers' shops of the rue de la Vieille Labterne, disgorged great streams of blood. Farther on, there were narrow, foul-smelling passageways, hidden stairs in the recesses of houses, and river banks where one's feet got bogged to the ankles in mud.

When they emerged again into the open air, the night was black and Angélique didn't know where she was. There was probably a small square with a fountain in the middle, for the murmur of water could be heard.

Nicholas's voice suddenly rose, quite close:

"Is it you, boys? You have the girl with you?"

One of the *narquois* held his lantern over Angélique.

"Here she is."

33

She saw the tall figure and the frightful face of the bandit Calembredaine, and she closed her eyes with horror. The sight made her panicky, even though she knew that he was Nicholas.

The chief slapped the lantern down with his hand.

"Have you gone out of your head carrying that dazzler? So the gentleman needs a light nowadays to go for a walk?"

"We didn't feel much like falling into the water under the Quai de Gesvres," the other protested.

Nicholas seized Angélique's arm rudely.

"Don't be afraid, my little pigeon. You know it's me," he said chaffingly.

He pushed her into the shelter of a porch.

"You, Peony-Jean, post yourself on the other side of the street, behind the corner-post. You, Martin, stay with me. Gobert over there. The others will stand watch at the cross-roads. You're at your post, Barcarole?"

A voice answered, as if dropping from the sky:

"I'm here, chief."

The dwarf was perched on a shop-sign.

From the porch, where she stood near Nicholas, Angélique could see right down the narrow street. It was feebly lit by a few lanterns hung in front of the smartest houses, and the central gutter, filled with refuse, gleamed like a dismal serpent.

The craftsmen's booths were shut tight. People were going to bed; behind the window-panes could be seen the round lights of candles. A woman opened a window to empty a pail into the street. She could be heard threatening a crying child that she would send for the Gruff Monk.

"I'll give you a taste of the Gruff Monk," growled Nicholas.

He added in a low, strained voice:

"I'm going to pay your dowry, Angélique. That's the way it's done in the beggars' world. A man pays to have his girl. Just like you buy a fine object that you're keen on."

"And it's about the only thing we do buy," jeered one of the cut-throats.

His chief silenced him with an oath. Hearing the sound of footsteps, the bandits froze and fell silent. They drew their swords without a sound. A man was coming up the street, hopping from one cobblestone to another to avoid dirtying his high-heeled shoes in the puddles.

"That isn't him," Calembredaine whispered.

34

The others sheathed their swords. The passser-by heard the click of weapons. He jumped with fright, dimly perceived the porch swarming with figures, and ran away, screaming:

"Help! Thieves! Murderers! Coat-snatchers! I'm being murdered!"

"Silly b——," came Peony-Jean's indignant growl from the other side of the street. "When we let someone pass quietly for once, without even taking his coat, he's got to go and bray like an ass! It's enough to make you sick!"

A soft whistle from across the street reduced him to silence.

"See who's coming, Angélique," Nicholas whispered, tightening his grasp on the young woman's arm.

Frozen and so completely numbed that she did not even feel the touch of his hand, Angélique stood waiting. She knew what was going to happen. It was inevitable. The thing had to be done. Her heart would not come alive again until *afterwards*. For everything was dead inside her, and hatred alone had the power of reviving her.

In the yellow light of the street lanterns, she saw two monks appear, arm in arm. She had no difficulty in recognising one of them as Conan Bécher. The other, fat and voluble, was discoursing in Latin with ample gestures. He seemed to be slightly drunk, for he kept pulling his companion now and then against the wall of a house, then with apologies led him back, wading in the gutter.

Angélique heard the alchemist's shrill voice. He too was talking in Latin, but his tone was one of outraged protest. As they came up to the porch, exasperation made him cry out in French:

"Now that's enough, Brother Amboise, your theories on baptism with meat-stock are a heresy! A sacrament is worthless if performed with water polluted by impure elements such as animal fats. Baptism with meat-stock! What a blasphemy! Why not with red wine while you're at it? That would suit you well, since you seem to have such a fancy for it."

With a jerk, the gaunt Franciscan friar freed himself from the clinging arm of Brother Amboise.

The fat monk was stammering in a drunkard's maudlin voice:

"Father, you grieve me. . . . Alas! I would have liked to convince you."

Suddenly, he emitted a demented shriek:

"Ah! Ah! *Deus coeli!*"

Almost at the same moment, Angélique noticed that Father Amboise was beside them under the porch.

"He's yours, boys," he whispered, passing without transition from the purest Latin to thieves' cant.

Conan Bécher had turned round.

"What's the matter with——"

He broke off, peering into the empty street with swimming eyes. His voice choked.

"Brother Amboise," he called. ". . . Brother Amboise, where are you?"

His haggard, worried face seemed to become even more sunken, his eyes popped out of their sockets, and his breath came in laboured gasps, as he took a few steps forward, casting terrified glances around him.

"Whoo! Whoo! Whoo!"

The dwarf Barcarole appeared on the scene with his sinister owl's hoot. He arched himself against the creaking sign, and with the bounding resilience of a giant toad he landed at the feet of Conan Bécher.

The monk gave a start and flattened himself against the wall.

"Whoo! Whoo! Whoo!" repeated the dwarf.

Performing a hellish dance before his terrorised victim, he multiplied his capers, grotesque salutes, grimaces and obscene gestures. He encircled him in a truly diabolic round.

Then a second hideous freak emerged from the darkness, with a jeering laugh. He was a hunchback with knock-knees, his legs and feet so deformed that he could move only by means of abrupt and horrible hip-jerks. But his figure was nothing compared with his monstrous face. For on his forehead he had a weird fleshy protuberance, red and pendulous.

The rattle that issued from the friar's throat was no longer human.

"Haah! . . . the demons!" he shrieked.

His long body suddenly caved in and he fell on his knees on the muddy pavement. His eyes bulged. His complexion turned waxen. Between the corners of his lips, dilated in a grimace of abject terror, two rows of rotten teeth could be seen chattering. Very slowly, as in the grip of a nightmare, he raised his two bony hands with their splayed fingers. His tongue moved with difficulty. He articulated:

"Have pity . . . Peyrac!"

The pronunciation of this name by the hated voice pierced Angélique's heart like a dagger. The gruesome scene released a reflex of madness in her. She began to scream wildly:

"Kill him! Kill him!"

And, without realising it, she bit into Nicholas's shoulder. He disengaged himself with a rough thrust, and pulled out the butcher's cutlass that served him as a weapon.

But suddenly there was a heavy silence in the street. Barcarole's voice rose:

"Why, I'm damned!" he said.

The monk's body had toppled over on its side at the foot of the wall.

The bandits drew closer. The chief bent over him and lifted up the motionless head; the lower jaw fell, showing the mouth wide open on a last cry of anguish. The eyes were staring and already glazed.

"No doubt of it, he's dead!" Calembredaine declared.

"We didn't even touch him," said the dwarf. "Isn't it true, Cockscomb, that we didn't touch him? We only made faces at him to get him into a funk."

"Well, you succeeded too well. He's died of it . . . died of funk."

"Damn funny," Barcarole repeated.

A window opened. A trembling voice queried:

"What's going on? Who's talking of demons?"

"Let's be off," Calembredaine ordered. "There's nothing left for us to do here."

In the morning, when Friar Bécher's body was found lifeless, yet carrying no trace of blows or wounds, people in Paris remembered the words of the sorcerer who had been burned on the Place de Grève: "Conan Bécher, I shall meet you before God's tribunal ere the month is out."

They consulted the calendar and saw that the month was ending. And crossing themselves profusely, the inhabitants of the rue de la Cerisaie, near the Arsenal, told of the strange cries that had pulled them out of their first slumber the night before.

The grave-diggers had to be paid double the fee to bury the cursed monk, and on his tomb was put this epitaph:

'Here lies Father Conan Bécher, a Franciscan monk, who

died from the vexations of the demons, on the last day of March 1661.'

The gang of Nicholas Calembredaine, the Illustrious Scamp, ended their night in the taverns.

All the public-houses between the Arsenal and the Pont-Neuf received a visit from them. They surrounded a white-faced woman with loose untidy hair, and made her drink.

The night was no longer black. It was red, red like wine, it blazed like a fire. Tables swayed, hearths revolved around their fiery axis, the stone floors rose to face-level.

Angélique was dead-drunk, and finally vomited helplessly. With her forehead resting against the wooden top of a table, a thought was born in her and rolled through her in a long wave of despair:

'Degradation! Degradation. . .'.'

Nicholas's imperative grip pulled her up and he stared at her with surprise and alarm.

"Are you sick? We haven't drunk anything yet, though. . . . We must celebrate our wedding. . . ."

Then, seeing that she was exhausted and that her eyes were closed, he picked her up in his arms and walked out.

The night was cold, but against Nicholas's chest she felt warm.

The Gutter-Poet of the Pont-Neuf, lying between the feet of the bronze horse, saw the great bandit pass, holding in his arms, as lightly as if she were a doll, a white form with long, untidy hair.

When Calembredaine walked into the big hall of the Tower of Nesle, a good many of his rogues and bawds were gathered around the fire. A woman rose yelling and threw herself upon him.

"Swine! You've taken another woman . . . they told me. And this while I was wearing myself out with a vicious party of musketeers . . . but I'll bleed you like a pig, and her too!"

Nicholas quietly put Angélique down on the ground and propped her up against the wall to prevent her from falling. Then he raised his big fist and the girl toppled over.

"Now, listen, all of you," said Calembredaine. "That girl over there—she is *mine*, and nobody else's. Anyone who dares to touch a hair of her head, or any woman who tries to harm her,

38

will have to deal with me. And you know what that means!...
As for the Marquise of the Polacks . . ."

He grabbed the girl again by a flap of her jacket and with a rough contemptuous shove sent her reeling among a group of card-players.

". . . you can do as you like with her."

Then, triumphantly, Nicholas Merlot, native of Poitou, former shepherd turned wolf, swung round towards the woman he had always loved and whom fate had restored to him.

CHAPTER 54

HE PICKED her up in his arms and started up the stairs of the Tower. He climbed slowly so as not to stumble, for the wine fumes were befogging his brain. Thus his ascent had a kind of solemnity.

Angélique abandoned herself to the embrace of his powerful arms. Her head was swimming. When he reached the top, Nicholas kicked open the door leading to the room that harboured the spoils of their thefts. Then he walked up to the litter of coats and dropped Angélique on to it like a parcel, crying:

"And now, the two of us."

The gesture as well as the triumphant laugh that widened the man's mouth pulled her out of the listless lethargy into which she had sunk ever since the last tavern. She roused herself with a jerk and ran to the window, where she clung to the bars without quite knowing why.

"Well," she shouted angrily over her shoulder, "what about the two of us, you nitwit?"

"I . . . but . . . I mean," he stuttered, completely dumb-founded.

She laughed insultingly.

"Did you by any chance imagine that you would become my lover—you, Nicholas Merlot?"

With two noiseless strides he was at her side with darkened brow.

"I'm not imagining anything," he said flatly, "I am sure of it."

"That remains to be seen."

"Nothing to be seen about it."

She stared at him defiantly. The red glow of a bargeman's fire, down on the river bank at the foot of the tower, illuminated them. Nicholas took a deep breath.

"Listen," he said in a low, threatening tone of voice. "I shall talk to you once more, because it's you and because you've got to understand. You have no right to refuse what I am asking. I have fought for you, I have killed the man you wanted me to, the Great Coesre has joined us: it's all in order with the underworld. You are mine."

"And suppose I won't have anything to do with the laws of the underworld?"

"Then you'll die," he said, and there was a flash in the depths of his eyes. "Of hunger or some other cause. But you won't come out alive, don't have any illusions on that score. Anyway, you no longer have any choice. Haven't you got that through your head yet?" he persisted, putting his clenched fist against the young woman's temple. "Hasn't this stubborn little ladylike mind of yours grasped what burned to cinders on the Place de Grève together with your sorcerer of a husband? Everything that used to stand between us, Footman and Comtesse, that no longer exists. I am Calembredaine, and you . . . you're nothing any more. Your people have deserted you. Those, over there. . . ."

He lifted his arm, pointing to the other side of the dark Seine, at the outlines of the Tuileries and the Louvre where lights were twinkling.

"For the people over there you no longer exist. And that's why you belong to the underworld . . . because that's the home of those who've been abandoned. . . . Here, there'll always be something for you to eat. You'll be protected. We'll avenge you, we'll help you. But don't ever betray us. . . ."

He fell silent, a little out of breath. She felt his burning breath on her shoulder. He brushed her lightly, and the ardour of his desire aroused in her an uneasy thrill. She saw him open his big hands and raise them to touch her, then he stepped back as though he did not dare.

He began to implore her very softly in dialect:

"My treasure, don't be mean. Why do you sulk at me? Isn't everything so simple? Here we are, both of us . . . alone . . . as in the old days. We've eaten well, drunk well. What else is

there to do now but love each other? You're not going to have
me believe that I frighten you?"

Angélique gave a scornful little laugh and shrugged her
shoulders.

He went on:

"Well, then? Come on! ... Remember. We always got on
so well together. We were made for each other, my baby.
There's no getting around that ... I knew you'd be mine. I
was hoping it. And now it's happened, you see! ..."

"No," she said, obstinately tossing her hair back over her
shoulders.

Beside himself, he screamed:

"Take care! I can take you by force, if I must."

"Just try, I'll scratch your eyes out with my nails."

"I'll have you held down by my guards," he yelled.

"Coward!"

He broke into a torrent of abuse.

She hardly heard him. With her forehead leaning against
the icy bars of the narrow opening like a prisoner who has no
hope left, Angélique felt under the sway of an overwhelming
weariness. "Your people have abandoned you ..." Like an
echo of the sentence Nicholas had uttered, others rang out,
cutting as a knife:

'I want to hear no more of you. You must *disappear*. You
will no longer have a rank, a name—or anything.'

And Hortense arose harpy-like, with a candle in her hand.

'Go away! Go away!'

Nicholas was right. He was right, this Calembredaine, this
Hercules with the wild, heavy blood, who was trembling behind her and swearing loud enough to make the old stones of
the Tower of Nesle crumble. His ragged clothes had the awful
smell of the city, but his flesh, perhaps, if you hugged it tight,
if you bit into it fiercely, might yield a little of the unforget-
table flavour of Monteloup? ...

With a sudden resignation, she passed in front of him and,
near the litter, began to unfasten her brown serge bodice.
Then she let her petticoat slip to the ground. In her shift, she
hesitated for a moment. The cold was biting on her flesh, but
her head was burning. Quickly she removed this last garment,
and lay down naked on the stolen cloaks.

"Come," she said calmly.

He had remained breathlessly silent. Her docility seemed

suspicious to him. He approached, watching her closely. He slowly stripped himself of his own rags. On the verge of reaching the climax of his most extravagant dreams, Nicholas, the former farmhand, stood trembling. The flickering light of the fire on the riverside below projected his gigantic shadow on the wall.

"Come," she said again. "I am cold."

She too had begun to tremble, from the cold perhaps, but also, before this tall, naked, expectant body, from impatience mingled with fear.

With a wolf's bound he was upon her. He crushed her in his arms as if to break her, and he gave great bursts of spasmodic laughter:

"Oh! This time it's real. Ah! this is good, you are mine. You won't escape me again, you're mine. . . . Mine! Mine! Mine!" he kept repeating, punctuating his virile delirium.

And with violent haste he possessed her.

A little later, she heard him sigh like a sated dog.

"Angélique," he murmured.

"You hurt me," she complained.

And, enveloping herself in a coat, she fell asleep.

He took her twice again during the night. She would emerge, numbed, from a heavy slumber to become the prey of this creature of darkness who grasped her, cursing, and had his will with her as he uttered loud, hoarse sighs, then fell in a heap at her side, mumbling disjointed phrases.

At dawn a whispering voice woke him.

"Calembredaine, get up," Pretty Boy was urging, "we've some accounts to settle at the Fair at Saint-Germain with the witches of Rodogone the Egyptian, who threw Mother Hurlurette and Father Hurlurot out on the street."

"I'm coming; but don't make any noise. The girl's still sleeping."

"No wonder. What a racket there's been in the Tower of Nesle this night! Even the rats couldn't sleep a wink. You certainly had your bit of fun. Funny, the way you've got to bellow when you make love."

"Shut up," growled Calembredaine.

"The Marquise of the Polacks didn't take it too much to heart. I must say I carried out your orders to the last detail. I've been petting her all night so that she wouldn't get the idea

42

of clambering up here with a knife. And the proof that she doesn't hold it against you is that she is waiting for you downstairs with a basinful of hot wine."

"All right. Get out."

When Pretty Boy had gone, Angélique ventured to cast a glance between her eyelashes.

Nicholas was up already, at the far end of the room, clothed in his uniform of unspeakable rags. His back was turned and he was leaning over a case in which he was foraging for something. To a woman gifted with shrewdness, the attitude of that back was highly significant. It was the posture of an extremely embarrassed man.

He closed the case again and, grasping something tightly in his fist, he came back to the bed. She quickly pretended to be asleep.

He leaned over her and called her under his breath:

"Angélique, do you hear me? . . . I've got to go. But before I go I'd like to tell you . . . I'd like to know . . . Are you very cross with me about last night? . . . It's not my fault. I couldn't help it. You are so beautiful! . . . Is it true that I hurt you? D'you want me to send for Big Matthieu of the Pont-Neuf to see to you? . . ."

He put his rugged hand on the pearly shoulder that peeped out of the blanket, and she could not help shivering.

"Answer me. I can see you're no longer asleep. Look what I've chosen for you. It's a ring, a genuine one, I had it appraised by a goldsmith on the Quai des Orfèvres. Look at it. Don't you want it? Here, I'm putting it beside you. . . .

"Tell me what you want, what would please you. Would you like some ham? A fine ham? They brought in a fresh one this morning, pinched from the pork-butcher in the Place de Grève while he was watching one of our chaps being hanged. . . . Do you want a new dress? . . . I've got that, too. . . . Answer me, or I'll get angry."

She deigned to slip a glance through her tousled hair and said haughtily:

"I want a big tub with plenty of hot water."

"A tub?" he repeated, dumbfounded.

He peered at her suspiciously.

"What for?"

"To wash myself, you big hog."

"All right," he said, reassured. "Polack will bring it up for

43

you. Ask for anything you like. And if you aren't pleased, just let me know when I come back."

He turned towards a small Venetian mirror that stood on the mantelpiece, and began to stick on his cheek the coloured wax pellet that helped to disfigure his face.

Angélique sat up with a jerk.

"That I won't stand for!" she said categorically. "I *forbid* you, Nicholas Merlot, to appear before me with that repulsive face of a rotten, lewd old man. Otherwise I should not be able to stand your touching me ever again."

An expression of childlike joy lit the brutal face.

"And if I obey . . . you'll let me again?"

She abruptly pulled up a coat flap over her face to hide the emotion produced in her by this gleam in the eyes of the bandit Calembredaine. For it was the familiar look of the little Nicholas, so frivolous and unstable, but 'not bad at heart', as his poor old mother used to say. Nicholas, as he stooped over the ravished body of his young sister, calling her softly 'Francine, Francine . . .'

So this is what life can do to a little boy, a little girl. Her heart swelled with pity for both of them. They were alone and abandoned by all.

"You'll let me love you again?" he murmured.

Then, for the first time since they had so strangely found each other again, she smiled at him.

"Perhaps."

Nicholas solemnly stretched out his arm and spat on the ground.

"Then I swear. Even if I risk getting nabbed by the sergeants and archers by showing my cleaned-up face right on the Pont-Neuf, you'll never see me as Calembredaine again."

He stuffed his wig and bandage into his pocket.

"I'll go and put on my disguise downstairs."

"Nicholas," she called out. "I've hurt my foot. Look. D'you think this Big Matthieu you talked about could do something about it?"

"I'll look in and see him."

Abruptly, he took the small white foot in both his hands and kissed it.

When he had left, she snuggled herself up and tried to go to sleep again. It was very cold once more but, well covered up

as she was, she did not feel it. A pallid winter sun was painting rectangles of light on the walls.

Angélique's body was tired and aching, yet she felt a kind of
well-being.

'It's good,' she thought to herself. 'It's like feeding one's
hunger or quenching one's thirst. One no longer thinks of
anything. It's good not to think.'

Near her the diamond ring was sparkling. She smiled. Anyway, she'd always be able to twist this fellow Nicholas round
her little finger!

When, in later days, Angélique thought back to this period
of her life, when she had fallen to the lowest depths and
mingled with the worst scum, she would murmur, dreamily
shaking her head: 'I was mad.'

And that is indeed, perhaps what enabled her to live in that
terrifying and pitiful world—madness, or rather a numbing of
her sensibilities, the slumber of the beast defending itself
against the harsh winter.

All her gestures and deeds responded to the very simplest
reflexes. She wanted food, warmth. A chilly need of protection brought her back to Nicholas's hard chest and made her
docile to his brutal and possessive embraces.

She, who had loved the finest linen and embroidered sheets,
was sleeping on a bed of stolen coats in whose wool there
lingered the smell of all the men of Paris. She was the prey
of an oaf, a farmhand turned bandit, who was jealous and
madly proud to be her master, and not only did she not fear
him, but she even found pleasure in the overwhelming attentions he paid her.

The objects she used, the food she ate, were entirely the
fruit of larceny if not of murder. Her friends were wretches
and criminals. Her home the ramparts, the corners of the
river banks, the low taverns; and her entire world consisted
of this feared and almost inaccessible sphere of the Court of
Miracles, where the officers of the Châtelet and the sergeants of
the Provost Marshal did not dare to venture, except in full
daylight. Too few in numbers in face of the dreadful army of
outcasts who then comprised one-fifth of the population of
Paris, the forces of law and order abandoned the nights to the
scum.

And yet, after murmuring 'I was mad', Angélique would

45

sometimes become dreamy as she thought of those days when she had reigned, at the side of the illustrious Calembredaine, over the old ramparts and bridges of Paris.

Calembredaine had turned the Tower of Nesle into his headquarters. And the other captains of the underworld became aware that this newcomer among the 'brothers' encircled the entire university district, held the approaches to the former gates of Saint-Germain, Saint-Michel and Saint-Victor, right down to the banks of the Seine in the substructures of the Tournelle.

Students with a fancy for duelling on the Pré-aux-Clercs, lower-class citizens happy to go fishing in the old moats of a Sunday, fine ladies on their way to visit their women friends in the Faubourg Saint-Germain or to see their confessors at the Val de Grâce, now had to hold their purses ready. A swarm of beggars would rise before them, stop the horses, bar the passage of the carriages in the narrow alleys of the gates or little bridges thrown over the moats.

Peasants or travellers from outside had to pay toll a second time to the threatening *drilles* whom they found posted in front of them when they had already been inside Paris for a long while. By making the passage as difficult as it was in the days of drawbridges, the men of Calembredaine revived the old city wall of Philippe-Auguste.

This had been a master-stroke in the kingdom of the underworld. The sagacious, greedy midget who ruled over it, Squat Rolin, the Great Coesre, did not interfere. Calembredaine paid in princely fashion. His love of open fighting, his bold decisions, placed at the disposal of an organising genius like Wood-Bottom, made him daily more powerful. From the Tower of Nesle he took the Pont-Neuf, the prize of Paris with its stream of goggle-eyed strollers, who let their purses be cut so easily that artists like Jactance got disgusted with stealing them. The battle of the Pont-Neuf had been terrible. It had lasted for several months. Calembredaine won eventually, because his men occupied the approaches. In abandoned flat-bottomed boats, moored to the arches or piles of bridges, he posted his beggars, who, though seemingly asleep, were in fact as many watchful sentinels.

Sallying out into subterranean Paris in the company of Lightfoot, Barcarole or Wood-Bottom, Angélique gradually

46

discovered the network of squalor and ransom, so carefully set up by her former playmate.

"You are smarter than I thought," she said to him one day. "There are some good ideas in that pate of yours."

And she lightly brushed his forehead with her hand.

Such gestures, with which she was not lavish, would bowl the bandit over completely. He took her on his knees.

"That surprises you, ha? . . . You wouldn't have expected that from a clodhopper like me? But I've never been a clod-hopper, never wanted to be one. . . ."

He spat scornfully on the flagstones.

They sat before the fire in the big room below the Tower of Nesle. Calembredaine's henchmen were foregathered there with a crowd of ragged tramps, come to pay court to the potentate of their gang. Every night, this stinking, vociferous rabble swarmed all over the place amid the screaming infants, the belchings and invectives that resounded under the domed roof, the clatter of tin tankards, and the unbearable stench of old rags and wine.

Wood-Bottom was perched on the table with the arrogance of a trusty manager and the sombre air of an unappreciated philosopher. Barcarole, his crony, gambolled from one group to another, exasperating the card-players. Rat-Poison was selling his day's hunt to some famished old hags. Thibault was turning the handle of his hurdy-gurdy while casting mocking glances through the slits in his straw hat, and Linot, his little follower, a mudlark with angel's eyes, was beating his cymbal. Mother Hurlurette and Father Hurlurot began to dance and the firelight threw their grotesque, lumbering shadows on the ceiling. This beggar couple, Barcarole said, had but one eye and three teeth between the two of them. Father Hurlurot was blind and scraped a kind of bow with two strings strung across it which he called a fiddle. His wife was one-eyed, heavy, with an enormous mane of grey hair falling from under her dirty linen turban; she played the castanets, while jigging her big, bloated legs, wrapped up in several layers of stockings. Barcarole said also that she must have been Spanish . . . a long while ago. All that remained were the castanets.

In Calembredaine's immediate suite there were also Light-foot, the ever-breathless former runner; Tabelot the hunch-back; Jactance the cut-purse; Prudent, a very timorous and whining thief, whose fears did not prevent him from being a party to all the burglaries; Pretty Boy, a *barbillon*, that is to say a pimp, who, when he rigged himself up as a prince, would have deceived the King himself; prostitutes, as uncaring as animals or yelling like harpies; a very few mountebanks (for most of their kind paid homage to Rodogone the Egyptian) and several rogues of lackeys who, between jobs where they robbed their masters, looked for receivers to buy their spoils. There also were disreputable students whom poverty had brought to the corruption of the underworld and who had finally thrown in their lot with it. In exchange for small services, they came here to play dice with the rogues. These talkers of Latin were called 'arch-henchmen' and they drew up the laws of the Great Coesre. Such a one was Big-Bag, who, in a monk's disguise, had lured Conan Bécher into an ambush.

The swindlers of public charity, the misshapen, the blind, the lame, the daytime moribunds, also had their place in the Tower of Nesle. The ancient walls which had seen the lascivious orgies of Queen Marguerite of Burgundy, and heard the dying groans of young men slaughtered after love-making, were ending their sinister careers by sheltering the worst riff-raff in creation. There were also among them real cripples, idiots, halfwits, monsters like Cockscomb with a strange appendage on his forehead.

An accursed world: children who were no longer like children, women who gave themselves to men on the straw flung on the stone floor, old men and women with the vacant stare of lost dogs; and yet there floated a carefree air of pleasure over this motley crowd. Poverty and squalor are unbearable only as a half-way house and for those who have means of comparison. The people of the Court of Miracles had neither a past nor a future.

Many a husky fellow, sound in limb but lazy, fattened here in idleness. Hunger and cold were the lot of the weak, the lot of those who were used to them. The uncertainty of the morrow did not worry anybody. What matter! The invaluable prize of this uncertainty was freedom, the right to crack one's lice in the sunshine whenever one felt like it. Let him come, the constable in charge of the poor! Let them build their hospitals and almshouses, the noble ladies and their chaplains! . . . The beggars wouldn't put their feet inside them of their own free will, for all the soup that was ladled out.

48

As if there wasn't better fare to be had at Calembredaine's table, replenished at the right places by his minions, who haunted the barges, roamed near the butcher's shops and slaughter-houses, and held up the peasants on their way to the market!

In front of the crackling fire of stolen logs, Angélique leaned against the sinewy thighs of Calembredaine.

"Do you know what I have been thinking of?" said Nicholas. "All those ideas I've had that enabled me to succeed in Paris came to me from our adventures and expeditions as children. We used to prepare them well in advance, do you remember? Well, when I found I had to organise all this, I sometimes said to myself——"

He broke off to ponder and passed his tongue over his lips. A youngster called Flipot, who was squatting at his feet, handed him a goblet of wine.

"Good," growled Calembredaine, downing the goblet. "Leave us to talk. You see," he went on, "I'd say to myself: What would Angélique have done? What exploit would her little brain have thought of next? And that would help me. . . ."

He ventured a caress while watching her out of the corner of his eye. He never knew how his amorous advances would be received. For a kiss she might jump at him with flashing eyes like those of a raging wild-cat, threatening to hurl herself from the top of the tower, abusing him with a fishwife's vocabulary which had not taken her long to pick up.

She would sulk for entire days, so icy that she impressed even Barcarole and caused Pretty Boy to stutter. Calembredaine would then collect his team and they would all question themselves, thunderstruck, about the causes of her moodiness.

At other moments she could show herself gentle, playful, almost tender. He had found her again. It was she . . . the dream of his lifetime! The child Angélique, barefoot, in rags, with wisps of straw in her hair, running along the paths.

At other times again she would become listless, as if absent, submissive to all he wanted of her, but so indifferent that he would leave her, alarmed and vaguely frightened.

A funny wench she was, the Marquise of the Angels!

As a matter of fact, she did not calculate at all. Her feminine instinct had dictated to her the only line of defence. As she had once subjugated the little peasant Merlot, so she was now besting the bandit he had become. . . . She avoided the danger of becoming his slave or his victim by too much docility or arrogance. She held him at her mercy, more by cajoling consents than by blunt refusals. And Nicholas's passion became more devouring every day.

This dangerous man, whose hands were soiled with the blood of many crimes, had reached the point of trembling lest he displease her.

That evening, seeing that the Marquise of the Angels did not have her 'black' look, he began to fondle her with pride. And she leaned languidly against his shoulder like a clinging vine. She ignored the circle of hideous, grinning faces that surrounded them. She allowed him to open her bodice, to kiss her violently on her mouth. Her emerald gaze filtered through her eyelashes, provocative and remote. Savouring inwardly the depth of her degradation, she seemed openly to display her pride at being the plaything of a feared master.

Such boldness made Polack scream with rage.

Calembredaine's former official mistress did not easily accept her sudden dismissal, especially since Calembredaine, with the cruelty of a true tyrant, had made her Angélique's servant. It was she who had to carry hot water up to her rival for her ablutions, which were such a startling custom for the beggar world that they were talked about as far as the Faubourg Saint-Denis. In her fury Polack would spill half the boiling water over her own feet, but such was the former farmhand's power over these people that she did not dare to utter a word when facing the woman who had supplanted her in her lover's favour.

Angélique received the big, dark girl's services and hate-filled glances with indifference. In the underworld cant, the Polack was a *ribaude*, that is to say a camp-follower. She had more battle tales to tell than a hoary Swiss mercenary. She could talk of cannons, arquebuses and pikes with the same ease, for she had had lovers in all military branches. She had even gone with officers, she would explain, for their sheer good looks, for those sweet lords more often had empty pockets than the pillaging soldier had. During a whole campaign she had lorded it over a regiment of Poles, hence her nickname.

In her belt she wore a knife that she pulled out at the least provocation, and she had the reputation of handling it expertly. When evening came and she had reached the bottom of a pitcher of wine, the Polack would talk of sackings and fire.

"Ah! those good war days! I'd say to the soldiers: 'Love me, boys, I'll kill your lice! . . .'"

And she would start to sing guardhouse ditties and kiss any former soldier within her reach.

They would finally kick her out forcibly. Then, in the wintry rain and wind, the Marquise of the Polacks would run along the banks of the Seine and hold out her arms towards the Louvre, invisible in the night.

"Hey! Majesty! Hey!" she would cry. "When will you give us a war? A good war! What are you doing up there, good-for-nothing, in your den? Where did we ever get such a bloody, battle-less King? A King without victories?"

When she was sober, Polack would forget her bellicose discourses and think only of reconquering Calembredaine. She deployed for this purpose all the resources of an unscrupulous character and a volcanic temperament. In her opinion, she would say, Calembredaine wouldn't take long to tire of this girl who never laughed and whose eyes at times did not appear to see you. It was a fact that they were 'countrymen'. That created ties; but she knew Calembredaine. That wouldn't be enough for him. And, damn it all, she'd be willing, if it came to that, to share him. Two women for one man wasn't so much, after all. The Great Coesre had six of 'em!

The situation finally reached its inevitable climax. It was brief but violent.

One evening, Angélique had gone to see Wood-Bottom in the hole where he lived by the Bridge of Saint-Michel. She had brought him chitterlings. Wood-Bottom was the only person in the gang for whom she had any esteem. She showed him little attentions, which he received with the air of a grumpy bulldog who considers them perfectly natural.

That evening, after sniffing the chitterlings, he stared hard at Angélique and said:

"Where are you going from here?"

"Back to Nesle."

"Don't. Stop on your way at Ramez's Inn, by the Pont-Neuf. Calembredaine is there with the gang and Polack."

He paused for a moment as if to give this time to sink in, then pressed her:

"Have you grasped what you've got to do?"

"No."

She was kneeling before him as was her habit, in order to be level with the truncated man. The floor and walls of his lair were made of mud. The only piece of furniture was a trunk of boiled leather in which Wood-Bottom stored his four jackets and his three hats. He was always very fastidious about his half-person. His lair was lit by a stolen church lamp fastened to the wall—a delicate piece of goldsmith's work, in silver-gilt.

"You walk into the tavern," Wood-Bottom explained ponti-fically, "and when you see what Calembredaine and Polack are up to, you grab whatever comes within your reach—tankard, a bottle—and you bash him on the head."

"Whom?"

"Calembredaine, of course! Never bother about the girl in a case like this."

"I've got a knife," said Angélique.

"Leave it alone, you don't know how to use it. Besides, to give a lesson to a beggar who's got mixed up about his mar-quise, there's nothing like a swipe on the head, believe me!"

"But I don't care a rap if that groundling deceives me," said Angélique with a haughty smile.

The cripple's eyes flared under his bushy eyebrows. He spoke very slowly.

"You haven't the right . . . I'll go further: you have no choice. Calembredaine is mighty among our folk. He's won you. He's taken you. You've no longer the right to scorn him. Nor to let him scorn you. He's your man."

Angélique felt a shudder, in which anger mingled with an obscure sensual thrill. Her throat constricted.

"I don't want it," she mumbled in a stifled voice.

The cripple burst into a loud, bitter laugh.

"I didn't want it either when a cannonball came and tore my two pins off at Nordlingen. But it didn't ask my opinion. You can't undo these things. You've got to accept them, that's all . . . learn to walk on a wooden platter. . . ."

The flame of the lamp threw into relief all the pimples that sprouted on Wood-Bottom's big face. Angélique thought he resembled an enormous truffle; a mushroom grown in the darkness and dampness of the earth.

"So you too had better learn to walk among beggars," he went on in a low, urging voice. "Do what I tell you. Or you'll die."

She tossed her hair back with a rebellious move.

"I am not afraid of death."

"I wasn't talking of that sort of death," he growled, "but of that other worse one, that of your own self. . . ."

He suddenly flew into a temper.

"You make me talk a lot of rubbish. I'm trying to make you understand, confound you! You haven't the right to let Polack crush you! You haven't the right . . . not you. You hear me?"

He was drilling a fiery gaze into her eyes.

"Come on, get up and walk! Take the bottle and the goblet over there, in the corner. Bring them here. . . ."

And after pouring out a bumper of brandy:

"Wash that down in one gulp and then—go to it. . . . Don't be afraid to hit hard. I know Calembredaine. He's got a hard nut."

As she entered the tavern of Ramez the Auvergnat, Angélique stopped on the threshold. The fog was almost as thick inside as out. The chimney was drawing badly and filled the room with smoke. A few workmen sat with their elbows propped on rickety tables, drinking in silence.

At the far end of the room, before the hearth, Angélique saw the four soldiers who composed Calembredaine's usual guard: Peony, Gobert, Riquet, La Chaussée, then Barcarole, hoisted on a table, Jactance, Prudent, Big-Bag, Rat-Poison, and finally Nicholas himself, holding on his knees a nude, dishevelled, half-sprawling Polack, bellowing tavern songs.

This was the Nicholas she hated, the hideous, disguised face of Calembredaine.

This sight, added to the drink Wood-Bottom had given her, roused her fighting spirit. With a nimble hand she seized a heavy tin tankard from a table and advanced towards the group. They were all too drunk to see her or recognise her. She found herself behind Nicholas and, gathering all her strength, she struck blindly.

There was a loud whoop from Barcarole. Then Nicholas Calembredaine swayed and toppled headlong into the embers in the hearth, dragging with him a screaming Polack.

There followed a tumult. The other patrons of the inn had rushed out. They could be heard shouting 'Murder!' while the *narquois* drew their swords and Jactance clutched at Nicholas, trying to pull him out. Polack's hair was beginning to catch fire. Barcarole ran across the table on which he was perched, seized a jug of water and emptied it over her head.

Suddenly a voice cried:

"Run, brothers! The police!"

The sound of approaching riders came from outside. A police sergeant of the Châtelet appeared on the threshold, a pistol in his hand, shouting:

"Stay where you are, ruffians!"

But the thick smoke and almost complete darkness in the tavern made him lose precious time. Grabbing the inert body of their chief, the bandits dragged him into the back room and fled by way of another exit.

"Hurry, Marquise of the Angels!" Big-Bag yelled.

She jumped over an upturned bench and tried to catch up with them, but a hard fist grasped her. A voice shouted:

"I've got the hussy, sergeant!"

Suddenly, Angélique saw Polack looming before her. The slut had raised her dagger.

'I am going to die,' Angélique thought in a flash. The blade gleamed as it slashed the darkness. The constable who was holding Angélique bent double and collapsed with a groan.

Polack knocked over a table into the legs of the policemen who were running towards them. She pushed Angélique towards the window and they both jumped into the lane outside. A shot rang out on their heels.

A few moments later the two women caught up with the party of Calembredaine's henchmen at the approaches of the Pont-Neuf. They had stopped to catch their breath.

"Phew!" sighed Peony-Jean, wiping his sweating brow with his sleeve. "I don't think they'll be following us this far, but this damned Calembredaine is made of lead, confound him!"

"They haven't nabbed anybody? You there, Barcarole?"

"Still here."

Polack explained:

"They had hooked the Marquise of the Angels, but I knifed the dog. Right in the belly. That finished him."

She showed her blood-spattered dagger.

The party got going again towards the Tower of Nesle, its numbers swelled by all the fellow-members who at this hour were loitering in their favourite spots.

The news spread from mouth to mouth.

"Calembredaine! The Illustrious Scamp is wounded!"

Big-Bag was explaining:

"It's the Marquise of the Angels who hit him with a tankard because he was fooling around with Polack. . . ."

"That's fair enough!" they said.

A man suggested:

"I'll go and fetch Big Matthieu." And he dashed away.

At the Tower of Nesle Calembredaine was laid on the table in the big room. Angélique stepped over to him, tore off his hateful mask and examined his wound. She was disconcerted to see him thus motionless and covered with blood; she had not had the impression of hitting him so hard; his wig should have protected him. But the bottom of the tankard had slipped and gashed his temple. Moreover, in falling, he had burned his forehead.

She ordered:

"Put some water on to boil."

Several youngsters rushed to obey her. Everyone knew that the Marquise of the Angels had a bee in her bonnet about hot water, and this wasn't the time to argue with her. She had clouted Calembredaine where even Polack hadn't dared carry out her threats. She had done so quietly, at the right moment, and properly. . . . It was on the level. They admired her and nobody had any sympathy for Calembredaine, for they knew he had a hard head.

Suddenly there was a fanfare outside. The door opened, and in it appeared Big Matthieu, the dentist-quack of the Pont-Neuf.

Even at this late hour he had taken care to put on his famous fluted ruff, slip his necklace of human molars round his neck, and have himself escorted by his cymbals and trumpet.

Big Matthieu, like all mountebanks, had one foot in the underworld, and the other in the anteroom of princes. All men were equal before the tooth-puller's tongs. And pain renders the most arrogant nobleman as well as the boldest brigand weak and credulous. Big Matthieu's healing tooth-pastes, beneficent elixirs and miraculous plasters made a universal man of him. The Gutter-Poet had composed a song for him, which the hurdy-gurdy grinders sang on street-corners:

> . . . And knowing of every bodily ill
> The secret source,
> He prescribed the very same pill
> For man and horse.

He attended rogues and whores out of an innate cordiality and to keep in their good books, and he attended the mighty out of greed and ambition. He could have made a sensational career among titled ladies, whom he would pat familiarly and treat indiscriminately as Highnesses, bawds or wenches. But after travelling throughout Europe, he had decided to end his days on the Pont-Neuf.

He gazed at the still motionless Nicholas with undisguised satisfaction.

"Now there's a bloody mess for you. Did *you* get him into that state?" he asked Angélique.

Before she had time to answer, he had gripped her jaw with a determined fist and was examining her mouth.

"Not a stump to draw," he said, with disgust. "Let's see lower down. Are you pregnant?"

And he kneaded her stomach so energetically that she uttered a cry.

"No. The box is empty. Let's see lower down. . . ."

Angélique jerked away to escape this thorough examination.

"You fat-bellied nostrum-pot!" she cried furiously. "You haven't been brought here to paw me, but to look after that man over there. . . ."

"Ho! Ho! The Marquise," roared Big Matthieu. "Ho! Ho! Ho! Ho! Ho!"

His laughter rose in crescendos till he almost brought the roof down; all the while he held his belly with both hands. He was a high-coloured giant of a man, invariably dressed in gaudy coats of orange or peacock-blue satin. He wore a wig under a finely plumed hat. When he descended into the underworld, among the grimy rags and repulsive scars, he was dazzling as the sun.

When he had stopped laughing, he noticed that Calembredaine had recovered consciousness. He was sitting up on the table with a wicked expression, with which he was really trying to hide a certain embarrassment. He did not dare look towards Angélique.

"What have you all got to crow about, you bunch of bastards?" he growled. "Jactance, you halfwit, you've let the meat get burned again. This place stinks of roast pig."

"Fool! You're the roast pig!" Big Matthieu roared, wiping tears of laughter into a chequered handkerchief. "And so is

Polack! Just look! Half her back is roasted! Ho! Ho! Ho! Ho! . . ."

And he laughed even more uproariously.

They had a lot of fun, that night, in the beggars' lair at the Tower of Nesle, opposite the Louvre.

CHAPTER 55

"TAKE A look over there," said Peony to Angélique, "that man walking down by the water with his hat over his eyes and his coat up to his moustache. . . . You've spotted him, eh? Well, he's a *grimaut*."

"A *grimaut*?"

"A policeman, if you prefer."

"How do you know?"

"I don't know; I smell it."

And the ex-soldier pinched his toper's nose, a bulbous, crimson appendage which had earned him the nickname of Peony.

Angélique leaned on the little hump-backed bridge that passed over the moats before the Nesle Gate. A pallid sun was dispelling the fog that had been hanging over the city for several days. The opposite bank, with the Louvre, was still invisible, but there was a mellowness in the air. Ragged children fished in the moats, while a lackey at the river's edge was washing two horses.

The man whom Peony had pointed out with the tip of his pipe-stem looked like a harmless stroller, like some shopkeeper taking an after-dinner walk on the banks of the Seine. He was watching the lackey rub down the beasts, and now and then raised his head towards the Tower of Nesle as if interested in this crumbling old vestige of a bygone era.

"You know who he is looking for?" Peony went on, blowing the smoke of his coarse tobacco into Angélique's face.

She drew away a little.

"No."

"You."

"Me?"

"Yes, you, the Marquise of the Angels."

Angélique gave a vague smile.

57

"You're a visionary."

"I'm a . . . what?"

"Never mind. I mean you're having notions. Nobody is looking for me. Nobody is thinking of me. I no longer exist."

"Maybe. But for the time being it's Martin the constable who no longer exists. . . . You remember, at Ramez the Auvergnat's? Big-Bag shouted to you: 'Hurry, Marquise of the Angels!' That stuck in the ears of those policemen, and when they found the archer with his belly open, 'The Marquise of the Angels,' they said to themselves, 'that's the hussy who's done him in.' And they're looking for you. I know it because we old soldiers sometimes get together for a drink with old war pals who've taken service at the Châtelet. You get to know things that way."

"Pah!" Calembredaine's voice said behind them, "it's nothing to get into a panic about. If we wanted to, we could dump that fellow down there into the river. What can they do against us? They're hardly a hundred, while we . . ."

He made a proud, possessive gesture as if gathering the whole city around him. From upstream, through the mist, came the clamour of the Pont-Neuf and its mountebanks.

A carriage began to drive over the bridge and they stepped aside to let it pass; but at the other end of the bridge the horses shied, for a beggar had thrown himself under their hooves. It was Black-Bread, one of Calembredaine's rogues, an old, white-bearded man, decked out with thick rosaries and pilgrim's shells.

"Have pity?" he intoned. "Take pity on a poor pilgrim on his way to Compostella to make a vow, and who hasn't the wherewithal to continue his pilgrimage. Give me a few *sols* and I shall pray for you on the grave of Saint-Jacquer."

The coachman dealt him a violent blow with his whip.

"Get back, devil's pilgrim!"

A lady put her head out of the carriage-window. Her half open cloak afforded a glimpse of beautiful jewels at her neck.

"What is going on, Lorrain? Hurry the horses up a bit. I want to be at the Abbey of Saint-Germain-des-Prés for compline."

Nicholas stepped forward and put his hand on the handle of the carriage door.

"Pious lady," he said, removing his tattered hat, "would you,

58

who are on your way to compline, refuse a gift to this poor pilgrim who is going to pray to God so far away in Spain?"

The lady stared at the black-bearded face that had appeared out of the dusk, scrutinised the creature whose torn tunic showed a wrestler's biceps, and whose belt held a butcher's knife. She opened her mouth wide and began to scream:

"Help! Help! Murd——"

Peony already had his rapier's tip against the coachman's belly. Black-Bread and Flipot, one of the gutter-snipes who had been fishing in the moat, were holding back the horses. Prudent arrived at a run. Calembredaine had jumped into the coach and was stifling the woman's cries with a brutal hand.

He cried to Angélique:

"Your kerchief! Hey! Your kerchief!"

Without knowing how, Angélique found herself in the carriage, smelling again the scent of iris powder, of satin and fine, gold-braided petticoats. Calembredaine had torn off her neckerchief and was stuffing it into the mouth of the captive woman.

"Hurry, Prudent! Tear her sparklers off! Take her money."

The woman struggled furiously. Prudent was sweating as he tried to unfasten the jewels, a little gold chain and a choker with a beautiful gold plaque encrusted with several large diamonds.

He got tangled up in it.

"Give me a hand, Marquise of the Angels," he whined. "I get muddled with all these gewgaws."

"Hurry up, we must be quick. She's slippery as an eel," Calembredaine grumbled.

Angélique's hands found the clasp. It was very simple. She had worn similar ones. . . .

"Give them the lash, coachman!" cried Peony's mocking voice.

The carriage hurtled down the Rue du Faubourg Saint-Germain with creaking wheels. The coachman, deeming himself lucky to have got off with a fright, lashed his horses. A little farther on, the woman's screams rang out again.

Angélique's hands were full of the exquisite weight of gold.

"Bring a candle," shouted Calembredaine.

In the Tower, they gathered around the table and gazed at the glittering jewels which Angélique had deposited there.

"A fine stroke!"

"Black-Bread will get his share, he started it."

"Still," sighed Prudent, "it was a risky thing. It was still daylight."

"You can't miss a chance like this, you'll learn, you clumsy, dithering fool. Ah! you're a light-fingered one, you are. If the Marquise hadn't given you a hand . . ."

Nicholas looked at Angélique and there was a strange, victorious smile on his lips.

And he flung her the gold chain. She pushed it back with horror.

"All the same," Prudent kept saying, "it was a risky deal. Not so smart, with a policeman only two steps away."

"There was the fog. He didn't see a thing, and if he heard anything he is still running. What could he do to us, eh? No, there's only one I am afraid of. But he hasn't been seen around for a long while. Let's hope he got himself bumped off somewhere. It's a shame. I'd have liked to have his hide, him and his blasted dog."

"Oh! the dog! the dog!" said Prudent, with bulging eyes. "He's had me here . . ."

And he raised his hand to his throat.

"The man with the dog," murmured Calembredaine, half closing his eyes, "but, come to think of it, I saw you with him one day, near the Petit Pont. You know him? . . ."

He approached Angélique and gazed at her musingly, then his face broke into his grim smile.

"You do know him," he repeated. "That's fine. You'll help us get him, won't you, now that you are one of ours?"

"He has left Paris. He'll never come back, I know it," said Angélique, tonelessly.

"Oh yes! he'll be back. . . ."

Calembredaine wagged his head, and the others did likewise. Peony grunted gloomily:

"The man with the dog always comes back."

"You'll help us, won't you?"

Nicholas had picked up the gold chain from the table.

"Take it, pet. You've earned it."

"No!"

"Why not?"

"I don't like gold," said Angélique, who was suddenly gripped by a convulsive shaking. "I loathe gold."

And she walked out, unable to stand this hellish circle any more.

The figure of the policeman had disappeared. Angélique walked along the banks. In the slate-coloured fog glowed the yellow pin-points of the lanterns fastened to the bows of the barges. She heard a boatman tune his guitar and began to sing. She walked on, towards the far end of the faubourg, whence came the scent of the countryside. When she stopped at last the night and the fog had muffled all sounds. She heard only the water whispering down below among the reeds, against the boats at their moorings.

She said softly, like a child who is afraid of too great a silence:

"Desgrez!"

A voice whispered in the folds of the night and the water: 'When evening falls on Paris, we two go hunting. We go down to the banks of the Seine, we roam under the bridges and piles, we stroll over the old ramparts, we dive into holes full of that vermin of beggars and bandits. . . .'

'The man with the dog will come back. . . . The man with the dog always comes back. . . .'

'And now, gentlemen, the time has come to make you listen to a solemn voice, a voice which, beyond all human turpitudes, has always sought to exhort the faithful to prudence. . . .'

'The man with the dog will come back. . . . The man with the dog always comes back. . . .'

Angélique hugged her shoulders with both hands to contain the cry that was bursting in her breast:

"Desgrez!"

But only silence answered her, a silence as deep as the snowy silence in which Desgrez had abandoned her. A silence as frozen as death, in which they had *all* abandoned her.

She took a few steps towards the river and her feet sank into the mud. Then the water rippled round her ankles. It was icy. . . . Would Barcarole say: 'Poor Marquise of the Angels, she can't have enjoyed much dying in cold water, she who was so fond of hot water'?

Among the reeds an animal moved, a rat probably. A little ball of wet hair brushed Angélique's calves. She gave a cry of disgust, recoiled, and hurriedly climbed up the bank again. But the clawing paws clutched at her petticoat. The rat was clambering up on her. She struck out in all directions to get rid of it. The animal began to cry shrilly. Suddenly Angélique felt around her neck the clasp of two icy little arms. She cried out with surprise:

"What's this? This isn't a rat! . . ."

Two boatmen were passing on the towpath with a lantern. Angélique called out to them:

"Hey there! Boatmen! Lend me your light!"

The two men stopped and eyed her suspiciously.

"A pretty wench!" said one of them.

"Don't move," said the other, "it's Calembredaine's wench. Keep still, if you don't want to be bled like a pig. He is jealous of this one. A real Turk!"

"Oh! A monkey!" exclaimed Angélique, who had at last managed to make out what type of animal was clinging to her.

The monkey continued to clasp her neck with his thin, long arms, and his black hunted eyes gazed at Angélique in almost human fashion. Although clothed in tiny red silk trunk-hose, he was shivering violently.

"Doesn't he belong to you or one of your pals?"

The boatmen shook their heads.

"Faith, no. He rather looks as if he belongs to one of the mountebanks of the Saint-Germain Fair."

"I found him down there. By the river."

One of the men swung the lantern in the direction towards which she pointed.

"There's someone down there," he said.

They approached and discovered a body stretched out in a sleeping position.

"Hey, man, a bit cold for sleeping out!"

As he did not move, they turned him over and gave a cry of fright, for he wore a red velvet mask. His long white beard flowed over his chest. His conical hat with a criss-cross of red ribbons, his embroidered shoulder-bag, his velvet trunks, tucked up at the legs with worn, muddy ribbons, were those of an Italian mountebank, one of those showmen of trained animals who came from Piedmont and wandered from fair to fair.

He was dead. His open mouth was already full of mud.

The monkey, still clinging to Angélique, uttered plaintive cries. The young woman bent down and removed the red mask. It revealed the face of an emaciated old man. Death had already ravaged it; his eyes were glassy.

"There's nothing left for it but to throw him into the river," said one of the boatmen.

But the other, who had crossed himself devoutly, said that one ought to fetch an abbé from Saint-Germain-des-Prés and see that this poor foreigner got a Christian burial.

Angélique left them noiselessly and walked back to the Tower of Nesle. She held the little monkey tightly to her bosom, as, shaking her head, she remembered. The tavern of The Trois Maillets was the place where she had first seen him. The monkey had made all the patrons laugh as he imitated their ways of drinking or eating. And Gontran had said, pointing the old Italian out to his sister: "Look, what a beauty, that red mask and that shimmering, snowy beard! . . ."

She also remembered that his master had called the monkey Piccolo.

"Piccolo!"

The monkey gave a sorrowful cry and pressed himself against her.

Angélique noticed only afterwards that she had kept the red mask in her hand.

At this very moment, Monsieur de Mazarin breathed his last. After having himself conveyed to Vincennes and handing his fortune to the King, who had refused it, the Cardinal departed this life, which he had appreciated to the full, having known its most varied facets.

He had bequeathed his deepest passion, power, to his royal pupil.

And raising towards the King his yellowed face, the Prime Minister had transmitted to him in a murmur the key to a sovereign's absolute power:

"No Prime Minister, no favourite. You alone the master . . ."

Then, spurning the Queen Mother's tears, the Italian had died.

The Peace of Westphalia with Germany, the Peace of the Pyrénées with Spain, the Northern Peace concluded by him under the auspices of France, all kept watch at his bedside.

The little King of the *Fronde*, of the civil war and the foreign wars, the little King, whose crown was threatened by the mighty, and whose cooking-pot was more than once knocked over while he roamed from town to town, henceforth appeared in Europe as the King of Kings.

Louis XIV ordered forty hours' prayers to be said and went into mourning. The Court had to follow his example. The whole kingdom was murmuring prayers before the altars for the hated Italian, and the knell tolled over Paris for two days without interruption.

Then, after having wept the last tears of a young heart determined to have no more to do with sentiment, Louis XIV with royal punctuality settled down to work. Meeting in his anteroom the President of the Assembly of the Clergy, who asked to whom he should henceforward turn concerning questions which the Cardinal used to settle, the King replied: "To me, Archbishop.

"No Prime Minister . . . no omnipotent favourite . . . I am the State, gentlemen."

The startled Ministers were standing before the young King whose love of pleasure had led them to indulge in different hopes. Like employees under supervision, they submitted their files. The Court smiled sceptically. The King had drawn up a time-table, hour by hour, comprising all his occupations, balls and mistresses, but work above all: intensive, unceasing, meticulous work. People wagged their heads. That wouldn't last, they said.

It was to last for fifty years.

On the other side of the Seine, in the Tower of Nesle, Barcarole's gossip brought an echo of the royal life to the underworld. Barcarole the dwarf was always well informed of what was going on at Court. For in his moments of leisure he would don the costume of a sixteenth-century 'buffoon' with bells and feathers, and act as door-keeper in the house of one of the greatest soothsayers of Paris.

"And however much those fine ladies veil and mask themselves, I recognise them all. . . ."

The names he mentioned and the details he gave left Angélique, who had known them all, in no doubt as to the fact that the brightest flowers of the King's entourage were frequent visitors to the shady lair of the fortune-teller in question.

The woman was called Catherine Monvoisin, known as La Voisin. Barcarole said she was terrifying and, above all, extraordinarily clever. Squatting in his habitual toad-like position near his friend Wood-Bottom, Barcarole would reveal in brief phrases to Angélique, who was alternately frightened and curious, the secret intrigues and the dreadful arsenal of weird practices and mystifications which he had occasion to witness.

What were they after, all those princes and noble ladies, who slipped out of the Louvre grey-cloaked and masked, to run through the muddy streets of Paris and knock at the door of a disreputable den, which was opened by a grimacing dwarf, to go and confide their most intimate secrets in the ear of a half-drunk woman? They were after those difficult things that cannot be obtained with money alone.

Love. Starry-eyed love, but also the love of ripe women who see their lovers slip from them and want to retain them, the love of ambitious, never contented women who wanted to climb higher, ever higher. . . .

They would come to ask La Voisin for magic philtres to shackle the heart, for aphrodisiacs to excite the senses. Others hankered after the legacy of an old uncle who would not die, or wanted to get rid of an elderly husband, or of a rival, or of a child to be born.

Abortionist, poisoner, witch—La Voisin was all these things.

What else did they want? To discover treasures, talk to the devil, conjure up a deceased person, kill by magic from afar? . . . All they had to do was pay a visit to La Voisin. It was merely a question of price, and La Voisin would find the requisite accomplices: an apothecary to concoct poisons, a lackey or chambermaid to steal letters, a debauched priest to hold black masses, or perhaps a baby to be sacrificed at the ritual moment by thrusting a long needle deep into its neck.

Plunged into the depths of the Court of Miracles by a false witchcraft trial, Angélique discovered, from Barcarole's accounts, the existence of real witchcraft. He disclosed to her the appalling corruption of the religious impulse which her century experienced with an intensity and a naïveté that future generations found hard to conceive.

Rotten Jean sold La Voisin many children for her sacrifices. It was through him, moreover, that Barcarole had become the soothsayer's door-keeper. Rotten Jean liked his work to be straightforward, properly done, and well organised.

Angélique could never meet this infamous character without a shudder. Whenever this small white-faced man, with the glassy eyes of a dead fish, sneaked into the room through the crumbling doorway, she trembled. A snake would not have been more terrifying.

For Rotten Jean was a child-merchant. Somewhere around the Faubourg Saint-Denis, in the very domain of the Great Coesre, there was a big mud hovel, about which even the most hardened rogues talked only in lowered voices. Day and night, there came from it the cries of martyrised innocents. Foundlings and stolen children were herded there. The frailest had their limbs twisted so that they could be hired out to beggar-women who would use them to arouse the pity of the passers-by. The prettiest little boys and girls, on the other hand, were carefully brought up and sold, when still quite young, to vicious noblemen who earmarked them well in advance for their dreadful pleasures. The luckiest were those who were bought by barren women, hungry for a child's smile in their home, or to appease a discontented husband, or else to make sure of a legacy by means of an apparent offspring. Quacks and mountebanks for a few *sols* would acquire sturdy children and train them to perform tricks.

A vast, ceaseless trade was carried on in this pitiable merchandise. Childred died by the hundreds. There were always fresh supplies; Rotten Jean was indefatigable. He went to see wet-nurses, sent his men into the countryside, picked up abandoned children, bribed the servants of public orphanages, kidnapped little Savoyards and Auvergnats who had come to Paris with their kerchiefs and their chimney-sweep material and who vanished without leaving a trace.

Paris had engulfed them, as it engulfed the weak, the poor, the lonely, the sick, the aged, pensionless soldiers, peasants driven from their land by the wars, ruined merchants. To all of them the underworld extended its nauseous welcome and offered all the resources of its industries.

Some learned to become epileptics, others to steal. Old men and women hired themselves out to form funeral processions. Girls prostituted themselves, and mothers sold their daughters. Sometimes a great nobleman would pay for the services of a party of hired assassins to dispatch an enemy. Or else the Court of Miracles served to provide a number of extras for riots that might influence the outcome of some Court intrigue. Paid to yell and shout abuse, the people of the underworld revelled in their task, and, faced with a circle of threatening tatterdemalions, many a Minister thought he was on the point of being thrown into the Seine by the rebelling capital and yielded to the pressure of his rivals.

It would also happen that on the eve of high festivals clerical figures could be seen to slip into the most dangerous lairs. Tomorrow the shrine of Saint-Opportune or Saint-Marcel would pass through the streets. The canons and chapter wished an appropriate miracle, occurring at the psychological moment, to revive the crowd's faith in the excellence of their relics. How could that be brought about, if not at the Court of Miracles? Well paid, the bogus blind, the bogus deaf, the sham paralytic would post themselves along the path of the procession and suddenly proclaim that they were cured, while shedding tears of joy.

Who could say that the people of the kingdom of the underworld were living in idleness?

Did not Pretty Boy have his hands full with his battalion of prostitutes, who brought him their wages, to be sure, but whose quarrels he had to settle and for whom he had to steal the finery they needed for their trade? Peony, Gobert, and all the ex-soldiers often spent a cold night out and had few spoils to show for it. For one coat they snatched, how many hours' waiting, how much shouting, what a hue and cry! . . .

And is it such fun to spit soap-bubbles when you are a sham epileptic, rolling on the ground in the middle of a circle of gaping spectators? Particularly when, at the end of the road, there is a lonely death waiting for you, among the reeds of the river-bank or, even worse, torture in the prisons of the Châtelet, torture that makes your nerves crack and your eyes pop, and the gibbet on the Place de Grève, the gibbet at the end of it all. . . .

In the kingdom of the underworld, Angélique, protected by Calembredaine and by Wood-Bottom's friendship, enjoyed a free and sheltered life.

She was untouchable. She had paid her fee by becoming the companion of a vagabond. The laws of the underworld are harsh. Calembredaine's jealousy was known to be unforgiving, and Angélique could find herself in the company of rough, dangerous men like Peony or Gobert in the middle of the night without running any risk of even the smallest equivocal gesture on their part. Whatever desires she might arouse, as

67

long as the chief had not lifted his ban she belonged to him alone. So that her life, though wretched to all appearances, was almost wholly divided between long hours of sleep and listlessness and aimless strolls through Paris. She was always sure of having something to eat and of finding a warming fire in the hearth of the Tower of Nesle.

She could have dressed properly, for the burglars sometimes brought back fine clothes, smelling of iris and lavender. But she had no fancy for that. She had kept the same brown serge costume, whose petticoat was by now becoming frayed. The same old linen bonnet held up her hair. But Polack had given her a special belt to hold her knife under her bodice.

"If you like, I'll teach you how to use it," she had suggested.

Ever since the night of the tin tankard and the slain archer, a mutual respect had grown between them, which was not far from becoming a friendship.

Angélique rarely went out in the day-time and never far. Instinctively she adopted the rhythm of life of her companions, to whom burghers, traders and archers abandoned the night. So it was one night that the past returned to her, loomed up and woke her so cruelly that she almost died of it.

Calembredaine's gang was burgling a house in the Faubourg Saint-Germain. It was a moonless night, the street was poorly lit. When Pick-Lock, a nimble-fingered youngster, managed to turn the latch of the small servants' entrance, they walked in without taking any great precautions.

"It is a big house, and there's only one old man in it with a maid who lives on the top floor," Nicholas explained. "We'll have all the time in the world to do the job."

And after lighting his dark lantern, he led them into the drawing-room. Black-Bread, who had frequently come to beg here, had given him a detailed plan of the premises. Angélique brought up the rear. It was not the first time that she had thus entered a house. In the beginning, Nicholas had not wanted to take her along.

"You'll get into a scrape," he said.

But she always did as she pleased. She did not follow them to steal. She just liked to sniff again the smell of sleeping houses. Tapestries, highly-polished furniture, the fragrance of cooking and pastries. She would touch the knick-knacks, put them down again. No voice ever rose within her to say: 'What are you doing here, Angélique de Peyrac?' Except that

68

night, when Calembredaine was burgling the house of the old scientist Glazer in the Faubourg Saint-Germain.

Angélique's hand had come against a torch and a candle on a pier-table. She lit it with her companions' lantern, then noticed a little door at the end of the room and pushed it inquisitively.

"Christ!" Prudent's voice whispered behind her, "what is this?"

The candle-flame was reflected in big, long-beaked glass bowls, and one could dimly make out intertwining copper tubes, earthenware pots with Latin inscriptions, coloured phials of all kinds.

"Whatever can this be?" Prudent repeated, perplexed.

"A laboratory."

Shrinking back, Prudent knocked over an alembic, which fell and broke with a tinkling noise. They left the room hurriedly. The drawing-room was empty. The others, having finished their raid, had gone. They heard a knock against the stone floor upstairs and an old man's voice shouted:

"Marie-Josèphe, you have again forgotten to lock up the cats. It's intolerable. I'll have to go down and see." Then, leaning over the landing, he cried:

"Is that you, Sainte-Croix? Have you come for the recipe?"

Angélique and her companion dashed into the kitchen, then into the pantry, on to which gave the small door that had been forced by the burglars. A few streets farther on, they stopped.

"Phew!" sighed Prudent, "I did have a fright. Who'd have thought we were dropping in on a sorcerer! . . . If only it won't bring us bad luck! Where are the others?"

"They must have gone home by another way."

"They might have waited for us. I can't see a thing."

"Oh! don't always complain, my poor Prudent. People like you must be able to see in the dark. "

But he gripped her arm and panted strangely.

"Listen."

"What is it?"

"Don't you hear? Listen . . ." he repeated in a tone of unspeakable terror.

And suddenly he uttered a groan.

"The dog! . . . The dog!"

Flinging his sack down, he ran away.

'The poor fellow is unhinged,' Angélique thought to herself, as she bent down mechanically to pick up the burglar's booty. Just then she, too, heard it. It came from the depths of the silent streets.

It was like a light, very fast gallop, drawing closer. Suddenly she saw the animal at the far end of the street, like a leaping, white phantom. Angélique, swept by a nameless panic, took to her heels. She ran like a madwoman, paying no heed to the cobblestones that twisted her feet. She was blind. She felt she was lost and wanted to scream, but no sound came from her throat.

The shock of the animal's leap at her shoulders threw her face-down in the mud. She felt his weight upon her, and against her neck the pressure of a jaw with fangs sharp as nails.

"Sorbonne!" she cried.

She repeated in a lower voice:

"Sorbonne!"

Then very slowly she turned her head. It was he, without any doubt, for he had released her at once. She raised her hand and stroked the big head of the Great Dane. He was sniffing her with surprise.

"Sorbonne, good old Sorbonne, you gave me such a fright. That is not nice, you know."

The dog suddenly gave her face a big lick with his rough tongue.

Angélique got up painfully. She had hurt herself badly in falling. She heard the noise of footsteps. Her blood congealed. Sorbonne . . . that meant Desgrez. Never one without the other. The man with the dog always comes back! . . .

With a bound, Angélique was on her feet.

"Don't betray me," she implored under her breath, turning to the dog. "Don't give me away."

She had only just time to hide in a doorway. Her heart throbbed as if it were going to break. She had a moment's mad hope that it might not be Desgrez. He had had to leave town. He could not come back. He belonged to a dead and buried past. . . .

The footsteps were quite close. They stopped.

"Well, Sorbonne," said the voice of Desgrez, "what's the matter with you? You did not catch the hussy?"

Angélique's heart was aching, so furiously did it beat against her chest.

70

This familiar voice, the lawyer's voice! 'And now, gentlemen, the time has come to make you hear a solemn voice, a voice which, beyond all human turpitudes . . .'

The night was deep and dark as a chasm. Nothing was visible, but Angélique might have reached Desgrez with two steps. She sensed his movements and guessed his perplexity.

"Confounded Marquise of the Angels!" he shouted—and she jumped in her hiding-place. "I'll be damned if she gives us the slip for long. Come on, sniff, Sorbonne, sniff. The hussy had the good idea of leaving her neckerchief behind in the carriage. With this, she won't be able to get away. Come, let's turn back towards the Gate of Nesle. That's where the track starts, I am sure."

He walked away, whistling for the dog, who lagged behind.

Sweat ran down Angélique's temples. Her legs were giving way. She decided finally to take a few steps out of her hiding-place. If Desgrez was roaming round the Gate of Nesle, it was wiser not to go back there.

She would try to make for Wood-Bottom's hovel and ask him to give her shelter for the rest of the night.

Her mouth was dry. She heard the murmuring water of a fountain. The little square on which it stood was dimly lit by a lamp in front of a haberdasher's shop.

Angélique approached and plunged her muddy face into the cool water. She sighed with relief.

As she straightened up, a strong arm encircled her waist while a brutal hand struck her mouth.

"I've got you, my pretty bird," said Desgrez's voice. "Do you think I'm thrown off the scent so easily?"

Angélique tried to free herself, but he was holding her in such a way that she could not move without crying out in pain.

"No, no, my little chicken, you won't get away," the policeman said with a dry laugh.

Paralysed against him, she recognised the familiar smell of his worn clothes: old serge, leather, ink and parchment, tobacco. It was Desgrez with his night-time face. She faltered, a single thought uppermost in her mind: 'If only he doesn't recognise me. . . . I'd die of shame. . . . If only I manage to run away before he recognises me!'

Still holding her with a single hand in a special grip, Desgrez raised a whistle to his mouth and gave three strident blows.

A few minutes later, five or six men arrived from the neighbouring streets. Angélique heard the clatter of their spurs and their sword-belts. They were the constables of the watch.

"I think I've got our bird," Desgrez called out.

"Well! This is a profitable night. We collared two burglars who were trying to get away. If we bring the Marquise of the Angels back as well, we'll have to grant that you've guided us well, sir. You do know the right corners. . . ."

"The dog was the one who guided us. With that hussy's kerchief, he just had to take us straight to her. But there was something I couldn't understand. She almost got away. . . . Do you know this Marquise of the Angels?"

"She's Calembredaine's woman. That's all we know. The only one of us who ever saw her at close range died—Constable Martin, whom she knifed in a tavern. But we can just pick up the wench you've got there, sir. If it's her, Madame de Brinvilliers will recognise her. It was still daylight when her coach was waylaid by the bandits, and she very clearly saw the woman who was her accomplice."

"Damn piece of cheek!" one of the men growled. "They are no longer afraid of anything, these bandits. To waylay the coach of the Police Lieutenant's own daughter, and in broad daylight in the middle of Paris!"

"They'll pay for it, don't you worry."

Angélique listened closely to this conversation. She was trying to keep stock-still in the hope that Desgrez might release his grip. She would leap, with a jerk, into the helpful darkness and run away. She was certain that Sorbonne would not pursue her. And those awkward fellows in their heavy uniforms would never be able to catch her. But the ex-lawyer seemed in no mood to forget his capture. He searched her with an expert hand.

"What is this?" he said.

She felt his hands sliding under her bodice. He gave a little whistle.

"A knife! Upon my word! And not a pen-knife, either, you can believe me. Well, sister, you don't seem very meek to me."

He slipped Rodogone the Egyptian's dagger into one of his pockets and continued his inspection.

She quivered as his rough, warm hand passed over her breasts and lingered there.

"Goodness, what a heart-beat!" Desgrez chaffed in an

undertone. "That doesn't sound like a clear conscience. Let's pull her under that shoplight and see what she looks like."

With a wrench she jerked herself free, but ten iron fists promptly grasped her, and a shower of blows rained upon her.

They dragged her into the light. Desgrez seized her hair with a rough hand and pulled her head back. Angélique closed her eyes. With those smears of mud and blood on her face, he might not recognise her if she closed her eyes. She shook so much that her teeth chattered.

The seconds that passed while she was thus exposed to the crude light of the candle seemed to her like centuries. Then Desgrez released her with a disappointed growl.

"No. It isn't she. It isn't the Marquise of the Angels."

The constables swore in unison.

"How do you know, sir?" asked one of them.

"I've seen her. She was pointed out to me one day on the Pont-Neuf. This girl looks rather like her but she's not the one."

"Let's take her along anyway. She might spit up some information."

Desgrez seemed to ponder, somewhat perplexed.

"There was something fishy about this, as a matter of fact," he went on musingly. "Sorbonne never makes a mistake. Well, he didn't grab this wench. He left her in peace when she was but a few steps away from him—that shows she isn't dangerous."

He concluded with a sigh:

"We've drawn a blank. Good thing you caught two burglars at least. Where did they break in?"

"In the rue du Petit-Lion. At an old apothecary's, a fellow called Glazer."

"Let's go back there. Perhaps we can pick up the scent."

"And what do we do about the girl?"

Desgrez seemed to hesitate.

"I wonder whether it wouldn't be better to let her go. Now that I know her face, I won't forget her. It may come in useful."

Without hesitation the constables released the young woman, and disappeared into the night with a great clatter of spurs.

Angélique slid out of the circle of light. She groped along the walls and found the darkness again with relief. But she could see something white by the fountain and heard the dog

73

Sorbonne's tongue smacking his lips as he drank. Desgrez's shadow was by his side.

Angélique grew motionless again. She saw Desgrez lift his hat and make a gesture in her direction. Something hard fell at her feet.

"Here," said the policeman's voice, "you can have your knife back. I've never stolen from a girl. And for a damsel walking at this time of night, it may be useful. Well, goodnight."

She could not reply.

"You don't say goodnight?"

She gathered up all her courage to breathe:

"Goodnight."

On the ringing cobblestones she heard Desgrez's heavy, nailed boots recede. Then once more she began to roam blindly through Paris.

CHAPTER 56

DAWN FOUND her on the edge of the Latin Quarter, near the rue des Bernardins. The sky was beginning to glow with pink tints above the roofs of the black colleges. She could see the reflection from candles lit by early-rising students in the attic windows. She passed others who were returning, yawning and bleary-eyed, from a bawdy-house, where wretched trollops had rocked these seedy youths for a few hours. They brushed by her in their dirty neck-bands, shabby serge clothes, and black stockings that sagged over their meagre calves.

The bells of the chapels began to ring.

Angélique reeled with fatigue. She was walking barefoot, for she had lost both her old shoes. Her face was dazed and vacant.

When she reached the Quai de la Tournelle, the scent of fresh hay was wafted to her—the first hay of spring. The barges were moored in a long line with their light and fragrant cargo. In the Parisian dawn they exhaled a breath of warm incense, the aroma of a thousand dried flowers, the promise of lovely days to come.

She slipped down to the bank. A few steps away, the boatmen were warming themselves around a fire and did not see her. She waded into the water and hoisted herself on to the prow of a barge. She delved voluptuously into the hay. Under the canvas cover the smell was even more intoxicating: moist, hot and charged with thunder like a summer day. Where could this hay have come from? From some silent, rich, fertile countryside, under a warm sun. This hay brought with it the quiet of vast, wind-dried horizons, of lofty skies filled with light.

Angélique lay down with outflung arms. Her eyes were closed. She was submerging, drowning in, the hay. She floated on a cloud of frail and poignant perfumes, and she no longer felt her aching body. Monteloup enveloped her and carried her away. The air had recaptured its flowery fragrance, its taste of dew. The wind caressed her. She floated slowly, drifting towards the sunshine. She was leaving the night and its horrors. The sun caressed her. For a very long time she had not been caressed like this.

She had been the prey of the savage Calembredaine. She had been the mate of the wolf who sometimes, during a brief embrace, had managed to wrest from her a cry of animal lust, the groan of a beast possessed. But her body had forgotten the sweetness of caresses. The light touch of flowers on the sensitive skin . . . long shivers that spread and bathe the abandoned body with tenderness. . . .

She floated towards Monteloup, finding again the smell of raspberries in the hay. On her burning cheeks, on her dry lips, the water of the brook showered cooling caresses. She opened her mouth and sighed 'Again!'

In her sleep, tears rolled down Angélique's face and trickled into her hair. They were not tears of sorrow, but of a too great sweetness.

She stretched her limbs, yielding herself up to those recaptured caresses . . . she let herself drift, cradled by the murmuring voices of the fields and the woods, which whispered into her ear:

'Don't cry . . . don't cry, my darling. . . . It's nothing. . . . No more misery. . . . Don't cry, poor little thing.'

Angélique opened her eyes. In the false twilight under the canvas she discerned a figure stretched out beside her in the hay. Two laughing eyes gazed at her.
She stammered:

75

"Who are you?"

The stranger put a finger to his lips.

"I am the wind. The wind from a little corner of the Berry countryside. When they mowed the hay, they mowed me flat with it. . . . Look, it's quite true, I'm flat."

He kneeled down and turned his pockets out.

"Not a single coin! Not a *sol*! Completely flat. Flattened with the hay. They put me into a barge and here I am in Paris. Funny thing to happen to a little country wind."

"But——" said Angélique. She passed her tongue over her lips, trying to assemble her thoughts.

The young man was dressed in a shabby black suit, which showed holes here and there. The linen band around his neck was in shreds, and the belt of his singlet emphasised his leanness. But he had a piquant face, which was almost handsome despite his pale hunger-drawn complexion. His long, thin lips seemed made for ceaseless chatter and for easy laughter about everything and nothing. His features were never in repose. He grimaced, laughed, mimicked. To this quaint physiognomy a shock of flaxen hair, the strands of which fell over his eyes, added something of peasant candour, which was belied by the cunning expression of his eyes.

While she was studying him, he continued his flow of talk.

"What can a little wind like me do in Paris? I who am used to blowing in the hedgerows will be blowing in the petticoats of ladies, and I'll be slapped for it. . . . I'll carry off the hats of churchmen and shall get excommunicated. They'll put me in jail in the towers of Notre Dame and I'll make the bells ring contrariwise. . . . What a scandal!"

"But——" Angélique said again, trying to sit up.

He promptly pushed her down again.

"Don't move . . . hush!"

'He is a mad student,' she said to herself.

He stretched out again, and, raising his hand, he caressed her cheek, murmuring:

"Don't cry any more."

"I am not crying," said Angélique, but she noticed that her face was wet with tears.

"I too like to sleep in the hay," the other went on. "When I slipped into the barge, I found you here. You were crying in your sleep. So I caressed you to comfort you and you said: 'Again!' "

76

"I did?"

"You did. I wiped your face and saw that you were very beautiful. Your nose has the delicacy of certain shells one finds on the beach. They are white and so delicate that they are almost translucent. Your lips are like the petals of clematis. Your neck is round and smooth. . . ."

Angélique was listening in a half-dream. Yes, it was really a very long time since any mouth had spoken such words to her. It seemed to be coming from far away and she was almost afraid that he was making fun of her. How could he say that she was beautiful when she felt crushed, tarnished, for ever sullied by this dreadful night when she had realised that she could no longer look the witnesses of her past in the face!

He continued to whisper:

"Your shoulders are two ivory balls. Your breasts cannot be compared to anything but themselves, so lovely are they. They are made to be held in the cupped hand of a man, and they have delicious little buds of rosewood colour, like the ones you see growing everywhere when spring comes. Your thighs are silky and slender. Your belly is a white satin cushion, bulging and firm, on which it is good to rest one's cheek."

"Well really, I should like to know how you can judge all that," said Angélique, taking offence.

"While you were asleep, I looked you over."

Angélique sat up abruptly in the hay.

"You insolent lout! Lewd oaf of a schoolboy! Devil's brood!"

"Hush! Not so loud. Do you want the lightermen to throw us overboard . . . ? Why are you so cross, gentle lady? When one finds a jewel on one's road, isn't it only right to examine it? One likes to know if it is of pure gold, if it's really as beautiful as it looks, in short, if it suits you or if it's wiser to leave it where it is. *Rem passionis suae bene eligere princeps debet, mundum examinandum.*"[1]

"And are you, by any chance, the prince whom the world is looking at?" Angélique inquired sarcastically.

He screwed up his eyelids with sudden surprise.

"You understand Latin, beggar wench?"

"For a beggar, you speak it well. . . ."

The student was chewing his lower lip in perplexity.

[1] A prince must choose with care the object of his affection, for the world is watching.

77

"Who are you?" he said softly. "Your feet are bleeding. You must have been running for a long while. What frightened you so?"

And as she did not reply:

"You have got a knife, there, which isn't at all like you. A terrible weapon, an Egyptian's dagger. Do you know how to handle it?"

Angélique looked at him maliciously from under her eyelashes.

"Perhaps."

"Oh!" he exclaimed, with a grimace, drawing away a little.

He pulled a stalk from the hay and began to nibble at it. His pale eyes grew dreamy. Soon she had the impression that he was no longer even thinking of her and that his mind was wandering in far-off regions. Who knows? Perhaps roaming in those towers of Notre Dame where he had said he would be jailed? Thus motionless and distant, his pallid face seemed less youthful. At the corners of his eyelids she discovered those crumpled marks that poverty or debauchery can imprint on a man's face in the prime of life.

He was ageless, anyway. His lean body in his too ample clothes seemed ethereal. She was afraid that he might disappear like a vision, and she touched his arm.

"Who are you?" she murmured.

His face came alive again and he turned towards her eyes which did not seem intended for daylight.

"I told you: I am the wind. And you?"

"I am the breeze."

He started to laugh and took her by the shoulders.

"What do the wind and the breeze do when they meet?" he murmured.

Gently he pressed against her. She found herself lying in the hay again, with, close above her, that long, sensitive mouth. There was a little fold in the expression of those lips which frightened her, she knew not why. An ironical, slightly cruel wrinkle. But the look in his eyes was tender and gay.

He remained thus until, drawn by his appeal, she was the first to make a movement towards him. Then he half stretched out upon her and kissed her.

The kiss lasted for a long time, the time of ten kisses slowly parted and found again. For Angélique's brutalised senses it was like a rebirth. Former delights revived, so different from

the coarse pleasures which had been dispensed to her—
though with so much ardour!—by the ex-farmhand.

'I was very weary a moment ago,' she thought, 'and now I
am no longer weary. My body does not seem sad and sullied
any more. So I am not quite dead after all. . . .'

She fidgeted a little in the hay, happy again to feel deep
within her the awakening of a subtle yearning which would
soon become a throbbing desire.

The man had sat up and, propped on one elbow, kept looking at her with a half-smile.

She was not impatient, only intent on the warm flow that
was spreading within her. Presently he would caress her again.
They had plenty of time, the whole long Parisian day of tramps
with nothing to do.

"It's funny," he murmured. "You have the refinements of a
great lady, which one would not expect from your tattered
petticoat."

She gave a little husky laugh.

"Really? Are you familiar with great ladies, Maître Pen-
pusher?"

"Sometimes."

He tickled the tip of her nose with a flower and explained:

"When I have too big a hole in my stomach, I hire myself
out to Maître Georges, at the Saint-Nicholas bath-house.
That's where the great ladies go, to add a little spice to their
mundane love affairs. Oh, it's true, I am not a beautiful brute
like Pretty Boy, and the favours of my poor undernourished
carcass are less well paid than those of the husky, hairy steve-
dores who reek of onions and black wine. But I have other
strings to my bow. Yes, my dear. Nobody in Paris has such a
hand-picked selection of smutty stories as I have. They have
rather a fancy for that to get into the mood. I make those
beauties giggle. That's what women need above all, a good
belly-laugh. Do you want me to tell you the story of the
hammer and the anvil?"

"Oh no!" Angélique said quickly, "please don't!"

He seemed touched.

"Little sweet! Funny little sweet! Isn't it odd! I've met
great ladies who were just like hussies, but I've never yet met
hussies who were like great ladies. You are the first. . . . You
are so beautiful, just like a dream. . . . Listen, do you hear the
chime of the Samaritaine on the Pont-Neuf? . . . It's almost

79

noon. Would you like to go on the Pont-Neuf and pinch a few apples for our dinner? And a bunch of flowers in which to bury your adorable little face? . . . We'll listen to Big Matthieu doing his patter and the hurdy-gurdy man making his wood-chuck dance. . . . And we'll thumb our noses at the constable who's looking for me to hang me."

"Why do they want to hang you?"

"Why, because . . . don't you know that they're always out to hang me?" he answered, surprised.

'He's definitely a little crack-brained, but he is funny,' she thought to herself.

She stretched herself. She wanted him to caress her again, but he seemed to be thinking of other things.

"Now I remember," he said all of a sudden, "I have seen you before on the Pont-Neuf. Don't you belong to the gang of Calembredaine, the Illustrious Scamp?"

"Yes, that is right. I belong to Calembredaine."

He recoiled with an air of comic terror.

"Oh dear! Oh dear! What scrape have I got into, incorrigible philanderer that I am! Are you by any chance the Marquise of the Angels whom our Scamp is so madly jealous of?"

"Yes, but——"

"Now, just look at these conscienceless females!" he exclaimed dramatically. "Couldn't you have said so before, wretch? Do you want to see my ugly turnip blood gush from my veins? Oh dear! Oh dear! Calembredaine! Isn't that just my luck! I've found the woman of my life and she turns out to be Calembredaine's . . . ! But never mind! The most adorable mistress of them all is life itself. Farewell, my sweet. . . ."

He seized a shabby old conical hat, such as schoolmasters wore, and, pulling it down over his fair shock of hair, he slipped out of the canvas cover.

"Be kind," he whispered with a smile, "don't tell your master of my boldness. . . . Yes, I can see you won't talk. You are a darling, Marquise of the Angels. . . . I'll think of you till the day they hang me . . . and even after. . . . Farewell!"

She heard his splash below the barge, then saw him running along the bank in the sunshine. Dressed entirely in black, with his pointed hat, his skinny legs, his threadbare coat streaming in the wind, he looked like a strange bird.

The boatmen who had seen him slipping out of the barge were throwing stones after him. He turned his pale face towards them and gave a roar of laughter. Then he disappeared suddenly, like a dream.

CHAPTER 57

THIS FANTASTIC apparition had cheered Angélique up and pushed into the background the bitter memory of her encounter with Desgrez the night before.

It was better not to think of it any more. Later, when she had struggled out of this dreadful mire, she would think of Desgrez again and wonder: 'Did he recognise me that night? Surely not. He would not have given me back my knife. . . . He would not have gone on talking to me in the same horribly vulgar way. . . . No, he didn't recognise me—I should have died of shame if he had!'

She shook her head and passed her hand through her hair to remove the wisps of dry grass. She would think of all this later. But for the present she must not break the charm of this new hour. She sighed with a tinge of regret. Had she really been on the point of deceiving Nicholas? The Marquise of the Angels shrugged and gave a short laugh. One does not deceive a lover of that kind. Nothing tied her to Nicholas, except slavery and squalor.

The young man's retreat a moment ago made her realise once again the powerful protection with which the bandit surrounded her in the murderous jungle of the underworld. Without him and his exclusive love, she would have sunk even lower.

In exchange, she had surrendered to him her body, the noble legacy of her high lineage, which he had dreamed about his whole life long.

They were quits.

Angélique waited for a moment before she slid down from the hay. As she touched the water, she found it was cold, but not icy and, gazing around her, she was dazzled by the light and realised that it was spring. Had not the student talked of fruit and flowers on the Pont-Neuf? As if by the stroke of a magic wand, Angélique discovered the blossoming of the gentle season.

The hazy sky was dappled with pink and the Seine wore its silver armour. Over its smooth, calm surface boats were passing. She could hear the water dripping from the oars. Lower down, the washerwomen's paddles answered the tick-tack of the mill-boats.

Hiding from the bargemen's sight, Angélique bathed herself in the cold water, which lashed her blood pleasantly; then, after putting her clothes on again, she walked along the banks till she reached the Pont-Neuf.

For the first time she saw the Pont-Neuf in all its splendour, with its beautiful white arches and its spontaneous, gay and indefatigable life. A ceaseless clamour rose from it, in which the shouts of the hawking artisans and the exhortations of the quacks and tooth-pullers mingled with the refrains of songs, the outbursts of ditties, the chimes of the Samaritaine, and the beggars' pleas.

A throng of strolling passers-by, coming and going, stopping, streaming on again, renewing itself endlessly, ever-busy and ever-curious—that was the Pont-Neuf.

Angélique began to walk through the loitering crowd, between two rows of shops and booths. She was barefoot, her dress was torn: she had lost her bonnet and her long hair hung over her shoulders all a-gleam in the sunshine. But that did not matter. On the Pont-Neuf bare feet jostled the stout shoes of craftsmen and the red heels of noblemen.

She stopped before the water-tower of the Samaritaine to look at its busy clock which marked not only the hours, but the days and the months, and set a carillon in motion, which the clock-maker, good Fleming that he was, had taken care not to omit. Angélique stopped before each shop: the toymaker's, the poultry-seller's, the bird-seller's, the fancy-goods merchant's, the ink- and paint-seller's, the puppet-player's, the dog-shearer's, the juggler's. She spotted Black-Bread with his shells, Rat-Poison with his rapier and its pitiful prey impaled on it, and also Mother Hurlurette and Father Hurlurot at the corner of the Samaritaine.

In the middle of a circle of spectators the blind old man was scraping his fiddle while the old hag bawled a sentimental ballad about a hanged man, and a corpse whose eyes the ravens ate, and all sorts of grim horrors, to which people listened with cocked ears and streaming eyes. Hangings and processions were the principal sports of the lower classes of Paris, they

82

were spectacles that cost nothing and made people deeply aware that they had both bodies and souls.

Mother Hurlurette bellowed her complaint with great conviction:

> *"Ecoutez tous ma harangue*
> *Quand je m'en irai*
> *À l'Abbaye de Monte-à-Regret*
> *Pour vous je prierai*
> *En tirant la langue."*[1]

You could see right into the back of her toothless mouth. A tear flowed from her eye and trickled into her wrinkles. She was frightful, admirable. . . .

When she had finished her song on a supreme *tremolo*, she moistened her big thumb and began to distribute leaflets which she was carrying in a bunch under her arm, crying:

"Who hasn't had his hanged man?"

As she passed near Angélique, she gave a shout of joy:

"Hey, Hurlurot, here's the kid! Lord, what a song and dance your man has made ever since this morning! He says the accursed dog has throttled you. He's talking and attacking the Châtelet with all the beggars and bandits of Paris. And the Marquise, the while, is taking a stroll on the Pont-Neuf . . . !"

"And why not?" Angélique protested haughtily. "You're taking a stroll here, aren't you?"

"I am working," said the old woman, bustling. "Now this song, you can't imagine what a seller it is. I'm always telling the Gutter-Poet: Give me hanged men. There's nothing sells better than hanged men. Here, you want one? No charge, because you are our Marquise."

"There'll be chitterlings for you tonight at the Tower of Nesle," Angélique promised her.

She walked away among the crowd, reading her sheet of paper:

> *"Ecoutez tous ma harangue*
> *Quand je m'en irai*
> *À l'Abbaye de Monte-à-Regret,*
> *Pour vous je prierai*
> *En tirant la langue . . ."*

---

[1] Listen, all, to my harangue, When from here I go away, To the Abbey 'Go-up-with-reluctance' (the gallows), For you I shall pray, As I stick out my tongue. . . .

In a corner at the bottom of the page there was the now familiar signature: the Gutter-Poet. A bitter memory of hatred rose in Angélique's heart. She cast a glance at the bronze horse on the bridge. There, they said, between the legs of the horse the Poet of the Pont-Neuf would sometimes go to sleep. The rogues respected his slumber. There was nothing to be stolen from him, anyway. He was poorer than the poorest beggar, always roaming, always hungry, always pursued, and always spurting some fresh scandal, like a jet of poison, through Paris.

'How is it that nobody has killed him yet?' Angélique wondered. 'I'd kill him gladly if I met him. But I'd first like to tell him why. . . .'

She crumpled the paper and threw it into the gutter. A carriage passed, preceded by its runners, who were skipping like squirrels. They looked magnificent with their satin liveries, their plumed hats. The crowd tried to guess who was inside the carriage. Angélique was gazing at the runners and thinking of Lightfoot.

The good bronze King Henri IV was gleaming in the sunshine and smiling above a flowerbed of red and pink parasols. The area before the monument was occupied by orange- and flower-sellers. A great single, unbroken shout announced the golden fruit:

"Portugal! Portugal!"

Handling their baskets of tuberoses, jasmine and roses with skilful hands, deftly pinning a carnation on the lapel of a jacket, the young flower-girls walked amid the crowd, while the older women watched over their stands set up under red parasols.

One of these florists engaged Angélique to help her make bouquets, and as the young woman did this very tastefully, the stallholder gave her twenty *sols*.

"You seem to me rather too old to be an apprentice," she said to Angélique after giving her and her wretched outfit a close look, "but a younger lass would take two years to learn to make bouquets like you do. If you'd like to work with me we could come to an understanding."

Angélique shook her head, clasped the twenty *sols* in her hand and left. She looked repeatedly at the few coins the flower-seller had given her. It was the first money she had ever earned.

She went to buy two fritters from a pastrycook and devoured them, while mingling with the strollers who laughed and gaped before the cart of Big Matthieu.

Resplendent Big Matthieu! He had set up shop opposite King Henri IV, undaunted by his smile or his majesty. Standing on his cart—a platform on four wheels surrounded by a balustrade, he addressed the crowd with a thunderous voice that could be heard from one end of the Pont-Neuf to the other.

His personal orchestra was composed of three musicians: a trumpeter, a drummer and a cymbal-player, who punctuated his speeches and covered, with an ear-splitting din, the wailing of the customers as he drew their teeth. Enthusiastic and tenacious, of prodigious strength and skill, Big Matthieu would always get the better of the most obstinate teeth, even if it meant making the patient kneel and lifting him from the ground at the end of his tongs. Whereupon he would dispatch his tottering victim to rinse out his mouth at the brandy-seller's.

In between customers, Big Matthieu would stride up and down his platform, the plume on his hat streaming in the wind, his double necklace of teeth displayed on his satin suit, his big sabre knocking against his heels, boasting of his great science and the excellence of his drugs, powders, electuaries and ointments of all kinds, concocted with lashings of butter, wax oil and a few harmless herbs.

"You see before you, ladies and gentlemen, the world's greatest personage, a virtuoso, a phœnix in his profession, the paragon of medicine, the successor of Hippocrates in direct descent, the investigator of nature, the scourge of all the faculties; you see with your own eyes a methodical, Galenic, Hippocratic, pathological, chemical, spagirical, empirical physician.

"I heal soldiers out of courtesy, the poor for love of God, and the rich merchants for their money.

"I am neither a doctor nor philosopher, but my ointment does as much as all the doctors and philosophers put together. Experience is worth more than knowledge. I have a pomade here to whiten the skin: it is snow-white, and as odoriferous as balsam and musk. . . .

"Now, here I have an ointment of inestimable value, for, listen well, gallant gentlemen and ladies, this ointment preserves him or her that uses it from the treacherous thorns of the roses of love."

And raising his arm lyrically:

> "Come, gentlefolk, and buy from me
> The nostrum for every malady,
> This admirable powder can
> Make a fool a witty man;
> The wicked rogue can mend his ways,
> And old dame and dotard end their days
> With lively company in bed.
> My ointment clears the dullest head. . . ."

This final sally, which he reeled off while rolling his enormous eyes, made Angélique burst out aloud with laughter. He noticed her and addressed a friendly wink to her.

'I laughed. Why did I laugh?' Angélique wondered. 'What he's saying is completely idiotic.'

But she felt like laughing.

Angélique closed her eyes for a moment. When she opened them again, she saw a few steps away, in the throng on the Pont-Neuf, Jactance, Big-Bag, Peony, Gobert, and the others, who were looking at her.

"Sister," said Peony, seizing her arm, "I'll burn a taper before the Eternal Father at Saint-Pierre-aux-boeufs. We thought we'd never see you again!"

"The jail of the Châtelet, or the General Hospital, was where we thought you were."

"Unless you'd been mauled to death by that cursed dog."

"They pinched Pick-Lock and Prudent. They were hanged this morning on the Place de Grève."

"We're going to have fun, my pretty one. D'you know why we're taking a daylight stroll on the Pont-Neuf? It's because young Flipot is going to pass his examination as a cut-purse."

Flipot had, for the occasion, swapped his rags for a violet serge suit and stout shoes in which he walked uneasily. He had even put a linen ruff round his neck and, with the plush-bag in which he was supposed to carry his books and pens, he impersonated rather convincingly a craftsman's son playing truant on the Pont-Neuf before the puppet-theatre.

Jactance was giving him a few last words of advice:

"Now listen, lad. Today it's not just a matter of cutting a purse, as you've done before . . . but we'll see if you're clever

86

enough to slip away in a scuffle and take the stuff with you. Understood?"

"Gy," Flipot answered.

Which is the proper way of saying 'yes' in thieves' cant. He snuffled nervously and passed his sleeve repeatedly under his nose.

His companions scrutinised the passers-by with care.

"Look, here comes a fine gentleman, with eyes only for his pretty lady, and they are on foot—that's a bit of luck! You've spotted the toff, Flipot? Here they are, stopping before Big Matthieu's. Now's the time! Here are your nippers, lad, now off to the pickings."

With a solemn gesture, Jactance handed the boy a pair of finely-honed scissors and pushed him into the crowd. His accomplices had already slipped among the audience around Big Matthieu.

Jactance's practised eye followed his apprentice's movements attentively. He suddenly started to shout:

"Look out! Monsieur, hey, Monsieur! They're cutting your purse! . . ."

Passers-by looked in the direction to which he was pointing and began to run. Peony yelled:

"Your Highness, take care! There's a brat having a go at you!"

The gentleman put his hand to his purse and found Flipot's hand there.

"Help! Cut-purse!" he screamed.

His lady companion gave a strident cry. There was prompt and total pandemonium. People were shouting, striking, gripping one another by the throat, bashing one another's heads, while Calembredaine's henchmen added to the scuffle with their cries and shouts.

"I've got him!"

"It's him!"

"Catch him! He's running away!"

"Over there!"

"Over here!"

Trampled children cried, women fainted. Booths were knocked over. Red parasols flew away into the Seine. The fruit-sellers, to defend themselves, began to pelt people with apples and oranges. Dogs jumped into the mêlée and rushed between people's legs in tight furry balls, yelping and slavering.

Pretty Boy passed from one woman to another, seizing staid citizens' wives by their waists, kissing them and petting them with extreme boldness, under the outraged eyes of their husbands, who vainly tried to beat him. Their blows fell on others, who avenged themselves by pulling off the wigs of the indignant husbands.

In the midst of this uproar Jactance and his accomplices were cutting purses, emptying fobs, snatching coats, while Big Matthieu from the top of his cart, amid the din of his ear-splitting orchestra, brandished his sabre and bellowed:

"Go to it, lads! Limber up! It's good for your health!"

Angélique had taken refuge on the steps of the terrace round the monument. Clutching the fence, she cried with laughter. It was a perfect climax for this day, exactly what she needed to sate the urge to cry and laugh which had been racking her ever since she had awakened in the hayboat under the stranger's caresses.

She could see Father Hurlurot and Mother Hurlurette clutching each other as they floated above the tide of the battle, like an enormous blob of dirty rags. Her laughter redoubled. She was choking with it. No, really, she was dying of laughter! . . .

"Is it so funny, wench?" a slow voice growled beside her.

And a hand seized her wrist. You don't recognise a *grimaut*, you smell him, Peony had said. Since that night, Angélique had learned to sniff whence danger would come. She went on laughing more softly, and put on an innocent look.

"Yes, it's funny, those people are fighting without knowing why."

"And maybe you know, eh?"

Angélique bent down to the policeman's face with a smile. Suddenly she seized his nose with a firm grip, twisted the nasal cartilage, and as he flung his head back under the impact of pain she smartly struck his protruding Adam's apple with the edge of her hand.

It was a hold Polack had taught her. Not rough enough to lay a policeman out but enough to make him let go.

Released, Angélique fled, bounding like a gazelle.

At the Tower of Nesle, everybody was coming back.

"We can count our bruises," Jactance said, "but what pickings, my friends, what pickings!"

And on the table they piled up coats, swords, jewels, clinking purses.

Flipot, black and blue as a truffled Christmas goose, had brought back the purse of the gentleman who had been assigned to him. He was made much of and ate at Calembredaine's table, with the veterans.

"Angélique," Nicholas murmured, "Angélique, if I hadn't found you again . . ."

"What would have happened?"

"I don't know. . . ."

He pulled her towards him and pressed her against his mighty chest as if to break her.

"Oh, please!" she sighed, freeing herself.

She went and leaned her head against the bars of the narrow window. The deep blue starry sky was reflected in the quiet waters of the Seine. The air was redolent with the scent of blossoming almond trees in the gardens and parks of the Faubourg Saint-Germain.

Nicholas came close to her and went on devouring her with his eyes. She was touched by the intensity of this unfailing passion.

"What would you have done if I hadn't come back?"

"That depends. If it was because you had been pinched by the constables, I'd have got the whole gang going. We'd have watched the jails, the hospitals, the chains of wenches. . . . We'd have made good your escape. If it was because the dog had strangled you, I'd have searched for the dog and his master everywhere to kill them. . . . If it was——"

His voice became hoarse.

"If it was because you'd gone off with another—I'd have found you anywhere, and I'd have had the other man's blood."

She smiled, for a pale, mocking face flashed through her memory. But Nicholas was shrewder than she thought, and his love for her sharpened his instincts.

"Don't imagine you can get away from me easily," he went on in a threatening tone of voice. ". . . We don't betray one another in the underworld, the way they do in high society, but if it happens, you die. There'd be no refuge for you anywhere. . . . There are too many of us, we are too powerful. We'd find you anywhere—in the churches, in the convents, even in the King's palace. We are well organised, you know. What I like best, in fact, is organising battles."

He opened his torn tunic and showed her a small bluish mark near his heart.

"Look, you see this? My mother always told me: 'That's your father's mark!' Because my father wasn't that fat, clod-hopping old Merlot. No, my mother had me by a soldier, an officer, somebody high up. She never told me his name, but sometimes, when Père Merlot wanted to thrash me, she'd cry to him: 'Don't touch the boy, he's got noble blood.' You didn't know that, did you?"

"A trooper's bastard! Something to be proud of," she said scornfully.

He crushed her shoulders between his Herculean hands.

"There are times I'd like to crack you like a nut. But now you're warned. If you ever deceive me——"

"Have no fear. Your embraces are more than enough for me."

"Why do you say that with such a nasty face?"

"Because one would have to be endowed with an exceptional temperament to ask for more. If you could only be a little gentler!"

"I? I am not gentle?" he roared, "I who adore you! Just say again that I am not gentle."

He raised a powerful fist. She shouted at him shrilly:

"Don't touch me, peasant! Brute! Remember Polack!"

He dropped his arm. Then, after scowling at her glumly, he heaved a deep sigh.

"Forgive me. You always get the better of me, Angélique."

He smiled and held his arm out awkwardly:

"Come, anyway. I'll try and be gentle."

She let herself be thrown on the litter and offered herself listlessly, indifferently, to the now familiar embrace. When he was satisfied, he remained nestled against her for a long spell. She felt against her cheek the rough bristle of his hair, which was cut quite short on account of his wig.

He said at last in a muffled voice:

"I know now . . . you'll never be mine. For it isn't only this I want, I want your heart."

"You can't have everything, my poor Nicholas," said Angélique, philosophically. "Once you had part of my heart, now you have my whole body. Once you used to be my friend

Nicholas, now you are my master Calembredaine. You've killed even the memory of the affection I had for you when we were children. But I'm attached to you, all the same, in a different way, because you are strong."

The man grew taut with pain. He growled and sighed again:

"I wonder whether I shan't be forced to kill you some day."

She yawned, trying to sleep.

"Don't talk rubbish."

CHAPTER 58

ONE SUMMER evening, Rotten Jean slipped into Calembredaine's lair at the Tower of Nesle. He came to see a woman called Teeming Fanny, who had ten children whom she hired out by turns to all and sundry. She had settled down comfortably to this sinecure, engaging in begging only for the fun of it, and in prostitution only out of habit, which after all did not hamper her breeding aptitude. Quite to the contrary.

Rotten Jean came to 'book in advance' the child she was expecting. She told him, as the shrewd business woman that she was:

"You'll have to pay more for him, for he'll have a club-foot."

"How do you know?"

"The fellow who made him had a club-foot."

"Oho!" Polack mocked her, laughing loudly, "aren't you lucky to know what he was like, the fellow who made him! Sure you're not getting mixed up?"

"*I'm* free to pick and choose," was the dignified reply.

And she went on spinning a distaff of dirty wool. She was an active woman and did not like to stay idle. The little monkey Piccolo jumped on to Rotten Jean's shoulders and quickly pulled a tuft of hair from his head.

"Horrible beast!" shouted the man, trying to ward him off with his hat.

Angélique was rather pleased with her pet's exploit. The monkey did not hide his repugnance for this tormentor of child martyrs. But as Rotten Jean was a creature to be feared, and since the Great Coesre, whose den he shared, held him in high esteem, she called the monkey back to her.

Rotten Jean rubbed his skull, growling abuses. He had

already warned the Great Coesre that these men of Calembre-daine's were an insolent, dangerous lot; they were lording it over the others, but there would come a day when the other bandits would rebel. And then . . .

"Come and have a drink," said Polack, to soothe him.

She poured him out a ladleful of boiling wine. Rotten Jean always felt cold, even in midsummer. He seemed to have cold blood in his veins. He had the glassy eyes of fish and their sticky, jelly-like skin.

When he had finished drinking, a rather frightening smile parted his lips over a row of black, rotten teeth. Thibault the hurdy-gurdy man was just coming in, followed by little Linot.

"Ah! here's the pretty little darling," said Rotten Jean, rubbing his hands. "Thibault, this time it's settled, I buy him from you and I'll give you—now hold tight!—fifty *livres*. A fortune!"

The old man cast an uneasy glance through the slit of his straw-hat.

"What do you want me to do with fifty *livres*? And besides, who'll beat my drum if I haven't got him any more?"

"You can train some other lad."

"But this one is my grandson."

"Well, then, don't you want to do the right thing by him?" said the odious fiend with a crafty grin. "Just consider that your grandson will be dressed in lace and velvets. I'm not telling you any lies, Thibault. I know who I'll sell him to. He'll become a Prince's favourite and later, if he's clever, he'll be able to aspire to the highest positions."

Rotten Jean caressed the child's brown curls.

"Would you like that, Linot? To have fine clothes, eat your fill out of gold-plate, and suck sweets all day?"

"I don't know," said the boy, with a pout.

A yellowish ray of sunshine through the open door lit his golden-brown skin. He had thick long lashes, big black eyes, cherry-red lips. He wore his rags gracefully. One could have taken him for a little lord disguised for a masquerade, and it seemed astonishing that such a flower could have bloomed on such a dunghill.

"Come on, come on! We'll get on very well together, we two," said Rotten Jean. And he slipped his white hand round the child's shoulders. "Come, my pretty one, come, my lamb."

"But I don't agree," the old man protested, and he began to tremble. "You've no right to take my grandchild away."

"I'm not taking him, I'm buying him. Fifty *livres*, that's fair, isn't it? And anyway, you keep quiet, or else you get nothing, so there!"

He brushed the old man aside and marched towards the door, dragging Linot after him. In front of the door he found Angélique.

"You can't take him away without Calembredaine's permission," she said very calmly.

And, taking the child by the hand, she brought him back into the room. Rotten Jean's waxen skin could blench no further, but he remained speechless for three long seconds.

"Well, I——" he raged, "well, I——!"

And pulling up a stool:

"Very well. I'll wait for him."

"You can wait till doomsday," Polack told him. "If she says no, you won't get the brat. He does whatever she wants," she added with a mixture of bitterness and admiration.

Calembredaine and his soldiers never returned before nightfall. He would call for a drink before attending to anything else. They would talk business afterwards.

While he was quenching his huge thirst, there came a knock at the door. This was not customary among the beggars. They all looked at one another, and Peony went to open, with drawn sword.

A woman's voice inquired from outside:

"Is Rotten Jean here?"

"Come in," said Peony.

The torches of resin, fixed in iron rings on the walls, illuminated the unexpected entrance of a tall girl draped in a cloak and a lackey in red livery, who was carrying a basket.

"We went to see you at the Faubourg Saint-Denis," the girl explained to Rotten Jean, "but there they told us you were at Calembredaine's. You've made us walk our legs off when it would have been just a hop from the Tuileries to Nesle."

While she spoke, she dropped her cloak and puffed up the lace frills of her bodice, righted the little gold cross that was dangling on a black velvet ribbon round her neck. The men's eyes sparkled at the sight of this buxom wench, whose flaming red hair was ill-concealed by a handsome bonnet.

Angélique had shrunk back into the shadow. A pearly sweat

93

had broken out on her temples. She had recognised Bertille, Madame de Soissons's chambermaid, who only a few months ago had acted as her go-between for the sale of Kouassi-Ba.

"You've got something for me?" asked Rotten Jean.

With a promising air, the girl lifted the napkin from the basket which the lackey had deposited on the table, and pulled a new-born baby out of it.

"There!" she said.

Rotten Jean scrutinised the baby with a dubious mien.

"Fat, well built," he said, pursing his lips. "I could give you thirty *livres* for him."

"Thirty *livres*!" she exclaimed, indignantly. "Do you hear that, Jacinthe? Thirty *livres*! Why, you haven't even looked at him! You're incapable of appraising the goods I'm bringing you."

She tore off the swaddling that covered the baby and exhibited it naked in the glow of the flames.

"Have a good look at it."

The little creature fidgeted vaguely.

"He's the son of a Moor," the maid whispered, "a blend of black and white. You know how beautiful mulattoes are when they grow up, with golden-coloured skin. One doesn't often come by them. Later, when he's six or seven, you'll be able to sell him as a page for a high price."

She gave a malignant guffaw.

"Who knows? You might even be able to sell him back to his own mother."

Rotten Jean's eyes were gleaming with greed.

"All right," he decided. "I'll give you a hundred *livres*."

"Hundred and fifty."

The infamous creature flung his arms up.

"You want to ruin me! Can you imagine how much it will cost me to bring up the brat, especially if I've got to keep him fat and strong?"

A sordid squabble followed. In order to haggle more effectively, with her fists on her hips, Bertille had put the baby down on the table, and everybody was crowding around and looking at it, a little fearfully. He was in no way different from any other new-born baby—his skin was perhaps just a trifle redder.

"And anyway, how do I know he's really a mulatto?" said Rotten Jean, having run out of arguments.

"I swear to you that his father was blacker than the bottom of a cooking-pot."

Teeming Fanny gave a terrified cry:

"Oh! I'd have been stiff with fright. However could your mistress . . ."

"Don't they say that a Moor need only look a woman in the eye to make her pregnant?" Polack inquired.

The servant gave a foul laugh.

"That's what they say . . . and even what they all keep repeating from the Tuileries to the Palais-Royal, ever since my mistress's condition attracted attention. It even got round to the King's own chamber. His Majesty said: 'Oh really? Then it must have been a very deep look!' And when he met my mistress in the anteroom, he turned his back on her. You can imagine how upset she was. When she'd been hoping all along that she might get him into her clutches! But the King has been furious ever since he's suspected that a black-skinned man was treated by her on the same terms as himself. And, worse luck, neither the husband nor the lover—that cad of a Marquis de Vardes—is prepared to assume the paternity.

"However, my mistress has more than one trick up her sleeve. She'll know how to put a stop to the tittle-tattle. To begin with, officially she won't be confined till December."

Bertille sat down, casting a triumphant glance around her.

"Pour me a drink, Polack, and I'll tell you how it's done. Now then, it's simple, you'll see. All you have to do is count on your fingers. The Moor left my mistress's service in February. If she is confined in December, he can't be the father, can he? So she'll let out the hoops of her dress a little and complain: Oh! my dear, this child does fidget so. He paralyses me. I don't know if I'll be able to go to the King's ball tonight. And then, in December, the confinement in great style, right in the Tuileries. That'll be the moment, Rotten Jean, to sell us a brand-new day-old baby. They can toss for who'll be the father. The Moor will be ruled out, that's all that matters. It's common knowledge that he's been rowing on the King's galleys ever since last February."

"Why was he sent to the galleys?"

"For a nasty affair of witchcraft. He was the accomplice of a sorcerer who was burned on the Place de Grève."

Despite her self-control, Angélique could not help casting a glance towards Nicholas. But he was drinking and eating with

95

indifference. She shrank farther back into the darkness. She would have liked to be able to leave the room, yet at the same time she was dying to hear more.

"Yes, a nasty affair," Bertille went on, dropping her voice, "that black devil was adept at casting spells and so he was sentenced. Actually, that's why La Voisin said it was no go when my mistress went to see her to get rid of the child."

Barcarole the dwarf jumped on to the table close to the servant's glass.

"Whoo! I've seen the lady and you, too; I've seen you several times, my pretty frizzy carrot. I am the little imp who opens the door at my famous mistress's, the fortune-teller."

"Indeed, I would have recognised you by your insolence."

"La Voisin would do nothing about it, because the child the Duchesse was bearing was the son of a Moor."

"How did she know?"

"She knows everything. She's a soothsayer."

"Just looking at the palm of her hand, she told her the whole story at once," the maid agreed, awe-stricken. "That it was a child of mixed blood, that the black man who begot it was familiar with the secrets of magic, and that she couldn't kill it, because it would bring bad luck to her who was also a witch. My mistress was awfully upset: 'What are we going to do, Bertille?' she said to me. She flew into a terrible rage. But La Voisin didn't give in. She said she'd help my mistress with the confinement at the proper time and that nobody would know anything about it. But that she couldn't do more. And she asked for a lot of money. The thing happened last night at Fontainebleau, where the whole Court is for the summer. La Voisin came with one of her men, a magician, Lesage. My mistress was delivered in a small house that belongs to La Voisin's daughter, quite close to the château. At dawn I took my mistress back, and in the early morning hours, dressed in all her finery and painted up to the eyes, she presented herself to the Queen, as is customary, since she's in command of the Queen's household. Now that'll baffle no end of people who are expecting to see her confined any day now. But they'll get nothing for their pains and gossip. Madame de Soissons is still expecting, she'll be delivered in December of a perfectly white child, and it is possible that Monsieur de Soissons may even recognise it."

A huge roar of laughter greeted the end of the story. Barcarole cut a caper, and said:

"I heard my mistress confide to Lesage that this Soissons business was as good as finding a treasure trove."

"Oh, she's a grasping one!" Bertille grumbled resentfully. "She demanded so much that all my mistress had left to give *me* was a little necklace to thank me for my help."

The maid gazed at the dwarf reflectively.

"As for you," she said suddenly, "I think you might make someone I know happy who is extremely highly placed."

"I've always thought that I was cut out for great things," Barcarole replied, pulling himself up on his bandy little legs.

"The Queen's dwarf has died, and that has sorely grieved the Queen, for anything upsets her now that she's pregnant. But her little midget woman is downright desperate. Nobody can console her. She needs a new companion . . . of her size."

"Oh! I'm certain this noble lady will find me attractive," cried Barcarole, clinging to the maid's petticoat. "Take me with you, pretty carrot, take me along to the Queen. Am I not good-looking and attractive?"

"It's true he is not bad-looking, is he, Jacinthe?" she said, amused.

"I am even handsome," the puny freak affirmed. "If nature had endowed me with a few more inches, I'd have been the most courted pimp. And when it comes to flirting with women, my tongue never stops wagging, believe me."

"The midget woman speaks only Spanish."

"I speak Spanish, German and Italian."

"We simply must take him with us," cried Bertille, clapping her hands. "It's an excellent business and will get us noticed by Her Majesty. Let's hurry. We've got to be back at Fontainebleau by morning, so that our absence won't be noticed. Shall we put you into the little mulatto's basket?"

"You are joking, Madame," protested Barcarole, assuming a lordly air.

They all laughed and congratulated themselves. Barcarole with the Queen! . . . Barcarole with the Queen! . . .

Calembredaine merely raised his nose above his bowl.

"Don't forget your pals when you become a lord," he said. And he made a meaningful gesture of rolling a coin between his thumb and his forefinger.

"You can bleed me if I forget you!" the dwarf protested.

And bounding towards the corner where Angélique was standing, he made a deep court bow.

"Goodbye, oh most beautiful lady, goodbye, sister, Marquise of the Angels."

The odd little fellow gazed up at her with his quick, strangely shrewd eyes. He added, aping the affected manners of a dandy:

"I do hope, my very dear, that we shall see each other again. I make a rendezvous with you . . . at the Queen's."

CHAPTER 59

THE COURT was at Fontainebleau. During the hot summer days there was nothing more delightful than this white château, immersed in its verdure, with its pond where the carp disported themselves, their snow-white old grandsire among them, wearing in his nostrils the ring of François the First. Water, flowers, groves . . .

The King worked, the King danced, the King hunted. The King was in love. The sweet Louise de la Vallière, all a-flutter at having aroused the passion of the royal heart, would languorously lift her magnificent blue-brown eyes to him. And in suggestive allegories, in which Diana hunting through woods and forests surrenders at last to Endymion, the whole Court vied in celebrating the ascent of this retiring, fair-haired girl, whose maidenly flower Louis XIV had only recently plucked.

Seventeen years of age and just emerged from the poverty of a numerous provincial family, isolated among Madame's maids-of-honour, wasn't there ample cause for Louise de la Vallière to tremble when all the nymphs and sylvans whispered in the moonlight as she passed: "There goes the favourite?" And all the bustle around her! She no longer knew where to hide the intensity of her love and the shame of her sin! But the courtiers knew the mechanism of their subtle profession as parasites. Through the King's mistress one gained access to the King; one could work up intrigues, obtain positions, favours, pensions. While the Queen, weighed down by her approaching maternity, remained withdrawn in her apartments with her inconsolable midget, the blazing summer days sparkled with an unbroken chain of balls and pleasures.

At informal suppers on the canal, as there was no room in the boats for the King's personal servants it was fun to see the Prince de Condé, instead of winning battles or plotting against the King, taking the dishes that were handed to him from a neighbouring boat and presented them to the King and his mistress, like a model footman.

On 11th August all the ladies went stag-hunting, on the 14th there was a country ball at which the King, disguised as a shepherd, danced with La Vallière. On the 18th there was a banquet in the forest, with small orchestras vying with the song-birds amid the shrubbery.

On the 25th a torchlight ball . . . love leading the dance. . . .

Sitting on the banks of the Seine, in the sweltering stench of Paris, Angélique watched the dusk descend on Notre Dame. Above the high square towers and the bulging hulk of the apse, the sky was yellow, specked with swallows. From time to time, a bird would flit past Angélique, grazing the bank with a shrill cry.

On the other side of the river, below the chapter-houses of the canons of Notre Dame, a long slope of clay marked the largest watering-point in Paris. At this hour a crowd of horses clambered down it, led by carters or coachmen. Their neighing concert rose in the pure evening sky.

Suddenly Angélique got up.

'I'm going to see my children,' she thought.

For twenty *sols*, a ferryman landed her at the port of Saint-Landry. Angélique walked down the rue de l'Enfer and stopped a few steps from the house of the proctor Fallot de Sancé. She had no intention of presenting herself at her sister's in the state she was in, with her petticoat in shreds, her unkempt hair tied with a kerchief, her down-at-heel shoes. But it had occurred to her that by taking up her stand nearby she might perhaps catch a glimpse of her two sons. For some time this desire had become an obsession with her, a need that grew more urgent with every passing day and that filled all her thoughts. Florimond's little face emerged from the well of dazed oblivion in which she had been plunged. She visualised him with his curly black hair under his little red hood. She heard him babble. How old was he now? Just over two years.

And Cantor? Seven months. She could not visualise him. He had been so tiny when she left him!

Leaning against the wall, near a cobbler's shop, Angélique kept an eye on the front of the house where she had lived when she was still rich and respected. A year ago, her equipage had cluttered up the narrow lane. From here she had set out for the King's entry, sumptuously dressed. And One-Eyed Kate had made her proposals from Fouquet, the Controller-General: "Accept them, my dear. . . . Isn't that better than losing your life?"

She had refused. And so she had lost everything, and she wondered she had not lost her life as well, for she no longer had a name nor the right to exist, she was dead in the eyes of all.

Time passed, and still nothing moved behind the façade of the house. However, behind the grimy window-panes of the solicitor's study the busy figures of the clerks could be perceived dimly. One of them came out to light the lantern.

Angélique went up to him.

"Is Maître Fallot de Sancé at home or has he gone to the country for the summer?"

The clerk took his time to inspect her suspiciously.

"Maître Fallot hasn't been living here for quite some time," he said. "He sold his office, his study, everything. He had some trouble over a witchcraft trial in which his family was involved. That did him harm in his profession. He's gone to set up in another district."

"And . . . you don't know in which district?"

"I don't," said the other haughtily. "And if I did I wouldn't tell you. You are no client for him."

Angélique was flabbergasted. For several days now she had been living entirely in the hope of seeing, were it only for a moment, the two faces of her children. She imagined them returning from their walk, Cantor in Barbe's arms, Florimond gaily trotting at her side. And now they too had vanished for ever from her sight!

She had to support herself against the wall, suddenly dizzy with grief. The cobbler, who was putting the boards of his shop up for the night and who had overheard the conversation, said to her:

"Were you as keen as all that to see Maître Fallot de Sancé? Was it about a lawsuit?"

"No," said Angélique, trying to control herself, "but I . . . I would have liked to see a girl who was in his employ . . . a girl called Barbe. Doesn't anybody in these parts know the proctor's new address?"

"As regards Maître Fallot and his family, I can't tell you anything, but when it comes to Barbe, I may be able to help. She is no longer with them. The last time she was seen she was working in a cook-shop in the rue de la Vallée-de-Misère, at the sign of 'The Brazen Cock'."

"Oh, thank you!"

Angélique was already running through the darkening streets. The rue de la Vallée-de-Misère, behind the prison of the Grand Châtelet, was the centre of the caterers of roast viands. Day and night, the squeals of poultry as their throats were cut and the noise of revolving spits before huge fires never stopped.

The eating-house of 'The Brazen Cock' was the last in the street and did not present a particularly engaging aspect. On the contrary, looking at it one might have thought that Lent had already started, for that is the only season which extinguishes the caterers' ovens, closes the butchers' shops and makes the pastrycooks yawn.

Angélique walked into a room that was dimly lit by two or three candles. Seated before a pitcher of wine, a burly man, with a grimy cook's cap on his head, seemed far busier drinking than serving his customers. The latter were not numerous, anyhow, and consisted mainly of craftsmen and impecunious-looking travellers. A slouching youngster with a greasy apron round his waist brought them some dishes whose composition could be guessed only with difficulty.

Angélique turned to the fat cook:

"Have you a servant here called Barbe?"

The man pointed to the kitchen at the back with an indifferent thumb.

Angélique saw Barbe. She was sitting before the fire and plucking a fowl.

"Barbe!"

The other raised her head and wiped her perspiring forehead.

"What do you want, wench?" she asked in a tired voice.

"Barbe!" repeated Angélique.

The servant's eyes grew round, then opened wide with amazement, and she uttered a stifled cry:

"Oh! Madame! . . . Will Madame excuse me. . . ."

"You mustn't call me Madame any more, as you can see," Angélique said curtly.

She let herself drop on the stone of the hearth. The heat was stifling.

"Barbe, where are my children?"

Barbe's round cheeks trembled as if she were going to burst out crying. She swallowed and finally managed to answer.

"They've been put out to nurse, Madame . . . outside Paris . . . in a village near Longchamp."

"My sister Hortense did not keep them with her?"

"Madame Hortense gave them straightway to a foster-mother. I went to see the woman once to give her the money you left me. Madame Hortense had ordered me to give her that money, but I didn't give her all of it. I wanted the money to serve the children. Afterwards, I couldn't return to the foster-mother . . . I had left Madame Hortense. . . . I had several places. . . . It's hard to earn one's living."

She was now talking hurriedly, avoiding Angélique's gaze. The latter pondered. Longchamp was not a very distant village. The ladies of the Court would sometimes drive out there for a promenade, to attend the nuns' service at the Abbey. . . . Barbe had nervously resumed plucking the fowl. Angélique had the feeling that someone was staring at her fixedly. Turning round she saw the kitchen-boy gazing at her open-mouthed, with an expression that left no doubt about the feelings that the sight of this beautiful woman in rags inspired in him. Angélique was accustomed to the lewd glances of men, but this time it annoyed her. She got up quickly.

"Where are you staying, Barbe?"

"Here, in a garret."

At this moment the landlord of 'The Brazen Cock' came in, with his cap awry.

"What the hell are you all doing here?" he demanded in a thick voice. "David, the customers are calling for you. . . . And when will this chicken be ready, Barbe? Upon my word, maybe I'll have to attend to the work while you are taking your ease! . . . And what is this beggarwoman doing here? Hey, out you go, out! And don't try and filch a capon. . . ."

"Oh! Monsieur Bourjus!" Barbe exclaimed, appalled.

But Angélique, this evening, was not in a passive mood. She put her fists on her hips and Polack's entire vocabulary rose to her lips.

"Shut up, you fat hogshead! I wouldn't take your decrepit cardboard cocks if you gave them to me. As for you, you ogling fledgling, you'd better drop your eyes and close your mouth if you don't want to get a swipe on the ear."

"Oh! Madame!" cried Barbe, even more appalled.

Turning to account the two men's amazement, Angélique whispered to Barbe:

"I'll wait for you in the courtyard."

A little later, when Barbe came out, with a candlestick in her hand, Angélique followed her up the rickety stairs to the loft which Maître Bourjus let to his maid.

"It's a very poor lodging, Madame," the poor girl said humbly.

"Don't apologise. I'm familiar with poverty."

Angélique took off her shoes to enjoy the coolness of the stone-flags and sat down on the bed, which was a curtainless pallet mounted on four legs.

"You must excuse Maître Bourjus," Barbe went on. "He isn't a bad man, but ever since his wife's death his mind wanders and he does nothing but drink. The kitchen-boy is a nephew of his. He brought him up from the province to help him, but he isn't very bright. So business isn't doing too well."

"If it's no inconvenience to you, Barbe," said Angélique, "could I spend the night here? I'll leave tomorrow at crack of dawn and go to see my children. Can I share the bed with you?"

"Madame is doing me a great honour."

"Honour!" said Angélique bitterly. ". . . Just look at me and don't talk like that."

Barbe burst into sobs.

"Oh! Madame," she stammered, "your beautiful hair . . . so beautiful! Who brushes it these days?"

"I do . . . occasionally. Barbe, don't cry so much, please!"

"If Madame will allow me," the maid murmured, "I have a brush here. . . . I might perhaps . . . since I happen to be here with Madame. . . ."

"If you like."

The maid's skilful hands disentangled the lovely, warmly gleaming locks. Angélique closed her eyes. The power of everyday gestures is considerable. The careful hands of a maid about her were enough to conjure up an atmosphere that was lost for ever. Barbe was snuffling.

"Don't cry," Angélique said again, "all this will be over some day. . . . Yes, I do believe it will. Not yet, I know, but the day will come. You cannot understand, Barbe. It's like a vicious circle from which one can't escape, except by death. But I'm beginning to think that I shall be able to escape, all the same. Don't weep, Barbe, my good girl. . . ."

They slept side by side. Barbe had to start work at the first light of dawn. Angélique followed her into the kitchen of the cook-shop. Barbe made her drink some hot wine and slipped two little pies into her hand.

Angélique walked along the road to Longchamp. She had passed the Gate of Saint-Honoré, and after following the long sandy rows of a promenade that was called the Champs-Elysées she reached the hamlet of Neuilly, where Barbe had told her she would find her children. She did not yet know what she was going to do. Watch them from afar, perhaps. And if Florimond happened to come near her in playing, she would try to lure him with the offer of a patty.

She asked someone the way towards the dwelling of Mère Mavaut, and as she approached it she saw children playing in the dust under the care of a girl of about thirteen. The children were rather dirty and uncared-for but they looked healthy. She vainly tried to recognise Florimond among them.

When a big woman in clogs came out of the house, she supposed that this was the foster-mother and decided to walk into the courtyard.

"I would like to see two children whom Madame Fallot de Sancé entrusted to you."

The peasant woman, who was a big, dark-haired, robust sort of woman, stared at her with undisguised distrust.

"Could you be bringing the money?"

"So there are arrears due to you for the months of foster-care?"

"Are there!" the woman exploded. "With what Madame Fallot gave me when I took them and what her maid brought me afterwards, I couldn't have fed them for more than a month. And ever since—not a *sou*, not a turnip! I went to

Paris to claim my due but they'd moved. Aren't those just the vulture ways of lawyers!"

"Where are they?" asked Angélique.

"Who?"

"The children."

"How do I know?" said the foster-mother with a shrug. "I am quite busy enough looking after the brats of those who pay."

The little girl, who had come closer, said quickly:

"The little one is over there. I'll show him to you."

She pulled Angélique along, led her through the main room of the farmhouse and brought her to the stable, where there were two cows. Behind the rack she discovered a box in which Angélique could dimly perceive, in the darkness, a child of about six months. He was naked, apart from a dirty rag over his belly, and he was greedily sucking one end of it.

Angélique seized the box and pulled it into the room to get a better look.

"I put him in the stable because it's warmer than in the cellar at night," the little girl whispered. "He's caked with crusts all over but he isn't skinny. It's I who milk the cows morning and evening, so I give him some every time."

Angélique gazed at the baby, horror-struck. This couldn't be Cantor, this hideous little larva covered with scabs and vermin. Anyhow, Cantor was fair-haired when he was born, and this child had brown curls. At that moment he opened his eyes and showed his bright, magnificent pupils.

"He has green eyes like yours," said the girl. "Would you be his mother?"

"Yes, I am his mother," said Angélique tonelessly. "Where is the elder one?"

"He must be in the dog's kennel."

"Javotte! Mind your own business!" the peasant woman shouted.

She was watching their doings with hostility but did not interfere, hoping perhaps that this shabby-looking woman might be bringing her money, after all.

The kennel was occupied by a most ferocious-looking mastiff. Javotte had to wheedle him out with all kinds of wiles and promises.

"Flo is always hiding behind Patou, he's afraid."

"Afraid of what?"

The girl cast a quick glance around.

"Of being beaten."

She pulled something out of the back of the kennel. A curly black ball appeared.

"Why, it's another dog!" cried Angélique.

"No, that's his hair."

"Of course," she murmured.

To be sure, such a shock of hair could only belong to the son of Joffrey de Peyrac. But beneath this thick, dark, bristling mane there was a poor grey little body, all skin and bones, covered with rags.

Angélique knelt down and parted the tousled thatch of hair with a trembling hand. She discovered the pale, drawn face, in which there gleamed two gaping black eyes. Although it was very hot, the child was shaken by a ceaseless shiver. His brittle bones protruded like nails and his skin was rough and dirty. Angélique stood up and strode towards the foster-mother.

"You're letting them starve to death," she said in a slow, heavy voice. "You're letting them die of want. . . . These children have had no care, no food for months. Nothing but the dog's left-overs and the morsels this girl saves from her own meagre fare. You are a wicked wretch!"

The peasant woman had gone very red. She crossed her arms over her bodice.

"Ha! That's a good one, that is!" she cried, choking with anger. "They clutter me up with penniless brats, disappear without leaving an address, and on top of that I've got to let myself be insulted by a highway tramp, a Bohemian, a gipsy, a . . ."

Without listening, Angélique had returned into the house.

She seized a towel that was hanging in front of the fireplace and grasping Cantor she set him up on her back, holding him in place with the towel tied over her chest, in the very manner in which gipsies carry their children.

"What are you going to do?" asked the foster-mother, who had followed her. "You aren't taking them away, are you? If you do, give me the money first."

Angélique foraged in her pockets and threw a few *écus* on the floor. The peasant-woman jeered.

"Ten *livres*! You are joking—they owe me at least three hundred. Come on, pay, or else I call the neighbours and their dogs and have you thrown out."

Tall and massive, she stood before the door with out-stretched arms. Angélique slipped her hand into her bodice and pulled out her dagger. The blade of Rodogone the Egyptian flashed in the semi-darkness with the same glint as her green eyes.

"Out of my way!" said Angélique in a hoarse voice. "Out of my way or I'll bleed you."

The woman shrank back, terrified. Angélique passed in front of her, holding the dagger pointed in the woman's direction, as Polack had taught her.

"Don't yell! Don't send any dogs or farmhands after me, or you'll be sorry. Tomorrow your farmhouse will go up in flames. . . . And you'll wake up with a slit throat. . . . Understand?"

When she reached the middle of the yard, she put the dagger back into her belt and, picking Florimond up in her arms, she fled towards Paris.

Panting, she threw herself back on the man-eating capital, where she had no other refuge for her two half-dead children than crumbling ruins and the fearsome kindliness of beggars and bandits.

Passing carriages raised clouds of dust that stuck to her perspiring face, but she did not slow down, oblivious of the weight of her too light double burden.

'This will end,' thought Angélique, 'it'll just have to end, I'll have to escape some day and bring them back to the living. . . .'

At the sight of the children, Calembredaine displayed neither anger nor jealousy, as she had feared, but a rather horrified expression came over his coarse, swarthy face.

"Are you mad?" he said. "Are you mad to bring your children here? Haven't you seen what they do to children here? Do you want them hired to go begging? . . . Or devoured by rats? . . . Or Rotten Jean to steal them from you? . . ."

Stricken by his unexpected reproaches, she clung to him.

"Where could I have taken them, Nicholas? Look at what's become of them—they were starving to death! I didn't bring them here for any harm to come to them, but to put them under your protection, because you are strong, Nicholas."

She nestled against him, forlorn, looking up at him in a way she had never done before. But he did not notice and shook his head, repeating:

"I shan't always be able to protect them . . . these children of noble blood. I just shan't."

"Why not? You are strong, you are feared."

"I am not as strong as all that. You've worn my heart out. When the heart gets involved, with people like us, one begins to trip up. Everything goes to pieces. I sometimes wake up at night and say to myself: 'Take care, Calembredaine—the gallows aren't such a long way off any more. . . .' "

"Don't talk like that. For once I'm asking you a favour. Nicholas, my Nicholas, help me to save my little ones!"

They were called the little angels. Protected by Calembredaine, they shared Angélique's sheltered life amidst crime and squalor. They slept in a big leather trunk padded with snug coats and fine sheets. They had fresh milk every morning. For their sake, Gobert or Peony would lie in wait for the milkmaids who were going to market at the Pierre-au-Lait with their copper cans on their heads.

Florimond and Cantor had aroused Angélique's passionate love. No sooner had she returned from Neuilly than she took them to see Big Matthieu. She wanted a salve for Cantor's sores, and for Florimond—what could one do to bring this trembling, spent little body back to life? He winced with fright even under her caresses. Broken-hearted, Angélique would hold him on her knees.

"When I left him, he had begun to talk," she said to Polack, "and now he no longer says anything."

Polack accompanied her to Big Matthieu. For them he lifted aside the crimson curtain which divided his platform in two, and ushered them like noble ladies into his private consulting-room. There could be seen an incredible jumble of dentures, suppositories, lancets, boxes of iris powder, pots and ostrich eggs as well as two stuffed crocodiles.

The master himself, with his august hands, applied a pomade of his own composition to Cantor's skin, and promised that it would be all right in a week. The prediction turned out to be correct: the crusts fell off and revealed a plump, peaceful little boy with white skin, closely curled brown hair, in the pink of health.

For Florimond, Big Matthieu was less encouraging. He picked the child up very cautiously, examined him, tried to make him smile, and handed him back to Angélique. Then he scratched his chin, with perplexity. Angélique was more dead than alive.

"What is the matter with him?"

"Nothing. He must eat; very little to begin with. Later, he must eat as much as he can. Perhaps that'll put some flesh on his bones. How old was he when you left him?"

"Twenty months, not quite two years old."

"It's a bad age for learning to suffer want and pain," said Big Matthieu, musingly. "It's better to get to know it at once, at birth—or else later. But for those little ones who are beginning to take a look at life, suffering shouldn't jump at them too suddenly with cruel surprise."

Angélique raised towards Big Matthieu eyes lustrous with unshed tears. She was wondering how this vulgar, bellowing brute could know such subtle things.

"Is he going to die?"

"Maybe not."

"Do give him a medicine, anyhow," she begged.

The quack poured a herb-powder into a small paper bag and recommended that the child be made to drink a decoction of it every day.

"It'll give him strength," he said. But he, who would talk so volubly of the virtues of his remedies, did not add any boasting patter.

After a moment's thought, he resumed:

"For a long time to come he should never again know hunger, cold or fear, he should no longer feel abandoned but see the same faces around him all the time. . . . What he needs is a medicine that can't be found in my jars—he needs to be happy. You understand, wench?"

She nodded her head. She was overwhelmed with amazement. Never had anyone talked to her about children in this way. In the society in which she had lived, it just wasn't done. But simple people had, perhaps, a deeper, shrewder insight . . .

A client, with a swollen cheek wrapped in a handkerchief, had clambered on to the platform, and the orchestra burst into a cacophony. Big Matthieu shoved the two women out, giving them a cordial slap on the back.

"Try and make him smile!" he cried after them before seizing his tongs.

Henceforward, in the Tower of Nesle, everybody tried his best to make Florimond smile. Father Hurlurot and Mother Hurlurette would dance for him, swinging their old legs for all they were worth. Black-Bread lent him his pilgrim's shells to play with. From the Pont-Neuf the men would bring back oranges, pastries, toy mills. A little Auvergnat boy showed him his woodchuck and a mountebank from the fairground of Saint-Germain came to exhibit his eight trained rats which danced the minuet to the sound of his violin.

But Florimond was frightened and hid his eyes. Piccolo the monkey was the only one who managed to interest him. However, despite his grimaces and capers, he did not succeed in making him smile.

The honour of bringing this miracle about came to Thibault the hurdy-gurdy man. One day, the old man began to play the song of 'The Green Mill'. Angélique, who was holding little Florimond on her knees, felt him start with a quiver. He lifted his eyes to her. His mouth trembled, revealed his tiny teeth, as small as rice-corns. And in a small, low, far-away voice he said:

"*Maman!*"

CHAPTER 60

SEPTEMBER CAME, cold and rainy.

"Here comes Homicide,"[1] Black-Bread growled, taking refuge by the fire, with dripping rags. The damp wood hissed in the hearth. For once, the burghers and wealthy traders of Paris did not wait for All Saints to unpack their winter clothes and get a blood-letting, according to the traditions which recommended this surrender to the surgeon's lancet four times a year, at the change of seasons.

But the noblemen and the beggars had other topics to worry them than talk of the rain and the cold. All the high personages at Court and in finance were stunned by the arrest of the exceedingly rich Controller-General of Finance, Monsieur

[1] Slang for 'winter'.

Fouquet. All the low personages of the streets were wondering about the turn which the struggle between Calembredaine and Rodogone the Egyptian would take.

The arrest of Monsieur Fouquet had struck like a bolt from the blue. Only a few weeks earlier, the King and the Queen Mother, received at Vaux-le-Vicomte by the sumptuous Controller-General, had once again admired the magnificent château designed by the architect Le Vau, contemplated the murals by the painter Le Brun, savoured Vatel's cooking, strolled through Le Nôtre's splendid gardens, which were cooled by waters piped by the engineer Francini and channelled into ponds, grottoes, jets and fountains. And finally the whole Court had been able to applaud, in the open-air theatre, a most witty comedy, *Les Fâcheux*, by a young playwright called Molière.

Then, when the last torches had been extinguished, everybody had gone to Nantes for the assembly of the Estates of Brittany. It was here that on a certain morning a musketeer by the name of d'Artagnan presented himself before Fouquet, as the latter was stepping into his carriage.

"That is not what you must ride in, sir," the officer said, "but enter this sedan chair with the bars at the windows which you see a few steps away."

"What? What does this mean?"

"That I am arresting you in the name of the King."

"The King is my master," murmured the Controller-General, who had gone very pale, "but for his glory I could have wished him to act more overtly."

The affair once again bore the seal of Mazarin's royal pupil. It was not without some resemblance to the arrest which had occurred a year ago of a great Toulousian vassal, the Comte de Peyrac, who had been burned as a sorcerer in the Place de Grève.

But amid the panic and alarm into which the Controller-General's fall from favour had plunged the Court, nobody thought of drawing a parallel in connection with the tactics adopted once again on this occasion.

The great gave little time to thought. However, they knew that Fouquet's accounts would show not only the traces of his peculations, but also the names of all those whose support he had paid for. There was even talk of certain highly compromising documents by which great noblemen and even

Princes of the blood had sold themselves to the crafty financier at the time of the *Fronde*.

No, no one as yet recognised in this second arrest—more spectacular and more strikingly sudden than the first—the same dictatorial hand.

Louis XIV alone, as he broke the seals of a dispatch advising him of uprisings in Languedoc, which had been fomented by a Gascon gentleman of the name of d'Andijos, sighed: "It was high time!"

The squirrel, struck by lightning at the height of his ascent, hurtled down from branch to branch. It was high time! Brittany would not rise up in arms for Fouquet, as Languedoc had rebelled for the other, that strange man who had had to be burned alive in the Place de Grève.

The nobility, on whom Fouquet had lavished his prodigality, did not defend him, for fear of following him into adversity. And the Controller-General's immense wealth would pour into the coffers of the State, which was only right. The artists—Le Vau, Le Brun, Francini, Le Nôtre, and even the gay Molière and down to Vatel—all the artists whom Fouquet had picked and kept with their teams of designers, painters, workmen, gardeners, actors, kitchen-boys, would henceforth work for a single master. They would be sent to Versailles, that 'house of cards' lost among forests and swamps, where Louis XIV had taken the gentle La Vallière into his arms for the first time. In honour of this burning, secret love, the most dazzling monument of all would be erected there to the glory of the Sun King.

As for Fouquet, prolonged investigations would be required. The squirrel would be locked up in a fortress. He would be forgotten. . . .

Angélique had no leisure to meditate over these fresh events. Fate decreed that the fall of the man to whom Joffrey de Peyrac had secretly been sacrificed was to follow close upon his victory. But for Angélique it came too late. She did not try to remember, to understand. . . . The great ones of the world passed, plotted, betrayed, returned to favour, disappeared. An authoritative and impassive young King levelled the heads around him with a relentless scythe. The little poison casket remained hidden in a turret of the Château du Plessis-Bellière.

Angélique was now but a nameless woman, who clasped her

children to her heart and watched winter approach with apprehension.

The Court was like an ant-heap demolished by a sudden vicious kick.

The underworld seethed in the expectation of a battle that promised to be terrible.

The Queen and the flower-sellers of the Pont-Neuf were waiting for a Dauphin.

The gipsies were coming into Paris. . . .

The battle of the Fair of Saint-Germain, which steeped the famous Parisian fairground in blood on its opening day, was a cause of bewilderment to all those who later tried to discover its origins.

Lackeys could be seen belabouring students, noblemen running their swords through the bodies of mountebanks, women were raped on the very pavement, coaches set afire. And nobody understood whence the first spark had come.

But one man was not unaware. He was a fellow called Desgrez, a man with book-learning and a variegated past. Desgrez had just been given the post of police-captain at the Châtelet. Greatly feared by all, he was beginning to be talked about as one of the cleverest policemen in the capital. The young man was subsequently to win renown by effecting the arrest of the greatest poisoner of the time and, perhaps, of all time, the Marquise de Brinvilliers, just as in 1678 he was the first to lift the veil from the famous poison drama which was to bespatter, by its revelations, even the steps of the throne.

Meanwhile, it was generally conceded at the close of the year 1661 that the policeman Desgrez and his dog Sorbonne were the two inhabitants of Paris who were most familiar with the city's nooks and corners and with its peculiar fauna.

For some time Desgrez had been following the rivalry which set two mighty bandit chiefs, Calembredaine and Rodogone the Egyptian, against each other for ownership of the area of the fairground of Saint-Germain. He also knew them to be rivals in love for the favours of an emerald-eyed woman who was called the Marquise of the Angels.

Shortly before the opening of the fair, he sensed the strategic moves inside the underworld. Although but a minor police officer, he managed, on the very morning of the opening of the fair, to wrest an authorisation from his superiors to bring up the entire police force of the capital to the approaches of the

Faubourg Saint-Germain. He could not prevent the outbreak of the battle, which spread with lightning speed and extreme fierceness, but he suppressed it just as suddenly and brutally as it had started, swiftly putting out the fires, organising in a defensive action the sword-bearing gentlemen who happened to be there, and effecting mass arrests. Dawn was just breaking after that bloody night when twenty rogues of note were led out of town to the grim common gibbet of Montfauçon.

To be sure, the fame of the Fair of Saint-Germain amply justified the bitter fight waged by the gangs of Paris ruffians for the monopoly of its 'pickings'. From October to December, and from February to Lent, the whole of Paris passed by there. The King himself was not above paying it a visit on certain evenings with his Court, and what a windfall for the cut-purses and coat-snatchers it was, this swarm of fabulous birds!

In the sixteenth century the monks of the Abbey of Saint-Germain-de-Prés, of which the fair-ground was a dependency, had enclosed it in high walls which were fitted with gates and guard-rooms. There was, however, no admission fee. Two large wooden market-halls, which housed traders and mounte-banks, were situated at the crossing of the rue du Four, the rue de Tournon and the rue des Quatre Vents. Towards the rue Garancière, there was a vast area reserved for the cattle market.

Inside the compound could be found four hundred bays composed of shops under covered arcades, set out in a vast chequerboard criss-crossed with lanes. All around them a spacious area was provided for open-air stands and for the traffic of coaches, sedan chairs and horses. The throng, how-ever, was so dense that one could hardly move.

There was nothing that wasn't sold at the Fair of Saint-Germain. The traders of the big provincial towns—Amiens, Rouen, Rheims—displayed samples of their business there. In the luxury shops there was a rush on dressing-gowns from Marseille, diamonds from Alençon, comfits from Verdun. The Portuguese sold ambergris and dainty porcelain. The Pro-vençal sold oranges and lemons. The Turk vaunted his Persian balsam, his scented essences from Constantinople. The Fleming offered his paintings and cheeses. It was like a Pont-Neuf extended to a world-wide scale amid a din of bells, flutes, reeds, and drums. The showmen of animals and freaks attracted vast crowds. One came to see rats dance to the sound of a fiddle and two flies fight a duel with two blades of straw.

Among the spectators a ragged mob brushed shoulders with the richly-clad upper classes. Everybody flocked to the Fair of Saint-Germain to find there, in addition to the most variegated and glittering displays, a free-and-easy way of life that could be had nowhere else.

Everything was organised for sensual bliss. Riotous debauchery sprouted side by side with a roaring trade in gluttony. Wine-shops gleaming with gold and mirrors were cheek by jowl with gambling dens for card games such as *brelan* and *lansquenet*. There wasn't a lad or a lass, stirred by the demon of love, who could not find satisfaction here.

But from time immemorial, the greatest attraction of the Fair of Saint-Germain had always been the gipsies. They were the princes of the fair, with their acrobats and fortune-tellers.

From midsummer onward one could see their caravans arrive, drawn by skinny old horses with braided manes, and loaded with women and children piled up higgledy-piggledy with their kitchen utensils, and stolen hams and chickens. The men, silent and arrogant, with long black hair under plumed hats, which shaded their flashing, coal-black eyes, carried long muskets over their shoulders.

The Parisians would stare at them with the same avid curiosity as their forefathers had done in 1427 when those eternal, dark-skinned wanderers had appeared before the walls of Paris for the first time. They had been called Egyptians, but were also referred to as Bohemians or Tziganes. The beggars acknowledged their influence on the origins of the laws of the underworld, and on All Fools' Day the Duc d'Egypte would walk abreast with the king of the underworld, and the high dignitaries of the Empire of Galilee preceded the arch-henchmen of the Great Coesre.

Rodogone the Egyptian, of gipsy origin himself, held of necessity a high rank among the rogues of Paris. It was only right and proper that he wanted to have sole command over the approaches to those magical sanctuaries, decorated with toads, skeletons and black cats, which the soothsayers, the 'brown witches' as they were called, set up in the centre of the Fair of Saint-Germain.

Calembredaine, however, as the master of the Gate of Nesle and of the Pont-Neuf, claimed this choice morsel for himself.

This rivalry could only end with the death of one or the other.

In the last days preceding the opening of the fair, numerous skirmishes broke out throughout the district. On the day before the opening, Calembredaine's troops had to retreat in disorder and take refuge in the ruined Tower of Nesle while Rodogone the Egyptian established a kind of protective cordon around the district along the ancient moats and the Seine.

Calembredaine's men gathered in the big hall around the table, from which Wood-Bottom was vociferating like a demon.

"I have seen this fight coming for months past. It's your fault, Calembredaine! Your woman has made you lose your wits. You are no fighter any more, so the other gang is getting cocky again. They feel that you are losing hold; they'll line up with Rodogone to knock you over. I saw Blue Mathurin the other night. . . ."

Standing before the fire, against which his mighty frame stood out black, Nicholas wiped his bloodstained torso, pricked by a dagger-blow. He yelled louder than Wood-Bottom:

"We know you're a traitor to the gang, that you assemble all the henchmen, that you go to see them, that you are preparing to take the place of the Great Coesre. But look out! I'll warn Squat Rolin. . . ."

"You son of a bitch! You can't do anything to me . . . ! Make no mistake, Calembredaine: if you retreat, you are done for. Rodogone will be merciless. It isn't just the fair-ground he wants, but your woman whom you snatched from him in the Churchyard of the Innocents. He wants her badly! He can't have her unless you disappear. It's him or you now."

Nicholas seemed to calm down.

"What do you want me to do? All his gang, all those damned Egyptians are out there, right under our noses, and after the whacking we have just got it's no good asking for more. We'd all get ourselves butchered."

Angélique went to her room, seized a cloak and put on her face the red velvet mask which she kept in a casket with other small odds and ends. Thus fitted out, she went down again amid the clamours.

The quarrel between Calembredaine and Wood-Bottom was assuming epic dimensions. The chief could easily have crushed the stunted man on his wooden platter, but Wood-Bottom's authority was such that he was the one who dominated the situation.

At the sight of Angélique in her red mask, they lowered their voices a little.

"What's this carnival for?" growled Nicholas. "Where are you going?"

"I'm merely going to make Rodogone's troops decamp. In an hour's time the place will be cleaned up, gentlemen. You'll be able to return to your posts."

Calembredaine took Wood-Bottom to witness:

"Don't you think she's becoming more crack-brained every day?"

"I do, but after all, if it gives her bright ideas, let her go ahead. One never can tell with this confounded Marquise of the Angels. She's reduced you to the state of a dish-cloth. The least she can do is repair the damage."

Angélique dashed through the night towards the Gate of Saint-Jacques, and there tried to cross the moat. One of Rodogone's Bohemians loomed up before her. She told him, in German gibberish, a complicated story of her being a shop-keeper at the Fair of Saint-Germain on her way back to her stall. He let this masked woman, wrapped in a black cloak, pass. She ran straightway to a friend of hers, a mountebank who owned three enormous, formidable bears. Angélique had won the hearts of those three bears and their old master, as well as that of the youngster who collected the money.

The deal was quickly settled, on the strength of her be-witching smile.

Ten o'clock was striking from the Abbey of Saint-Germain-des-Prés when Rodogone's men, keeping watch along the old moats, saw an enormous growling mass advancing towards them in the misty moonlight. One of them, who tried to make out exactly who was trying to force their blockade, had his chest clawed by a mighty paw which tore his tunic and a sizeable lump of flesh.

The others, without waiting for more ample explanations, jumped over the ramparts. Some of them ran down to the Seine to warn their accomplices, but they too had received the same unpleasant visit. Most of the bandits were already in the river swimming to the Louvre bank and other more healthy places. To brawl, to kill one another in a frank duel with beggars and rogues, held no terror for valiant hearts. But none of Rodogone's men felt any inclination to grapple with a bear which, when it reared up on its hind legs, measured twice six feet!

Angélique calmly reappeared at the Tower of Nesle and notified the company that the whole district had been cleared of undesirables. Calembredaine's staff went to reconnoitre and had to admit the fact.

Wood-Bottom's hollow bursts of laughter made the ladies of the Faubourg tremble behind their bed-curtains.

"Oh la la! That Marquise!" he kept on repeating. "Talk about a miracle! . . ."

But Nicholas did not take the same view.

"You've made a deal with them to betray us," he said, crushing Angélique's wrists. "You've gone and sold yourself to Rodogone the Egyptian?"

To appease his jealous fury, she had to explain her manœuvre.

This time, Wood-Bottom's hilarity shook the rafters like a roll of thunder. Some neighbours appeared at their windows and shouted they'd come down with their swords or halberds to teach a lesson to those scoundrels who wouldn't let decent people sleep. The half-man paid no heed. Dragging himself from cobblestone to cobblestone, he passed through the entire Faubourg Saint-Germain, roaring with laughter. For years to come, the beggars, gathered around a fire, would tell the story of the Marquise of the Angels and the three bears! . . .

This supreme stratagem did not prevent the final drama. Police-captain Desgrez was well advised when, on the morning of the first of October, he went to see Monsieur de Dreux d'Aubray, seigneur of Offémont and Villiers, Civil Lieutenant of the City of Paris, and persuaded him to post all his available police forces at the approaches to the fairground of Saint-Germain.

The day, however, passed quietly. Calembredaine's men were in control among the swelling crowd. At dusk the coaches of high society began to drive up.

Amid the thousands of torches lit at every stand, the fair

assumed the appearance of an enchanted palace. Angélique was at Calembredaine's side and together they watched the varying fortunes of an animal fight: two bulldogs against a wild boar. The crowd, who adored these cruel spectacles, crushed against the fences around the small arena.

Angélique was a little tipsy, having drunk muscatel, raw cider and cinnamon water in succession at the lemonade-vendor's stand. Lavishly and without scruples she spent the money from a purse which Nicholas had handed her. She was collecting puppets and pastries for Florimond.

For once, in order to pass unnoticed—for he had an inkling that the policemen were lying in wait—Nicholas was closely shaven and dressed in a somewhat more decent outfit than his ordinary disguise. With his wide hat concealing his disquieting eyes, he looked like an impecunious country bumpkin who had come to have fun at the fair.

Everything was forgotten. It was the Fair of Saint-Germain. The lights were reflected in shiny eyes; one remembered the fine fairs of one's childhood in hamlets and villages.

Nicholas had put his arm around Angélique's waist. It was his particular way of holding her. It gave her the impression of being completely enclosed in one of those iron hoops that are riven round a prisoner's waist. But this forceful hold was not always unpleasant. Tonight, for instance, enfolded in this sinewy arm, she felt slim and supple, weak and protected. Her hands full of sweets, toys and small scent-flasks, she was en-thralled by this animal fight, was shouting and stamping with the public when the fierce, black mass of the boar, tossing off his attackers, sent one of the dogs flying, with a ripped belly, from the tip of his tusks.

Suddenly, facing them from the other side of the arena, she saw Rodogone the Egyptian.

He was holding a long, thin dagger poised on his finger-tips. The weapon came whizzing over the animal fight. Angélique jumped aside, pulling her companion with her. The blade passed a few centimetres from Nicholas's neck and landed in the throat of a curio-dealer. Struck as if by lightning, the man flung up his arms in a spasm, unfolding the flaps of his gaudy-coloured cloak. For a moment he looked like an enormous pinned butterfly. Then he crumpled up on the ground.

It was the spark that made the Fair of Saint-Germain explode.

CHAPTER 61

Towards midnight Angélique, together with some ten women and wenches, two of whom belonged to Calembredaine's gang, was thrown into one of the low jails of the Châtelet. When the heavy door slammed upon her, she still seemed to hear the clamour of the frenzied crowd, the shouts of the beggars and bandits caught in the implacable net of the archers and police-men and brought in cart loads from the Fair of Saint-Germain to the common jail.

"Nice mess we're in," a bawd said. "Isn't that just my luck! For once I take a stroll away from Glatigny, and of course I get myself nabbed. I wouldn't put it past them to give me a taste of the rack for not having remained in the reserved district."

"Does it hurt to be put on the rack?" a chit of a girl asked.

"Oh God! I've still got my veins and nerves strung out like marshmallow from it. Ah, when the executioner put me on it I shouted: 'Sweet Jesus! Virgin Mary have pity on me!'"

"Me," said another, "I had a hollow horn pushed right down my gullet and they poured in nearly six kettles full of cold water. If only it had been wine! I thought I'd burst like a pig's bladder. Afterwards, they carried me before a good fire, in the kitchen of the Châtelet, to make me come round."

Angélique listened to the voices coming from the foul-smelling darkness. The idea that she too would doubtless be tortured in the course of the preliminary questioning—which was obligatory for all the accused—did not even enter her head. One thought alone was uppermost in her mind: 'My little ones—what will become of them? . . . Who will look after them? Maybe they'll be forgotten in the Tower. And the rats will eat them . . . .'

Although it was icy and damp in the dungeon, sweat oozed from her brow. Squatting on some straw strewn on the ground, she leaned against the wall, her arms clasped around her knees, trying not to tremble and to find arguments to put her mind at rest.

'One of the women will surely look after them. They are a careless, incapable lot, but they do remember to give bread to their children. . . . They'll give some to mine. Anyhow, if Polack is there they'll be all right. And Nicholas will watch over them. . . .'

But hadn't Nicholas been arrested, too? Angélique thought

back to those moments of panic when, running from lane to lane to escape from the bloody brawls, she had been stopped everywhere by a wall of archers and sergeants.

Angélique tried to remember if Polack had been able to leave the fairground before the clash. When she last saw her, Polack was dragging along a young provincial, who seemed at once alarmed and thrilled, towards the banks of the Seine. But they might have stopped on the way at all sorts of shops, or had a drink at a tavern.

Summoning all her will-power, Angélique managed to convince herself that Polack had not been caught, and this thought calmed her a little. From the depth of her anguish, an imploring appeal rose to her lips and forgotten words of prayer came back mechanically:

'Take pity on them! Protect them, Virgin Mary. . . . I swear to you,' she repeated to herself, 'that if my children are saved, I shall tear myself out of this degrading quagmire. I shall run away from this gang of thieves and criminals. I shall try to earn my living by the work of my hands. . . .'

She thought of the flower-seller and drew some plans. The hours that passed seemed less long to her.

In the morning there was a great rattling of locks and keys, and the door was opened. A constable of the watch directed the light of a torch towards them. The daylight that came through the loop-hole beyond the six-foot-thick wall was so dim that one could not see much in the dungeon.

"Here are the marquises, lads," a constable cried hilariously. "Step forward, girls. It looks like a fine harvest."

Three more soldiers of the watch came in and stuck the torch into a ring on the wall.

"Come on, pretty ones, you won't give us trouble, will you?"

And one of the men pulled a pair of scissors from under his tunic.

"Take off your cap," he said to the woman who was near the door. "Bah! grey hairs. Never mind, we'll make a few *sous* on them, anyway. I know a barber over at the Place Saint-Michel who uses them for cheap wigs for elderly clerks."

He cut off the grey hair, tied it with a piece of string and flung it into a basket. His companions inspected the heads of the other prisoners.

"It isn't worth while cropping mine," one of them said. "You sheared me only a short while ago."

"Why, that's true," said the jovial constable, "I remember you, little mother. Hi! Hi! It looks as if you've taken a fancy to this lodging-house!"

A soldier approached Angélique. She felt a coarse hand groping for her hair.

"Hi! pals," he called out, "we've got a tasty bit here! Bring the torch a little closer so we can take a good look."

The resinous flame lit the fine sheath of curly auburn hair, which fell free as the soldier untied Angélique's bonnet. There was an admiring whistle.

"Why, that's a peach, that is! Not fair hair, of course, but it's got a sheen. We'll be able to sell that to Maître Binet in the rue Saint-Honoré. That fellow isn't particular about the price, but he *is* particular about quality. 'Take those parcels of vermin away,' he says to me, whenever I bring him the hair of jail-birds. 'I don't make wigs out of worm-eaten hair!' But this time he won't be able to turn up his nose."

Angélique raised her two hands to her head. They were not going to cut her hair; it was inconceivable!

"Oh no, don't do that!" she begged. But a hard fist slapped her wrists down.

"Now then, my pretty one, you shouldn't have come to the Châtelet if you wanted to keep your thatch on your head. We've got to make our little profit, don't you see?"

And with much clicking of steel, the scissors cropped the shiny curls which Barbe had brushed so reverently but a short while ago. When the soldiers had left, Angélique passed a trembling hand over her bare nape. Her head seemed to have become quite small and light.

"Don't blubber," one of the women said, "it'll grow again. Provided, that is, you take care not to be nabbed again. Because the men of the watch are the devil's own reapers. Hair is fetching a good price in Paris, what with all those bumpkins up from the country who want to wear wigs."

The young woman tied her bonnet up again, without answering. Her companions thought she was crying, because she was shaken by nervous shudders. But the incident was already forgotten. It was unimportant, after all. The only thing that mattered to her was the fate of her children.

The hours crept on with unbearable slowness. The cell in which they were crowded was so small that they could hardly breathe. One of the women said that it was a good sign that they had been put into this small cell. It was the cell called 'the in-between'. It was used for locking up those whom they were uncertain whether or not to consider in a state of arrest.

"After all, we weren't doing anything wrong when they picked us up," she said. "We were at the fair, like everyone else. And that everybody went there is proved by the fact that they didn't search us, for the women-warders of the Châtelet were also there, to have a bit of fun."

"So were the police," remarked another prostitute sourly.

Angélique touched Rodogone the Egyptian's dagger below her clothes.

"A piece of luck they didn't search us," the first woman repeated.

"They will, don't you worry," her companion retorted.

Most of the women displayed scant optimism about their prospects. They told stories of prisoners who had remained locked up for ten years before anyone remembered them. And those among them who were familiar with the Châtelet described the prisons contained in the sinister fortress. There was the dungeon 'End of Comfort', full of filth and reptiles, where the air was so foul that one could not keep a candle lit in it; the 'slaughterhouse', thus called because it was filled with the nauseous smells from the big butcher's shop nearby; the 'Chains', a big hall where the prisoners were shackled to one another; 'Barbary', 'Balsam', which meant 'grotto', and still others: the 'Well', the 'Bottle-Dungeon', which was in the form of an inverted cone. Here the prisoners stood with their feet in the water and could neither hold themselves upright nor lie down. Generally, they would die after a fortnight's detention. Finally, the women lowered their voices to talk of the *oubliettes*, the underground dungeon from which no one ever returned.

A grey light seeped through the small barred window. It was impossible to guess what time it was. An old woman removed her down-at-heel shoes, tore the nails from the sole and stuck them in the other way, with their points outwards. She showed this odd weapon to her companions and advised them to do likewise in order to be able to kill the rats that would appear at night.

Towards midday, however, the door was opened noisily and halberdiers made the prisoners come out and led them through endless corridors to a large hall covered with blue tapestries adorned with yellow fleurs-de-lis.

At the back of the room, on a semicircular platform, there stood a kind of pulpit of carved wood, surmounted by a painting representing Christ on the Cross and by a small needlework canopy. A man in a black robe with a small neckband trimmed with white, and wearing a white wig, sat there. Another, holding a bundle of parchments, was at his side. They were the Provost of Paris and his lieutenant.

Court ushers, tipstaffs and soldiers of the Royal Watch surrounded the group of women and girls. They were pushed to the foot of the platform and had to pass before a table where a court clerk took down their names.

Angélique was at a loss when she was asked her name: she no longer had a name. . . . Finally she said she was called Anne Sauvert, taking the name of a village in the neighbourhood of Monteloup.

Sentence was quickly passed. There was pressure of work at the Châtelet that day. They had to sift fast. After putting a few questions to each one of the detained women, the Provost's lieutenant read out the list that had been handed to him and declared that "all the above-mentioned persons were sentenced to be publicly whipped, and would then be taken to the General Hospital, where devout women would teach them to sew as well as to pray to God".

"We're let off cheaply," one of the prostitutes whispered to Angélique. "The General Hospital isn't like a prison. It's the workhouse. You get put there by force but no watch is kept. It won't be hard to run away."

Then a group of some twenty women was taken into a vast hall on the ground floor, and the sergeants made them line up along the wall. The door opened and a very tall and corpulent soldier walked in. He wore a handsome brown wig over a flushed face cut in two by a black moustache. With his blue tunic tightly stretched over his fat-pillowed shoulders, his wide belt over his bulging midriff, his enormous cuffs covered with braid, his sword and his outsize neckband tied with thick, golden tassels, he looked rather like Big Matthieu, but without the latter's good-natured joviality. His deep-set eyes under the bushy brows were small and hard.

He was shod in high-heeled boots, which further increased his impressive height.

"That's the officer of the watch," whispered Angélique's neighbour. "Oh! he's terrible; he's called the Ogre."

The Ogre passed along the line, making his spurs click on the stone-flags.

"Ho! Ho! sluts, you'll get a good tanning! Come on, off with the jackets. And those who scream too loud had better look out: there'll be an extra stroke for them."

Those women who already had experience of the ordeal of the whip obediently removed their bodices. Those who wore a shift let it slip down over their arms and hang over their petticoats. The archers went to the others who showed some hesitation and brutally stripped them to the waist. One of them half tore Angélique's bodice as he pulled it off. She hastened to bare her torso herself, fearing they might notice her dagger.

The captain of the watch walked up and down, inspecting the women lined up before him. He stopped among the younger ones and a glint flashed in his small, pig-like eyes. Finally, with a peremptory gesture, he indicated Angélique.

With a chuckle of connivance, one of the archers made her step forward.

"Come on, take all this rabble away," the officer ordered, "and let it sting! How many are there?"

"A score, sir."

"It's four o'clock in the afternoon. Finish with it before sundown."

"Yes, sir."

The archers shepherded the women out. In the courtyard Angélique saw a tumbrel piled with switches, which was to follow the wretched procession to the place reserved for public beatings, near the Church of Saint-Denis-de-la-Châtre.

The door was closed again. Angélique remained alone with the officer of the watch. She cast a surprised, anxious glance at him. Why wasn't she sharing the fate of her companions? Would she be taken back to prison?

It was icy cold in the low, domed hall, whose medieval walls oozed with moisture. Although there was still daylight outside, darkness was falling and a torch had already been lit. Shivering, Angélique crossed her arms and clasped her shoulders with her hands, not so much, perhaps, to defend herself against the cold as to conceal her breasts from the Ogre's weighty gaze.

He advanced with a heavy tread and coughed.

"Well, my little chicken, do you really feel like getting your pretty white back skinned?"

As she did not answer, he insisted:

"Answer me! Do you really feel like it?"

Angélique evidently could not say that she did. So she decided to shake her head.

"Well, then, we may be able to do something about it," the soldier said in a sugary tone. "It would be a pity to damage such a pretty chicken. We two might come to an understanding, perhaps?"

He slipped a finger under her chin to force her to raise her head. He whistled with admiration.

"Phew! What beautiful peepers! Your mother must have drunk buckets of absinthe while she was carrying you! Come on, give me a smile."

His fat fingers slyly caressed the fragile neck, stroked the round shoulders. She recoiled, unable to check a shudder of revulsion. His belly heaved with laughter. Her green eyes stared at him fixedly. At last, though he towered over her, he was the first to give signs of embarrassment.

"It's a deal, isn't it?" he went on. "You'll come with me into my apartment. And afterwards you'll go back to the others, but the archers will leave you alone. You won't get a whipping. . . . Are you pleased, my baby?"

He burst into hearty laughter, then pulled her towards him with a vigorous arm and began to plant fat, resounding, greedy kisses on her face.

The touch of that moist mouth, with its smell of tobacco and red wine, revolted Angélique, who writhed like an eel to slip out of his embrace. The belt and the braid of his uniform were chafing her breasts. She finally managed to free herself and hastened to slip her torn jacket on as best she could.

"Hey, what's this?" said the astonished giant. "What's come over you? Didn't you understand that I want to spare you a whipping?"

"Thank you very much," said Angélique firmly, "but I prefer the whipping."

The Ogre's mouth dropped wide open, his moustache quivered and he turned crimson, as if the strings of his neckband were suddenly choking him.

"Wha-at . . . what are you saying? . . ."

"I prefer to be whipped," Angélique repeated. "His Honour

126

the Provost of Paris sentenced me, I must not evade the verdict."

And she stalked resolutely towards the door. With a single stride he caught up with her and gripped her by the neck.

'Oh, good God!' thought Angélique. 'Never again will I seize a chicken by its neck; it's a most horrid feeling!'

The captain scrutinised her attentively.

"You seem an odd sort of wench to me," he said, panting a little. "For what you've just said I could trounce you with the flat side of my sabre and leave you for dead on the floor. But I don't want to hurt you. You are pretty, and well set up. The more I look at you, the more I take a fancy to you. It would be silly if we two couldn't make a deal. I can do you a favour. Listen, don't sulk! Be nice to me, and when you are back with the others, well . . . maybe the warder who escorts you will look the other way. . . ."

In a flash Angélique saw a chance to escape. Florimond's and Cantor's little face danced before her eyes.

Distraught, she looked at the brutal, red face which was bending over her. It was impossible! She could never do it! Besides, there were ways of getting out of the General Hospital. . . . And even on the way there she might have a try. . . .

"I prefer the General Hospital!" she shouted, beside herself. "I prefer . . ."

The rest was lost in a tornado. Shaken so hard that she lost her breath she heard a shower of thundering abuse coming down upon her. An open door gaped bright before her and she was flung through it like a ball.

"I want this strumpet drubbed till her skin hangs in shreds!" roared the captain.

And the door slammed like a thunder-clap.

Angélique had landed sprawling amid a group of the civilian watch who had just arrived to stand guard for the night. Most of these were peaceful craftsmen and shopkeepers who only grumblingly assumed this charge, which was imposed on the guilds alternately. They constituted the 'sitting' or 'sleeping' watch.

They had only just started to pull out their playing cards and their pipes when this half-naked girl was flung into their midst. The captain's order had been yelled at such a pitch that nobody had grasped a word of it.

"Another one whom our valiant captain has abused," said one of them. "One can't say love makes him tender."

"He has plenty of success, though, his nights are never lonely."

"What the hell, he picks them out of the prisoners' lot and lets them choose between the jail and his bed."

"If the Provost knew about it, he'd give him hell."

Angélique had struggled to her feet, badly bruised. The men of the watch gazed at her good-humouredly. They were filling their pipes and shuffling their cards. Hesitantly, she walked to the door of the guardroom. Nobody stopped her. She found herself outside in the vaulted passage of the rue Saint-Leufroy, which led, by way of the fortress of the Châtelet, from the rue Saint-Denis to the Pont-au-Change.

People were coming and going. Angélique realised that she was free. She began to run, madly.

CHAPTER 62

"Psst! Marquise of the Angels—look out! Don't go any farther!"

Polack's voice stopped Angélique as she was approaching the Tower of Nesle. She turned round and saw the girl beckoning to her from the shadow of a porch. She walked across to her.

"Well! My poor girl," the other sighed. "We're in a nice fix! Talk about a round-up! Luckily, Pretty Boy had just turned up. He got himself a tonsure by a 'brother' and afterwards he told the constables he was a friar. So while he was being transferred from the Châtelet to the jail of the Bishopric, he bolted."

"Why do you stop me from going to the Tower of Nesle?"

"Why, Rodogone the Egyptian and all his gang are there."

Angélique went white. Polack went on:

"You should have seen the way they turned us out! No time even to take our clothes! Still, I was able to save your little casket and your monkey. They are in the rue du Val-d'Amour, in a house where Pretty Boy's got friends and where he put up his women."

"What about my children?" asked Angélique.

"As for Calembredaine, nobody knows what's become of

him," Polack continued volubly. "Maybe he's in prison. . . . Maybe he's been hanged. . . . Some say they saw him jump into the Seine. He may have managed to get out of town. . . ."

"I care not a damn about Calembredaine," said Angélique through clenched teeth.

She had gripped the woman by the shoulders and was digging her nails into her flesh.

"Where are my babies?"

Polack's big black eyes stared at her with bewilderment, then she lowered her eyelids.

"I didn't want them to, I assure you . . . but the others had the upper hand. . . ."

"Where are they?" Angélique repeated in a toneless voice.

"Rotten Jean took them . . . with all the kids he found there."

"He's taken them away to . . . the Faubourg Saint-Denis?"

"Yes. That's to say, he took Florimond. Not Cantor. He said he was too fat to be hired out to beggars."

"What did he do with him?"

"He . . . he's sold him . . . yes, for thirty *sous* . . . to some Bohemians who wanted a child to train as a tumbler. . . ."

"Where are those Bohemians?"

"How do I know?" protested Polack, freeing herself moodily. "Pull in your claws, kitten, or you'll hurt me. . . . What can I tell you . . . ? They were Bohemians . . . and they were pulling out. They were sick of the battle of the night. They were leaving Paris."

"Which way did they go?"

"Less than two hours ago they were seen heading towards the Gate of Saint-Antoine. I came back to scout around here, for I had a hunch I might run into you. You're a mother, and mothers have a way of walking through walls. . . ."

Angélique felt torn by a heartrending pain. She thought she was going mad.

Florimond, down there, in the hands of infamous Rotten Jean, crying and calling for his mother! . . . Cantor carried away to an unknown destination, lost for ever!

"I must go after Cantor," she said, "perhaps the Bohemians haven't yet gone far."

"You're off your head, my poor Marquise."

But Angélique had already started off. Polack followed her.

"After all," she said resignedly, "we might as well try. I

129

have a little money. Perhaps they'll be willing to sell him back to us. . . ."

It had been raining during the day. The air was damp and smelled of autumn. The pavements gleamed.

The two women followed the right bank of the Seine and left Paris by the Quay of the Arsenal. On the horizon, over the countryside, the low sky shone deep red through a break in the clouds. A cold wind was rising. People in the suburb told them that they had seen the gipsies near the bridge of Charenton.

They walked fast. Polack now and again shrugged and swore, but she did not protest. She followed Angélique with the fatalism of a woman who had done a lot of walking and camp following, without understanding why, in all sorts of weather and over all sorts of roads.

As they reached the bridge of Charenton, they noticed camp-fires lit in a field, in a hollow by the road. Polack stopped.

"That's them," she whispered, "we are in luck."

They approached the encampment. A clump of big oaks provided shelter for the tribe. Canvas stretched from branch to branch was the gipsies' only covering on this rainy evening. Women and children sat round the fires. They were roasting a sheep on a rough spit. Some lean horses grazed a little way off.

Angélique and her companion advanced cautiously.

"Mind you don't rub them the wrong way," Polack whispered. "You can't imagine how wicked they are! They'd impale us on their spits with no more ado than they spit their sheep and pass on to other things. Just let me do the talking. I know their lingo a little. . . ."

A tall gawk of a fellow, with a fur cap on his head, moved away from the firelight and came up to them. The two women gave the underworld's sign of recognition; the man responded to it haughtily. Thereupon Polack proceeded to explain the object of their visit. Angélique could not understand a word of what they said. She was trying to guess from the gipsy's face what he was thinking, but the darkness was impenetrable now, and she could not make out his features. At last, Polack pulled out her purse; the man weighed it in his hand, gave it back to her and walked away towards the firelight.

"He says he'll talk to the men of his tribe."

They stood waiting, frozen by the wind from the plain. Then the man returned with the same noiseless, lithe step.

He uttered a few words.

"What does he say?" asked Angélique, breathlessly.

"He says that . . . they don't want to return the child. They think he's pretty and graceful. They are already fond of him. They say they are satisfied."

"But that isn't possible! . . . I want my child!" cried Angélique.

She made a move to rush towards the camp. Polack held her back forcibly. The gipsy had drawn his sword. Others were approaching. The trollop dragged her companion towards the road.

"Are you mad? . . . D'you want to die?"

"It isn't possible," Angélique kept repeating. "We've got to do something. They can't take Cantor away . . . far, far away. . . ."

"Don't make such a fuss, that's the way life is! Sooner or later children leave. . . . A little sooner, a little later, it comes down to the same thing. What about all the children *I* had! Do I even know where they are? You go on living just the same!"

Angélique shook her head, to shut out that voice. The rain had begun to fall, thick and fast. They had to do something! . . .

"I have an idea," she announced. "Let's go back to Paris."

"That's right, let's go back to Paris," Polack agreed.

They began to walk again, stumbling into puddles. Angélique's feet were bleeding in her shabby shoes. The wind smacked her drenched skirt against her legs. She felt faint. She had not eaten anything for twenty-four hours.

"I can't go on," she murmured, stopping to catch her breath. "And yet we must be quick, very quick. . . ."

"Wait, I can see some lanterns behind us. They must be riders on their way to Paris. We'll ask them to give us a ride on the crupper."

Polack boldly planted herself in the middle of the road. When the group had come level with them, she shouted to them in the husky voice which she knew how to render cajoling:

"Hi there! Gallant gentlemen! Won't you take pity on two poor girls in distress? We'll thank you prettily."

The riders reined in their mounts. All that could be seen of them was their cloaks with upturned collars and their soaked hats. They exchanged a few words in a foreign language. Then a hand reached down to Angélique and a young voice said in French:

"Climb up, pretty lady."

The hand had a strong grip and the young woman found herself comfortably seated sideways, behind the rider. The horses resumed their trot.

Polack was laughing and, seeing that the man who had lifted her up was a foreigner, she began to exchange jokes with him in a rugged German which she had picked up on the battlefields.

Angélique's companion said without turning round:

"Hold on tight, my girl. My mount has a hard trot and the saddle is narrow. You might fall off."

She obeyed and passed her arms around the young man's body, clasping her icy two hands over his warm chest. This warmth revived her. She let her head drop against the stranger's broad back and enjoyed a moment's rest. Now that she knew what she had to do, she felt calmer. From the riders' talk she gathered they were a party of Protestants returning from the Temple of Charenton.

They rode into Paris. Angélique's companion paid the toll fee for her at the Gate of Sainte-Antoine.

"Where shall I take you, my beauty?" he asked, turning round this time to try and catch a glimpse of her face.

She shook off the numbness that had begun to creep over her.

"I would not like to take too much of your time, sir, but you would greatly oblige me by taking me as far as the Grand Châtelet."

"Angélique," cried Polack, "you're going to do something silly. Be careful!"

"Leave me . . . and give me your purse. I may still need it."

"Oh well, after all . . ." muttered the girl, shrugging her shoulders.

She had jumped down and was profusely thanking her cavalier in the German tongue; he seemed both delighted and embarrassed by this lusty heartiness.

Angélique's rider raised his hat to take leave of the others, then spurred his horse through the wide and almost empty streets of the Faubourg Saint-Antoine. A few minutes later he stopped before the prison of the Châtelet which Angélique had left but a few hours ago. She jumped down. Big torches fixed under the main arch of the fortress lit up the place. In their reddish light Angélique got a better look at her obliging companion. He was a young man of twenty or twenty-five, in the comfortable but simple clothes of a burgher.

She said:

"I am sorry you had to part from your friends on my account."

"It's of no importance. Those young fellows don't belong to my company. They are foreigners. I am French and live at La Rochelle. My father, who is a shipowner, sent me up to Paris to get some business experience in the capital. I joined up with those foreigners because I had met them at the Temple of Charenton, where we had been attending a burial service. So you see you have in no way upset my plans."

"Thank you, sir, for reassuring me so graciously."

She held out her hand. He took it and she saw a grave and kindly young face bending towards her with a smile.

"I'm glad to have obliged you, my dear."

She watched him ride away among the jostling crowd and bloodstained stands of the rue de la Grande Boucherie. He did not turn round, but this encounter had given the young woman fresh courage.

She walked resolutely through the arched gateway and presented herself at the door of the guardroom. An archer stopped her.

"I want to speak to the captain of the Royal Watch."

The man gave her a wink of connivance.

"The Ogre? Well, go ahead, my pretty one, since you find him to your liking."

The hall was blue with pipe-smoke. As she walked into it, Angélique mechanically smoothed her wet petticoat. She noticed that the wind had once more torn off her bonnet and she was ashamed at the thought of her shorn head. She untied her neckerchief, put it over her head and tied the two ends under her chin.

Then she advanced towards the back of the room. Against the fire in the hearth there loomed the black, impressive silhouette of the captain. He was holding forth noisily, his long-stemmed pipe in one hand, a glass of wine in the other. His listeners were yawning and rocking on their chairs. They were used to his bragging.

"Look, here's a wench comes to see us," one of the soldiers remarked, glad of this interruption. The captain gave a start and turned purple as he recognised Angélique. She did not give him time to recover his wits and cried:

"Listen to me, Captain, and you, gentlemen of the watch, come and help me! Gipsies have kidnapped my child and are carrying it away from Paris. At the moment they are camping near the Bridge of Charenton. I beg of you, do come with me, a few of you, and force them to return my child to me. They will have to obey if they are ordered to by the watch. . . ."

There followed a stupefied silence, then one of the men burst out laughing.

"Damn my eyes! Why, this is the cheekiest wench I ever saw! Ho! Ho! A skirt who expects the watch to get moving to—haha! This is too funny! Who do you think you are, Marquise?"

"She's dreaming, she thinks she is the Queen of France."

The laughter spread to the whole room. Whichever way she turned, Angélique saw nothing but open mouths and shoulders heaving with irrepressible laughter. The only one who did not laugh was the captain, and his crimson face assumed a terrible expression.

'He's going to throw me into prison, I'm lost,' thought Angélique.

She looked around, panic-stricken.

"It's a baby boy of eight months," she cried. "He is as pretty as an angel. He resembles your children who are sleeping in their cradles at this moment, near their mother. . . . And the gipsies will take him away with them, far, far away. . . . He'll never see his mother again. . . . He won't know his homeland nor his King. . . . He'll . . ."

Sobs stifled her. The laughter faded from the mirthful faces of the soldiers and watchmen. There were some more guffaws, then an exchange of embarrassed glances.

"Damn it all," said an old soldier with a scar-stitched face, "if the beggar-wench has her heart set on her baby. . . . There are enough of them who abandon their brats at street-corners. . . ."

"Silence!" roared the captain.

He planted himself before the young woman.

"So," he said with threatening calm, "not only are you a shiftless slut sentenced to be whipped, but you dare to come here swaggering and taking on airs and consider it quite natural to call out a military patrol! What do you offer in exchange, Marquise?"

She looked at him fervently:

"Myself."

The colossus's eyes narrowed, and he gave a start.

"Come over here," he decided abruptly.

And he pushed her into an adjoining room that served as a record-office.

"What exactly do you mean?" he growled.

Angélique swallowed, but she did not flinch.

"I mean that I'll do whatever you want."

A mad fear gripped her: perhaps he no longer wanted her, considered her beneath him. The lives of Cantor and Florimond were suspended on the lust of that brute.

The Ogre became meditative, and Angélique was trembling. He finally held out his hands, seized her under her armpits to pull her rudely towards him.

"What I want," he said, looking fierce, "what I want. . . ."

He hesitated; she did not suspect how much timidity this hesitation concealed.

"I want a whole night," he concluded. ". . . You understand? Not just a short hop as I offered you before—a whole night."

He let her go and took his pipe again with a vengeful scowl.

"That'll teach you to play the coy maiden! Well? Is it a deal?"

Unable to speak, she gave an affirmative sign.

"Sergeant!" roared the captain.

A subordinate came running.

"The horses and five men. And stir your stumps!"

The small troop stopped within sight of the gipsies' camp. The captain gave his orders:

"I want two men over there behind the little wood, in case they feel like making for the open country. You stay here, wench."

With the intuition of animals used to the night, the gipsies were already looking towards the road and forming into groups. The captain and the archers advanced, while the men he had appointed were effecting a turning manœuvre.

Angélique remained in the shadows. She heard the voice of the captain of the watch, who, swearing profusely, was explaining to the chief of the tribe that all those people, men, women and children, were to line up before him. They were going to take a count. It was a compulsory formality, on account of the previous night's events at the Fair of Saint-Germain. Afterwards, they would be left in peace.

Reassured, the nomads obeyed. They were familiar with meddlesome police habits the world over.

"Come on, girl," the captain's voice bawled.

Angélique rushed forward.

"This woman's child is among you," the officer went on. "Give him back or you'll be run through."

Just then Angélique saw Cantor. He was asleep against the brown breasts of a gipsy woman. With the roar of a tigress, Angélique bounded towards the woman and wrested the baby, who was beginning to cry, from her. The gipsy woman screamed, but the chief of the tribe rudely told her to be quiet. The sight of the mounted archers, whose halberds pointing towards them were gleaming in the firelight, had made him realise that all resistance was futile.

He made much show of arrogance, however, and remarked that they had paid thirty *sous* for the child. Angélique flung them at him.

Her arms closed passionately around the plump, smooth little body. Cantor evinced little liking for this somewhat brutal appropriation. With the gift for self-adjustment which he had shown ever since his birth, he obviously had settled down very happily on the gipsy woman's lap. The trotting horse on which Angélique was riding pillion behind an archer rocked him to sleep, a thumb in his mouth. He did not seem to suffer from the cold, although he was stark naked in the manner of gipsy children. She put him against her bosom, underneath her bodice, holding him with one arm, while clinging with the other to the archer's belt.

Back in Paris honest folk were closing their windows and snuffing their candles. Noblemen and burghers were setting out towards theatres or taverns. Intimate suppers were prolonged by a few glasses of rosolio and gallant kisses.

The clock of the Châtelet was striking ten o'clock. Angélique jumped down and ran towards the captain.

"Let me take my child to a place of safety," she begged him. "I swear I'll come back tomorrow night."

He looked ferocious.

"Ah! don't trick me! There'd be hell to pay!"

"I swear it."

And, at a loss how to convince him of her good faith, she crossed two fingers and spat on the ground, like the people of the underworld when they make an oath.

"All right," said the captain. "I haven't often seen that oath broken. I'll be waiting for you . . . but don't let me wait too long. Meanwhile, come and give me a little peck on account."

But she jumped back and fled. How did he dare to touch her when she was holding her precious baby in her arms! Men didn't respect anything!

The rue de la Vallée-de-Misère was just behind the Châtelet. It was but a few steps away. Never slowing her pace, she reached 'The Brazen Cock', passed through the restaurant and walked into the kitchen.

Barbe was there, still wearily plucking the feathers of an old cock. Angélique dropped the child into her apron.

"Here's Cantor," she gasped. "Look after him, protect him. Promise me you won't abandon him, whatever happens."

The stolid Barbe hugged the baby and the fowl to her breast with the same gesture.

"I swear it to you, Madame."

"If your master Bourjus flies into a rage . . ."

"I'll let him holler, Madame. I'll tell him that it is my child, and that a musketeer fathered it."

"Very well. . . . Now, Barbe . . ."

"Madame?"

"Take your rosary."

"Yes, Madame."

"And start praying to the Virgin Mary for me. . . ."

"Yes, Madame."

"Barbe, have you some brandy?"

"Yes, Madame, on the table, over there. . . ."

Angélique gripped the bottle and took a long swig from it. She thought she would collapse on the stone floor and had to lean against the table. But after a moment she could see clearly again and felt a beneficent warmth flooding through her.

Barbe was staring at her with popping eyes.

"Madame—where is your hair?"

"How am I to know where it is?" Angélique snapped. "I've better things to do than go and look for my hair."

She strode firmly towards the door.

"Where are you going, Madame?"

"I am going to fetch Florimond."

CHAPTER 63

AT THE corner of a mud house stood the statue of the god of the *argotiers*: a Heavenly Father stolen from the church of Saint-Pierre-aux-boeufs. Blasphemies and obscenities were the prayers that his people addressed to him.

Beyond it, through a maze of repulsive, stinking lanes, one entered the kingdom of darkness and horror. The statue of the Heavenly Father marked the boundary beyond which no solitary archer or policeman could venture without risking his life. Nor would respectable people cross this frontier. What would they have been doing anyway in this nameless slum, where crumbling black houses, mud hovels, decrepit carts and carriages, old mills and barges, transported here goodness knows how, served as homes to thousands of families who were themselves nameless and rootless and had no place of refuge except in the underworld.

Angélique knew she had entered the realm of the Great Coesre by the even deeper darkness, by the silence of a different quality which suddenly shrouded her. The songs from the taverns faded into the distance. There were no taverns here, no lights, no songs. Nothing but unadulterated squalor, with its filth, its rats, its roaming dogs. . . .

Angélique had been here before, in this reserved district of the Faubourg Saint-Denis, but only in daytime and with Calembredaine. He had pointed out to her the Great Coesre's own stronghold, a strange house of several storeys, which must have been a former convent, for one could still see bell-towers and the ruins of a cloister among the mounds of earth, old planks, poles and pebbles with which it was shored up to prevent it from collapsing. Propped up on all sides, wobbling and rickety, displaying the gaping wounds of its arcades and vaulted windows, cocking with a swagger the plumes of its turrets, this was indeed the castle of the Beggar King!

The Great Coesre lived here with his court, his women, his arch-henchmen, his idiot. And here too, under the wings of the great master, Rotten Jean stored his merchandise of stolen children—bastards or legitimate.

The moment Angélique stepped into this fearsome district she began looking for that house. Her instinct told her that Florimond was there. She walked, protected by the pitch-black darkness. Passing figures took no interest in this ragged woman who resembled the inhabitants of the wretched hovels. If anyone had approached her, she would have got off without rousing any suspicions. She was sufficiently familiar with the language and manners of the underworld.

She wore the only disguise that could enable her to pass through this hell with impunity: the disguise of poverty and degradation.

She had to be careful, however, not to be recognised. Two gangs that were rivals of Calembredaine's were living in this district. What would happen if rumour got around that the Marquise of the Angels was loitering here? The nocturnal hunt of wild beasts in the heart of the forest is less ruthless than men are when in pursuit of one of their own kind, in the heart of a city!

For greater safety, she stooped and smeared her face with mud.

At this hour the house of the Great Coesre distinguished itself from the others by the fact that it was lit up. Here and there at the windows one could see the russet, star-shaped glow of a meagre night-light, made up of a bowl full of oil into which an old rag was dipped. Hiding behind a boundary post, Angélique watched it for quite a while. The house of the Great Coesre was also the noisiest one. It was the meeting-place of beggars and bandits, as the Tower of Nesle used to be. Calembredaine's men were being received here. As it was a chilly night, all the doors had been boarded up with old planks.

Angélique at last approached one of the windows and looked through a slit between two boards. The room was packed with people. She recognised some faces: the Little Eunuch, Jean the Greybeard, the arch-henchman with his flowing beard, and finally, Rotten Jean.

He was holding his white hands out to the flames and talking to the arch-henchman.

"Now that's what I call a successful operation, my dear dominie. Not only did the police do us no harm, but it greatly helped us to scatter the gang of that impudent Calembredaine."

"I consider you are somewhat wide of the mark in saying that the police did us no harm. Fifteen of our men were hanged, practically without a judgment, at the gibbet of Montfauçon! And we aren't even sure that Calembredaine was among them!"

"Pshaw! Anyway, his head's smashed and he won't be able to get back where he was for a long time . . . if he ever reappears, which I doubt. Rodogone has occupied all his places."

The Greybeard sighed.

"So one day we'll have to fight Rodogone. That Tower of Nesle, which commands the Pont-Neuf and the Fair of Saint-Germain, is a formidable strategic position. Formerly, when I was teaching history to some scamps at the college of Navarre——"

Rotten Jean was not listening.

"Don't be pessimistic about the future of the Tower of Nesle. As far as I'm concerned, I don't mind a little revolution like that from time to time. What a fine haul I made at the Tower of Nesle! Some twenty brats of good quality who will yield a good profit in clinking coins."

"Where are your little cherubs?"

Rotten Jean gestured towards the cracked ceiling.

"Up there, under lock and key. . . . Madeleine, my girl, come here and show me your suckling."

A fat, bovine woman removed a nursing baby from her breast and held it out to the odious creature, who picked it up and lifted it admiringly.

"Isn't he a beauty, the little Moor? When he's big, I'll dress him up in a sky-blue suit and sell him at Court."

At that moment, one of the beggars began to play on his reed-pipe and two others began to dance a peasant reel. Angélique could no longer hear what Rotten Jean and the Greybeard were saying.

But there was something she now knew for certain. The

children kidnapped from the Tower of Nesle were in this house, and apparently in a room situated above the main hall.

She walked very slowly around the house. She found an opening that gave on to the staircase. She slipped off her shoes and walked barefoot. The winding stairs led to a corridor on the first floor. The walls and floor were covered with a rough-cast mixture of earth and straw. To her left she saw an empty room in which a small lamp was glimmering. There were chains fixed to the wall. Whom did they chain up in this place? . . . Whom did they torture? . . . She remembered that people said that during the civil wars Rotten Jean had young men and isolated peasants kidnapped for re-sale to the recruiting-sergeants. . . . The silence of this part of the house was frightening.

Angélique continued to advance. A rat brushed past her and she stifled a cry.

Now a new sound seemed to be coming from the bowels of the house.

They were groans and distant weeping, which gradually became more distinct. Her heart gave a jump; they were the moans of children. She imagined Florimond's face with his terrified black eyes, the tears running down his pale cheeks. He was afraid of the dark. He was calling. . . . She advanced more quickly. She climbed another flight of stairs, passed through two rooms; small lamps shed their grimy light. She noticed there were copper gongs on the walls; together with bundles of straw scattered over the floor and a few mugs lying on the ground, these constituted the only furnishings of this sinister dwelling-house.

She guessed that at last she was nearing her goal. She distinctly heard the mournful concert of children's sobs.

Angélique entered a small room to the left of the corridor which she had been following for a while. A little light glimmered in a recess, but there was nobody here. And yet that was where the sounds came from. She noticed at the end of the room a heavy door studded with locks. It was the first door she had come across, for all the other rooms were wide open.

A small barred opening had been cut out of the door-panel. She could not see anything through it, but realised that the children were locked up in that dungeon without light or air. How could she attract the attention of a terrified two-year-old?

The young woman glued her lips to the grille and called out softly:

"Florimond! Florimond!"

The sobbing calmed down a little, then a voice whispered from inside:

"Is it you, Marquise of the Angels?"

"Who is there?"

"It's me, Linot. Rotten Jean bundled us off with Flipot and the others."

"Florimond is with you?"

"Yes."

"Is he crying?"

"He was but I told him that you'd come and fetch him."

"Be patient, I'll get you out," Angélique promised. She stepped back and examined the door. The locks seemed stout, but perhaps there was a means of loosening the hinges from the crumbling walls. She began to scratch the stonework with her nails.

Then she heard a strange noise behind her. It was like a chuckle, stifled at first, but gradually mounting, mounting till it became a roar of laughter.

Angélique veered around, and in the doorway she saw the Great Coesre.

The monster was slumped in a low cart mounted on four wheels. This was the way in which, propelling himself with his two hands, he moved through the corridors of his fearsome labyrinth.

From the threshold of the room he fixed the young woman with his cruel gaze. And, paralysed by terror, she recognised the fantastic apparition of the graveyard of the Saints-Innocents.

He continued to laugh with guffaws and horrible hiccups which shook his crippled torso and his two short, limp and spindly legs. Then, without ceasing to laugh, he started to move again. Fascinated, her eyes followed the movements of the creaking little chariot. He was not moving towards her, but swerved across the room, and suddenly she noticed on the wall one of those copper gongs she had seen in the other rooms. An iron bar was lying on the ground.

The Great Coesre was about to strike the gong, and in answer to his call there would come rushing, from the depths of the house, towards Angélique, towards Florimond, all the beggars, all the bandits, all the demons of this hell. . . .

The eyes of the beast with the slashed throat were turning glassy.

"Oh! you've killed him," said a voice.

On the same threshold on which the Great Coesre had appeared a moment ago stood a young girl, hardly more than a child, with a Madonna face.

Angélique stared at the blade of her dagger, red with blood. Then she said in a low tone of voice:

"Don't call, or I'll be obliged to kill you, too."

"Oh no! I won't call, I'm so glad you killed him!"

She came closer.

"Nobody had the courage to kill him," she murmured. "They were all afraid. And yet he was only an abominable little man."

Then she raised her black eyes towards Angélique.

"But now you must run away, quickly."

"Who are you?"

"I am Rosine—the Great Coesre's last wife."

Angélique slipped her dagger into her belt. She reached out a trembling hand and placed it on that fresh, pink cheek.

"Rosine, help me. My child is behind that door. Rotten Jean has locked him up. I *must* have him back."

"The double key to the door is there," said the girl. "Rotten Jean lets the Great Coesre keep it for him. It's in his cart."

She bent towards the motionless, repulsive heap. Angélique did not look. Rosine straightened up.

"Here it is."

She herself inserted the keys into the keyholes, the locks creaked. The door opened. Angélique rushed into the dungeon and seized Florimond, whom Linot was holding in his arms. The child was not weeping, he wasn't screaming, but he was icy cold, and he hugged her so tightly with his thin little arms that she could not get her breath.

"Now help me to get out of this place," she said to Rosine.

Linot and Flipot clung to her petticoats. She freed herself.

"I can't take you all with me."

She wrenched herself from the grimy little hands, but the two urchins ran after her.

"Marquise of the Angels, Marquise! don't leave us!"

Suddenly Rosine, who had pulled them towards a staircase, put a finger to her lips.

"Hush! Someone's coming up."

A heavy step resounded on the floor below.

"It's Bavottant, the idiot. Come this way."

She began to run wildly. Angélique followed her with the two children. As they came out into the street, an inhuman roar mounted from the heart of the Great Coesre's palace. It was the idiot Bavottant giving vent to his sorrow before the corpse of the royal freak on whom he had for so long lavished his tender cares.

"Let's run!" Rosine said again.

The two of them, followed by the panting boys, streaked through the tunnel of dark lanes. Their bare feet slipped over the sticky stones. At last the young girl slowed down.

"Here are the lights," she said. "This is the rue Saint-Martin."

"We must go farther. They may be after us."

"Bavottant can't talk. Nobody'll understand; maybe they'll even think he was the one who killed him. They'll put up another Great Coesre. I'll never go back there. I'll stay with you because you killed him."

"What if Rotten Jean manages to find us?" asked Linot.

"He won't find you. I'll defend you all."

Rosine pointed, far up the street, to a wan light that made the glow of the lanterns seem pale.

"Look, the night's over."

"Yes, the night is over," Angélique repeated grimly.

CHAPTER 64

AT THE Abbey of Saint-Martin-des-Champs there was a soup-kitchen for the poor every morning. The fine ladies who had attended early Mass would help the nuns in this pious task of charity.

The paupers who sometimes had had no other place to sleep but the angle of a boundary post found a moment's respite in this large refectory. Each one was given a bowl of hot soup and a roll.

That's where Angélique landed eventually, carrying Florimond, and followed by Rosine, Linot and Flipot. They were, all five of them, covered with mud and filth and their faces were drawn. They lined up with a whole swarm of destitutes and sat down on long benches before wooden tables. Serving-maids appeared, carrying big soup tureens.

The smell was fairly appetising, but before sating her hunger Angélique wanted Florimond to eat. Gently she raised the bowl to the baby's lips.

Only then did she see him in the dim daylight that came through a stained-glass window. His eyes were half closed, his nose was pinched. . . . He was breathing very fast, as if his heart, strained by terror, could not find its normal rhythm. Apathetically, he let the broth spill out of his lips. The warmth of the liquid, however, revived him. He gave a hiccup, managed to swallow a sip, then held out his hands towards the bowl and drank greedily.

Angélique gazed at the poor, miserable little face under its dark, tousled shock of hair.

'So this is what you have done,' she said to herself, 'with the son of Joffrey de Peyrac, the heir of the Comtes de Toulouse, the child of the Floral Games, born for light and gladness. . . .'

She was awakening from a long numbness, contemplating the horror and ruin of her life. A savage fury against herself and against the world flooded her like a tide. At that moment, when she should have been stricken and emptied of all substance after that horrible night, she felt permeated by a stupendous force.

"Never again . . ." she said, "never again will he be hungry . . . or cold . . . or afraid. I swear it."

But weren't hunger, cold and fear lying in wait for them at the gate of the Abbey?

"I must do something. Immediately."

Angélique looked around her. She was but one of those wretched mothers, one of those 'poor' to whom nothing is owed, and over whom those richly dressed ladies were bending out of charity before returning to their gossiping in the literary 'alcoves' or to their Court intrigues. With a mantilla placed over their hair to hide the brilliance of their pearls, an apron pinned to their velvets or silks, they went from one to the other. A maidservant followed them, carrying a basket from which the ladies drew cakes, fruit, sometimes a pie or half a chicken, the scraps of princely tables.

"Oh! my dear," said one of them, "you *are* brave, in your condition, to come here so early in the morning to distribute alms. May God bless you."

"I do indeed hope so, my dear."

The little laugh that followed seemed familiar to Angélique. She looked up and recognised the Duchesse de Soissons, to whom the red-haired Bertille was holding out a prune silk cloak. The Duchesse wrapped herself up in it snugly.

"God didn't arrange things too well when he obliged women to carry in their womb for nine months the fruit of a moment's pleasure," she said to the abbess who was escorting her to the door.

"What would there be left to us nuns, if all the minutes of this worldly life were filled with pleasure?" replied the nun, with a smile.

Angélique rose abruptly and held her son out to Linot.

"Take Florimond."

But the baby clung to her, uttering piercing cries. She resigned herself to keeping him with her, and told the others:

"Stay there, don't move."

A carriage waited in the rue Saint-Martin. As the Duchesse de Soissons was about to climb into it, a shabbily-dressed woman, holding a child in her arms, came up to her and said:

"Madame, my child is dying of hunger and cold. Order one of your lackeys to take, to the address I shall give him, a barrow full of firewood, a basin of soup, bread, blankets and clothes."

The noble lady stared at the beggar-woman with surprise.

"You are rather bold, my daughter. Did you not receive your bowl of soup this morning?"

"I can't live on a bowl of soup, Madame. What I am asking for represents little of your great wealth: a barrow full of firewood and food which you will send me until I can manage without it."

"Incredible!" the Duchesse exclaimed. "Do you hear that, Bertille? The impudence of these beggar-wenches is becoming more incredible every day! Leave me, woman! Don't touch me with your dirty hands, or I'll have you thrashed by my lackeys."

"Take care, Madame," said Angélique under her breath, "take care lest I talk of Kouassi-Ba's child!"

The Duchesse, who was tucking up her petticoats to step into the carriage, remained with one foot in the air.

Angélique continued:

"I know a house in the Faubourg Saint-Denis where a Moor's child is being brought up. . . ."

"Talk more softly," Madame de Soissons muttered, enraged. "Now what's all this about?"

And, to keep herself in countenance, she opened her fan and waved it, which served no useful purpose since a sharp, cold wind was blowing.

"I know of a Moor's child being raised. . . . He was born in Fontainebleau on a day I know, to a woman whose name I could give to anyone who'd be interested. Wouldn't the Court be amused to learn that Madame de Soissons has been carrying a child in her womb for thirteen months?"

"Oh! the swine!" cried the beautiful Olympe, whose southern temperament always got the better of her.

She stared hard at Angélique, trying to recognise her, but the young woman lowered her eyes, convinced that in her present sorry state nobody would dream of identifying her with the radiant Madame de Peyrac.

"Enough of this!" the Duchesse de Soissons said, infuriated. And she strode hurriedly to her carriage. "You deserve to be caned. I'll have you know that I don't like to be made a fool of."

"The King doesn't like to be made a fool of either," murmured Angélique, who was following her.

The noble lady went crimson and threw herself back against the velvet cushions, patting her skirts with much agitation.

"The King! . . . The King! . . . To hear a shiftless beggar-wench talk of the King! It's intolerable! Well, then? . . . What do you want? . . ."

"I told you, Madame. Very little: a barrow full of firewood, warm clothes for myself, my baby and my little boys aged eight and ten, a little food. . . ."

"Oh! how humiliating to be spoken to in this way!" said Madame de Soissons, biting into her lace handkerchief. "And to think that that fool of a police lieutenant is congratulating himself that the operation of the Saint-Germain Fair has made those overwhelming bandits draw in their horns. . . . What are you waiting for to close the carriage doors?" she cried to her flunkeys.

One of them jostled Angélique to carry out his mistress's order, but she did not accept defeat and again approached the carriage.

"May I present myself at your hôtel in the rue Saint-Honoré?"

"Present yourself," the Duchess said curtly.

So it happened that Maître Bourjus, caterer in viands in the rue de la Vallée-de-Misère, saw a strange procession arrive in his courtyard, as he was starting on his first pint of wine and thinking sadly of the gay ditties which Madame Bourjus used to hum at this hour.

A family of tatterdemalions, made up of two young women and three children, preceded a footman in the cherry-red livery of a great household, who was pulling a cartload of firewood and clothes. To complete the picture, a little monkey, perched on top of the cart, seemed delighted to be taken for a ride and was making faces at the passers-by. One of the little boys held a hurdy-gurdy, whose strings he was gaily strumming.

Maître Bourjus jumped up, swore, hit his fist on the table and arrived in the kitchen just as Angélique was handing Florimond into Barbe's arms.

"What . . . what's this? . . ." he stuttered, beside himself. "Are you going to tell me that this one is yours, too? And I who took you for a decent, respectable girl, Barbe?"

"Maître Bourjus, listen to me. . . ."

"I'll listen no more to anything! You are making my cookshop into a foundling asylum! I am disgraced. . . ."

He flung his chef's cap down on the ground and ran out to call for the watch.

"Keep the two babies warm," Angélique advised Barbe. "I'll go and light the fire in your room."

Madame de Soissons's dumbfounded and indignant lackey had to carry the logs up to the seventh floor by a rickety staircase, and put them down in a small room which was not even furnished with a curtained bed.

"And mind you tell Madame de Soissons to have the same things brought to me every day," Angélique told him.

"Look here, wench, if you want my advice . . ."

"I don't want your advice, peasant, and I forbid you to address me familiarly," Angélique cut him short in a tone which accorded ill with her torn bodice and her cropped head. The lackey walked down the stairs, feeling—like Master Bourjus—that he was disgraced.

A little later, Barbe climbed the stairs, carrying Florimond and Cantor in her arms. She found Linot and Flipot lustily blowing upon a magnificent log-fire. The heat was suffocating, and they all had flushed cheeks. Barbe related that the land-lord was still incensed and that his tantrums were frightening Florimond.

"Leave them with us now that it's warm up here," said Angélique, "and go and attend to your duties, Barbe. You aren't cross that I've come to you with my babies?"

"Oh! Madame, it's a great joy for me."

"And those poor children, we must put them up too," said Angélique, pointing to Rosine and the two little boys. "If you knew where they come from!"

"Madame, my poor little room is yours."

"Ba-a-arbe! . . ."

Maître Bourjus was roaring in the courtyard. The entire neighbourhood echoed with his screams. Not only had his house been invaded by beggars, but his servant was losing her head. She had let a spit-load of six capons burn. . . . And what was that shower of sparks issuing from the chimney-stack—a chimney in which no fire had been made for five years? Everything would go up in flames! . . . This was his final ruin. Ah, why had Madame Bourjus died! . . .

The cooking-pot sent by Madame de Soissons contained meat-stock, soup and fine vegetables. There were also two loaves of bread and a jug of milk. Rosine went down to fetch a pail of water from the well in the courtyard, and they heated the water on the andirons. Angélique washed her two children, wrapped them in fresh clothes and warm blankets. Never again would they be hungry, never again cold! . . .

Cantor was sucking a chicken bone picked up in the kitchen. He babbled away as he played with his little feet. Florimond did not yet seem to have recovered fully. He would fall asleep, then wake up crying. He shivered, and she did not know whether it was from fever or fear. But after his bath he perspired profusely, then fell into a peaceful slumber.

Angélique sent Linot and Flipot out of the room and, in her turn, washed in the tub which normally served for the ablutions of the modest serving-maid.

"How beautiful you are!" Rosine exclaimed. "I don't know you, but you must surely be one of Pretty Boy's girls."

Angélique was scrubbing her head energetically and found that washing one's hair was really very easy when one hadn't any left.

"No, I am the Marquise of the Angels."

"Oh! So it's you!" cried the young girl, dazzled. "I've heard so much about you. Is it true that Calembredaine was hanged?"

"I don't know, Rosine. As you see, we are in a very simple, very decent little room. There's a crucifix on the wall. You mustn't talk of all that any more."

She slipped on her coarse linen shift, a dark-blue serge skirt and bodice, which were part of the cart-load that had been sent. Angélique's slender figure was lost in these rough, shapeless garments; but they were clean, and she felt a profound relief as she dropped her old tattered rags on the floor.

She took a small mirror from the casket she had gone to retrieve from the rue du Val d'Amour. There were all sorts of interesting things which she cherished in this casket, among them a tortoiseshell comb. She arranged her hair. Her face under the short crop seemed like a stranger's to her.

"Did the police crop your hair?" Rosine asked.

"Yes . . . oh well! It'll grow again. But, Rosine! what have I there?"

"Where?"

"In my hair. Look!"

Rosine looked.

"It's a strand of grey hair," she said.

"Grey hair!" Angélique repeated, horrified. "But it can't be! I . . . only yesterday I still hadn't any, I am sure."

"It's come just like that. Last night, perhaps?"

"Yes, last night."

With limp legs, Angélique went to sit down on Barbe's bed.

"Rosine . . . Have I grown old?"

The young girl, kneeling before her, examined her gravely, then stroked her cheek.

"I don't think so. You have no wrinkles, and your skin is smooth."

Angélique arranged her hair as best she could, trying to hide the unfortunate strand underneath the others. Then she tied a black satin scarf around her head.

"How old are you, Rosine?"

"I don't know. Fourteen perhaps, or fifteen."

"I remember you now. I saw you at the graveyard of the Saints-Innocents one night. You were walking in Great Coesre's procession, and your breasts were bare. It was winter. Weren't you dying of cold, naked like that to the waist?"

Rosine raised her big, dark eyes towards Angélique, who could read a vague reproach in them.

"You said yourself, we mustn't talk of all that any more," she murmured.

At that moment Linot and Flipot started drumming on the door. They came in gaily. Barbe had slipped them surreptitiously a frying-pan, a piece of fat and a jar of dough. They were going to make pancakes.

There was no gayer place in Paris that evening than the little room in the rue de la Vallée-de-Misère. Angélique tossed the pancakes; Linot strummed on Thibault's hurdy-gurdy. Polack had found the instrument against a boundary-stone and had given it back to the old musician's grandson. Nobody knew what had become of the old man in the scuffle.

A little later, Barbe came up with a candlestick. She said that no customer had come to the shop that night and that Maître Bourjus had locked up in disgust. To top the innkeeper's misfortune, his watch had been stolen. Thus Barbe was free earlier than usual. As she finished talking, her eyes fell on a strange assortment of objects placed on the wooden chest in which she stored her clothes. There were two tobacco-graters, a string-purse with a few *écus*, buttons, a hook, and right in the middle——

"But . . . that's Maître Bourjus's watch!" she exclaimed.

"Flipot!" cried Angélique.

Flipot assumed an air of modesty.

"Yes, I did it. When I went down to the kitchen for the pancake dough."

Angélique grabbed him by the ears and shook him hard.

"If you start again, you cut-purse sprout, I'll throw you out and you can go back to Rotten Jean."

Disconsolately, the boy went to lie down in a corner of the room, where he promptly fell asleep. Linot did likewise, then Rosine, half sprawled across the pallet. The babies were slumbering again.

Kneeling before the fire, Angélique was the only one who

stayed awake with Barbe. She could hear no sound, for the room overlooked a courtyard and not the street, which at this hour was beginning to fill up with gamblers and revellers.

"There's nine o'clock striking from the Châtelet," said Barbe.

She was surprised to see Angélique raise her brow with a drawn expression on her face, then get up abruptly. For a moment the young woman remained gazing at the sleeping Florimond and Cantor. Then she walked towards the door.

"I'll see you tomorrow, Barbe," she whispered.

"Where is Madame going?"

"There remains one more thing for me to do," said Angélique. "After that, it will be all over. Life can begin again."

CHAPTER 65

IT WAS but a few steps from the rue de la Vallée-de-Misère to the Châtelet. From 'The Brazen Cock' one could see the pointed roofs of the big tower of the fortress.

Angélique soon found herself in front of the main gate of the prison, flanked by two turrets and surmounted by a bell-tower and a clock.

As on the previous night, the arched gateway was lit by torches. Angélique walked up to the gate, then shrank back and began to wander around in the neighbouring streets, hoping that a miracle might destroy the sinister castle whose thick walls had already withstood the onslaught of half a dozen centuries. The adventures of this last day had almost erased from her memory the promise she had given to the captain of the watch. But Barbe's words had recalled it to her mind. Now the hour had come for her to keep her word.

'Come on,' she said, 'lingering here won't help. I have to go through with it.'

She turned back towards the prison and, under the arch, stepped aside to make room for a funeral procession that was coming out. In the lead walked a man holding a smoking torch. Two porters carrying a bier marched behind him. Two more stretchers followed, and in their wake the air was permeated with cadaverous odours so strong that they surpassed the fetid stench of the adjacent streets.

The stretchers, by order of the Lieutenant of Police, were transporting three drowned men who had been deposited in the lower jail for several days and who had not been identified. They would be passed on to the nuns of the Hospital of Saint-Catherine, at a few hundred steps' distance from the Châtelet; these nuns were called upon by their statutes to wash, shroud and bury this sad human carrion in a special grave.

Angélique shuddered and hastened into the guardroom.

"Ah! there you are," said the captain.

He was seated, smoking, his two feet on the table.

"I didn't believe she'd come back," said one of the men.

"I did," the captain asserted. "I have seen men go back on their word, but a skirt never. So, my sweet? . . ."

She lowered an icy glance on the flushed face. The captain reached out with his hand and heartily pinched her backside.

"You'll be taken to the surgeon so that he can give you a wash and see that you aren't sick. If you are, he'll apply some pomade. I am a finicky fellow, you know. Off you go!"

A soldier escorted Angélique to the surgery. They found the surgeon in amorous conversation with one of the prison matrons.

Angélique had to lie down on a bench and submit to the revolting examination.

"You can tell the captain that she is clean as a whistle and fresh as a daisy," the surgeon shouted after the disappearing soldier. "We don't often come across the likes of her in this place!"

The matron took her to the captain's room, pompously christened his 'apartment'. She remained alone in this room, which had barred windows like a jail, and thick walls ill-concealed by frayed, threadbare tapestries. A torch on the table, placed next to a sabre and an inkstand, did little to dispel the shadows under the vaulted ceiling. The room smelled of old leather, tobacco and wine. Angélique remained standing by the table, unable to sit down or do anything, sick with nervousness and gradually, as the time passed, completely frozen, for the place exuded a chilly moisture.

At last she heard the rumbling noise of the captain in the corridor, and he walked in, uttering a stream of curses. He flung his sword and pistol on the table, sat down panting and commanded, as he held out his foot to Angélique:

"Take my boots off!"

Angélique's blood gave just one turn.

"I am not your servant!"

"Well, I'm damned!" muttered the captain, putting his hands on his knees to take a better look at her.

Angélique told herself that she was mad to provoke the Ogre's wrath at the very moment when she was completely at his mercy. She tried to soften her answer.

"I'd do so gladly, but I don't know anything about military dress. Your boots are so big and my hands are so small. Look."

"It's true they are small," he conceded. "You have the hands of a duchess."

"I can try to . . ."

"Never mind, sparrow," he growled, pushing her back.

He seized one of his boots and began to pull at it, writhing and grimacing. There was the sound of steps on the flagged corridor, and a voice called:

"Captain! Captain!"

"What's the matter?"

"They've brought in a corpse, fished out near the Petit-Pont."

"Put him in the morgue."

"Yes . . . only he's got his belly slashed. You'll have to make a report."

The captain blasphemed enough to make the nearby church tower come crashing down, and rushed out.

Angélique waited again, more and more chilled. She was beginning to hope that this whole night would pass in this way, or that the captain would not come back, or—who knows? —might himself get knifed, when the Châtelet echoed once more with the roars of his mighty voice. A soldier accompanied him.

"Remove my boots," he told him. "All right. Now out! And you, wench, hop into bed instead of standing there, stiff as a ramrod, with your teeth chattering."

Angélique turned away and walked over to the alcove. She began to undress. There was a big lump in the pit of her stomach. She wondered whether she ought to take off her shift, and finally decided to keep it on. She climbed into the bed and, despite her apprehension, had a feeling of well-being as she slipped under the blankets. The featherbed was soft, and she gradually began to warm up. With the sheet up to her chin, she watched the captain undress.

He was something of a phenomenon: he creaked, panted, groaned, grumbled, and the shadow of his enormous figure covered an entire wall-panel.

He removed his superb brown wig and placed it carefully on a wooden stand. Then, after energetically scratching his skull, he proceeded to take off his other clothes.

Deprived of his boots and wig and stark naked, the captain of the watch was still an imposing figure. She heard him splash in a pail of water, then he emerged again, with a towel modestly tied around his loins.

At that moment, there was again a knocking at the door.

"Captain! Captain!"

He went to open it.

"Captain, it's the watch come back saying that a house has been burgled in the rue des Martyrs and . . ."

"Damn and blast you!" the captain thundered, "when will you realise that if there's any martyr about, it's me! Can't you see that I have a warm little chicken in my bed who's been waiting for me for three hours!"

He slammed the door, shot the bolt resoundingly and stood there for a moment, naked and colossal, reeling off curses and abuse. Then, somewhat mollified, he tied a scarf around his skull, making the two ends puff coquettishly over his forehead.

Finally, picking up the torch, he stepped gingerly towards the alcove.

The cowering Angélique, with the sheet up to her chin, watched the advance of this ruddy giant whose horned head threw a grotesque shadow on the ceiling. Relaxed by the warmth of the bed, numbed by the long wait and already close to sleep, she found this apparition so ludicrous that she suddenly could not help giggling.

The Ogre stopped, gazed at her with surprise and a jovial expression split his merry face.

"Ho! Ho! The baby's giving me a smile! Why, that's unexpected! For you certainly know how to freeze a fellow with icy glances! But I see you're not averse to a bit of fun either. Hey! Hey! You're laughing, sweetheart! That's fine! Hee! Hee! Hee! Hee!"

He began to laugh heartily, and he looked so funny with his cap and his candlestick that Angélique positively choked in her pillow. At last, with streaming eyes, she managed to control herself. She was furious with herself, for she had promised herself to be dignified, indifferent, granting just what had to be, and here she was laughing like a trollop trying to put a customer at ease.

"That's fine, sweetie, that's fine," the captain repeated, well pleased. "Now move over to make a little room for me."

The 'little room' he asked for almost released a fresh outbreak of mirth on Angélique's part. But at the same time she was gripped by the thought of what she was about to submit to. While he was hoisting himself into the bed, she shrank back to the other side, curled up and stayed there, mute with revulsion.

The mattress sagged under the enormous bulk which slumped on it. The captain had blown out the candle. His hand pulled the curtains of the alcove, and in this fusty darkness the strong smell of wine, tobacco and boot-leather became unbearably intense. He was breathing hard and muttering indistinct curses. At last he groped on the mattress near him and his big paw came down on Angélique, who stiffened.

"There! There!" he said. "You're like a wooden puppet. This is no time for that, my beauty. However, I don't want to rush you. I'll talk nice to you, because it's you. A while ago, just from the way you looked at me as if I was no bigger than a pea, I could tell you didn't much fancy the idea of going to bed with me. And yet I am a good-looking man and generally the ladies like me. But it's hopeless trying to understand women. . . . I like you, though, and that's a fact. I'm really smitten! You're not like other girls. You're ten times prettier. I've been thinking of nothing but you ever since yesterday. . . ."

His podgy fingers were pinching and patting her affectionately.

"You aren't used to it, it looks like. And yet, pretty as you are, you must have had hundreds of men! Anyhow, as far as we two are concerned, I'll be frank with you. Earlier this evening, when I saw you in the guardroom, I thought to myself that with your high and mighty airs you might get me all tied up in a knot. That sort of thing can happen to the best of us. So, to be sure not to let you down and be caught short, I downed a whole pitcher of spiced wine. But woe and alas! ever since that moment I've been bedevilled with all this business of thieves and corpses. As if all these people were getting themselves murdered on purpose to annoy me.

"I have spent three hours running from the records to the morgue, with this damned cinnamon-wine heating my blood. So now I'm right and ready, I'm making no bones about it. But still, it would be nicer for both of us if you'd show a little good will too, don't you think?"

This speech had a calming effect on Angélique. Unlike most women, even her physical reflexes and reactions responded to reason. The captain, who was no fool, had guessed it intuitively. You don't take part in sacking a number of towns and raping heaven knows how many women and girls of all races and nationalities without collecting a little experience! . . .

He was rewarded for his patience by finding a beautiful, supple body against him which, though in silence, offered itself docilely to his desire. With a grunt of pleasure he took hold of it and possessed it with great vigour but without brutality.

Angélique had no time to feel revulsion. Buffeted by this embrace as if by a fierce whirlwind, she found herself free almost instantly.

"There, that's done," sighed the captain.

With the flat side of his big hand he rolled her like a log to the other side of the bed.

"Now sleep your fill, my pretty slut. We'll have another go in the morning, and then we'll be quits."

Two seconds later, he was snoring noisily.

Angélique thought that it would take her a long time to fall asleep, but this supreme exercise coming after the fatigues of the last hours, added to the comfort of a soft, warm bed, plunged her at once into a deep sleep.

When she woke up in the darkness, it took her quite a while to realise where she was. The captain's snores had become less loud. It was so hot that Angélique removed her shift, as the rough linen irritated her delicate skin.

She was no longer frightened, but she felt vaguely troubled. She was uneasy, and it wasn't on account of the Ogre's big, sleeping hulk, but because of something else . . . something indefinable and frightening.

She tried to fall asleep again and tossed from side to side. At last she pricked up her ears. Then she became aware of the dim, diffused sounds which had drawn her from her slumber, despite herself. They were like the sound of voices, very distant voices which had all fallen into a single plaintive moan. It never stopped. When one sound receded, another one took its place. And suddenly she understood: they were the *prisoners*.

What had reached her ears through the floor and the massive walls were the muffled moans, the cries of despair, of the unfortunates who were fettered, freezing, fighting off the jail-rats with their shoes, fighting against the water, against death. Criminals were blaspheming against the name of God, the innocent were praying to Him. Others, broken by the torture of the 'question', half asphyxiated, exhausted by hunger and cold, were gasping in the throes of death. These things accounted for the grim, mysterious noises.

Angélique shivered. The fortress of the Châtelet weighed upon her with all its centuries and all its horrors. Would she ever find the open air again? Would the Ogre let her go? He was sleeping. He was strong and mighty. He was the master of this hell.

Very softly she drew closer to the huge mass that snored at her side and was surprised to find some charm in his thick hide as she put her hand on it.

The captain moved and almost crushed her as he turned over.

"Hi! Hi! the little quail is wake," he said in a thick voice.

His outstretched arm pulled her towards him, and she felt submerged in this welter of muscular flesh that rippled under his skin. The man yawned noisily. Then he drew the curtains aside and saw a grey light dimly paling behind the window-bars.

"You are an early bird, my kitten."

"Those noises—what are they?"

"They are the prisoners. They're having less fun than we are."

"They are suffering. . . ."

"They aren't put there to have fun. You're lucky, you know, to have been let off. Why, you're better off in my bed than on the other side of the wall on the straw. Isn't that true?"

Angélique nodded with so much conviction that the captain was delighted.

He seized a pint of red wine from the bedside table and took a long draught. His Adam's apple rose and fell in his powerful throat. He offered the tin pot to Angélique.

"Your turn."

She accepted, for she felt that this alone could save her from despair between the sinister walls of the Châtelet: the brutal well-being of drunkenness and lust which produce oblivion.

He encouraged her:

"Drink, kitten, drink, my beauty. It's fine wine, it'll do you good."

When she finally sank back, her head was spinning; the strong, pungent liquor fogged her brains. Nothing mattered any more except being alive.

He turned towards her heavily, but she no longer feared him. She even felt a ripple of pleasure when he stroked her with his big hand, not very gently, but in an energetic, experienced way. Those caresses, which were more like a rough massage than a zephyr's breath, gave her a genuine feeling of relief. He kissed her in peasant fashion, with big, greedy, noisy smacks, which surprised Angélique and made her want to giggle.

Then he took her in his hairy arms and calmly laid her out across the bed. She realised that he was determined this time to take full advantage of his windfall, and she closed her eyes. She was determined, anyway, not to remember the moments that followed.

Still, it was not quite as dreadful as she had imagined. The Ogre was not vicious. He behaved rather like a man who is unaware of his weight and size but, despite this burden which left her half crushed and flattened, she had to admit that she had not been far from experiencing a certain pleasure at finding herself the prey of this colossus, full of strength and drive. Afterwards, she felt as light as a feather.

The captain was dressing and humming a military march.

"By Jove," he kept repeating, "you gave me no end of pleasure. And I'd been so afraid of you! . . ."

The surgeon of the Châtelet came in, armed with his shaving-dish and his razors. Angélique finished dressing while her cumbrous lover-for-a-night let the barber tie a towel round his neck and lather his face. He continued to display much satisfaction.

"You were jolly well right, barber: fresh as a daisy!"

Angélique did not know how to take her leave. The captain suddenly flung a purse on the table.

"That's for you."

"I have already been paid."

"Take it," roared the captain, "and go!"

When Angélique found herself outside the Châtelet, she had not the courage to return straightway to the rue de la Vallée-de-Misère, which was too close to the terrible prison. She walked down to the Seine. On the Quai des Morfondus the boatmen's wives had set up 'baths' for women during the summer months. The 'baths' consisted of some wooden posts holding up a canvas covering and driven into the mud. The women would climb down to them in shift and bonnet.

The bargeman's wife to whom Angélique paid her fee, exclaimed:

"Are you crazy to want to take a dip at this hour? It's chilly, you know."

"Never mind."

The water was cold indeed, but after a moment, Angélique found it very pleasant. Since she was the only customer, she swam around a little among the posts. When she had dried and dressed herself, she walked for a while along the banks, enjoying the warm autumn sun.

'It's over,' she said. 'I want no more poverty, no more dreadful things like killing the Great Coesre, or difficult ones like sleeping with a captain of the watch. It's not my kind of life. I like fine linen, beautiful clothes. I want my children never to know hunger or cold again. I want them to be well-dressed and respected. I want them to have a name again. I want to have a name myself. . . . I want to become a great lady again. . . .'

PART SIX:

THE INN OF THE RED MASK

CHAPTER 66

As ANGÉLIQUE was sneaking as quietly as possible into the courtyard of the inn of 'The Brazen Cock', Maître Bourjus, armed with a ladle, emerged and hurled himself upon her.

She had been expecting something of the sort, and just had time to dodge behind the small well.

"Get out, beggar wench, trollop!" bawled the landlord of 'The Brazen Cock'. "What sins have I committed to deserve this invasion by fugitives from the General Hospital, Bicêtre . . . or worse. I know what a shorn head like yours means. . . . Go back to the Châtelet, where you come from—or else I'll have you sent back there. . . . I don't know what prevented me from calling the watch last night. . . . I am too kind-hearted. Ah! what would my sainted wife say if she saw her shop thus disgraced!"

Angélique, while dodging the ladle-thrusts, began to shout louder than he:

"And what would your *sainted* wife say of such a disgraceful husband . . . who starts drinking at the crack of dawn?"

The innkeeper stopped motionless. Angélique seized her advantage.

"And what would she say to her shop covered with dust and to a window-dressing of six-day-old chickens, shrivelled like parchment, and to her empty cellar, and to her unpolished tables and benches? . . ."

"Why, the devil——!" he spluttered.

"And what would she say to a blaspheming husband? Poor Madame Bourjus looking down on such a mess from up there in Heaven! I can assure you that she doesn't know how to hide her shame before the angels and all the saints in Paradise!"

Maître Bourjus's expression became ever more bewildered. He finally slumped down heavily on the lip of the well.

"Alas!" he moaned, "why did she have to die? She was such a sprightly housewife, always gay and resolute. I don't know what keeps me from seeking oblivion at the bottom of this well!"

"I can tell you what it is: it's the thought of her greeting you up there and saying: 'Ah! So it's you, Maître Pierre . . .' "

"Maître Jacques, if you please."

" 'So it's you, Maître Jacques! I can't say I'm proud of you. I always said you didn't know how to manage on your own. Worse than a child . . . ! You've certainly proved it! When I see what you have done with my shining, beautiful shop, so spick and span during my lifetime, when I see our beautiful shop-sign all rusty and creaking so loud on windy nights that it keeps the neighbours awake, and my pewter, my pie-dishes, my fish-kettles, all scratched because your fool of a nephew cleans them with ashes instead of using special soft chalk. . . . And when I see you letting yourself be cheated by all the rascally poultry-mongers and wine-merchants, who sell you de-combed cocks for capons and barrels of verjuice for fine wine, how do you expect me, who used to be a devout and honest woman, to make the most of Heaven? . . .' "

Angélique stopped, out of breath. Maître Bourjus seemed entranced.

"It's true," he stammered, "it's true—she'd talk just like that. She was so . . . so . . ."

His heavy jowl quivered.

"It's no good snivelling," said Angélique roughly, "that isn't the way to avoid the broomstick-thrashing that is waiting for you up there. The only way is to get down to work, Maître Bourjus. Barbe is a good girl, but slow by nature; you've got to tell her what to do. Your nephew seems to me a rare half-wit. And customers don't walk into a shop where they are welcomed by a growling watch-dog."

"Who growls?" asked Maître Bourjus, assuming a threatening air.

"You do."

"I do?"

"Yes. Your wife, who was so gay, would not have stood you for three minutes with that scowl you have, sitting before your pot of wine."

"And you think she would have tolerated an insolent, dirty wench of your kind in her yard?"

"I am not dirty," Angélique protested, pulling herself up, "my clothes are clean, look at them."

"Do you think she would have stood for letting your cut-purse breed of impudent ragamuffins help themselves in her kitchen? I caught them gorging themselves with bacon in my larder and I am sure that they were the ones who stole my watch."

"Here's your watch," said Angélique, disdainfully pulling it out of her pocket. "I found it under the staircase. You must have lost it when you went up to bed last night, dead-drunk."

She held out the watch to the innkeeper across the well, and added:

"You see I am not a thief either. I could have kept it."

"Don't let it fall into the well!" he said, frantically.

"I'd be glad to hand it to you, but I am afraid of your ladle."

Muttering a curse, Maître Bourjus flung his weapon on the ground. Angélique came closer to him, with a roguish air. She had the feeling that her night with the captain had taught her a few things about the art of winning over curmudgeons and standing up to brutes. It had given her an ease of manner which might be useful in the future.

She did not hurry to return the watch but examined it with much interest.

"It's a beautiful watch."

The innkeeper's face lit up again.

"Isn't it? I bought it from a pedlar from the Jura, those highlanders who spend the winter in Paris. They have real treasures in their pockets, but, mind you, they won't show them to everybody, not even to princes—they want to know whom they are dealing with."

"They prefer to deal with real business men rather than with gullible fools . . . especially for these mechanical gadgets which are genuine works of art."

"That's just it: genuine works of art," the innkeeper repeated, as his silver watch-case gleamed in the pale sunshine. He put it back into his pocket, fastened the numerous chains and charms to his button-holes, and again cast a suspicious glance at Angélique.

"I really wonder how this watch could have dropped out of my pocket, as you insinuate. And I also wonder where you get that ladylike talk, when only the other night you were rattling off thieves' cant to make one's hair stand on end. I've a feeling you are trying to bamboozle me like the strumpet you are."

Angélique remained unruffled.

163

"It's not easy talking to a man like you, Maître Jacques," she said in a tone of gentle reproach, "you know women too well."

The innkeeper crossed his short arms over his paunch and looked fierce.

"I know them and they can't pull the wool over my eyes."

He allowed a heavy silence to settle, his eyes fixed on the guilty woman, who hung her head.

"Well, then?" he said, peremptorily.

Angélique, who was taller than he, thought he was very funny, round as a barrel, with his cap over one ear, and his frozen gaze. However, she said humbly:

"I'll do whatever you tell me, Maître Bourjus. If you turn me out with my two babies, I shall go. But I don't know where to go, nor where to take my little ones to shelter them from the cold and rain. Do you think your wife would have turned us out? I am staying in Barbe's room. I am not disturbing you. I have my own firewood and food. The boys and the girl who are with me could render you small services: carry water, scrub floors. The babies will remain in the attic. . . ."

"And why should they stay up in the attic?" bawled the innkeeper. "Children don't belong in a pigeon-coop, but in the kitchen, by the hearth, where they can keep warm and toddle around. These beggar-wenches are all the same. Less heart than wild beasts! You get those nippers down into the kitchen, if you don't want me to get cross. Besides which, you're likely to start a fire there any moment, with those wooden tiles up there! . . ."

Angélique mounted, with elfin nimbleness, the seven storeys that led to Barbe's attic. On a landing, she passed a furtive figure whom she recognised as the landlord's nephew. The kitchen boy flattened himself against the wall and cast a resentful glance at her. She smiled at him, determined to make friends in this house where she was anxious to resume a respectable life.

"Good morning, little one."

"Little?" he growled, giving a start. "I'd like to point out that I could comfortably eat patties off the top of your head. I was sixteen last Michaelmas."

"Oh! excuse me, Monsieur! What a shocking mistake on my part! Would your gallantry go so far as to forgive me?"

The youngster, who was visibly unaccustomed to such talk, shrugged awkwardly and stammered:

"Might be."

"You are too kind. I am touched. And would your good upbringing likewise go so far as not to talk so familiarly to a lady of quality?"

The poor apprentice cook seemed on the rack. He had rather fine black eyes in this thin, white face. His self-assurance was completely gone. Angélique, who had started to climb the stairs again, stopped.

"With that accent of yours, you're bound to be a southerner, aren't you?"

"Yes . . . M'dame . . . I am from Toulouse."

"Toulouse!" she cried. "Oh! a brother countryman!"

And she jumped at his neck and kissed him.

"Toulouse!" she repeated.

The kitchen boy was red as a tomato. Angélique said a few words to him in the *langue d'oc*, and David's excitement knew no bounds.

"You, too, come from there?"

"Almost."

She was ludicrously happy about this encounter. What a contrast! To have been one of the great ladies of Toulouse and to have come down to hugging a kitchen boy because he had that sunny accent on his tongue, with a whiff of garlic and flowers!

In the garret she found Rosine scratching her head while looking with cow-like eyes at Florimond and Cantor as they played. Barbe was downstairs. The boys had gone 'for a stroll'. In underworld slang, that meant they had gone begging for alms.

"I don't want them to go begging," said Angélique categorically.

"You don't want them to steal, you don't want them to beg. What do you want them to do, then?"

"I want them to work."

"But that *is* work!" protested the girl.

"No. Now rouse yourself! Help me take the children down to the kitchen. You'll look after them and help Barbe."

She was happy to leave the two babies in this vast, warm, fragrant domain. The fire was blazing in the hearth with a new ardour.

'Never again shall they be cold, or hungry!' Angélique said to herself again. 'Upon my word, I couldn't have taken them to a better place than a cook-shop!'

Florimond seemed stiffly awkward in his little grey-brown muslin frock, his yellow serge top and green serge apron. A bonnet, also of green serge, covered his head. These colours made his frail little face look even more sickly. She felt his forehead and put her lips in the hollow of his little hand to see if he was feverish. He seemed well enough, though a little fretful and grumpy. As for Cantor, since morning he hadn't stopped trying to undo the swaddling-clothes into which Rosine had wrapped him. In the basket into which he had been put he stood up, naked as a little Cupid, and tried to get out to catch the flames.

"The poor child hasn't been raised properly," remarked Barbe with concern. "Has he even had his arms and legs swaddled and bound, as they should be? He will never hold himself straight and may even get humpbacked."

"At the moment, he seems rather sturdy for a nine-months-old," said Angélique, who was admiring the plump thighs of her younger child.

But Barbe was not reassured. Cantor's freedom of movement worried her.

"As soon as I have a free moment, I'll cut some strips of linen to bind him. But it is out of the question this morning. Maître Bourjus seems in a frenzy. Imagine, Madame, he has ordered me to scrub the floors, polish the tables, and even run down to the Temple to buy soft chalk in order to give his pewter a shine. I'm at my wits' end. . . ."

"Ask Rosine to help you."

After she had got all her family settled, Angélique set out gaily for the Pont-Neuf.

The flower-woman did not recognise her. Angélique had to remind her of the day when she had helped her make up bouquets and been complimented by her.

"Well! How do you expect me to recognise you!" the woman exclaimed. "That day you had hair on your head and no shoes on your feet. Today you have shoes and no hair. Still, your fingers haven't changed, I hope? . . . Come along and sit down with us. There is no lack of work, with All Saints' Day in the offing. There'll be flowers wanted soon for the graveyards and churches, to say nothing of the pictures of the departed."

Angélique sat down under the red parasol and set about her task conscientiously and skilfully.

But the Pont-Neuf was very quiet that day. She did not even hear Big Matthieu's roaring voice, for he had moved his wheeled platform and his band to the fairground of Saint-Germain. The Pont-Neuf was in eclipse. There were fewer strollers, fewer mountebanks, fewer beggars. Angélique was glad of it.

The flower-sellers were talking, with copious lamentations, of the battle of the Fair of Saint-Germain. Apparently, the corpses of this particularly bloody brawl were still being counted. But, for once, the police had been equal to their task. Since that famous evening, one could see flocks of beggars led by the constables in charge of the poor on their way to the General Hospital, or chain-gangs of convicts bound for the galleys. As for executions, each new day dawned on two or three hanged men on the Place de Grève.

There followed a fervent discussion of the finery the ladies of the Pont-Neuf—flower and orange sellers—would wear when, together with the fish-wives of the central market, they would go to present their compliments, as Paris stall-keepers, to the young Queen in confinement and to Monsieur le Dauphin.

"In the meantime," said Angélique's employer, "there's something else worrying me. Where will our guild go and feast, to celebrate worthily the day of Saint-Valbonne? The innkeeper of the 'Bons-Enfants', last year, swindled us like a highway robber. I'll never put another *sou* into his till."

Angélique joined in the conversation, to which she had listened silently.

"I know of an excellent eating-house in the rue de la Vallée-de-Misère. The prices are moderate and they serve succulent and novel dishes."

She quickly enumerated specialities of the table of Gay Learning, which she had helped prepare in the old days:

"Crayfish-patties, turkeys stuffed with fennel, braised lamb tripe, not to mention almond-paste with pistachio, rissoles, aniseed wafers. But moreover, ladies, you will eat in that restaurant something that even His Majesty Louis XIV has

167

never seen on his table: small, oven-hot, feather-light *brioches* with a dab of chilled liver-paste inside. A real marvel!"

"Humph! wench, you make our mouths water," cried the flower-sellers, their faces already flushed with gluttony. "And where may that be?"

"At 'The Brazen Cock', the last cook-shop in the rue de la Vallée-de-Misère as you go towards the Quai des Tanneurs."

"Why, I don't think the fare's so good there. My man, who works at the Great Butcher's shop, sometimes goes and has a snack there, and he says it's a gloomy, unprepossessing place."

"You are ill-informed, my dear. Maître Bourjus, the land-lord, has with him his nephew, only just up from Toulouse, who is a first-rate cook and knows all sorts of southern dishes. There's also a monkey at 'The Brazen Cock' which makes no end of grimaces. And a hurdy-gurdy player who knows all the songs of the Pont-Neuf. In short, there's everything one's heart desires to enjoy oneself in good company."

"Well, my girl, you seem to have an even greater gift for 'barking' than for making bouquets! I'll go with you to that eating-house."

"Oh no! Not today. The cook from Toulouse has gone down to the country to pick cabbages personally for a fried ham stew which is his own secret. But tomorrow night we'll be expecting you, you and two ladies of your guild, to discuss the menu that would suit you."

"And what are you doing in that cook-shop?"

"I am a relative of Maître Bourjus," declared Angélique. "My husband was a small pastrycook. He had not passed his examination yet to become a master cook, when he died of the plague last winter. He left me in dire poverty, for we had con-tracted big debts with the apothecary for his illness."

"Don't we know all about apothecaries' bills!" sighed the good women, sympathetically, raising their eyes to the sky.

"Maître Bourjus took pity on me and I help him in his trade. But as customers are rare I try to make a little extra money."

"What's your name, dearie?"

"Angélique."

Thereupon she rose and said she was going, in order to in-form the innkeeper at once of their impending visit.

While she walked quickly towards the rue de la Vallée-de-Misère, she marvelled at the number of lies she had told in a single morning. She did not try to understand why the idea had come over her to recruit customers for Maître Bourjus. Had she wanted to show her gratitude to the innkeeper who in the end had not driven her out? Was she hoping to get a reward from him? She did not ask herself any questions. She drifted with the current which drove her to do now one thing, now another. She was impelled by the sharpened instinct of a mother defending her little ones.

From one lie to another, from one idea to another, from one bold stroke to another, she would succeed in saving herself, in saving her children.

CHAPTER 67

THE FOLLOWING morning, Angélique rose at the first light of dawn and roused Barbe, Rosine and the children.

"Everybody up! Don't forget that the flower ladies are coming to see us about the guild banquet. We must put up a good show."

Flipot grumbled.

"Why is it always we who do the work?" he asked. "Why is that sluggard David still snoring and not going down to the kitchens till the fire is lit, the pot on the boil and the whole room swept? You ought to shake him up, Marquise!"

"Look here, boys, I am no longer the Marquise of the Angels and you aren't beggars any more. For the moment, we are servants—maids and errand-boys. And soon we'll be respectable citizens."

"F——!" said Flipot. "I don't like respectable citizens. They are people whose purses you cut and whose coats you snatch. I don't want to become a respectable citizen."

"And what are we supposed to call you if you aren't the Marquise of the Angels any more?" Linot wanted to know.

"Just call me Madame."

"Well, aren't we grand!" mocked Flipot.

Angélique boxed his ear so resoundingly that he realised at once that she meant it. She checked the two boys' appearance. They were dressed in the shabby clothes sent by the Duchesse de Soissons, patched and ugly, but clean and neat. Moreover, they had stout nailed boots, in which they walked awkwardly but which would protect them against the cold all winter.

"Flipot, you'll accompany me to the market with David. Linot, you'll do as Barbe tells you. You'll go and fetch water and firewood. Rosine will mind the babies and the spits in the kitchen."

Flipot sighed very sadly:

"Not much fun, this new job. As beggars and cut-purses you lead a high-class life. One day, you have plenty of money: you eat till you burst and drink enough to drown in. Another day, you have nothing. So, in order not to be hungry, you lie down in a corner and sleep as long as you like. Whereas here it's drudgery all the time and filling your belly with stew."

"If you want to go back to the Great Coesre, I won't stop you."

"Oh no! Anyway, we haven't the right any more. We'd be knifed. Phut!"

Angélique sighed.

"What you miss is adventure, poor little lads. I can understand. But then, there's the gibbet at the end of the road. Whereas on this road we'll be less rich perhaps, but we'll become persons worthy of respect. Now off with you!"

The little squad clattered down the stairs. On one of the landings Angélique stopped, drummed on the door of young David's room and finally walked in.

"Get up, apprentice!"

The youngster popped a dumbfounded face out of the sheets.

"Up, up, David Chaillou!" Angélique repeated gaily. "Don't forget that from now on you are a famous cook, whose recipes all Paris will be clamouring for."

Maître Bourjus, jostled, groaning, excited despite himself, and galvanised by Angélique's authority, consented to handing her a fairly well-lined purse.

"If you are afraid I might rob you, you can follow me to the market," she told him. "But you'd be better advised to stay here and prepare the capons, turkeys, ducks and joints. You must realise that the ladies who'll be coming here want to find a setting that inspires confidence. An empty 'show-case' or a display of dusty fowl, a dark room reeking of stale tobacco, an air of poverty or straitened circumstances, won't tempt people who are out for a feast. Even if I promised them an exceptional treat, they wouldn't believe me."

"But what are you going to buy this morning, since these people haven't decided on their choice yet?"

"I'm going to buy the décor."

"The . . . what?"

"Everything that's needed to make your eating-house look attractive: rabbits, fish, cold meat, fruit, fine vegetables."

"But I'm not a general caterer!" lamented the burly man. "I deal in *roast viands*. Do you want to get the guilds of master cooks and pastrycooks on my neck?"

"What can they possibly do to you?"

"Women never have the least notion of serious questions," groaned Maître Bourjus, flinging up his short arms. "The jurymen of those guilds can sue me, haul me to court. In short, you're going to ruin me!"

"You're ruined anyway," Angélique told him bluntly. "So you've nothing to lose by trying something else and shaking yourself out of your torpor. Get started on your fowl and then take a look round the port of the Grève. I heard the wine-crier announce a fresh arrival of good vats from Burgundy and Champagne."

In the Place du Pilori, Angélique did her shopping, trying hard not to get too badly cheated. David complicated things by constantly repeating:

"This is much too fine! This is much too expensive! What's my uncle going to say? . . ."

"Dunderhead!" she finally threw at him. "Aren't you ashamed, you, a lad of the south, to look at things so pettily, like a cold-hearted miser! Don't tell me you are from Toulouse."

"But I am!" protested the apprentice. "My father was Monsieur Chaillou. Doesn't that name mean anything to you?"

"No. What exactly did your father do?"

The lanky David seemed disappointed, like a child deprived of his sweet.

"But you know, surely! The big grocer, in the Place de la Garonne! The only one who sold exotic herbs to enhance the fragrance of dishes!"

'In those days I didn't do the shopping myself,' Angélique thought.

"He brought back all sorts of unknown things from his

171

voyages, for he had been a cook on the King's vessels," David went on. "You know . . . he was the one who wanted to start selling chocolate in Toulouse."

Angélique made an effort to extract from her memory an incident which the word chocolate conjured up in her mind. Yes, there had been talk of it in the drawing-rooms. The protest of a Toulousian lady came back to her. She said:

"Chocolate? . . . But that's what Indians drink!"

David seemed much upset, for Angélique's opinion had already assumed outstanding importance in his eyes. He moved closer to her and said that he would tell her a secret which he had never yet entrusted to anyone, not even to his uncle.

He assured her that his father, a great traveller in his young days, had tasted the chocolate of various foreign countries where it was manufactured from beans imported from Mexico. Thus he had been able to convince himself, in Spain, Italy and even in Poland, of the excellence of this new product which had a pleasant taste and remarkable medicinal qualities.

Once David had launched out on this subject, he seemed to be inexhaustible. In his eagerness to retain the interest of the lady of his thoughts, he began to expound, in strident tones, all that he knew about the question.

"Pshaw!" said Angélique, who was listening with only one ear, "I have never tasted this stuff and I don't feel tempted to. They say that the Queen is crazy about it. But the whole Court is embarrassed by this peculiar fancy and makes fun of her."

"That's because the people at Court aren't used to chocolate," argued the apprentice cook. "My father thought so, too, and he obtained letters patent from the King to make this new product known. But alas, he died, and as my mother was already dead I'm the only one left to make use of this patent. I don't know how to go about it. That's why I haven't mentioned it to my uncle. I am afraid he might make fun of me and my father. He always says that my father was crazy."

"You have those letters patent?" Angélique asked suddenly.

David almost fainted under the radiance of those green eyes.

"You have the patent?" Angélique repeated.

"Yes," he breathed.

"What date does it bear?"

"28th May 1659, and the authorisation is valid for twenty-nine years."

"This means that for twenty-nine years you alone are authorised to manufacture and market this exotic product?"

"Well, yes. . . ."

"We'd have to find out whether chocolate is dangerous," murmured Angélique musingly, "and if the public would take a fancy to it. Have you tried it yourself?"

"Yes."

"What do you think of it?"

"Well," said David, "I find it rather sickly sweet. But adding a little pepper or pimento gives it a stronger flavour. Still, I personally prefer a good glass of wine any time," he added with a swaggering air.

"Mind the water!" cried a voice above them.

They had only just time to jump aside to avoid a foul-smelling shower. Angélique gripped the youngster's arm. She felt him tremble.

"I wanted to tell you," he stammered hurriedly, "I have never seen a . . . a woman as beautiful as you."

"Of course you have, my poor boy," she said, exasperated. "You need but look around instead of biting your fingernails and shuffling along like a dying fly. Meanwhile, if you want to please me, tell me about that chocolate of yours instead of paying me superfluous compliments."

Then, seeing his pitiful expression, she tried to comfort him. She told herself that she'd be unwise to snub him. He might turn out to have possibilities, with that patent of his. She said laughingly:

"I am no longer, alas, a girl of fifteen, my lad. Look, I am old. I have grey hair already."

From under her bonnet she pulled the strand of hair that had so strangely turned grey during the terrifying night at the Faubourg Saint-Denis.

"Where is Flipot?" Angélique went on, looking around. "Is that little scamp playing truant by any chance?"

She was a little worried, fearing that Flipot, stimulated by the dense crowd, might again put into practice the teachings of Jactance the cut-purse.

"You oughtn't to pay any attention to that rascal," said David, in a tone of intense jealousy. "I saw him just now exchanging a sign with a beggar, covered with sores, who was asking for alms before the church. Then he made off . . . with the basket on his back. My uncle will fly into such a temper!"

"You always see the black side of things, my poor David."

"I never have any luck!"

"Let's turn back, we'll find that little scamp."

But the urchin was already reappearing at a run. Angélique liked the look of him, with his bright sparrow eyes, his red nose, his long, lank hair under his big battered hat. She was getting attached to him as well as to young Linot, whom she had twice wrested from Rotten Jean's claws.

"Guess what, Marquise of the Angels!" panted Flipot, forgetting her orders in his excitement. "Do you know who is our new Great Coesre? Wood-Bottom, yes, our Wood-Bottom of the Tower of Nesle!"

He dropped his voice and added in a frightened murmur:

"They said to me: 'Beware, kids, hiding as you are in the petticoats of a traitress!' "

Angélique felt her blood turn to ice.

"Do you think they know that it was I who killed Squat Rolin?"

"They didn't say anything. And yet . . . there was Black-Bread talking of how you went to fetch the policemen against the gipsies."

"Who was there?"

"Black-Bread, Lightfoot, three old women of our gang and two 'epileptics' of another."

The young woman and the child had been exchanging these words in thieves' cant which David could not understand, but he readily recognised the terrifying intonations. He was both perturbed and awed to find his new flame so uncannily familiar with that ubiquitous and elusive scum that played such an important part in the life of Paris.

Angélique did not speak the whole way back, but as soon as she had crossed the threshold of the inn she resolutely tossed aside her apprehensions.

'It may well be, my girl,' she told herself, 'that you will wake up one fine morning with a slit throat, floating in the Seine. It's a risk you've been running for a long while. When the princes aren't after you, the beggars are. Never mind! You've got to fight, even if it's your last living day. You can't get out of difficulties without tackling them resolutely and doing your share. . . . Wasn't it the steward Molines who said that to me a long time ago? . . .'

"Come, children!" she cried aloud. "Those ladies of the

174

florists' guild must melt like butter in the sun when they step over this threshold."

The ladies were charmed indeed when, at dusk, they walked down the three steps leading to 'The Brazen Cock'. Not only was the air permeated with a delicious smell of scones, but the appearance of the room was both appetising and original.

The big fire in the hearth crackled and spread its golden light. With the aid of some candles placed on the neighbouring tables, it shone on the pewter plate and utensils, artistically set out on the sideboards: pots, pitchers, fish-kettles, pie-dishes. Moreover, Angélique had requisitioned the few pieces of silver-plate Maître Bourjus kept jealously locked up in his coffers, two ewers, a vinegar-cruet, two egg-cups, two rinsing bowls. The latter were richly decorated with fruit—grapes and pears—and set out on the tables with beautiful decanters of red and white wine which sparkled with ruby and gold glints in the firelight. These were the details that most surprised the flower-sellers.

Having often been called upon to bring their wares to the princely homes of the great, they found the arrangement of the silver, fruit and wine vaguely reminiscent of the parties given by the nobility, and they felt secretly flattered.

As shrewd business women, they did not want to display their satisfaction too openly and cast critical glances at the hares and hams hanging from the rafters, sniffed distrustfully at the dishes of pork-butchery, cold meat and fish covered with green sauce, prodded the poultry with experienced fingers. The *doyenne* of the guild, who was called Mère Marjolaine, at last found some fault with this perfect picture.

"It's lacking flowers," she said. "This calf's head would look quite different with two carnations in its nostrils and a peony between its ears."

"Madame, we did not attempt to compete, by means of even a spray of parsley, with the skill and gracefulness which you display in this realm where you reign supreme," Maître Bourjus replied very gallantly.

The three sprightly ladies sat down before the fire and a jug of the best wine was brought up from the cellar. The charming Linot, seated on the hearthstone, turned the handle of his hurdy-gurdy, while Florimond played with Piccolo.

175

The menu for the festive meal was settled in the most cordial atmosphere, and an agreement was quickly reached.

"There, now!" moaned the innkeeper, when he had eventually ushered the flower-women to the door with many bows. "What are we going to do with all this stuff on the tables? The artisans and workmen will be coming for their beef-salad. They won't eat these delicacies, let alone pay for them. Why this needless expense?"

"You surprise me, Maître Jacques," protested Angélique. "I thought you were more of a business man. This needless expense has enabled you to hook an order which will bring you in ten times what you spent today. Without counting all the extras these ladies may order once the feast really gets going. We'll make them sing and dance, and the passers-by in the street will want to join in the fun when they see an eating-house where people are having such a good time."

Although Maître Bourjus did not want to show it, he was inclined to share Angélique's sanguine expectations. The bustling activity he displayed in the preparations for the feast of Saint-Valbonne made him forget his penchant for the bottle. Bouncing on his short legs, he rediscovered his culinary skill and his commanding voice for use on merchants, as well as the natural, unctuous affability of all self-respecting innkeepers. Angélique having eventually persuaded him that a well-to-do appearance was necessary to the success of his enterprise, he had even ordered a complete kitchen boy's outfit for his nephew and another for Flipot. Enormous cooks' caps, jackets, trousers, aprons, together with tablecloths and napkins, were sent to the laundresses and came back stiff with starch and white as snow.

On the morning of the great day, Maître Bourjus went up to Angélique, smiling and rubbing his hands.

"My dear," he said, beaming with kindness, "it is a fact that you have brought back to my house the gaiety and liveliness with which my wife used to fill it. And this has given me an idea. Come with me for a moment."

Encouraging her with a wink of connivance, he beckoned her to follow him. She climbed up the winding stairs behind him. On the first landing they stopped. As Angélique entered Maître Bourjus's bedroom, a fear came over her which had not occurred to her before. Was the innkeeper by any chance harbouring the plan of asking her, who was so auspiciously beginning to replace his wife, to extend her services in this ticklish rôle yet further?

The sly smile on his face, as he closed the door and walked over to the wardrobe, was not of the kind to reassure her. In a sudden panic Angélique wondered how she was going to face this appalling situation.

Would she have to give up her beautiful projects, leave this comfortable roof, set out once more with her two children and her miserable little family? Yield? Her cheeks burned at the thought of it, and with anxious eyes she looked around the shopkeeper's room with its big bed behind green serge curtains, its two small armchairs, its walnut cabinet containing a wash-basin and a silver ewer.

Above the fireplace there were two pictures representing scenes of the Passion and, placed on racks, the weapons which were the pride of every craftsman and burgher: two small rifles, a musket, an arquebus, a pike and a sword with silver hilt and guard.

Angélique heard him pant and struggle noisily in the small adjacent closet.

He emerged from it, pushing a vast chest of blackened wood before him.

"Give me a hand, girl."

She helped him pull the trunk into the middle of the room. Maître Bourjus wiped his brow.

"There," he said, "I've been thinking—anyway, it's you who've kept saying that for this banquet we should look as resplendent as Swiss guards, all of us. David, the two kitchen-boys, and myself, we'll all be on parade. I shall put on my brown silk hose. But you, poor girl, won't do us proud despite your pretty face. So I've been thinking . . ."

He broke off, hesitated, then opened the trunk. In it, care-fully stored and scented with a bit of lavender, were Madame Bourjus's petticoats, her bodices, bonnets, neckerchiefs, her handsome black cloth hood with satin squares.

"She was a little plumper than you," said the innkeeper in a muffled voice, "but with some pins here and there . . ."

He wiped away a tear with one finger, and growled:

"Don't stand there staring at me! Make your choice."

Angélique lifted out the clothes. They were modest gar-ments of simple material, but their velvet trimmings, brightly-

177

coloured linings and fine linen showed that the landlady of
'The Brazen Cock' had, towards the end of her life, been one
of the most well-to-do merchant's wives in the district. She
had even owned a little red velvet muff with a gold floral
pattern, which Angélique tried on her wrist with undisguised
pleasure.

"A folly!" grunted Maître Bourjus with an indulgent smile.
"She had seen it in the Palace arcades and couldn't stop talking
about it. I would tell her: 'Amandine, what will you do with
a muff like that? It is more suited to some noble lady of the
Marais district who wants to play the coquette in the Tuileries
gardens or on the Cours-la-Reine on a sunny winter day.'—'All
right,' she'd answer, 'so I'll go and play the coquette in the
Tuileries or on the Cours-la-Reine.' And that made me go
wild! I made her a present of it last Christmas. How delighted
she was! . . . Who'd have thought that a few days later . . .
she'd . . . be dead. . . ."

Angélique checked her emotion.

"I am sure she is happy up there in Heaven to see how kind
and generous you are. I won't wear this muff, for it's a
hundred times too beautiful for me. But I gladly accept your
gift, Maître Bourjus. I shall have a look to see what suits me.
Could you send Barbe up to me so that she can help me to
make the alterations?"

She made a note, as the first step towards her self-appointed
goal, that she was standing there before a looking-glass with a
lady's-maid at her feet. With her mouth full of pins, Barbe
too seemed to feel this, for she was multiplying her 'Madames'
with evident satisfaction.

'And to think that my entire fortune consists of the few *sous*
the flowerwomen of the Pont-Neuf gave me!' Angélique
thought, amused.

She had chosen a green serge bodice and petticoat trimmed
with black satin. An apron of black satin with tiny gold flowers
completed her outfit as a well-to-do shopkeeper's wife.
Madame Bourjus's ample bosom did not make it possible to
adjust the bodice exactly to Angélique's small, firm, high
breasts. A pink neckerchief with green embroideries concealed
the somewhat gaping neckline.

In a small bag Angélique found the dead landlady's simple
jewels: three gold rings set with cornelians and turquoises, two

crosses, earrings, as well as eight beautiful rosaries, one of which was of black jet beads and the others of crystal-glass.

Angélique went downstairs again, wearing under the starched bonnet which concealed her shorn hair the agate-and-pearl earrings, and, round her neck, a little gold cross held by a black velvet ribbon. The good innkeeper did not hide his joy at seeing how attractive she looked.

"By Saint Nicholas, you look just like the daughter we had always hoped for and never had! We dreamed of her sometimes. She'd be fifteen, sixteen years old now, we'd say. She'd be dressed like this or like that. . . . She'd come and go in our shop, gaily laughing with the customers. . . ."

"It's kind of you, Maître Jacques, to pay me such lovely compliments. Alas! I am no longer fifteen or even sixteen . . . I am the mother of a family. . . ."

"I don't know what you are," he said, much moved, shaking his big, ruddy face. "You don't seem quite real. Ever since you've come swirling into my house, the times don't seem the same any more. I am not so sure you won't vanish one day the way you've come . . . It seems so far away now, that evening when you came out of the night with your hair hanging on your shoulders and saying to me: 'Haven't you a maid called Barbe?' It rang in my skull like a peal of a bell. . . . Perhaps, it meant that you would have a rôle to play here."

'I should hope so,' Angélique thought. But she protested, in an affectionately scolding voice:

"You were drunk, that's why you heard bells ringing in your head!"

The banquet of the guild of Saint-Valbonne was a success. Three baskets of flowers had served for table decorations. Maître Bourjus and Flipot, in sparkling array, did the honours of the house and served the dishes. Rosine helped Barbe in the kitchen. Angélique went from one to the other, watched over the spits and cauldrons, gaily answered the diners' cordial greetings, and encouraged David's talents with alternating compliments and reproaches, for he had been promoted to master cook in southern specialities for the occasion. Actually, she had not compromised herself by representing him as a talented master of the profession. He knew a great many things, and his idleness alone, and perhaps a lack of opportunities, had so far prevented him from showing his capacities.

Subjugated by Angélique's high spirits, overjoyed by her approval, guided by her, he surpassed himself. He was given an ovation when she dragged him, blushing crimson, into the room. The ladies, enlivened by the good wine, found he had fine eyes, asked him indiscreet and naughty questions, kissed, patted and tickled him. . . .

Linot picked up his hurdy-gurdy and there followed songs, with raised glasses, then roars of laughter when Piccolo did his turn, mercilessly aping the oddities of Mère Marjolaine and her companions.

A party of musketeers, strolling along the rue de la Vallée-de-Misère on the look-out for amusement, heard the outburst of gay, feminine voices and came tearing into the inn of 'The Brazen Cock', clamouring for 'roasts and pints'.

The evening then took a turn which would definitely have been frowned upon by Saint-Valbonne, if that kindly Provençal saint, who loved sunshine and gaiety, had not been naturally indulgent towards the inevitable disorder produced by gatherings of flower-sellers and gallant soldiers.

The Angelus sounded from the steeple of the church of Sainte-Opportune. With flushed cheeks, drooping eyelids, her arms aching from carrying jugs and dishes, her lips burning from a few bold, moustachioed kisses, Angélique revived when she saw Bourjus counting his gold pieces with circumspection.

She cried:

"Did we work well, Maître Jacques?"

"We certainly did, my girl. It's a long while since my shop saw such revels! And those gentlemen didn't prove such bad payers, as I feared from their plumes and rapiers."

"Do you think they'll send their friends to us?"

"That's quite possible."

"Now this is what I propose," declared Angélique. "I continue to help you with all my children: Rosine, Linot, Flipot, and the monkey. And you'll give me a quarter of your profits!"

The innkeeper frowned.

"We'll draw up a contract before a notary," she continued, "but we'll keep it secret. You don't have to tell your neighbours about your affairs. Tell them that I am a young relative whom you have taken in, and that we are working as a family. You'll see, Maître Jacques, I have a feeling that we are going to do a roaring trade. The whole district will be boasting of your business skill, and people will envy you. Mère Marjolaine spoke to me tonight of the banquet of the orange-sellers' guild of the Pont-Neuf, which falls on Saint-Fiacre's Day. Believe me, you have a real interest in keeping us here. Now, here's what you owe me for the present."

She quickly counted out the share due to her and went away, leaving the good man perplexed but convinced that he was a very bold business man.

Angélique walked out into the yard to breathe the fresh morning air. She clasped the gold pieces tightly in her hand against her chest. These gold pieces were the key to freedom. Maître Bourjus had certainly not been robbed by the deal. Angélique reckoned that, since her little troupe would have the advantage of feeding on the leavings of the banquets, her earnings would eventually constitute a fortune. It would then be time to try and launch out into something else. For example, why not work the patent which David Chaillou claimed he held and which concerned the manufacture of an exotic drink called chocolate? The simple people would probably not take much fancy to that drink, but the fops and *précieuses*, always avid for novelties and oddities, might possibly set the fashion for it.

Angélique imagined the carriages of noble ladies and be-ribboned lords stopping in the rue de la Vallée-de-Misère.

She shook her head to dispel these day-dreams. One must not look too far, or too high. Life was still precarious, un-stable. First of all, she must save up, save up like an ant. Wealth is the key to freedom, the right not to die, not to see your children die, the right to see them smile. 'If my posses-sions had not been put under seal,' the young woman told her-self, 'I'd surely have been able to save Joffrey.' She shook her head again. She must no longer think of that. For whenever she did, a longing for death would creep into her veins and she was gripped by a desire to sleep for ever.

She would never again think of it. She had other things to do. She had to save Florimond and Cantor. She would save up, save up! . . . She would lock up her gold in the wooden casket, that precious relic of sordid times where she had already placed the dagger of Rodogone the Egyptian. Next to the now useless weapon, she would pile up gold, the weapon of power.

Angélique raised her eyes towards the wet sky, where the golden glints of dawn were paling, making room for a weighty, leaden grey. The brandy-seller was crying his wares in the street. A beggar, at the entrance to the courtyard, chanted his plaintive lay. Gazing at him, she recognised Black-Bread. Black-Bread, with all his rags, all his sores, all his shells of the eternal pilgrim of poverty.

Gripped by fear, she ran to fetch a chunk of bread and a bowl of soup and brought them to him. The tramp stared at her fiercely from under his bush white eyebrows.

CHAPTER 68

FOR SEVERAL days Angélique divided her talents between Maître Bourjus's pots and pans and Mère Marjolaine's flowers. The florist had asked her to help her out, for the birth of the royal heir was imminent, and the flower-sellers were flooded with work.

One day in November, as they were sitting on the Pont-Neuf, the palace clock began to strike. The jack-o'-the-clock of the Samaritaine seized his hammer, and in the distance could be heard the booming shots of the cannon of the Bastille.

The entire population of Paris went mad with joy.

"The Queen's given birth! The Queen's given birth!"

Breathlessly, the crowd counted:

"Twenty, twenty-one, twenty-two . . ."

At the twenty-third cannon-shot people began to grab one another's arms. The bell-ringing, chimes and salvoes continued showering on a delirious Paris. No more doubt: a *boy*!

"A Dauphin! A Dauphin! Long live the Dauphin! Long live the Queen! Long live the King!"

Everybody embraced and kissed. The Pont-Neuf burst into song. People formed in jubilant throngs. Booths and work-shops put up their shutters. The fountains spouted streams of wine. At long tables, set up in the streets by the King's foot-men, pastries and preserves were served. In the evening there was a great display of fireworks.

When the Queen had returned from Fontainebleau and settled down again at the Louvre with the royal baby, the city guilds made ready to present their compliments to her.

Mère Marjolaine said to Angélique:

"You will come along. It's not very regular, but I shall select you as the apprentice to carry my flower-baskets. You'll like that, won't you, to see the home of Kings, the beautiful Louvre? The rooms there are larger and loftier than churches, it seems!"

Angélique did not dare refuse. The good woman was doing her a great honour. Moreover, though she hardly admitted it to herself, she was eager to find herself once more in a place which had been the scene of so many events and dramas in her life. Would she catch a glimpse of the Grande Mademoiselle, swollen-eyed with tears of emotion; or the insolent Duchesse de Soissons; the witty Lauzun; the sombre de Guiche; de Vardes? . . . Who among those great lords and ladies would dream of seeing, amid the stall-keepers, the woman who, not so long ago, used to pass through the corridors of the Louvre, in her court dresses, with burning eyes, followed by her impassive Moor, going from one to the other, perturbed at first, then imploring, begging for an impossible mercy for a husband condemned in advance? . . .

On the appointed day she found herself in the palace court-yard, where the flower and orange sellers of the Pont-Neuf and the fish-wives of the Halles mingled their sonorous voices and their starched petticoats. They were accompanied by their wares, which vied in beauty, if not in aroma.

Baskets of flowers, hampers of fruit and kegs of herrings were to be placed side by side before Monseigneur the Dauphin, whose tiny hand had to touch them all, the soft roses, the sparkling oranges and the beautiful silvery fish.

As the ladies, in a noisy, odoriferous group, were mounting the stairs that led to the royal apartments, they passed the Apostolic Nuncio, who had just presented a layette to the heir-presumptive to the throne of France, the Pope's traditional gift 'in token of his recognition of him as the elder son of the Church'.

In the anteroom where they were told to wait, the good women went into raptures over the wonders extracted from the three red velvet cases with silver fittings.

They were then led into the Queen's bedroom. The ladies of the merchant guilds knelt down and made their speeches. Kneeling with them on the brightly-coloured carpets, Angélique saw the Queen lying in a sumptuous robe in the semi-darkness of the richly-gilded bed. She still had the same somewhat set expression which she had displayed at Saint-Jean-de-Luz, fresh from the sombre palaces of Madrid, but French fashions and hairstyle were less becoming to her than the fantastic attire and the hairdress puffed up with false locks which had then framed with severe and ample lines the face and figure of the young idol betrothed to the Sun King.

Queen Maria-Theresa, a happy young mother and a loving wife reassured by the King's attentions, deigned to smile at the brash, gaudy group which had succeeded the unctuous company of the apostolic embassy at her bedside. The King was at her side. He was smiling.

Gripped by a cruel emotion at finding herself at the King's feet amid these humble women, Angélique was as if blind and paralysed. All she saw was the King.

Later, when she was outside again with her companions, they told her that the Queen Mother had been present, as well as Madame d'Orléans and Mademoiselle de Montpensier, the Duc d'Enghien, the Prince de Condé's son, and a number of young men and women of their households.

She had not seen anyone but the King, who was smiling, standing on the steps by the Queen's big bed. She had felt greatly frightened. He did not resemble the young man who had received her at the Tuileries and whom she had so much wanted to shake by his shirt-frill. On that day they had faced each other like two young creatures endowed with equal strength, fighting each other fiercely, each of them convinced that he deserved victory.

What madness! How could she have failed to grasp at once that there was in this sovereign, under the outward appearance of a still vulnerable sensitivity, an indomitable character which, throughout his life, would never tolerate the least encroachment on his authority! From the start, the King was fated to triumph, and for her failure to understand this Angélique had been broken like a reed.

She followed the group of apprentices on their way to the service quarters to reach the palace gates. The members of the guilds were staying on to attend a big banquet, but the apprentices were not admitted to this feast.

As they passed through the pantries, where elaborate dishes and piles of viands were waiting to be carried into the halls,

Angélique heard someone whistling behind her: one long, two short. She recognised the signal of Calembredaine's gang and thought she was dreaming. Here, at the Louvre? . . .

She turned round. In an open doorway a small silhouette cast its shadow on the stone floor.

"Barcarole!"

She rushed up to him with a surge of genuine pleasure. The dwarf preened himself, proud and full of dignity.

"Come in, sister. Come in, my very dear Marquise. Let's indulge in a little chat."

She laughed.

"Oh, Barcarole! how handsome you look! And how well you talk!"

"I am the Queen's midget," said Barcarole, very smugly.

He showed her into a kind of small parlour and made her admire his satin singlet, which was half orange, half yellow and held in at the waist by a belt with many bells. He then went into a series of capers and somersaults so that she might appreciate the jingle-jangle he produced. With his hair cut at nape-length just above the enormous fluted ruff and his pleasant face carefully shaven, the dwarf seemed happy and healthy. Angélique told him that she found him years younger.

"As a matter of fact, that's rather what I feel like," Barcarole agreed modestly. "Life does not lack in comfort and I believe that, on the whole, people here are rather fond of me. I am happy to have reached the summit of my career at my age."

"How old are you, Barcarole?"

"Thirty-five. It's the height of maturity, the fullness of man's moral and physical development. Come along, sister. I want to introduce you to a noble lady for whom, I won't hide it from you, I harbour tender feelings . . . which she reciprocates."

With the swaggering air of a conquering lover, the dwarf led Angélique very mysteriously through the gloomy maze of the Louvre's service quarters. He ushered her into a dark room where she saw, sitting behind a table, a woman of about forty years, who was extremely plain and swarthy, and who was in the process of heating something on a small silver-gilt cooker.

"Dona Thérésita, I present to you Dona Angelica, the loveliest madonna in Paris," Barcarole announced pompously.

The woman bored dark, shrewd eyes into Angélique, and

spoke a sentence in Spanish, in which the words 'Marquise of the Angels' could be distinguished. Barcarole winked at Angélique.

"She is asking whether you are the Marquise of the Angels that I keep telling her about. You see, sister, I don't forget my friends."

They had walked round the table and Angélique noticed that Dona Thérésita's tiny feet barely reached over the edge of the stool on which she was perched. This was the Queen's she-midget.

Angélique seized her petticoat between two fingers and made a little curtsy to show the respect in which she held this high-ranking lady. With a movement of her head, the midget motioned the young woman to sit down on another stool, while she continued to stir her mixture slowly. Barcarole had jumped on to the table. He was cracking and nibbling hazel-nuts and telling stories in Spanish to his companion. A beautiful white greyhound came to sniff Angélique and lay down at her feet.

"This is Pistolet, the King's greyhound," said Barcarole, introducing him, "and here are Dorinde and Mignonne, the greyhound bitches."

It was warm and quiet in this part of the palace where the two midgets indulged in sweet dalliance between capers. Angélique's nose quivered with curiosity at the scent wafted to her from the saucepan. It was a pleasant, indefinable smell, dominated by a tang of cinnamon and red pepper. She examined the ingredients spread on the table: hazel-nuts and almonds, a spray of red pepper, a pot of honey, a half-crushed sugar-loaf, cups filled with aniseeds and pepper-corns, boxes of cinnamon powder. And lastly, a kind of bean which she did not know.

Absorbed in the operation she was performing, the she-midget seemed little inclined to engage in conversation with the newcomer. However, Barcarole's voluble speeches eventually wrested a smile from her.

"I told her," he explained to Angélique, "that you found me years younger and that I owed this to the happiness which she gives me. My dear, I really am in clover here! To tell the truth, I'm getting too staid and settled. It sometimes worries me. The Queen is a most kindly woman. When she is too sad, she calls me to her and pats my cheeks, saying: 'Ah! my poor boy! My poor boy!' I am not used to such manners. They bring tears to my eyes—can you imagine, me, Barcarole!"

"Why is the Queen sad?"

"Well, she's beginning to suspect that her husband is cuckolding her!"

"It is true, then, what they say about the King having a favourite?"

"Of course! He's hiding her, his La Vallière. But the Queen is bound to find out eventually. Poor little woman! She isn't very subtle and she knows nothing about life. You see, sister, the life of princes, when you look at it closely, isn't so different from that of their humble subjects. They play each other dirty tricks and quarrel in their homes, just like brigands and hussies. You ought to see her, the Queen of France, when she's waiting at night for her husband to come, while he is having sport in another woman's arms. If there's one thing we French can be proud of, it's our master's amorous capacity. Poor little Queen of France!"

There was no doubt that Barcarole the cynic had now become a compassionate philosopher. He saw Angélique smile and winked at her.

"Makes you feel good, doesn't it, Marquise of the Angels, to indulge in fine sentiments at times, to feel you are honest, brave, and earning your living by good hard work?"

She did not answer, for the dwarf's cloying tone was not to her liking. To change the subject, she inquired:

"Can you tell me what Dona Thérésita is brewing so painstakingly? This dish has an odd smell that I can't put a name to."

"Why, it's the Queen's chocolate."

Angélique promptly rose and went to have a look in the saucepan. She saw a thick, blackish product in it which did not look very appetising. Through the intermediary of Barcarole she engaged in a conversation with the midget-woman, who told her that the completion of the masterpiece which she was about to concoct required a hundred cocoa beans, two corns of chili or Mexican pepper, a handful of aniseed, six roses of Alexandria, a clove of campeachy, two drams of cinnamon, twelve almonds, twelve hazel-nuts and half a sugarloaf.

"That seems to me awfully complicated," said Angélique, disappointed. "Is it good? Could I taste it?"

"Taste the Queen's chocolate! An impious beggar-wench

like you! What a heresy!" cried the dwarf with mock indignation.

Although the midget-woman also considered this a rather bold request, she condescended to hold out to Angélique a little of the pasty mixture on a golden spoon. The paste was so highly-seasoned that it burnt her mouth, and it was also inordinately sweet. Angélique said out of politeness:

"It's excellent."

"The Queen couldn't do without it," commented Barcarole. "She has several cups a day, but they are brought to her secretly, for the King and the whole Court are making fun of her passion for it. At the Louvre there is none but Her Majesty the Queen Mother, who is Spanish too, who also drinks it."

"Where can one obtain these cocoa beans?"

"The Queen has them brought specially from Spain, through the intermediary of the ambassador. They must be roasted, pounded and cleansed."

He added under his breath:

"I can't understand anyone making such a fuss about this horror!"

Just then, a little girl came rushing in and asked in hurried Spanish for Her Majesty's chocolate. Angélique recognised Philippa. It was alleged that the child was a bastard offspring of King Philip IV of Spain and that the Infanta Maria-Theresa, finding her abandoned in the corridors of the Escorial, had had her brought up. She had been among the Spanish suite which had crossed the Bidassoa.

Angélique got up and took leave of Dona Thérésita. The dwarf showed her out to the small gate that opened on to the quay.

"You haven't asked me how I have been getting on," Angélique said to him.

She suddenly had the impression that the dwarf had changed into a pumpkin, for all she could see of him was his huge orange silk hat. Barcarole was looking down at the ground. Angélique sat down on the doorstep in order to be at the same level as the little fellow; she looked into his eyes.

"Answer me!"

"I know how you've been getting on. You have dropped Calembredaine and are the prey of fine sentiments."

"You sound as if you were accusing me! Haven't you heard of the battle of the Fair of Saint-Germain? Calembredaine has disappeared. As for me, I managed to escape from the Châtelet. Rodogone is at the Tower of Nesle."

"You no longer belong to the underworld."

"Nor do you."

"Oh yes, I do! I'll always belong to it. It's my kingdom," said Barcarole with a strange solemnity.

"Who told you all this about me?"

"Wood-Bottom."

"You've seen him again?"

"I went to pay him homage. He is our Great Coesre now. I expect you are not unaware of it?"

"No, indeed."

"I went to fork out a purse full of *louis d'or*. Whoo! Whoo! my dear, I was the richest toff at the gathering."

Angélique took the dwarf's hand, a curious, round, podgy little hand, like a child's.

"Barcarole, are they going to harm me?"

"I believe there's not a woman in Paris whose pretty skin clings less closely to her body than yours."

"It can't be helped. I'll die, but I could never turn back. You can tell Wood-Bottom so."

The Queen's dwarf veiled his eyes with a tragic gesture.

"Ah! what a painful thing to see such a pretty girl with her throat slit!"

As she was going out, he caught her by her petticoat.

"Between you and me, it would be better if you told Wood-Bottom so yourself."

From the month of December onward, Angélique gave all her time to the business of the cook-shop. The number of customers was increasing. News of the successful feast of the flower-sellers' guild had spread like wildfire. 'The Brazen Cock' was beginning to specialise in guild banquets. Trades-people, happy to 'wet their gills' and guzzle in good company and for the greater glory of their patron saints, came to feast here under the freshly-varnished rafters, which were invariably adorned with the choicest game and pork-butchery.

Gradually there began to appear at 'The Brazen Cock' parties of libertines, dissolute and rakish philosophers, who professed the right to all sensual enjoyments, a contempt of women and the denial of God. It was not easy to dodge their foraging hands. Moreover, they were extremely fastidious in their choice of food. But Angélique, though she was some-times appalled by their cynicism, counted much on them to give her establishment a justified renown which, in turn, would bring to it customers of higher standing.

With perspiring brow, her cheeks flushed by the kitchen-fire, her fingers stained and greasy, Angélique went about her task without giving a thought to anything but the present. It did not cost her any effort to laugh, exchange banter, slap down a boldly searching hand. And stirring sauces, mincing herbs and garnishing dishes amused her.

She remembered that, when still a little girl at Monteloup, she had loved to lend a hand in the kitchen. But it was in Toulouse above all that she had taken a liking to gastronomy, under the guidance of the fastidious Joffrey de Peyrac, whose table at the Gay Learning was famed throughout the kingdom. To revive certain recipes and recollect certain hallowed principles of the culinary art sometimes caused her a melancholy joy.

When winter came, Florimond fell seriously ill. His nose ran; his ears were suppurating.

Twenty times a day, Angélique would snatch a moment to dash up the seven flights of stairs to the garret where the feverish little body was fighting its lonely battle against death. She trembled every time she approached the litter and heaved a sigh of relief when she saw that her son was still breathing. She would gently caress the big, bulging forehead from which pearls of sweat poured.

"My love! My treasure! Let me keep my frail little boy! ... I'll ask nothing else of life, dear God. I'll go to church again, have Masses said. But leave me my little boy. . . ."

On the third day of Florimond's illness, Maître Bourjus gruffly 'ordered' Angélique to move into the big bedroom on the first floor, where he no longer slept since his wife's death. Could a child be properly nursed in an attic no larger than a wardrobe, where six people including a monkey were crammed at night? These were real gipsy ways, the manners of a heart-less beggar-wench! . . .

Florimond recovered, but Angélique stayed on in the big first-floor bedroom with her two children, while a second attic was allotted to Flipot and Linot. Rosine continued to share Barbe's bed.

"And moreover," concluded Maître Bourjus, flushing angrily, "I'd like you to stop insulting me by the daily sight of a rascally footman flinging firewood down in my courtyard under the noses of all my neighbours. If you want to warm yourself, you can help yourself from the wood-pile."

So Angélique informed the Duchesse de Soissons through her lackey that she required her gifts no longer and thanked her for her charitable help. She tipped the flunkey on his last visit. The latter, who had never recovered from his first day's bewilderment, nodded his head.

"I've been compelled to do all sorts of things in my life, and that's a fact, but never have I seen a woman like you!"

"That would have been only half a misfortune," retorted Angélique, "if I hadn't been obliged to see you too."

Lately, she had been sharing out parts of the food and clothes sent by Madame de Soissons among the beggars and tramps who, in growing numbers, were gathering at the approaches to 'The Brazen Cock'. Among them there appeared many a well-known face, scowling and taciturn. She silently entreated these paupers to grant her the right of freedom. But they became more exacting every day. Their swarm of rags and crutches assailed her refuge ever more threateningly. Even the customers of 'The Brazen Cock' protested against this invasion, complaining that the neighbourhood of the inn was more pauper-ridden than the church doors. Their smell and the sight of their running sores did not stimulate one's appetite.

Maître Bourjus stormed, with, for once, unfeigned rage.

"You attract them like a civet-cat attracts snakes and woodlice. Stop giving them alms and rid me of this vermin, or I'll be obliged to part with you."

She protested hotly.

"Why do you imagine that your shop is more besieged by beggars than the other shops? Haven't you heard the rumours of famine spreading through the country? They say that the starving peasants are swarming into the cities like armies, and that the destitute are growing in numbers. . . ."

But she was frightened.

There followed three terrible months.
Cold and famine increased. The beggars became threatening.

Angélique made up her mind to go and see Wood-Bottom. She ought to have done so a long time ago; it had been Barcarole's advice. But she felt faint at the thought of finding herself again before the house of the Great Coesre.

Once more she had to overcome her fears, pass a new stage of her journey, win a new battle. On a black and icy night she made for the Faubourg Saint-Denis.

She was taken before Wood-Bottom. He squatted deep in his mud-built house, on a kind of throne, amid the smoke and soot of oil lamps. The copper basin was before him on the ground. She threw a heavy purse into it and presented another gift: a huge roast shoulder of mutton, and a loaf of bread, which were rare delights at that period.

"It's none too soon," growled Wood-Bottom. "I have been expecting you, Marquise, for a long time. Do you know that you are playing a dangerous game?"

"I know that I owe it to you that I am still alive."

She went close up to him. On either side of the cripple's throne there stood the nightmarish members of his fearsome retinue: the Big and the Little Eunuch, with their insignia of fools, the broom and the pike with a dead dog impaled on it, and Jean the Greybeard, with his streaming beard and his birches, the emblems of the former master of the college of Navarre.

Wood-Bottom, still wearing an impeccable stock, had a magnificent hat with two rows of red plumes.

Angélique gave pledge that every month she would bring him, or have brought to him, the same amount and promised that his 'table' would never lack for anything. But in exchange she asked to be left free to lead her new life. She also demanded that the beggars be ordered to evacuate the doorstep of 'her' eating-house.

She saw from Wood-Bottom's face that she had at last acted in a proper manner; and that he considered himself satisfied.

On leaving him, she gravely dropped a curtsy.

In 1663, Angélique turned to account the enforced leisure of the Lenten fast to carry out three projects that she had set her heart upon.

First of all, she moved house. She had never cared for this tightly-wedged and busy district in the shadow of the Great

Châtelet. In the lovely borough of the Marais she found a two-storey lodging comprising three rooms which seemed a palace to her.

It was situated in the rue des Francs-Bourgeois, not far from where it crossed the rue Vielle-du-Temple. Under Henri IV, a financier had started building there a handsome town house of brick and ashlar. However, ruined by the wars or perhaps by his crooked dealings, he had had to leave it unfinished. Only the gateway, flanked by two lodges, at the approach to the big inner courtyard, had been completed. A little old woman, who was the owner of the building, lived on one side of the vaulted entrance. She rented the other lodge to Angélique at a reasonable price.

On the ground floor two heavily-barred windows lit a passage that led to a tiny kitchen and to a fairly spacious room which Angélique took for herself. The large room on the upper floor was reserved for the children, who moved into it with their governess, Barbe, who had left Maître Bourjus's employ to enter into that of 'Madame Morens', which was the name Angélique had decided to adopt. Some day she would perhaps be able to add the nobiliary particle to it. Thus the children would bear their father's name: de Morens. And later, she would try to claim for them his rank, if not his heritage.

She had wild hopes. Money can do anything. Had she not already a place of her own?

Barbe had left the restaurant without regrets. She did not like the cookery trade and was happy only with 'her babies'. For some time she had devoted herself entirely to them. To take her place, Angélique had engaged two kitchen-maids and a scullion. What with Rosine, who was growing into a fresh and sprightly serving-maid, Flipot as kitchen boy, and Linot more particularly in charge of the customers' entertainment and of selling scones and rissoles, the staff of 'The Brazen Cock' was becoming impressive.

At the rue des Francs-Bourgeois, Barbe and the children would enjoy the quiet.

On the evening they moved in, Angélique never stopped running upstairs and downstairs in her excitement. There was not much in the way of furniture: a bed in each room, a small cot for the children, two tables, three chairs, square plush cushions to sit on. But the fire danced in the hearth, and the big room was redolent with the aroma of pancakes. That's how the house-warming was celebrated.

Patou the dog wagged his tail, and the little nursemaid Javotte smiled at Florimond, who smiled back at her.

For Angélique had gone out to Neuilly to fetch Florimond's and Cantor's former companions in misfortune. When she decided to settle down in the rue des Francs-Bourgeois, Angélique had thought of their needing a watch dog. The Narais district was isolated and dangerous at night, with its big empty spaces, its garden patches that separated the dwelling-houses. Angélique was assured of Wood-Bottom's protection, but in the darkness thieves could make a mistake. And there came back to her mind the memory of the little girl to whom her two children undoubtedly owed their lives, and the dog who had sheltered Florimond in his misery.

The foster-mother did not recognise her, for Angélique was wearing her mask and had come in a hired carriage. For the offered sum of money, the woman was all smiles and gladly parted with the girl, who was her niece, and with the dog. Angélique wondered about Florimond's possible reaction, but the two newcomers seemed to arouse in him nothing but pleasant memories. It was Angélique herself who felt a twinge as she looked at Javotte and Patou, remembering Florimond in his kennel.

That evening, she had been extravagant. She had bought toys. Not those paper-mills or hobby-horses that could be acquired for a few *sous* on the Pont-Neuf. But toys which were said to be manufactured in Nuremberg: a little gilt-wood carriage with four dolls, three little glass dogs, an ivory whistle and, for Cantor, a painted wooden egg that contained several smaller ones.

Looking at her little family, Angélique said to Barbe:

"Barbe, some day these two young gentlemen will go to the Academy of Mont-Parnasse, and we shall present them at Court."

And Barbe answered, clasping her hands:

"I do believe it, Madame."

Just then, the crier of the dead passed through the street.

"Hark, all you who are asleep in bed,
Pray God for the dead . . ."

Angélique rushed furiously to the window and poured a pail of water over his head.

Angélique's second move was to change the sign over the eating-house of 'The Brazen Cock', which, in view of her success, became the tavern of 'The Red Mask', named after the red mask she wore habitually in her dining-rooms. The young woman had great ambitions, for, apart from a wrought-iron sign hanging over the street which would depict a carnival mask, she wished to have a painted sign placed above the entrance door.

One day, as she was returning from the market, she came to a sudden stop before a gunsmith's shop. Its sign represented an old soldier with a white beard, about to drink wine out of his helmet, while his pike, leaning near him, was sparkling with its steely glints.

"But that's old Guillaume!" she cried.

She dashed into the shop, and the shopkeeper told her that the masterpiece above his door was the handiwork of a painter by the name of Gontran Sancé who lived in the Faubourg Saint-Marcel.

With throbbing heart, Angélique ran to the address she had been given. On the third floor of a modest-looking house, a small, smiling, pink young woman opened the door. In the studio Angélique found Gontran at his easel amidst his canvases and paints: azure, red-brown, ash-blue, Hungarian green. . . . He was smoking his pipe and painting a naked little cherub, whose model was a lovely little baby girl of a few months, lying on a blue velvet carpet.

To begin with, the visitor, who was masked, talked of the gunsmith's sign. Then, lifting her mask with a laugh, she made herself known. She had the feeling that Gontran was sincerely delighted to see her again. He was looking more and more like their father, and had his way of placing his hands on his knees, when listening, like a horse dealer. He told Angélique that he had passed his examination and married the daughter of his former master, Van Ossel.

"But you've married beneath you!" cried Angélique, appalled, the moment the little Dutchwoman had gone out into the kitchen.

"What about you? If I understand correctly, you are the hostess of a tavern and are pouring out drinks to people some of whom are certainly of a much lower rank than I."

After a moment's silence he went on, not without shrewdness:

"And you've come rushing to see me, without hesitation or false shame! Would you have hurried in the same way to announce your present state to Raymond, who has just been appointed confessor to the Queen Mother; or to our sister Marie-Agnès, who is maid-of-honour to the Queen, and who plays the whore at the Louvre, according to the rules of that swarm of beauties; or even to young Albert, who is a page to the Marquis de Rochant?"

Angélique admitted that she hadn't kept very close track of her family. She asked what had become of Denis.

"He is in the army. Father is jubilant. At last a de Sancé in the King's service! Jean-Marie, the last born, is at college. Raymond may possibly obtain a church living for him, for he is on the best possible terms with the King's confessor, who has the nomination sheets. We'll end up having a bishop in the family."

"Don't you think that we are a funny lot?" asked Angélique, nodding. "There are de Sancés right up and down the ladder."

"Hortense is hovering somewhere in between, with her solicitor of a husband. They have a great many connections, but live rather meanly. With this business of having to buy back their office, they haven't been paid a penny by the State for almost four years."

"Do you see them?"

"Yes. As I do Raymond and the others. They are none of them very proud to see me. But they are all glad to have their portraits painted."

Angélique hesitated briefly.

"And . . . when you meet . . . do you ever talk of me?"

"Never!" the painter said harshly. "The memories connected with you are too terrible. It was a catastrophe, a collapse that shattered our hearts. Such as they are. Luckily, few people knew that you were our sister—you, the wife of a sorcerer who was burned on the Place de Grève!"

However, while he spoke, he had taken her hand into his, which was stained with paints and scarred by acids. He parted her fingers, touched the small palm that showed traces of blisters and burns from the oven, and he placed his cheek on it with caressing affection, a gesture that he used to make in his early childhood. . . .

Angélique's throat ached so much that she thought she would start to cry. But she had not cried for too long now! Her last tears had been shed well before Joffrey's death. She had lost the habit.

She withdrew her hand and said almost curtly, as she looked at the canvases leaning against the wall all around her:

"You make beautiful things, Gontran."

"Yes. And yet the great noblemen presume to treat me familiarly, and the bourgeois look down on me haughtily, because I make them with my hands, these beautiful things. Would they rather I worked with my feet? And why should the handling of a sword represent a less manual and less contemptible work than the handling of a brush?"

He shook his head and a smile lit his face. Marriage had made him gayer and more talkative.

"Little sister, I am full of confidence. Some day, we'll go to Court, we'll both of us go to Versailles. The King calls for artists in great numbers. I shall paint the ceilings of the apartments, the portraits of Princes and Princesses, and the King will say to me: 'You make beautiful things, sir.' And to you he will say: 'Madame, you are the most beautiful woman in Versailles.'"

They both burst out laughing together.

CHAPTER 69

IN THE autumn dusk Angélique strolled on the Pont-Neuf. She had come to buy flowers and took advantage of the opportunity to wander from shop to shop.

She stopped before Big Matthieu's platform, and her heart gave a jump. Big Matthieu was pulling a tooth from a man kneeling before him. The patient's mouth was open and distended by the operator's forceps, but Angélique recognised his stiff, straw-coloured hair, and his shabby black coat. It was the man of the hay-boat.

The young woman elbowed her way through to the front row.

Although it was rather cold, Big Matthieu was sweating profusely.

"*Ventre-saint-gris*, as the fellow across the street would say,[1] this is a hard one. My God, it's hard!"

He paused in his labour, to wipe his brow, removed the instrument from his victim's mouth and asked him:

"Does it hurt?"

The other turned his face towards the people who were watching, smiled and shook his head. There was no doubt. It was he, with his pallid face, his long mouth, his grimaces of a fazed loon!

"You see, ladies and gentlemen!" Big Matthieu bawled. "Isn't it amazing? Here's a man who's not in pain, though, believe me, his teeth are like granite! And by what miracle is he not in pain? Thanks to this miraculous ointment with which I rubbed his gum before the operation. This little bottle, ladies and gentlemen, contains oblivion for all ailments. You *feel no pain* with me, because of this miraculous ointment, and you have your teeth pulled out without even noticing it. Come, my friend, let's get back to work."

The other eagerly opened his mouth. With much swearing and groaning, the quack grappled again with the recalcitrant jaw. At last, with a shout of triumph, Big Matthieu brandished the obstreperous tooth at the end of his tongs.

"Here we are! Did it hurt, my friend?"

The other got up, still smiling. He made a sign of denial.

"Can I say more? Here's a man whose ordeal you could see for yourselves, and who is walking away fit and fresh. Thanks to the miraculous ointment, which I am the only one to use among empirical practitioners, nobody will ever again have the slightest hesitation in getting rid of those stinking stumps that disgrace the mouth of an honest Christian. You'll go to have your tooth pulled out with a smile. Don't hesitate any longer, ladies and gentlemen. Come forward! There's no more pain. *Pain is dead*."

Meanwhile, the customer had put on his hat with its pointed crown and clambered down from the platform. Angélique followed him. She would have liked to go up to him, but wondered whether he would recognise her.

He walked along the Quai des Morfondus, below the Palace of Justice. At a few steps' distance, Angélique saw his weird, lean silhouette floating in the mist rising from the Seine.

[1] The favourite oath of Henri IV, whose statue stands on the Pont-Neuf.

Once again, he did not seem quite real. He walked very slowly, stopping, then walking on again.

Suddenly he vanished. Angélique gave a little cry. But she realised that the man had merely gone down the three or four steps from the quayside to the riverbank. Without a moment's thought, she, too, descended the steps and almost knocked against the stranger leaning against the quay wall. He was bent double and groaning hoarsely.

"What is it? What's wrong with you?" asked Angélique. "Are you ill?"

"Oh! I am dying," he moaned feebly. "That brute almost wrenched my head off. And my jaw is dislocated, I am sure."

He spat out a thin trickle of blood.

"But you said it didn't hurt?"

"I didn't say anything. It would have been quite beyond me. Happily Big Matthieu paid me well for playing this little comedy."

He groaned, spat again. She thought he was going to faint.

"It's stupid! You should never have accepted it," she said.

"I haven't had anything to eat for three days."

Angélique put her arms around the stranger's emaciated torso. He was taller than she, but so light that she felt almost strong enough to carry his poor carcass.

"Come on, you'll eat well tonight," she promised him. "And it won't cost you anything. Not a *sol* . . . or a tooth."

Back at the inn, she dashed into the kitchen, looking for something that might suit a victim of starvation and the tooth-puller's care. There was a meat broth and a fine ox tongue garnished with cucumbers and gherkins. She brought him all this, together with a pitcher of red wine and a big jar of mustard.

"Go ahead and start with this. We'll see to the rest later."

The poor devil's long nose quivered.

"Oh! the subtle perfume of soups," the stranger murmured, sitting up as if he was coming back to life. "Blessed essence of the vegetable gods!"

She left him in order that he might sate his hunger undisturbed. After giving her orders and seeing that everything was ready for the arrival of customers, she went into the pantry to prepare a sauce. It was a tiny room into which she withdrew whenever she had to concoct a particularly difficult dish.

After a few moments, the door opened and her guest passed his head through the opening.

"Tell me, my dear, you are the little beggar-wench who knows Latin, aren't you?"

"I am . . . and I am not," said Angélique, who did not know whether she was cross or pleased that he had recognised her. "I am now the niece of Maître Bourjus, the landlord of this tavern."

"In other words, you are no longer under the fearful jurisdiction of Monsieur Calembredaine?"

"God forbid!"

He slipped into the room, walked up to her with his lithe step, took her by the waist and kissed her lips.

"Well! You seem to have regained your strength all right!" said Angélique when she could get her breath again.

"Who wouldn't? I have been looking for you all over Paris for a long time, Marquise of the Angels!"

"Hush!" she said, looking around, frightened.

"Don't be afraid. There are no constables in the diningroom. I didn't see any and, believe me, I know them all. So, little wench, you know how to feather your nest, I can see. You had your fill of hay-boats? I left a pale, wasting, grimy little flower, who sobs in her sleep, and I find a plump goodwife, comfortably settled. . . . And yet it's you all right. Your lips are still as good, but they taste of cherries now, and not of bitter tears. Do come again. . . ."

"I am in a hurry," said Angélique, pushing back the hands that tried to imprison her cheeks.

"Two seconds of bliss are worth two years of life. Besides, I'm still hungry, you know!"

"Do you want some pancakes and jam?"

"No, I want *you*. Seeing you and touching you is all I need to sate my appetite. I want your cherry lips, your peach-like cheeks. Everything about you is edible. One cannot dream of anything better for a famished poet. . . . Your flesh is tender. It makes me want to bite it. And you are warm . . . ! It's wonderful."

"Oh, you are impossible!" she protested, freeing herself. "Your declarations, with their lyrical and vulgar hodge-podge, drive me mad!"

"That's what I want. Come, don't pretend you're coy."

With an imperious gesture which proved the return of his

strength he pulled her towards him again and, throwing her head back into the crook of his arm, he started to kiss her.

The sound of a wooden ladle knocking hard against the table pulled them brutally apart.

"By Saint Jacques!" Maître Bourjus was yelling. "It's that accursed gazetteer! That devil's henchman, that slanderer, in my house, in my pantry, making free with my wench! Out with you, marauder, or I'll kick you right out into the street!"

"Have pity, sir, have pity on my pants! They are so worn already that your august foot might provide an indecent spectacle for the ladies."

"Out of here, rascal, pen-pusher, nail-biter! You disgrace my shop with your rags full of holes and your mountebank's hat."

But the other, making faces, laughing and holding his threatened backside with both hands, had run towards the street entrance. He thumbed his nose and disappeared.

Angélique said, a little cravenly:

"The fellow came into my pantry and I couldn't get rid of him."

"Hmm!" growled the innkeeper. "You didn't seem so displeased for once. There, there, my dear, don't protest. That isn't what puts my back up: a little petting now and then livens up a pretty girl. But honestly, Angélique, you disappoint me. Aren't there plenty of respectable people patronising this place? Why do you have to pick a journalist?"

The King's favourite, Mademoiselle de La Vallière, had a somewhat large mouth. She also had a slight limp. People said that this gave her a special gracefulness and did not prevent her from dancing delightfully, but the fact was there: she limped.

She had no bosom. People would compare her to Diana, talk of the charm of hermaphrodites, but the fact was there: she was flat-chested. Her skin was dry. The tears caused by the royal infidelities, humiliations at Court, and remorse had put dark rings around her eyes. She was becoming thin and dry. Finally, as a result of her second maternity, she suffered from an intimate disability of which Louis XIV alone knew the details. Louis XIV . . . and the Gutter-Poet.

And, out of all these hidden or admitted misfortunes, out of these physical handicaps, he made an astonishing pamphlet, full of wit, but so wicked and crude that even the least prudish citizens avoided showing copies to their wives, who promptly asked their servants for them.

> If you limp and have just turned fifteen
> Have no bust to boast of, nor senses that are keen,
> If for parents you have God knows whom,
> If, a fresh maid, you make sons in the anteroom,
> Then the first man in the realm to you will make love:
> La Vallière is the proof thereof.

So the song began.

These lampoons could be found all over Paris, at the Hôtel Biron, where Louise de La Vallière was living, at the Louvre and even in the Queen's apartment. The latter, on seeing her rival thus depicted, laughed for the first time in a long while and rubbed her little hands with joy.

Wounded and dying of shame, Mademoiselle de la Vallière flung herself in the first carriage that came along and asked to be taken to the convent of Chaillot, where she wanted to take the veil.

The King gave orders for her to return and show herself at Court. He sent Monsieur Colbert to fetch her. This recall was the result not so much of indignant tenderness as of the enraged defiance of a sovereign whom his people dared to make fun of, but who was beginning to fear that his mistress was no feather in his cap.

The smartest sleuths in the police were set in pursuit of the Gutter-Poet.

This time nobody doubted that he would be hanged.

Angélique was getting ready to go to bed in her little room in the rue des Francs-Bourgeois. Javotte had just withdrawn with a curtsy. The children were asleep.

Running feet were heard outside. The sounds were muffled by a thin film of snow that had begun to fall, very slowly, on this December night. There was a knocking at the door. Angélique slipped on her dressing-gown and went to pull back the peep-hole.

"Who is there?"

"Open quickly, little wench, quickly. The dog!"

Without taking time to think, Angélique pulled back the bolt. The journalist stumbled into her. At the same moment, a white mass rose out of the darkness, leaped and took him by the throat.

"Sorbonne!" shouted Angélique.

She dashed forward, and her hand touched the mastiff's wet pelt.

"Let him go, Sorbonne. *Lass ihn! Lass ihn!*"

Sorbonne growled, his fangs solidly dug into his victim's collar. But after a moment Angélique's voice sank into him. He wagged his tail and consented to release his prey, though continuing to growl.

The man gasped:

"I am dead!"

"No, you aren't. Come in quickly."

"The dog will stay outside the door and warn the policeman."

"Come in, I tell you!"

She pushed him inside herself, then stayed in the archway, pulling the door shut behind her. She held Sorbonne tightly by his collar. In the entrance of the porch she saw the snow swirl in the light of a lantern. She finally distinguished the approach of a muffled step, the step that one always heard following the dog, the step of the policeman François Desgrez.

Angélique stepped forward.

"Are you looking for your dog, Maître Desgrez?"

He stopped, then he, too, stepped under the porch. She could not see his face.

"No," he replied very calmly. "I am looking for a pamphleteer."

"Sorbonne was passing. Imagine, I used to know your dog. I called him and he came to me."

"He must certainly have been enchanted, Madame. You were taking a breath of air on your doorstep in this delightful weather?"

"I was just closing my door. But we are talking in the dark, Maître Desgrez, and I am sure you can't guess who I am."

"I don't have to guess, Madame, I know. I have known for quite some time that you live in this house, and as there isn't a tavern in town that I do not know, I have seen you at 'The Red Mask'. You call yourself Madame Morens and you have two children, the elder of whom is called Florimond."

"One cannot hide anything from you. But since you know who I am, why did we have to meet by accident?"

"I was not certain that my paying a call would please you, Madame. The last time we saw each other, we parted on very bad terms."

Her mind's eye conjured up the night of her flight in the Faubourg Saint-Germain. It seemed to her that not a drop of saliva was left in her mouth.

She asked in a toneless voice:

"What do you mean?"

"It was snowing as it is tonight, and the postern of the Temple was no less dark than your porch."

Angélique smothered a sigh of relief.

"We weren't on bad terms. We had been defeated, that isn't the same thing, Maître Desgrez."

"You mustn't call me Maître any more, Madame, for I've sold my lawyer's practice, and have been struck from the university roll. However, I sold it very well, and was able to buy the office of a police-captain, on the strength of which I devote myself to a more lucrative and no less useful task: the hunting down of wrongdoers and ill-intentioned individuals of this city. Thus, from the heights of eloquence I've sunk into the depths of silence."

"You still talk just as well, Maître Desgrez."

"When the occasion arises. I then recapture a liking for oratorical phrases. This is no doubt why I have been specially charged to attend to those who indulge in incontinence of speech or writing: poets, journalists, pen-pushers of all types. Thus, tonight I am after a virulent personage, named Claude Le Petit, also called the Gutter-Poet. This chap will no doubt have occasion to bless you for your interference."

"Why so?"

"Because you stopped us short while he went on running."

"I apologise for having kept you."

"Personally, I am delighted, although the small *salon* in which you are receiving me is not very cosy."

"Forgive me. You must come again, Desgrez."

"I shall, Madame."

The snowflakes were falling more thickly. The policeman put up the collar of his coat, took a step, then stopped.

"Something has just come back to me," he said. "This Gutter-Poet wrote some pretty cruel libels at the time of your husband's trial. Let me see. . . ."

"Oh, stop it, for pity's sake!" cried Angélique, putting her hands to her ears. "Don't even mention those things. I no longer remember anything. I don't want to remember. . . ."

"The past, then, is dead for you, Madame?"

"Yes, the past is dead!"

"It's the best that could happen to it. I shall not mention it again. Goodbye, Madame, and . . . goodnight!"

Angélique, with chattering teeth, bolted the gate again. She was frozen to the marrow from standing in the cold, with no clothes on but her dressing-gown. And added to the cold was the emotion of having met Desgrez again and having heard his revelations.

She went back into the room and closed the door. The fair-haired man was sitting on the hearthstone, his arms clasped around his bony knees. He resembled a cricket.

The young woman leaned against the door. She said tonelessly:

"You are the Gutter-Poet?"

He smiled.

"Gutter? Certainly. Poet? Perhaps."

"You are the one who wrote those . . . infamies about Mademoiselle de La Vallière? Can't you let people love each other in peace? The King and that girl have done all they could to keep their love secret, and you go spreading the scandal in loathsome terms! The King's conduct is blameworthy, no doubt. He is a young, fiery man who has been married by force to a Princess without wit or beauty."

He sneered.

"How you defend him, my sweet! Has the *Franc-Ripault* twisted your heart-strings?"

"No, but I loathe to see a respectable and royal feeling besmirched."

"There's nothing respectable, or royal, in the world."

Angélique crossed the room and leaned against the other end of the fireplace. She felt faint and tense. The poet looked up at her. She saw the red points of the flames dance in his eyes.

"Didn't you know who I was?" he asked.

"Nobody told me, and how could I have guessed? Your pen is impious and licentious, whereas you . . ."

"Go on."

"You had seemed to me kind and gay."

"I am kind with little beggar-wenches who weep in hay-boats, and I am ruthless with princes."

Angélique sighed. She could not seem to get warm. She motioned with her chin towards the door.

"You must go now."

"Go!" he exclaimed. "Go, when that dog Sorbonne is only waiting to get his fangs into my hose? And that devil's policeman is getting his chains ready?"

"They aren't in the street."

"Yes, they are. They are waiting for me in the dark."

"I swear to you they have no inkling that you are here."

"How do you know? Don't you know those two pals, my sweet, you who have belonged to Calembredaine's gang?"

Quickly she motioned him to be silent.

"You see? You yourself feel that they are lying in wait outside in the snow. And you want me to go away!"

"Yes, go away!"

"You are driving me out?"

"I am."

"And yet I haven't done you any harm, have I?"

"Yes, you have."

He looked at her searchingly, then held out his hand.

"If that's so, let's be reconciled. Come."

And as she remained motionless:

"We are both of us hunted by the dog. What will become of us if we, too, fall out?"

He continued to hold out his hand.

"Your eyes have become hard and cold like emeralds. They no longer have that sunny light of a little brook under green leaves which seems to be saying: Love me, kiss me. . . ."

"Does the brook say all that?"

"Your eyes do, when I am not your enemy. Do come!"

She yielded suddenly and squatted down beside him. He promptly put his arm around her shoulders.

"You are trembling. You no longer have the self-confident mien of my hostess. Something has frightened you, hurt you. The dog? The policeman?"

"It's the dog. And the policeman. And you too, Monsieur Gutter-Poet."

"Oh, baneful trinity of Paris!"

"Do you, who know everything, have any idea of who I was before I joined up with Calembredaine?"

He gave a pout of annoyance and pulled a face.

"No. Since I have met you again, I have more or less

grasped how you have managed in between and how you got around your innkeeper. But before Calembredaine, well, no, the track stops there."

"It's better so."

"What annoys me is that I have an idea that this devil of a policeman is one up on me and knows all about your past."

"Are you vying with each other in collecting information?"

"It happens quite frequently that we pass information on to one another."

"At heart, you're much alike."

"A little. But there's a great difference between us, all the same."

"What difference?"

"I can't kill him, but he can take me for a ride to death. If you hadn't opened your door to me tonight, I should now be at the Châtelet through his good offices. I'd already have grown three inches thanks to Maître Aubin's rack, and tomorrow at dawn I'd have swung at the end of a rope."

"And why do you say that *you* can't kill him?"

"I cannot kill. The sight of blood makes me sick."

She began to laugh at his grimace of disgust. The poet's sinewy hand touched her neck.

"When you laugh, you are like a little pigeon."

He bent over her face. In his tender, mocking smile she saw the dark breach caused by Big Matthieu's forceps, and it made her want to cry and love this man.

"That's good," he murmured. "You are no longer frightened. It's all going away. . . . There is only the snow falling outside, and we here, snug and warm—— I don't often have such a grand lodging! You are naked under that gown? Yes, I can feel it. Don't move, my love. . . . Don't say anything. . . ."

His hand slid, pushed back the gown to follow the line of the shoulder, slipped further down. He laughed as a shiver passed through her.

"Here are the burgeons of spring. And yet it's winter! . . ."

He took her lips. Then he stretched out before the fire and gently pulled her towards him.

> Do I not hear, just hark! my sweet,
> The brandy-crier in the street?
> I do believe, fooling apart,
> It's time, my love, that we should part. . . .

The poet had put on his big hat and his coat full of holes. Dawn had come, thick with snow, and through the whiteness of the silent street the brandy-merchant was stumbling like a bear, muffled up to his nose.

Angélique hailed him. He poured out a small glass of spirits for both of them on the doorstep. When the fellow had passed on, they smiled at each other.

"Where are you off to, now?"

"To report a new scandal to the people of Paris. Monsieur Brienne caught his wife with her lover this night."

"This night? How can you possibly know?"

"I know everything. Farewell, my love."

She held him back by the flap of his coat and said:

"Come back."

He did come back. He would arrive in the evening, scratch at the window according to a prearranged signal. She would open the door noiselessly. And in the warm little room, beside this garrulous, caustic or loving companion, she would forget the day's hard work. He would tell her of the latest scandals, at Court and in town. That amused her, for she knew most of the people concerned.

"I am rich with the fears of all those who fear me."

But he attached no importance to money. She tried in vain to dress him more decently. After a good dinner, which he would accept without even making a move to open his purse, he would disappear for a week, and when he showed up again, hungry, gaunt and grinning, she would question him in vain. Why, since he was on excellent terms with the underworld gangs of Paris, did he never join them in their occasional carousals? He had never put in an appearance at the Tower of Nesle. And yet, as one of the important personages on the Pont-Neuf, he could have occupied a place of honour. And with all the secrets he knew, he could have made no end of people 'cough up'.

"It's more fun to make them weep or gnash their teeth," he would say.

He was willing to be helped only by the women he loved. A little flower-seller, a harlot, a maidservant had the right, after surrendering to his caresses, to pamper him a little. They would tell him: "Eat, little one," and tenderly watch him wolf down his food.

Then he would fly away. Like the flower-girl, the harlot or the maidservant, Angélique sometimes felt an urge to hold him back. Lying in the snug warmth of the bed beside this long body, whose embrace was so swift and light, she would pass an arm around his neck and pull him towards her. But already he had opened his eyes, seen the daylight behind the small, lead-framed window-panes. He would jump out of bed and dress hurriedly.

The fact was that he could never stay in one place. He was possessed by a craving which was rare at that time and which in all times has to be dearly paid for: a craving for liberty.

CHAPTER 70

ANGÉLIQUE PUT down her pen on the writing-desk and re-read with satisfaction the account she had drawn up.

She had just returned from 'The Red Mask', where she had witnessed the arrival of a noisy party of young noblemen whose Genoa-point lace collars and wide 'canons' spoke well of their solvency. They were masked, which was further proof of their high rank. Certain high-placed personages at Court did indeed prefer to remain incognito when visiting the taverns.

As would frequently happen nowadays, the young woman had left it to Maître Bourjus, David and the scullions to receive these high-class customers. Now that the inn's reputation was established and that David's hand had become practised in concocting its culinary specialities, Angélique did less of the work herself, and devoted more of her time to purchasing and to the financial management of the establishment.

It was the close of the year 1664. The situation had gradually progressed to a state of affairs which would have made the whole rue de la Vallée-de-Misère burst with laughter had one predicted it three years earlier. Without as yet having bought up Maître Bourjus's house, which was her secret intention, Angélique had in fact become its hostess. The innkeeper remained its owner, but she paid all the expenses and her share in the profits had increased in proportion. In the end, Maître Bourjus was the one who received the smaller share. He was quite satisfied to be rid of worries and to live opulently in his own inn, while putting aside a little nest-egg for his old age. Angélique was free to amass all the money she liked. All that Maître Bourjus asked was to stay under her wing, and to feel himself surrounded by her far-sighted and peremptory affection. Speaking of her, he would sometimes say 'my daughter' with so much conviction that many customers of 'The Red Mask' did not doubt their relationship. Inclined to melancholy and always convinced that his end was near, he would tell all and sundry that his will, without disregarding his nephew's interests, would greatly benefit Angélique. David, anyway, could not take offence at his uncle's decisions in favour of a woman who continued to dazzle him completely.

Angélique shook the sand off the sheet of paper on which she had drawn up the accounts. She gave an indulgent laugh.

"I am in a nice fix, with my three tender-hearted cooks all doting on me for different reasons! Their profession probably accounts for it—the warmth of the kitchen fire makes their hearts melt like turkey grease."

Javotte came in to help her undress and brush her hair.

"What's that noise?" inquired Angélique.

"I don't know. It sounds like a rat that keeps nibbling at the door."

The noise increased. Angélique went into the vestibule and realised that the gnawing sound did not come from the bottom of the door but from the little spy-hole half way up. She pulled the shutter aside and gave a little cry of horror, for a small black hand slipped through the grating and reached towards her.

"It's Piccolo!" cried Javotte.

Angélique pulled back all the bolts, opened the door, and the monkey rushed into her arms.

"What's the matter? He's never yet come here on his own. It's as if—why yes, he looks as if he's broken his chain."

She carried the little animal into her room and put him down on the table.

"Good Lord!" exclaimed the maid, laughing. "He *has* got himself into a state! His fur is all red and sticky. He must have fallen into the wine-barrel."

Angélique, who was caressing Piccolo, found indeed that her fingers were stained and sticky. She sniffed them and immediately felt herself go pale.

"This isn't wine," she said, "it's blood!"

"He's hurt?"

"I'll see."

She removed his embroidered singlet and his hose, both of which were wet with blood. But the little animal showed no trace of wounds, though he was shaken by convulsive trembling.

"What is the matter, Piccolo?" said Angélique softly. "What's happened, little friend? Explain yourself!"

The monkey stared at her with his bright, dilated eyes. Suddenly he jumped back, caught hold of a little box of sealing-wax and began to walk with grave steps, shaking the little box in front of him.

"Oh! the little rascal!" cried Javotte, giggling. "First he frightens us, and then he starts aping Linot with his tray of scones. Isn't he extraordinary, Madame?"

But the monkey, after walking all round the table imitating the little biscuit-seller, now seemed perturbed again. He turned, glanced around, shrank back. His little snout puckered, with a piteous, frightened expression. He lifted his face to the right, then to the left. He seemed to be imploring some invisible persons. At last he appeared to struggle, to fight. He abruptly dropped the box he was holding, contracted his two hands over his belly and fell backward with a shrill scream.

"But what's the matter with him? What's the matter?" stammered Javotte, bewildered. "He is ill. He's gone crazy!"

Angélique, who had watched the monkey's performance very attentively, strode quickly to her wardrobe, took her cloak from the peg and put on her mask.

"I believe some harm has come to Linot," she said hoarsely, "I must go to the tavern immediately."

"I am coming with you, Madame."

"If you like. You carry the lantern. But take the monkey up to Barbe first, so that she can clean him and warm him up and give him some milk to drink."

The forebodings of a tragedy assailed Angélique. Despite the comforting words which Javotte kept murmuring, she never doubted for a moment that the monkey had been present at a dreadful scene. But the facts surpassed her worst fears. Hardly had she reached the entrance to the Quai des Tanneurs, when the impact of a rushing shape almost knocked her over. It was Flipot, wild with horror.

She gripped his shoulders and shook him to make him recover his wits.

"I was just going to fetch you, Marquise of the Angels," stuttered the boy. "They've . . . they've killed Linot!"

"Who, they?"

"They . . . those men, the customers."

"Why? What happened?"

The poor kitchen-boy swallowed and said hurriedly, as if reeling off a lesson learned by heart:

"Linot was in the street with his basket of scones. He was singing: 'Scones! Cakes! Who's calling for the cake-man . . . ?' One of the customers in the tavern, one of those masked gentlemen, you know, with a lace collar, said: 'There's a pretty voice. I feel a sudden fancy for scones. Let someone fetch the fellow.' Linot came. And the gentleman said: 'By Jove, the boy's even more attractive than his voice.' He took Linot on his knees and began to kiss him. Then others came and wanted to kiss him too—they were all as drunk as fiddlers. Linot dropped his basket and started to shout and kick them. One of the noblemen drew his sword and thrust it into Linot's belly. Another one also drove his sword into him. Linot fell; and there was blood spurting out of his belly all over the place."

"Didn't Maître Bourjus try to come between them?"

"He did, but they killed him."

"What? What are you saying? Whom?"

"Maître Bourjus."

"You're going mad!"

"No, it's not me, it's they who are mad. When Maître Bourjus heard Linot scream, he came out of the kitchen. He said: 'Gentlemen! Please, gentlemen!' But they jumped at him. They were laughing and bashing him and shouting: 'Big barrel! Big vat!' It even made me giggle. And then one of them said: 'I recognise him, he's the former landlord of "The Brazen Cock" . . . !' Another said: 'You don't look very brazen for a cock to me, I'll dress you for the oven.' He took a big meat-knife, they all rushed towards him and they . . .'"

The boy ended his tale with a forceful gesture which left no doubt about the horrible mutilation which the poor innkeeper had suffered.

"He was braying like a donkey! But you can't hear him any more. David, too, wanted to stop them. They took a lunge at

212

his head with their swords. When we saw that, David and I and the other kitchen-boys and the maids and Suzanne, we all ran like the devil!"

The rue de la Vallée-de-Misère had an unusual air. Always bustling in this carnival season, it was still full of customers who packed the eating-houses, singing and clinking their glasses. But towards the far end of the street there was an abnormal crowd of white figures with high caps on their heads. The neighbouring innkeepers and their scullions, armed with larding-pins and skewers, were massed outside the tavern of 'The Red Mask'.

"We don't know what to do!" one of them shouted to Angélique. "Those devils have barred the door with stacked benches. And they've got a pistol. . . ."

"We must send for the watch."

"David has run to call them, but . . ."

The landlord of 'The Plucked Capon', the neighbour of 'The Red Mask', said, lowering his voice:

"Footmen stopped the watch in the rue de la Triperie. They told them that the customers who were making merry at 'The Red Mask' were very high-ranking noblemen, lords of the King's suite, and that the constables of the watch would find themselves in a devilish mess if they put their noses into this business. David nevertheless went right on to the Châtelet, but the footmen had already warned the guards. They told him at the Châtelet that he should straighten things out with his customers himself."

An appalling din issued from the tavern of 'The Red Mask': uproarious laughter, bibulous songs and such savage shouts that the good innkeepers' hair stood on end under their tall caps.

Tables and benches had been piled before the windows. It was impossible to see what was going on inside, but one could hear the sounds of breaking glass and crockery and, from time to time, the thudding report of a pistol shot, probably aimed at the fine flagons of precious crystal with which Angélique had adorned the tables and the mantelpiece.

Angélique caught a glimpse of David. He was as white as his apron, and the napkin tied around his forehead was stained with a star of blood. He went up to her and told her, stammering, the complete story of the dreadful saturnalia. The noblemen

213

had behaved with overbearing arrogance from the start. They had already been drinking in other taverns. They had started by upsetting a full, almost boiling, soup tureen over the head of one of the kitchen boys. Then there had been no end of trouble chasing them out of the kitchen, where they had wanted to seize Suzanne, notwithstanding her being an unprepossessing prey. Finally, there had been those tragic happenings with Linot, whose sweet face had filled them with odious desires. . . .

"Come on," said Angélique, gripping the young man's arm. "We must have a look. We'll go through the courtyard."

Twenty hands held her back.

"Are you crazy? . . . They'll run you through! They are wolves!"

She tore herself away and, pulling David along, went into the yard. From there she passed into the kitchen.

The kitchen door leading to the dining-room had been carefully bolted by David before he had run away with the other servants. Angélique heaved a sigh of relief. At least the substantial provisions which she had stored there had not been subjected to the blackguards' destructive fury.

With the young boy's help, she pushed the table against the wall and hoisted herself up to the fanlight which, half way up, made it possible to look inside.

She saw the devastated dining-room, strewn with plates and dishes, soiled cloths and broken glass. The hams and hares had been unfastened from the rafters. The drunken wretches were stumbling over them, shoving them aside with kicks of their boots. The obscene words of their songs, their curses and blasphemies could now be heard distinctly.

Most of them were grouped around one of the tables near the hearth. From their attitudes and their increasingly thick voices it could be guessed that they would soon collapse in a heap. In the firelight, the sight of those gaping, bawling mouths under the black masks had something sinister about it. The sumptuous clothes were spattered with wine and sauce, perhaps with blood.

Angélique tried to see the bodies of Linot and the innkeeper. But as the candles were knocked over, the back of the room was in darkness.

"Which one was the first to attack Linot?" she asked under her breath.

"The little man over there, at the corner of the table, the one with the flow of pink ribbons on his lavender singlet. He seemed the one who set the tone and got them all going."

Just then, the man whom David had pointed out scrambled to his feet with difficulty and, raising his glass in a shaking hand, cried in a falsetto voice:

"Gentlemen, I drink the health of Astrée and Asmodée, the princes of friendship."

"Oh! that voice!" exclaimed Angélique, recoiling.

She would have recognised it anywhere. It was the voice which, in her worst nightmares, still woke her at times: "Madame, you're going to die!"

So it was *he*—always he. Was he chosen by hell to incarnate unceasingly for her the demon of a malevolent fate?

"Was he the first to strike Linot with his sword?" she asked.

"Perhaps—I don't remember. But the tall one behind him, with the red rhinegrave, he struck him, too."

That man, too, had no need to remove his mask for her to recognise him.

The King's brother and the Chevalier de Lorraine! She was now certain that she could put names to all the other masked faces!

One of the drunks started to throw the chairs and stools into the fire. One of them seized a bottle and, from a distance, flung it across the room. The bottle burst in the fireplace. It was brandy. A huge flame spurted and at once set fire to the furniture. A hellish blaze blew, roaring, through the chimney, and fire-brands crackled on the stone floor.

Angélique hurtled down from her perch.

"They'll set the house on fire. We must stop them!"

But the apprentice nervously clasped her in his arms.

"Don't go. They'll kill you."

They struggled for a moment. Her anger and the fear of fire gave her added strength. She managed to free herself and push David away.

Angélique adjusted her mask. She, too, did not care to be recognised. Resolutely she drew back the bolts and noisily pulled open the kitchen door.

The appearance of this woman draped in a black cloak and with that strange red mask on her face caused a moment's stupefaction among the revellers. The singing and shouting faded.

"Oh! The red mask!"

"Gentlemen," said Angélique in a resounding voice, "have you lost your mind? Do you not fear the King's wrath when public rumour will acquaint him with your crimes?"

From the bewildered silence that followed she felt that she had flung out the only word—the King!—which was able to penetrate into the drunkards' befogged brains and light a spark of lucidity in them.

Turning her advantage to account, she stepped boldly forward. Her intention was to reach the hearth and pull from it the flaming furniture in order to confine the blaze and thus avert a chimney-fire.

At that moment she saw underneath the table the horribly mutilated body of Maître Bourjus. Beside him, the boy Linot, his belly torn open, his face as white as snow and as peaceful as an angel's, seemed asleep. The blood of the two victims mingled with the trickles of wine that flowed among the broken bottles.

The horror of this spectacle paralysed her for a second. Like a tamer of wild beasts who, panic-stricken, looks away for a moment, she lost control of the savage pack.

"A woman! A woman!"

"That's what we need!"

A brutal hand came down on Angélique's neck. She caught a violent blow on her temple. Everything went black. She was choked with nausea. She no longer knew where she was.

A woman's voice somewhere screamed shrilly and ceaselessly . . .

She realised that it was she who was screaming.

She was lying on the table, and the black masks were bending over her with wild gasps of laughter. Her wrists and ankles were held down by iron fists. Her petticoats were brutally lifted.

"Who's turn? Who'll have a go at the wench?"

She screamed, as one screams in a nightmare, in a paroxysm of terror and despair.

A body flattened upon her. A mouth stuck to her mouth.

Then so deep a silence fell that Angélique thought she had really lost consciousness. Such, however, was not the case. Her tormentors had stopped their noisy revelry and stood as if frozen. Their befuddled and terrified gaze followed something at floor level that Angélique could not see.

The man who a moment ago had climbed on the table and was about to rape the young woman had hurriedly slipped down. Feeling that her arms and legs were free again, Angélique sat up and quickly pulled down her long skirts. She was bewildered. It was as if a magician's wand had suddenly petrified the frenzied madmen.

Slowly she let herself slide to the floor. Only then did she see the dog Sorbonne, who had knocked over the little man in the lavender singlet and was gripping his throat firmly between his fangs. The dog had come in by the kitchen door and his attack had been swift as lightning.

One of the profligates stammered:

"Call your dog back. . . . Where . . . where's the pistol?"

"Don't move," commanded Angélique. "If you make but one move, I'll order the dog to throttle the King's brother!"

Her legs trembled under her like those of a broken-down horse, but her voice was clear.

"Don't move, gentlemen," she repeated, "or you will *all* bear the responsibility for his death before the King."

Then she very calmly took a few steps. She looked at Sorbonne. He was holding his victim as Desgrez had taught him. At a single word, the iron jaws would crush this panting flesh completely, make the bones crack. Indistinct gurgles escaped from Monsieur d'Orléans's throat. His choking face was violet.

"*Warte*," Angélique said softly.

Sorbonne lightly wagged his tail to show that he had understood and was waiting for orders. Around them, the perpetrators of the orgy remained motionless. They were all too drunk to grasp what was happening. They only saw that Monsieur, the King's brother, was on the verge of being throttled, and that was enough to scare them.

Angélique, without taking her eyes off them, opened one of the drawers of the table, took a knife and went up to the man in the red rhinegrave, who was standing nearest to her.

Seeing her raise her knife, he shrank back.

"Don't move!" she said in a tone that brooked no reply. "I don't intend to kill you. I only want to know what a murderer in laces looks like."

And with a swift gesture she cut the string that held up the mask of the Chevalier de Lorraine. When she had gazed into the handsome face, ravaged by debauches, which she knew

217

only too well for having seen it loom over her in the Louvre on a night she would never forget, she went towards the others.

Dazed and in the last stages of inebriation, they let her do her will and she recognised them all, every one of them: Brienne, the Marquis d'Olonne, the good-looking de Guiche, his brother Louvignys and that other who, when she uncovered his face, tried to murmur with a mocking grimace:

"Black mask against red mask."

It was Péguilin de Lauzun. She also recognised Saint-Thierry, Frontenac. An elegant nobleman, sprawled on the ground amidst puddles of wine and vomit, was snoring. Angélique's mouth filled with hatred and bitterness as she identified the features of the Marquis de Vardes.

Ah! the King's fine young men! She had formerly admired their glittering plumage, but the hostess of 'The Red Mask' was now entitled to see the image of their rotten souls!

Three among them were unfamiliar to her. One of these, however, conjured up a memory, but it was so vague that she could not define it. He was a tall, lanky boy, wearing a magnificent, golden-blond wig. Not as drunk as the others, he was leaning against one of the pillars of the room and pretending to file his fingernails. When Angélique approached, he did not wait for her to cut the strings of his mask but pushed it up himself, with a graceful, casual gesture. His very pale blue eyes had an icy, scornful expression. She was troubled by it. The nervous tension which had kept her going was at its breaking-point; a great fatigue gripped her. Sweat ran from her brow, for the heat in the room had become unbearable.

She went back to the dog and took him by the collar to make him release his prey. She had hoped that Desgrez would appear, but she remained alone and abandoned among these dangerous ghosts. The only presence that seemed real to her was Sorbonne's.

"Get up, gentlemen," she said in a tired voice. "And now go away, all of you. You have done enough harm."

Tottering and, holding their masks in one hand and dragging with the other the slumped bodies of the Marquis de Vardes and the King's brother, the courtiers departed. In the street they had to defend themselves with their swords against the scullions, who, armed with their skewers, pursued them with angry, outraged shouts.

Sorbonne sniffed the blood and growled, baring his black jowls. Angélique pulled the little cake-seller's light body towards her and caressed his pure, icy brow.

"Linot! Linot! My sweet little boy . . . poor little seed of wretchedness . . ."

A clamour from outside tore her out of her despair.

"Fire! Fire!"

The chimney-flue had caught fire and it had spread to the lofts of the house. The splinters were beginning to fall in the hearth, and a thick smoke filled the room.

Angélique rushed out, carrying Linot in her arms. The street was bright as in broad daylight. Customers and landlords pointed with horror at the sheaf of flames that wreathed the roof of the old house. A shower of sparks rained on the neighbouring roofs.

People ran towards the Seine, close by, to form a chain of pails and tubs. But the fire had started at the top. The water had to be carried up the stairs of the neighbouring houses, for the staircase of 'The Red Mask' was crumbling.

Angélique, followed by David, tried to go back into the inn to pull out Maître Bourjus's body. But they had to retreat, choked by the smoke. They then dashed into the kitchen through the courtyard and carried out at random all that they could lay their hands on.

Meanwhile, the Capuchins had arrived. The crowd acclaimed them. The people loved these monks, whose rules included the obligation to help the victims of fires and who had eventually come to constitute the only fire-brigade of the city. They brought with them ladders and iron hooks as well as long, leaden pumps that could send mighty sprays of water a great distance.

As soon as they had reached the site of the fire, they rolled up the sleeves of their cassocks and, without heeding the flaming splinters that fell upon their skulls, they dashed into the adjacent houses. They emerged on the roofs and started to break up everything around them with their big hooks. Thanks to their vigorous measures, the blazing house was isolated, and as no wind was blowing the fire did not spread to the rest of the district. There had been fear of one of those terrible disasters that befell Paris two or three times in a century, owing to its serried mass of old wooden houses.

A great breach, heaped with rubble and cinders, now gaped

on the spot where only yesterday had stood the gay tavern of 'The Red Mask'. But the fire had been put out.

Angélique, with blackened cheeks, gazed at the ruin of her hopes. By her side was the dog Sorbonne.

'Where is Desgrez? Oh, I'd like to see Desgrez,' she thought. 'He'll tell me what to do.'

She took the mastiff by his collar.

"Take me to your master."

She did not have far to go. A few yards away, in the darkness of a porch she perceived the policeman's hat and big coat. He was calmly shredding some tobacco.

"Good evening," he said in an equable voice. "Bad night, isn't it?"

"You were here, only a couple of steps away!" exclaimed Angélique, gasping. "And you didn't come!"

"Why should I?"

"Didn't you hear me shout?"

"I didn't know it was you, Madame."

"Never mind! It was a woman shouting."

"I can't dash to the rescue of all women who shout," declared Desgrez, good-humouredly. "Still, believe me, Madame, had I known it was you, I would have come."

She grumbled resentfully:

"I doubt it!"

Desgrez sighed.

"Haven't I risked my life and my career for you before? I might well have risked them a second time. Alas, Madame, you are a deplorable habit in my life, and I am much afraid that, despite my innate prudence, it'll some day be the death of me."

"They held me on a table—they tried to rape me."

Desgrez looked down upon her sarcastically.

"Is that all? They might have done worse."

Angélique passed her hand over her brow in bewilderment.

"That's true! I felt a kind of relief when I saw that that was all they wanted. And then Sorbonne arrived . . . just in time!"

"I've always had great confidence in this dog."

"*You* sent him?"

"Obviously."

The young woman gave a deep sigh and, with a spontaneous impulse of weakness and apology, she leaned her cheek against the young man's rugged shoulder.

"Thank you."

"You see," Desgrez went on in the calm tone of voice that both exasperated and soothed her, "I'm only *apparently* a member of the State police. In fact, I am above all the King's policemen. It's not my task to interfere with the delightful sport of our noble lords. After all, my dear, you've surely seen enough no longer to be ignorant of the kind of world you belong to? Who wouldn't follow the fashion? Drunkenness is a joke, debauchery pushed to the point of lewdness a sweet failing, orgies pushed to the point of crime a pleasant pastime. Red heels and Court bows in the daytime; love, gambling-dens and taverns at night. Doesn't that make for a well-filled life? You are mistaken, my poor dear, if you imagine these people are to be feared. In actual fact, their little amusements present no danger! The only enemy, the worst foe of the kingdom, is the man who with a single word can corrode their might: the pamphleteer, the journalist, the lampooner. Personally, I am after lampooners."

"Well! You can start hunting," said Angélique, straightening up, with clenched teeth, "for I promise you plenty of work."

A sudden idea had flashed across her mind.

She moved away and began to walk. Then she turned back.

"There were thirteen of them. Among them three whose names I do not know. You must get them for me."

The policeman lifted his hat and bowed.

"At your service, Madame," he said, finding again the tone of voice and the smile of the lawyer Desgrez.

CHAPTER 71

As AT their first meeting, she discovered Claude Le Petit asleep in a hay-barge over by the Arsenal. She woke him up and told him the events of the night. All her hopes had been annihilated. The libertines in lace and ribbons had once again devastated her life as thoroughly as any army of plunderers devastates the country it passes through.

"You must avenge me," she kept saying, with fever-bright

eyes. "You alone can do it. You alone, because you are their greatest enemy. Desgrez said so."

The poet yawned with a loud snap of his jaws, and rubbed his pale lashes, still dusty with sleep.

"You're a strange woman," he said at last.

He took her by the waist to pull her towards him. She freed herself impatiently.

"Do listen to what I am telling you!"

"You aren't a beggar-wench any more, but a great lady who's giving her orders. All right: I am at your command, Marquise. Anyhow, I've got the idea. With whom do you want me to start? With Brienne? I remember that he courted Mademoiselle de La Vallière, and that he dreamed of having her painted as the Magdalene. Ever since, the King can hardly bear him. Thus we'll cook Brienne's goose for His Majesty's dinner."

He turned his pale, handsome face towards the east, where the sun was rising.

"Yes, it should be quite possible for dinner. Maître Gilbert's press works fast when it's a question of multiplying the echo of my teeth-gnashing against the powers that be. Did I ever tell you that Maître Gilbert's son was sentenced to the galleys long ago for goodness knows what trifling offence? An excellent thing for us, isn't it?"

And pulling an old goose quill from his tunic, the Gutter-Poet began to write.

Day was breaking. All the bells of the churches and convents were gaily ringing the Angelus.

Towards the end of the morning, the King, leaving the chapel where he had gone to hear Mass, passed through the anteroom where petitioners were waiting for him. He noticed that the stone floor was littered with white leaflets which an embarrassed footman was hurriedly picking up as if he had only just seen them. But a little farther on, as he was going down the stairs that led to his apartment, Louis XIV came upon the same disorder and showed his displeasure.

"What does this mean? It's raining the parchments here like autumn leaves on the Cours-la-Reine. Give me that, please."

The Duc de Créqui stepped forward, red as a turkey.

"Your Majesty, this rigmarole is of no interest whatsoever. . . ."

"Ah! I see what it is," said the King, impatiently holding

out his hand. "Some more scurrilous outpourings by the damned Gutter-Poet of the Pont-Neuf, who slips like an eel through the archers' fingers and manages to deposit his filth right in my palace, under my feet. Give it to me, if you please. . . . It's his pen, indeed! When you see the Civil Lieutenant and His Honour the Provost of Paris, you may convey my compliments to them, gentlemen. . . ."

Sitting down to dinner, in front of three partridges stuffed with raisins, a fish casserole, a roast with cucumbers and a dish of whale-tongue fritters, Louis XIV placed on the table before him the grimy piece of paper, on which the printer's ink was still so wet as to stain his fingers. The King was a hearty eater and had long ago learned to dominate his emotions. So his appetite was not troubled by what he read. But when he had finished reading, the silence reigning in the room, where generally the courtiers chatted pleasantly with their master, was as heavy as in a crypt.

The pamphlet was written in crude, scurrilous language, whose words nevertheless stung like darts.

It related the exploits of Monsieur de Brienne, first gentleman to the King, who, not content with trying to snatch 'the nymph with the moonlight hair' from a master to whom he owed everything, not content with causing a permanent scandal by his discord with his wife, had gone to an eating-house in the Rue de la Vallée-de-Misère the night before. There this valiant young man and his companions had first assaulted a young cake-seller, then stabbed him with their swords. They had attacked the landlord, who had died of his wounds, split the head of the latter's nephew, raped the daughter and capped their sport by setting fire to the shop, of which nothing but ashes remained.

"By Saint Denis!" said the King. "If this thing is true, Brienne deserves the gallows. Has someone among you heard of these crimes, gentlemen?"

The courtiers stammered, and alleged that they had little knowledge of the events of the night. The King, perceiving a young page who was helping the officers of the King's table, asked him point-blank:

"And you, my child, who are surely inquisitive and prying, as befits one of your age, tell me a little of what's being said on the Pont-Neuf this morning."

The youngster blushed, but answered without too much embarrassment:

"Sire, they're saying that all that the Gutter-Poet reports is perfectly true and that it happened last night at the tavern of 'The Red Mask'. I myself was returning from a spree with some friends when we saw the flames, and we ran to see the fire. But the Capuchins had already got the better of it. The district is up in arms."

"Did they say that the fire was caused by some noblemen?"

"Yes, but they didn't know the names, because they wore masks."

"What else do you know?"

The King's eyes bored into the page's. The boy, who was already an adept courtier, trembled lest he utter a word that might injure his career. But, obedient to the command of those imperious eyes, he lowered his head and whispered:

"Sire, I saw the body of the little cake-seller. He was dead, and his belly was ripped open. A woman had pulled him out of the fire and was holding him in her arms. I also saw the innkeeper's nephew, with his forehead bandaged."

"And the landlord?"

"They hadn't been able to recover his body from the blaze. People say——"

The page tried to smile with the laudable intention of producing a little light relief, "—people say it was a fine death for a roast meat caterer."

But the King's face remained frozen, and the courtiers quickly put their hands over their lips to hide an expression of unseemly gaiety.

"Have Monsieur de Brienne brought to me," said the King. "And you, my lord," he said, turning to the Duc de Créqui, "convey to Monsieur d'Aubray the following instructions: first, to collect all information and particulars about last night's incident and have the report brought to me at once; secondly, any carrier or seller of these leaflets is to be immediately arrested and taken to the Châtelet. Finally, any passer-by who is caught picking up or reading one of these leaflets will be heavily fined and risks prosecution and imprisonment. I also want the most energetic measures to be taken immediately to apprehend the printer and the man Claude Le Petit."

The Comte de Brienne was found at his home, where he had

been put to bed by his valets and was heavily sleeping off his drunkenness.

"My dear friend," the Marquis de Gesvres, captain of the guard, told him, "you see me obliged to carry out a painful duty. Though nothing definite has been said, I believe I have actually come to arrest you."

And he shoved under the other's nose the poem which he had been reading with relish on the way.

"This is the end of me," declared Brienne in a thick voice. "News travels fast in this kingdom! I haven't yet managed to . . . evacuate all the wine I drank in that damn tavern and I'm already called upon to foot the bill."

"Monsieur," Louis XIV said to him, "for various reasons, a conversation with you is distasteful to me. Let us be brief. Do you, or do you not, admit having taken part last night in the infamous outrages denounced in this leaflet?"

"Sire, I was there, but I did not commit all those turpitudes. The Gutter-Poet himself admits that I am not the one who murdered the little cake-vendor."

"Who did, then?"

The Comte de Brienne remained silent.

"I approve of your not entirely throwing upon others a responsibility which you amply share. That much can be seen from your face. Unhappily for you, Monsieur, you were unfortunate enough to be recognised. You will pay for the others. The people are murmuring . . . and they have reason to. So justice must be done, and done quickly. I want people to be able to say on the Pont-Neuf tonight that Monsieur de Brienne is in the Bastille . . . and that he will be severely punished. Personally, I am delighted at this opportunity to rid myself of a face whose sight I have found increasingly hard to bear. You know why."

Poor Brienne sighed, thinking of the timid kisses he had tried to steal from the tender La Vallière at a time when he was still unaware of his master's inclination for this pretty person.

It meant that he was paying at the same time for an innocent little flirtation and a shameless orgy. There was one more gentleman in Paris to curse the poet's pen. On the way to the Bastille, the carriage conveying Brienne was stopped by a flock of fishwives from the central market. They waved the leaflets and their carving-knives and demanded that the prisoner be handed over to them so that they could submit him to the same treatment that had been meted out to the poor master-cook Bourjus.

Brienne breathed freely only after the heavy prison gates had closed upon him.

But the next morning a new shower of white sheets flooded Paris. The King was flabbergasted to find the epigram underneath the plate of a snack which he was just about to eat before setting out for the Bois de Boulogne to go deer-hunting.

The hunt was called off, and Monsieur d'Olonne, Master of the Royal Hunt, left in the opposite direction from that which he had intended to take. That is to say, instead of going down the Cours-la-Reine, he went up the Cours Saint-Antoine, which led to the Bastille.

The new verse did indeed name him specifically as having held down Maître Bourjus while the latter was being murdered.

> Each day to one his account we'll render,
> And the last day we'll tell by whose shameful hand
> Was murdered a child, sweet and tender,
> A high-sounding name, known all over the land:
> Who killed the little cookie-vendor?

After that came Lauzun's turn. His name was being shouted in the streets as he was riding in his carriage to the King's *petit levée*. Péguilin promptly made the horses turn round and took the road to the Bastille.

"Get my apartment ready," he told the Governor.

"But, your lordship, I have received no orders concerning you."

"You will, have no fear."

"But where is your warrant of arrest?"

"Here," said Péguilin, handing to Monsieur de Vannois the printed sheet of paper which he had just bought for ten *sols* from a scrubby ragamuffin.

Frontenac preferred to flee without waiting his turn. Vardes strongly advised him against this course of action.

"Your flight is tantamount to a confession. It'll denounce you for certain. Whereas by continuing to act as if you were innocent you might perhaps slip through this cascade of denunciations. Look at me: do I look worried? I joke, I laugh. Nobody suspects me, and the King himself has confided to me how much this business upsets him."

"You'll stop laughing when your turn comes."

"I have an idea that it won't come. 'They numbered thirteen,' says the song. And so far only three have been named and it's already being asserted that some of the arrested papersellers have disclosed under torture the master-printer's name. In a few days, the shower of leaves will stop, and everything will return to normal."

"I do not share your optimism as regards the short duration of this painful season," remarked the Marquis de Frontenac, putting up the collar of his travelling-cloak with a shiver. "Personally, I prefer exile to prison. Farewell."

He had reached the German frontier when his name appeared, and passed almost unnoticed. Indeed, only the day before, Vardes had been delivered up to public obloquy, and in such terms that the King had been outraged. The Gutter-Poet had in fact gone so far as to accuse this 'worldly villain' of being the author of the Spanish letter which, two years ago, had found its way into the Queen's apartment for the sole purpose of acquainting her charitably with her husband's infidelities with Mademoiselle de La Vallière. This accusation opened an unhealed wound in the sovereign's heart, for he had never been able to put his finger on the guilty party, and more than once had talked about it with Vardes, asking for his advice. While he was questioning the captain of the Swiss guards and summoning Madame de Soissons, de Vardes's mistress and accomplice; while his sister-in-law, Henriette of England, also implicated in the affair of the Spanish letter, threw herself at his feet, and de Guiche and the Petit Monsieur argued angrily in private with the Chevalier de Lorraine; the list of criminals of the tavern of 'The Red Mask' imperturbably continued to offer a new victim to the crowd every day. Louvignys and Saint-Thierry, who had resigned themselves beforehand and made the necessary arrangements, learned one fine morning that Paris knew the exact number of their mistresses and their amorous peculiarities. Such details spiced the habitual refrain:

> . . . by whose shameful hand
> Was murdered a child, sweet and tender?
> Who killed the little cookie-vendor? . . .

Profiting by the King's discomfiture at the revelations made about Vardes, Louvignys and Saint-Thierry were merely requested to relinquish their posts and withdraw to their country houses.

A wind of excitement blew over Paris.

"Whose turn next? Whose turn next?" song-sheet sellers yelled each morning. The sheets were torn from the vendors' hands. From the street up to the windows, people would shout 'the name' of the day.

In high society, it became a habit to whisper mysteriously, when meeting one another:

"Now, who may well have killed the cookie-vendor? . . ."

And they would giggle covertly.

Then a rumour began to spread, and the laughter faded. At the Louvre an atmosphere of panic and profound embarrassment superseded the amusement of those who, with their conscience at rest, hilariously followed the developments of this head-chopping game. The Queen Mother was repeatedly seen proceeding in person to the royal palace to converse with her younger son. At the approaches to the palace where the Petit Monsieur was staying, groups of hostile, silent bystanders loitered. Nobody as yet spoke, nobody voiced an assertion, but the rumour got around that the King's brother had taken part in the orgy at 'The Red Mask', and that it was *he* who had murdered the little cake-vendor.

Desgrez was the one who told Angélique of the first reactions at Court. On the very morning after the outrage, while Brienne, on his way to the Bastille, was having trouble in getting there, the policeman knocked at the door of the little house in the rue des Francs-Bourgeois, to which Angélique had withdrawn.

She listened with a set face to his report of the King's words and decisions.

"He imagines he'll get off with Brienne," she murmured through clenched teeth. "But look out! It's only starting. The

228

less guilty ones are the first to be dealt with. It'll go higher and higher, till the day when the scandal will break and Linot's blood will splash on the steps of the throne."

She wrung her pale, icy hands with passion.

"I just now brought him to the Churchyard of the Saints-Innocents. All the market-wives left their stalls and followed the poor little creature who had received nothing from life but his beauty and sweetness. And vicious princes had to come and snatch his only possession from him: his life. But for his funeral he had the most beautiful procession."

"Those ladies of the fish-market are at this moment giving a little escort to Monsieur de Brienne."

"Let them hang him, set his carriage on fire, set the royal palace ablaze! Set fire to all the castles on the outskirts: Saint-Germain, Versailles. . . ."

"Fire-brand! Where would you go and dance, then, once you are a great lady again?"

She looked at him fixedly, and shook her head.

"Never, never again shall I be a great lady. I've tried everything, then lost everything again. They are too strong for me. Have you the names I asked you for?"

"Here they are," said Desgrez, pulling a scroll of parchment from his coat. "The result of a strictly personal investigation, and known only to me: Were seen to enter the tavern of 'The Red Mask' on this evening of October 1664: Monsieur d'Orléans, the Chevalier de Lorraine, His Lordship the Duc de Lauzun."

"Oh please! spare me the titles," sighed Angélique.

"I can't help myself," said Desgrez, laughingly. "I am, as you know, a most respectful official of the régime. We were saying: 'de Brienne, de Vardes, du Plessis-Bellière, de Louvignys, de Saint-Thierry, de Frontenac, de Cavois, de Guiche, de La Vallière, d'Olonne, de Tormes.' "

"De La Vallière? The favourite's brother?"

"The very one."

"That's too wonderful," she murmured, her eyes shining with the joy of revenge. "But . . . wait, that makes fourteen. I had counted thirteen."

"To begin with, they were fourteen, for the Marquis de Tormes was with them. He's a man of middle age who likes to take part in youthful sprees. However, when he realised Monsieur's designs on the little boy, he withdrew, saying:

'Goodnight, gentlemen, I have no wish to accompany you along these tortuous paths. I like to go my quiet little way and shall calmly go to bed with the Marquise de Raqueneau.' As everyone knows, that plump lady is his mistress."

"An excellent story to make him pay for his cowardice!"

Desgrez gazed for a moment at Angélique's set face and he smiled thinly.

"Malevolence becomes you well. When I first knew you, you were rather the pathetic type—the type that attracts the hounds."

"And when I first knew *you*, you were the frank, gay, affable type. Whereas now I could hate you at times."

She cast at him the shaft of her green eyes and ground through her teeth:

"Devil's policeman!"

The policeman gave a laugh of amusement.

"Madame, to hear you talk, one might think that you had hobnobbed with guttersnipes."

Angélique shrugged her shoulders, went over to the fireplace and picked up a log with a pair of tongs.

"You are frightened, aren't you?" went on Desgrez, with the drawl of the lower-class Parisian. "You are frightened for your little Gutter-Poet. This time, I might as well warn you, he'll end up on the gibbet."

The young woman avoided giving an answer, though she felt like shouting: 'He'll never end up on the gibbet! You can't catch the poet of the Pont-Neuf. He'll fly away like a lean bird and perch on the towers of Notre Dame.'

She was in a state of excitement that strained her nerves to breaking-point. She stirred the fire, keeping her face lowered over the flames. There was a small burn on her forehead, caused by a flaming cinder from the night before. Why didn't Desgrez go away? And yet she was glad he was there. An old habit, probably.

"What name did you say?" she cried suddenly. "Du Plessis-Bellière? The Marquis?"

"So it's you who insist on titles now! Well, yes, it's indeed the Marquis du Plessis-Bellière, marshal of the King's camp . . . the victor of Norgen, you know."

"Philippe!" murmured Angélique.

How had she failed to recognise him when he had pushed up his mask and dropped on her the same cold blue eyes which formerly he used to lower so scornfully on his cousin in her grey dress? Philippe du Plessis-Bellière! The Château du Plessis rose before her eyes, floating like a white water-lily above the pond. . . .

"How strange, Desgrez! That young man is a relative, a cousin, of mine who used to live a few miles from our castle."

"And now that the little cousin goes to play with you in taverns, you are going to spare him?"

"Perhaps. There were thirteen of them, after all. With the Marquis de Tormes, the score's complete."

"Aren't you somewhat imprudent, my dear, to tell all your secrets to a devil's policeman?"

"What I'm telling you won't help you to discover the Gutter-Poet's printer, nor how the leaflets get into the Louvre. And, anyway, you won't give *me* away!"

"No, Madame, I won't give *you* away, but I won't deceive you either. This time the Gutter-Poet will swing!"

"That we'll see!"

"Alas, Madame, I'm afraid that we shall indeed," he retorted. "Goodbye, Madame." .

After he had left, it took her some time to calm her spasmodic shivering. The autumn wind whistled through the rue des Francs-Bourgeois. The storm swept Angélique's heart along with it. She had never felt such a raging inner turmoil. Anguish, fear, pain, were familiar to her. But this time she sank into a sharp, tearless desperation which refused to be soothed or comforted.

CHAPTER 72

The Marquis de la Vallière, realising that his turn would come, decided to confess to his sister, at the Hôtel Biron, where Louis XIV had settled his favourite. Though frightened and appalled, Louise de La Vallière advised her young brother to make a clean breast of it to the King.

This he did.

"It would pain me, if I chastised you too harshly, and brought tears to a pair of lovely eyes that are dear to me," said His

Majesty. "Leave Paris, Monsieur, and join your regiment in Roussillon. We shall suppress the scandal."

This, however, did not prove a simple matter. The scandal did not care to be suppressed. Despite arrests, imprisonments and tortures, each day, with the regularity of a natural phenomenon, a new name would appear. Soon now would come the turn of the Marquis de La Vallière, of the Chevalier de Lorraine, of the King's brother! All the printing-houses were searched and watched. Most of the paper-sellers on the Pont-Neuf were locked up in the dungeons of the Châtelet.

But the pamphlets still found their way right into the Queen's bedroom!

A watch was kept on the comings and goings at the Louvre, the entrances were guarded like those of a fortress. Any person entering in the early morning hours—water-carriers, milkmaids, footmen—were searched bodily. The windows and passages had sentinels posted before them. It was impossible for any man to leave the Louvre or enter it unnoticed.

'Any man, yes, but perhaps half a man?' Desgrez wondered, strongly suspecting the Queen's dwarf, Barcarole, of being Angélique's accomplice.

The beggars at the street-corners were her accomplices, who would hide a bundle of sheets under their rags and strew them on the steps of churches and convents; as were the armed ruffians who, at night, after stripping a belated citizen of his valuables, would give him 'in exchange' some leaflets to read 'as a consolation'; as were the flower-women and orange-sellers of the Pont-Neuf; or Big Matthieu, who, under the pretext of offering prescriptions free of charge to the honoured customers, distributed the latest versifications of the Gutter-Poet.

And, last but not least, there was the new Great Coesre himself, Wood-Bottom, into whose hide-out, on a moonless night, Angélique had dispatched three cases filled with pamphlets which revealed the names of the last five guilty persons. A police raid in the stinking lairs of the Faubourg Saint-Denis was most unlikely. It did not seem an opportune moment to besiege a district whose surrender could not be obtained without a pitched battle.

Vigilant though they were, archers, constables and sergeants could not be everywhere. The night still reigned supreme, and the Marquise of the Angels, helped by her 'men', was able to transfer the cases, without a hitch, from the university district to Wood-Bottom's stronghold.

Two hours later, the police came to arrest the printer and his employees. A paper-seller, jailed in the Châtelet, was made to swallow five kettles of cold water by the hangman's hand, and revealed the master-printer's name. At the printer's they found evidence of his guilt, but no trace of future denunciations. Some people nursed the hope that no fresh sheets had yet been printed, but in the morning Paris learned of the cowardice of the Marquis de Tormes, who, instead of defending the little cake-seller, had left his boon companions, saying:

"Goodbye, gentlemen. I'm off to bed with the Marquise de Raqueneau, according to my little habit."

The Marquis de Raqueneau was perfectly aware of his conjugal misfortune. But hearing it shouted from the roof-tops, he found himself obliged to go and challenge his rival. The duel was fought and the husband was killed. Monsieur de Tormes was putting his cloak on, when the Marquis de Gesvres appeared and showed him the warrant for his arrest. The Marquis de Tormes, who had not yet seen the incriminating pamphlet, thought he was being taken to the Bastille because he had fought a duel.

"Only four more! Only four more!" the street-urchins chanted as they formed a dancing chain.

"Only four more! Only four more!" the mob yelled under windows of the royal palace.

The guards dispersed the booing, jeering crowd with whips.

Harried and hunted from hiding-place to hiding-place, Claude Le Petit eventually took refuge with Angélique. He was paler than ever, though a beard blackened his face.

"This time, my sweet, there's a smell of burning in the air," he said with a contorted smile. "I've got a feeling I won't be able to slip through the meshes of their net."

"Don't talk like that! You yourself told me a hundred times that you'll never be hanged."

"That's the way one talks as long as nothing has yet impaired one's strength. And then, suddenly, there is a crack, your strength is slipping and you see clearly."

He had been injured in escaping through a window. He had had to break the panes and twist the leaden frames. She made him lie down on the bed, bandaged him, fed him. He followed her movements attentively, and she was perturbed not to see the usual mocking glint in his eyes.

"*You* are the crack," he said abruptly. "I should never have met you . . . nor loved you. Ever since you woke me up in that hay-boat I knew that you'd made a valet of me."

"Claude," she said, wounded, "why do you try to pick a quarrel with me? I . . . I felt that you were very close to me, that you'd do anything for me. But if you like, I'll become more ceremonious."

She sat down on the edge of the bed and took his hand, and cupped her cheek in it tenderly.

"My poet . . ."

He pulled his hand away and closed his eyes.

"Ah!" he sighed, "that's what's so bad for me. Near you, I start to dream of a life in which you'd be there all the time. I begin to reason like any fool of a worthy citizen. I say to myself: 'I would like to come home every night to a warm, bright house, where she'd be waiting for me! I'd like to find her in my bed every night, warm and plump and yielding to my desire. I would like to have a respectable pot-belly, stand on my doorstep at dusk and say "my wife" when talking of her to the neighbours.' That's what knowing you does to a fellow. And I begin to notice that the tables in the taverns are hard pillows to sleep on, that it's chilly between the legs of a bronze horse, and that I am alone in the world, like a masterless mongrel."

"You talk like Calembredaine," said Angélique, dreamily.

"You cracked him, too, for, at bottom, you are only an illusion, fugitive as a butterfly, ideal, transparent, intangible. . . ."

"You're going to leave Paris," she decided. "Your task is finished, since the last pamphlets are written, printed and safely stored."

"Leave Paris? I? But where would I go?"

"To your old nurse, that woman you told me of, who brought you up in the Jura mountains. It will soon be winter, the roads will be snowbound and nobody will look for you there. You will leave my house, which isn't safe, and hide at Wood-Bottom's. At midnight, this very night, you'll make for the Gate of Montmartre, which is always very poorly guarded.

234

You'll find a horse there, and in the saddle-bag you'll find money and a pistol."

"All right, Marquise," he said, yawning.

He got up to go.

His submissiveness alarmed Angélique more than any rash recklessness would have. Was it tiredness, fear, or the effect of his injury? He seemed like a sleepwalker. Before leaving, he gave her a long, unsmiling look.

"Now," he said, "you are very strong, and you can leave us by the roadside."

She did not understand what he meant. Words no longer penetrated her mind, and her body ached as if it had been beaten. She did not wait to see the slight, black figure of the Gutter-Poet walk away in the fine drizzle.

In the afternoon she went to the cattle market at the Fair of Saint-Germain, bought a horse which cost her part of her savings, then went to the rue du Val-d'Amour to 'borrow' a pistol from Pretty Boy.

It was arranged that towards midnight Pretty Boy, Peony and a few others would take the horse to the Gate of Montmartre. Claude Le Petit would meet them there, with some of Wood-Bottom's trusted men. This small escort of armed men would accompany him through the suburbs till he reached the countryside.

Once her plan was mapped out, Angélique found some calm again. In the evening she went up to the nursery, then to the garret where she was lodging David. The youngster was running a high temperature, for his wound had begun to fester for lack of proper care.

Later, back in her room, Angélique began to count the hours. The children and servants were asleep; Piccolo the monkey had settled down on the hearth-stone. With her elbows propped on her knees, Angélique gazed into the fire. In two hours, in one hour, Claude Le Petit would be out of danger. She would breathe more easily, and then she would go to bed and try to sleep. Since the fire in the tavern of 'The Red Mask' it seemed to her that she had forgotten what it was like to sleep.

The steps of a horse resounded on the cobblestones, then stopped. There was a knock at the door. With beating heart, she pushed the small shutter aside.

"It's me, Desgrez."

"Do you come as a friend or as a policeman?"

"Open the door. I'll tell you afterwards."

She pulled back the bolts, thinking that a policeman's visit was most unpleasant, but at heart she was glad to see Desgrez rather than to stay alone and feel every minute of her watch fall like a drop of molten lead on her heart.

"Where is Sorbonne?" she asked.

"He isn't with me tonight."

She noticed that under his wet cloak he wore a red cloth singlet trimmed with black ribbons and adorned with a neckband and lace cuffs. With his sword and his spurred boots, he looked very much like a minor provincial nobleman, proud to find himself in the capital.

"I have just left the theatre," he said gaily. "Quite a delicate mission with a beautiful lady. . . ."

"You're no longer tracking down gutter-pamphleteers?"

"It was realised, perhaps, that on this occasion I wouldn't quite give my all. . . ."

"You've refused to have anything more to do with it?"

"Not exactly. I am given every freedom, you know. They know I have methods of my own."

He stood before the fire, rubbing his hands to warm them. He had put his black gauntlets and his hat on a stool.

"Why didn't you become a soldier in the King's army?" asked Angélique, admiring the dashing figure cut by the formerly shabby lawyer. "You'd be considered a handsome man, and you're far from dull. . . . Don't move—I'll get you a jug of white wine and some scones."

"No, thanks! Despite your gracious hospitality, I think I'd better withdraw. I still have an errand over at the Gate of Montmartre."

Angélique started violently and cast a glance at her watch: half past eleven. If Desgrez were to ride to the Gate of Montmartre now, there was every likelihood that he might run into the Gutter-Poet and his accomplices. Was it a coincidence that he wanted to go to the Gate of Montmartre, or had this devil of a man had wind of something? No, that was impossible! She made a sudden decision.

Desgrez was putting his coat on.

"Already!" Angélique protested. "What extraordinary manners you have! You arrive at an impossible hour, pull me out of bed and you slip away as soon as you come."

236

"I didn't pull you out of bed. You weren't even undressed. You were day-dreaming before the fire."

"Exactly . . . I was bored. Come on, sit down."

"No," he said, tying the cord of his collar. "The more I think, the more it seems to me that I'd better hurry."

"Oh, these men!" she protested, with a pout. She racked her brains to find a pretext for retaining him.

It was not so much for the poet as for Desgrez himself that she feared the encounter which would inevitably result if she let him go to the Gate of Montmartre. The policeman had a pistol and a sword, but the others were armed too, and they were numerous. Moreover, Sorbonne was not with his master. In any case, there was no point in Claude Le Petit's escape being accompanied by a scuffle in which a police-captain of the Châtelet stood a good chance of being killed. She simply had to prevent it.

But Desgrez was already leaving the room.

'Oh, this is too silly!' thought Angélique. "If I'm not able to hold a man up for a quarter of an hour, I wonder what God's made me for!'

She followed him into the anteroom and, as he reached for the doorknob, she put her hand on his. The tenderness of the gesture seemed to surprise him. He hesitated slightly.

"Goodnight, Madame," he said with a smile.

"It won't be a good night for me, if you go," she murmured. "The night is too long . . . when one is alone."

And she leaned her cheek against his shoulder.

'I am behaving like a courtesan,' she thought, 'but never mind! A few kisses will gain me time. And even if he demands more, why not? We are old acquaintances after all.'

"We've known each other for such a long time, Desgrez," she said aloud. "Has it never occurred to you that between us . . ."

"It's not like you to fling yourself at a man's head," said Desgrez, baffled. "What's the matter with you tonight, my dear?"

But his hand had left the doorknob and he took her by the shoulder. Very slowly, as if reluctantly, his other arm came up and surrounded the young woman's waist. However, he did not press her towards him. He was holding her rather like a dainty, fragile object that one does not know what to do with. Still, she sensed that the policeman Desgrez's heart was beating a little faster. Wouldn't it be fun to ruffle this indifferent, invariably self-controlled man?

"No," he said at last. "No, I have never thought that we might go to bed together. For me, you see, love is something very ordinary. In this, as in many other things, I'm unfamiliar with luxury, and it doesn't tempt me. Cold, hunger, poverty and my masters' canings were not apt to give me a fastidious taste. I am a man of the tavern and the brothel. What I ask of a girl is to be a good, sound animal, a comfortable piece of goods that one can do with as one likes. To speak quite frankly, my dear, you're not my type."

She listened with a certain amusement, her head in the crook of his shoulder. On her back she felt the warmth of Desgrez's two hands. He did not scorn her quite as much as he liked to pretend. A woman like Angélique made no mistake about it. There were too many bonds between her and Desgrez. She gave a stifled little laugh.

"You talk as if I were a luxury article . . . not comfortable, as you say. No doubt you are admiring the sumptuousness of my dress, of my home?"

"Oh! the dress has nothing to do with it. You'll always keep that consciousness of your superiority which shone through in your eyes on that distant day when a certain shabby commoner of a lawyer was introduced to you."

"Many things have come to pass since then, Desgrez."

"Many things will never pass, and among them the arrogance of a woman whose ancestors were with Good King Jean II at the Battle of Poitiers in 1356."

"You always know everything about everybody, policeman that you are!"

"Yes . . . just like your friend, the Gutter-Poet."

He took her by her shoulders and, gently but firmly, held her away from him to look into her face.

"Well? . . . So it's true that he was to be at the Gate of Montmartre at midnight?"

She trembled, then thought that by now the danger was over. Far away, a clock was chiming the last strokes of midnight. Desgrez caught the flash of triumph in her eyes.

"Yes . . . yes, it's too late," he murmured, nodding his head dreamily. "So many people had planned to meet tonight at the Gate of Montmartre! Among others, the Civil Lieutenant himself, and twenty archers of the Châtelet. Perhaps, if I had

238

arrived a little sooner. I could have advised them to go and wait for their game elsewhere. . . . Or else I might have given a sign to the imprudent game to make for the open country by some other route. . . . But now, I believe. . . . yes, I do believe it is too late. . . ."

Flipot went out early in the morning to fetch fresh milk for the children from the market of the Pierre-au-lait. Angélique had only just sunk into a brief, fitful slumber, when she heard him racing back. Forgetting to knock at the door, he stuck his tousled head through the opening. His eyes were popping out of their sockets.

"Marquise of the Angels," he gasped, "I've just seen . . . the Gutter-Poet . . . in the Place de Grève."

"In the Place de Grève? . . ." she repeated. "But he must be completely mad! What's he doing there?"

"He's sticking his tongue out," answered Flipot. "They've hanged him!"

CHAPTER 73

"I HAVE promised Monsieur d'Aubray, the Civil Lieutenant of Paris, who in turn has given a similar pledge to the King, that the last three names of the list will not be disclosed to the public. This morning, despite the hanging of the author of these pamphlets, the name of the Comte de Guiche has been flung to the public for Parisians to feast on. His Majesty has fully realised that the condemnation of the principal offender would not stop the hand of imminent justice from descending upon Monsieur, that is to say, his own brother. On my part, I gave His Majesty to understand that I knew the accomplice or accomplices who, despite the pamphleteer's death, were determined to continue his work. And, I repeat, I promised that the last three names would not appear."

"They shall appear!"

"No!"

Angélique and Desgrez once more faced each other, on the very spot where Angélique had put her head on the policeman's shoulder the night before. The eyes of the two antagonists were like crossed swords.

The house was empty. Only David, wounded and feverish, was upstairs in the loft. There was hardly any noise from the street. The ripples of the popular outcry did not penetrate into this aristocratic district.

"I know where the bundles of leaflets are hidden which you still propose to distribute," said Desgrez. "I can ask for the army's co-operation, attack the Faubourg Saint-Denis and have all the rogues cut to pieces who'd try to oppose the police in their search of the Great Coesre's house. There is a simpler way, however, of settling the matter. Listen to me, little fool, instead of glowering at me like a furious kitten—Claude Le Petit is dead. It had to be. His impudence had gone on for too long and the King will never permit the rabble to judge him."

"The King! The King! Your mouth is full of him. You used to have more pride in the old days!"

"Pride is a sin of youth, Madame. Before indulging in pride, one must know whom one's up against. I have clashed with the King's will and it almost broke me. The demonstration is conclusive: the King is the stronger. So I am on the side of the King. In my opinion, Madame, you, who have two children to look after, would be well-advised to follow my example."

"Silence, you disgust me!"

"Haven't I heard something about letters patent that you are anxious to obtain for manufacturing an exotic drink—or something of the kind . . .? And don't you think that a large sum of money, say 50,000 *livres*, would come in handy to promote some kind of business? Or else some privilege might help, an exemption of dues or I don't know what? A woman like you is surely not short of ideas. The King is prepared to grant whatever you ask in exchange for your definite and immediate silence. Now this is a good way of putting an end to this drama to everyone's benefit. The Civil Lieutenant will receive congratulations, I'll be promoted to a new post, His Majesty will heave a sigh of relief, and you, my dear, having got your boat afloat again, will continue to forge ahead towards the most exalted destiny. Come on, don't tremble like a filly under the trainer's whip. Think it over. I'll come back for your answer in two hours. . . ."

Paris felt the spirit of insurrection welling up again. The city remembered that the Gutter-Poet had been the first, back in 1650, to hurl the arrows of the *mazarinades*. As long as he

240

was alive, as long as one could be sure that his stinging tongue would trumpet abroad the latest grievances, one could let the old ones sleep. But now that he was dead, the people were gripped by panic. They had the impression of being suddenly gagged. Everything rose again to the surface: the famines of 1656, of 1658, of 1662, the new taxes. What a pity the Italian was dead! They would have burned his palace . . .!

Chains of dancers formed along the quays, shouting:
"Who stabbed the little cake-vendor?"

While others were beating out the rhythm:
"Tomorrow . . . we'll know! Tomorrow . . . we'll know!"

But the next day the city did not have its daily flowering of white leaflets. Nor on the following days. Silence fell again. The nightmare faded. People would never know who had killed the little cake-vendor. Paris realised that the Gutter-Poet was truly dead.

He had, in fact, told Angélique so himself.
"Now you are very strong and you can leave us by the road-side."

During the long nights in which she did not find a moment's rest, she would see him before her, looking at her with eyes as pale and brilliant as the waters of the Seine when the sun shines upon them.

She had not been able to bring herself to the Place de Grève. It was quite enough that Barbe had taken the children there, as if to a sermon, without afterwards sparing her the slightest detail of the sinister picture: the Gutter-Poet's fair hair fluttering over his bloated face, his bagging black stockings over his spindly calves, his ink-horn and goose quill which the hangman had, superstitiously, left at his belt.

When, on the third day, she got up after a sleepless night, she said to herself:
'I cannot bear this life any longer.'

On the evening of that day she was to call on Desgrez, at his home in the rue du Pont Notre-Dame. From there he was to take her to some important persons with whom a secret agreement was to be drawn up that would put an end to this strange affair.

Angélique's proposals had been accepted. In exchange, she would hand to whom it might concern the three cases of printed but undistributed pamphlets, with which the gentlemen of the police would no doubt make a big bonfire.

And life would start all over again. Angélique would once more have a lot of money. She would also enjoy the sole privilege of manufacturing and marketing throughout the kingdom the drink called chocolate.

'I cannot bear this life any longer,' she repeated to herself.

She lighted her candle, for it was not yet dawn. The mirror on her dressing-table cast back at her the reflection of a wan, drawn face.

'Green eyes,' she said to herself. 'A colour that brings bad luck. Yes, it's true, I bring bad luck to those I love . . . or who love me.'

Claude the poet? . . . Hanged. Nicholas? . . . Disappeared. Joffrey? . . . Burned alive.

Slowly she passed her two hands over her brows. Inwardly she was trembling so violently that she could hardly breathe. And yet the palms of her hands were icy.

'What am I doing here, fighting against all these strong and powerful men? That isn't my place. A woman's place is in her home, beside a husband she loves, near the warmth of a hearth, in the tranquillity of a house, with a child sleeping in a wooden cot. Do you remember, Joffrey, the little château where Florimond was born? . . . The mountain-storm rattled against the window-panes and I sat on your knees; I leaned my cheek against yours. And I looked with a little fear and a wonderful confidence at your curious face, on which the fire-light was playing. . . . How gaily you could laugh, showing your white teeth! Or else I'd lie down in our big bed and you would sing for me, with that deep, velvety voice which seemed to reverberate from the mountains. Then I'd fall asleep and you would lie down beside me in the cool, embroidered sheets, scented with iris. I had given you much. And you, you had given me everything. . . . And I would tell myself, in my dreams, that we would be happy for ever. . . .'

She stumbled through the room, fell on her knees by the bed, buried her face in the crumpled sheets.

'Joffrey, my love! . . .'

The cry, stifled for so long, burst forth.

'Joffrey, my love, come back, don't leave me alone. . . . Come back.'

But he would never come back, she knew. He had gone too far away. Where could she go and find him? She had not even a grave to pray on. . . . The ashes of Joffrey had been scattered by the winds of the Seine.

Angélique rose, her face tear-stained.

She sat down at the table, took a white sheet of paper and sharpened her pen.

"When you read this letter, gentlemen, I shall have ceased to live. I know that to put an end to one's own life is a great crime, but for this crime God, who sees into the depths of our souls, will be my only refuge. I throw myself upon His mercy. I entrust the fate of my sons to the justice and graciousness of the King. In exchange for a silence on which the honour of the royal family depended and which I respected, I entreat His Majesty to take fatherly care of these two little lives, which started out under the sign of the greatest misfortune. If the King does not give them back the name and inheritance of their father, the Comte de Peyrac, may he at least offer them the means of subsistence in their childhood and, later, the education and funds necessary for their establishment. . . ."

She went on writing, adding certain particulars concerning the life of her children, asking also for protection of the young, orphaned David Chaillou. She then wrote a letter for Barbe, begging her never to leave Florimond and Cantor, and bequeathing to her the few things she owned, clothes and jewels. She slipped the second letter into an envelope and sealed it.

After that she felt better. She washed herself and dressed, then spent the morning in the nursery. The sight of the children did her good. But she was not troubled by the thought that she would leave them for ever. They did not need her any more. They had Barbe, whom they knew and who would take them to Monteloup. They would grow up in the sunshine and the fresh country air, far from the filth and stench of Paris.

Even Florimond had lost his dependence on his mother. She would return, late at night, to a home which they had turned into their own little kingdom, with the two maids, the dog Patou, their toys and their birds. Since it was Angélique who brought toys home, they would rush up to her when they saw her and, tyrannically, grumblingly, would always clamour for something new. That day, Florimond pulled at his little red dress and said:

"Maman, when will I have trunk-hose, like a boy? I am a man now, you know!"

"Darling, you already have a big felt hat with a beautiful

pink plume. Many little boys of your age are quite content with a hood like Cantor's."

"I want trunk-hose!" shouted Florimond, flinging his trumpet on the floor.

Angélique slipped away, fearing a fit of temper which would have obliged her to punish him.

After the midday meal, she took advantage of the children's sleep to put on her cloak and leave the house. She took the sealed envelope with her. She would hand it to Desgrez and asked him to take it to the famous secret meeting-place. Then she would leave him and walk along the Seine. She would have a few hours' time before her. She intended to take a rather long walk. She wanted to reach the countryside and carry away, as her last vision, the sight of autumn-yellow meadows and golden trees, breathe for the last time the smell of moss, which would remind her of Monteloup and her childhood. . . .

CHAPTER 74

ANGÉLIQUE waited for Desgrez in his new house. The décor had changed since that first visit which Angélique had paid him, years ago, in one of the tumbledown houses on the Petit-Pont.

He now had a house of his own on the very rich Pont Notre-Dame, which was almost new and displayed the gaudy taste of wealthy bourgeois, its house-fronts adorned with terminals in the forms of gods holding fruit and flowers, its medallions of kings, its statues, all painted in gaudy 'natural' colours.

The room into which Angélique had been shown by the caretaker reflected the same middle-class affluence. But the young woman hardly cast a glance at the vast bed with its canopy supported by twisted columns or at the writing-desk covered with objects in gilt-bronze. She did not ask herself any questions about the circumstances to which the lawyer could owe this modest wealth. Desgrez was both a presence and a memory. She had the impression that he knew everything about her, and this was restful. He was hard and indifferent, but solid as a rock. With her last message in his hands, she could die with her mind at peace: her children would not be abandoned.

The open window overlooked the Seine. The sound of oars could be heard. It was a fine day. The air was warm. A gentle autumn sun shone on the black-and-white stone floor.

At last Angélique heard in the passage the clicking spurs of a resolute stride. She recognised Desgrez's step. He came in, and showed no surprise.

"I greet you, Madame. Sorbonne, my friend, stay outside, with your muddy feet."

Once again, he was dressed, if not elegantly, at least prosperously. A black velvet braid emphasised the collar of the ample coat which he threw over a chair. But she recognised the old Desgrez by the casual way in which he tossed off his hat and his wig. Then he unfastened his sword. He seemed in an excellent mood.

"I've just come back from Monsieur d'Aubray's. Everything is going splendidly. My dear, you are going to meet all the notables of commerce and finance. There is even talk of Monsieur Colbert himself attending the meeting."

Angélique smiled politely. These words seemed futile to her and did not shake her out of her stupor. She would not have the honour of making Monsieur Colbert's acquaintance. At the very hour when these omnipotent persons would foregather, the body of Angélique de Sancé, Comtesse de Peyrac, Marquise of the Angels, would drift upon the current between the golden banks of the Seine. She would be free then; out of reach of all. And perhaps Joffrey would come to meet her. . . .

She gave a start, for Desgrez was still talking.

"What were you saying?"

"I was saying that you were early for the appointment, Madame."

"Actually, that's not what brings me here. I was only passing, for a charming dandy is waiting to take me to the Palace arcades, where I want to have a look at the latest novelties. I might even go on to the Tuileries afterwards. These amusements will help me spend the time till the fateful hour of the meeting. But I have an envelope here that rather encumbers me. Could you keep it for me? I'll collect it on my way back."

"At your service, Madame."

He took the sealed envelope and, going to a small strong-box on a sidetable, he opened it and put the envelope inside.

Angélique turned away to pick up her fan and gloves. It was all quite simple. Just as simply, she would go for her walk, without hurrying. All that was needed, at a given moment, was to swerve a little towards the Seine. . . . The sunshine would make the water gleam like a black-and-white stone floor. . . .

A creaking sound made her lift her head. She saw that Desgrez was turning the key in the door. Then, with a very natural air, he slipped the key into his pocket and came back towards the young woman.

He towered over her. He was smiling, but his eyes had a red glow. Before she could make a gesture of defence, he picked her up in his arms. He murmured, his face over hers:

"Come, my pretty little animal."

"I don't want you to talk to me in this way!" she shouted. And she burst into sobs.

It had come over her all of a sudden. A storm of tears, a cloudburst of sobs, tearing her heart out, choking her.

Desgrez carried her to the bed. For a long while he sat looking at her quietly, with close attention. Then, when the violence of her despair had calmed down a little, he began to undress her. She felt the touch of his fingers on her neck as he unfastened her bodice with the dexterity of a chambermaid. Bathed in tears, she no longer had the strength to resist.

"You are wicked, Desgrez," she sobbed.

"No, my sweet, no, I'm not wicked."

"I thought that you were my friend. . . . I thought that—— Oh! my God! I am so unhappy."

"Tut! Tut! what an idea!" he said in a tone of scolding indulgence.

With a nimble hand, he raised the wide petticoats, unfastened her garters, rolled down her silk stockings, removed her shoes.

When she had nothing left but her shift, he stepped aside and she heard him undressing, whistling, and flinging his boots, his singlet, his belt into the four corners of the room. Then, with a leap, he joined her on the bed and pulled the curtains.

In the warm twilight of the alcove, Desgrez's hairy body seemed red under a black velvety bloom. The man had lost none of his dash.

"Hopla, my girl! What's all this moaning about? No more

246

weeping! We're going to have a good laugh. Come over here!"

He pulled off her shift and at the same time gave her such a resounding wallop on the back that she rounded, raging with humiliation, and dug her sharp little teeth into his shoulder.

"Oh! you bitch!" he cried. "This deserves punishment!"

But she was struggling fiercely. They grappled. She shouted the lowest invectives that she could think of. Polack's entire vocabulary poured forth, and Desgrez laughed like mad. This outburst of laughter, the sparkle of the white teeth, the acrid smell of tobacco which mingled with his virile perspiration, shook Angélique to the marrow. She was sure she hated Desgrez, even wished his death. She shouted that she would kill him with her knife. He laughed even more. At last he managed to crush her under him and sought her lips.

"Kiss me," he said. "Kiss the policeman. . . . Obey, or I'll give you such a thrashing that you'll be sore for three days. . . . Kiss me. Better than that. I am sure you can kiss very well. . . ."

She could no longer resist the imperious commands of that mouth which was biting her pitilessly at every refusal. She yielded.

She yielded so completely that, a few moments later, her desire flung her blindly against the body that had vanquished her. Desgrez's gaiety in love was prodigious, inexhaustible. Angélique caught it like a fever. The young woman told herself that Desgrez was treating her without any respect, that nobody had ever treated her thus, not even Nicholas, not even the captain. But, with her head thrown back against the edge of the bed, she heard herself laughing like a shameless strumpet. She felt very hot now.

At last the man pulled her back to him. For a second, she glimpsed a different face: closed eyelids, a passionate gravity, a face from which all cynicism had faded, all irony had vanished under the urge of a single feeling. The next moment she felt that she was his. And he laughed again, a gluttonous, savage laughter. She hated him for it. Just then she yearned for tenderness. A new lover always roused in her, after the first embrace, a reflex of astonishment and fright, perhaps of revulsion.

Her excitement subsided. A leaden fatigue came over her. She let herself be taken, inertly, but he did not seem to take offence. She had the impression that he was treating her like any streetwalker. She pleaded, tossing her head from side to side.

"Let me alone . . . let me alone!"

But he persisted.

Everything went black. The nervous tension that had sustained her during the last days snapped before a crushing fatigue. She was at the end of her tether. She was emptied of strength, of tears, of passion. . . .

When she awoke, she was sprawled on the devastated bed, her arms and legs flung out like a starfish. in the very position in which slumber had caught her. The bed-curtains were tucked up. A circle of pink sunshine was dancing on the stone floor. She could hear the water of the Seine under the arches of the bridge of Notre Dame. Another sound mingled with it, closer by: a sort of busy, muffled scratching.

She turned her head and saw Desgrez, who was writing at his desk. He was wearing his wig and a starched white neckband. He seemed very calm and absorbed in his work. She gazed at him without understanding Her memories remained indistinct. Her body seemed of lead, but her head felt quite light. She became aware of her unchaste posture and drew her legs together.

At that moment Desgrez raised his head. Seeing that she was awake, he put down his pen on the inkstand and came over to the bed.

"How are you? Did you sleep well?" he asked in a perfectly courteous and natural voice.

She stared at him stupidly. She was not quite certain about him. Where had she seen him terrifying, brutal, lecherous? In her dream, probably.

"Sleep?" she stammered. "Did I sleep? For how long?"

"Well, for three hours now I've had this charming spectacle before my eyes."

"Three hours!" repeated Angélique, pulling up the sheet to cover herself. "But that's terrible! What about the appointment with Monsieur Colbert?"

"You have an hour left to get ready."

He went into the next room.

"I have a comfortable bathroom and all that a lady requires for her toilet: rouge, powder, patches, perfume."

He came back, holding on his arm a silky dressing-gown, which he flung to her.

"Put that on and hurry up, my dear."

A little dazed and with the feeling that she was moving on a cloud of cottonwool, Angélique proceeded to bathe and dress. Her clothes were carefully folded on a trunk. Before the mirror was set out a great array of accessories which were, to say the least, astonishing in this bachelor's wardrobe: jars of white and vermilion paints, black cream for eyelids, a whole range of scent-bottles.

Slowly, Angélique's memory returned. Not without difficulty, for her mind seemed unable to collect her thoughts. She remembered the resounding slap with which the policeman had stunned her. Oh! it was abominable! He had treated her like a slut, without any respect. She was sure now that he knew that she was the Marquise of the Angels. What was he going to do with her now . . .?

She heard the goose quill scratch. Desgrez got up and inquired:

"Can you manage? Can I serve as a lady's-maid?"

Without waiting for her answer, he came in and began skilfully to tie the laces of her petticoat.

Angélique no longer knew what to think.

At the recollection of the caresses he had forced upon her, she felt numbed by shame. But Desgrez's mind seemed to be on other things altogether. She would have thought she had dreamed it, had not the mirror shown her the face of a sensual, sated woman, her eyelids dark from the fatigue of lust and lips swollen from the sting of kisses. What a disgrace! Even for the least knowing eyes, her features bore the mark of the violent love-making into which Desgrez had driven her. Mechanically, she put two fingers over her swollen lips, which continued to smart painfully.

She met Desgrez's eyes in the mirror. He gave a little smile.

"Oh yes! it shows," he said. "But it's of no importance. The grave persons whom you are going to meet will be all the more impressed . . . and perhaps vaguely envious."

Without answering, she smoothed her curls and stuck a patch on her cheek. The policeman had fastened his belt and was picking up his hat. . . . He really did look elegant, although his dress maintained a sombre, somewhat austere note.

"You are mounting the rungs of the social ladder, Monsieur Desgrez," and Angélique, with an effort to imitate his casualness. "Here you are, wearing a sword, and your apartment is that of a prosperous bourgeois."

"I receive a good many visitors. And, you see, their type is changing peculiarly. Is it my fault if the tracks I follow lead to ever higher places? Sorbonne is getting old. When he dies, I won't replace him, for it isn't the slums any more that hide the worst murderers of our times. One has to look for them in other places."

He seemed to ponder, then added, nodding his head:

"In the drawing-room, for instance. . . . Are you ready, Madame?"

Angélique picked up her fan and motioned 'yes'.

"Shall I return your envelope to you?"

"What envelope?"

"The one you entrusted to me when you came here."

The young woman frowned. Then she remembered, and a slight flush rose to her forehead. Was it the envelope which contained her last will and which she had handed to Desgrez with the intention of killing herself afterwards?

Kill herself? What a peculiar idea! Why ever had she wanted to kill herself? This really wasn't the moment for it. When for the first time in years she was at last on the point of seeing the successful end of all her endeavours, when she held the King of France practically at her mercy! . . .

"Yes, yes," she said hurriedly. "Give it back to me."

He opened the strong-box and held the sealed envelope out to her. But he held on to it just as Angélique was about to grasp it, and she looked up at him inquiringly. Desgrez's gaze had its glint again which seemed to penetrate like a shaft of light into the very depths of her soul.

"You wanted to die, didn't you?"

Angélique stared at him like a child caught in the act. Then she dropped her head and nodded.

"And now?"

"Now . . .? I don't know any more. At any rate, I certainly don't intend to forgo turning to account the cravenness of these people when I can use it to my advantage. It's a unique opportunity and I am convinced that, if I manage to start a fad for chocolate, I'll be able to rebuild my fortune."

"Excellent."

He took back the envelope and threw it into the fire. Then he came back towards her, still calm and smiling.

"Desgrez," she whispered, "how did you guess? . . ."

"Oh, my dear!" he exclaimed, laughing. "Do you think I'm fool enough not to find there's something suspicious about a woman who comes to me with a wild look and no powder or rouge on her face and who tells me she has a date to strut along the Palace arcades? . . . Besides——"

He seemed to hesitate.

"I know you too well," he pursued. "I saw straightway that something was up, that it was serious, and needed prompt and vigorous action. In view of my friendly intentions, you will forgive me, won't you, Madame, for having somewhat mal-treated you?"

"I don't know yet," she said, with a rankling grudge. "I shall think it over."

But Desgrez began to laugh, with a warm, friendly look in his eyes. It humiliated her. But at the same time she told herself that she had no better friend in the world. He added:

"One more bit of advice, Madame, if you will allow a modest policeman to make so free: always look ahead. Don't ever turn back towards your past. Avoid stirring up its ashes—those ashes that were scattered to the four winds. For every time you think of it, you will have a longing for death. And I shall not always be there to rouse you in time. . . ."

Masked and, as a further precaution, with blindfolded eyes, Angélique was taken in a carriage with drawn curtains to a small house in the suburb of Vaugirard. The bandage over her eyes was removed only when she found herself in a draw-ing-room lighted by a few torches, in which four or five wigged persons were assembled. Stiff and formal, they seemed rather vexed at seeing her.

Had it not been for Desgrez's presence, Angélique would have feared that she had been lured into an ambush which she would not leave alive, but there was nothing underhand about the intentions of Monsieur Colbert, a bourgeois with a cold, stern face. None more than this commoner, who disapproved of the licentiousness and squandering at Court, could admit the merits of Angélique's petition to the King. The sovereign himself had realised it, somewhat perforce, it is true, under the impact of the Gutter-Poet's scandal-sheets. Angélique was quick to sense that the arguing was merely a matter of form. Her own position was impregnable.

When she left the learned gathering two hours later, she took with her the promise that a gift of 50,000 *livres* would be remitted to her from the King's own coffers for the reconstruction of the tavern of 'The Red Mask'. The letters patent for the manufacture of chocolate, granted to young Chaillou's father, would be confirmed. Angélique would be mentioned by name, and it was specified that she would not come under the jurisdiction of any guild.

All kinds of facilities for obtaining the raw materials were granted to her. Finally, by way of reparation, she asked to become the owner of one share in the newly-founded East India Company. This last request caused some surprise. But these financiers saw that the young woman was very well primed on business affairs. She pointed out that as her business was particularly concerned with exotic commodities, the East India Company would surely welcome a client who had every interest in seeing the Company prosper and enjoy the support of the greatest fortunes of the kingdom.

Monsieur Colbert admitted, with a growl, that the claims of this young person, though obviously considerable, were relevant and well-founded. She got all she asked for. In exchange, Police Lieutenant d'Aubray's minions were to proceed to a hovel in the open country, where they would find a case filled with leaflets which bore in bold letters the names of the Marquis de La Vallière, the Chevalier de Lorraine, and of Monsieur, the King's brother.

In the same carriage with closed shutters that took her back to Paris, Angélique tried to contain her elation. It did not seem proper to be happy, especially when she remembered from what horrors this triumph had emerged. But, after all, if everything proceeded as planned, there was little to stop her from becoming one of the richest women in Paris. She would go to Versailles, she would be presented to the King, she would recapture her rank, and her sons would be brought up as young noblemen.

For the return journey her eyes were not blindfolded, for the night was black. She was alone in the carriage, but, absorbed in her dreams and calculations, the journey seemed short to her. Around her she heard the clattering hooves of the horses of a small escort.

Suddenly the carriage stopped and one of the curtains was raised. In the light of a lantern she saw Desgrez's face leaning through the carriage-window. He was on horseback.

"I leave you here, Madame. The carriage will take you home. In two days I shall see you again to hand you what is your due. Is all well?"

"I think so. Oh! Desgrez, it's wonderful. If I can manage to get this chocolate venture started, I am sure I'll make a fortune."

"You'll manage. Three cheers for chocolate!" said Desgrez. He doffed his hat, bowing, kissed her hand.

"Farewell, Marquise of the Angels!"

She gave him a little smile.

"Farewell, policeman!"

CHAPTER 75

ANGÉLIQUE walked along the banks of the Seine, reviewing the various stages of her journey since that evening when she had been summoned before Monsieur Colbert in great secrecy.

First, there had come the chocolate-house which had very shortly become *the* fashionable meeting-place of Paris. The shop-sign read 'At the Spanish Midget's'. It had received a visit from the Queen, delighted no longer to be the only one in Paris to drink chocolate. Her Majesty had come escorted by her midget-woman and by her dwarf, the dignified Barcarole.

Spurred by her success, Angélique had set up branch establishments in several small towns in the neighbourhood of Paris: at Saint-Germain, Fontainebleau and Versailles, and even in Lyons and Nantes.

She showed particular acumen in the choice of those whom she put in charge of these new enterprises. She granted them great advantages but demanded honest book-keeping and stipulated in the contract that unless the establishment showed continuous progress in the first six months of its existence, the manager would be replaced. Spurred by this threat, the latter would display a feverish activity to convince the provincials that it was their duty to drink chocolate.

All this enabled her to make a great deal of money.

Lost in her calculations, Angélique became aware that she had left the riverside and had taken the rue du Beautreillis. The busy traffic in this street brought her back to reality. Walking on foot among water-carriers and maids on errands was not in keeping with her new status. No longer wearing the short petticoats of women of the people, she looked woefully at the mud-stained hem of her heavy skirts.

A sudden jostling among the crowd crushed her against the wall of a house. She protested violently. The burly citizen who almost squashed her turned round to shout:

"Patience, pretty lady. It's the Prince passing by."

A wide carriage-gate had indeed just opened and a coach-and-six was coming out. Through the window Angélique had just time to glimpse the sullen profile of the Prince de Condé. Some people shouted:

"Long live the Prince!"

Curtly he raised his lace-ruffed sleeve. For the people, he always remained the victor of Rocroi. Unfortunately, the Peace of the Pyrénées had forced him into a retirement which was not at all to his liking.

When he had gone, the traffic resumed. Angélique passed in front of the courtyard of the mansion he had just left. She glanced into it. For some time now, her beautiful apartment in the Place des Vosges had no longer satisfied her. She, too, dreamed of owning a mansion with a carriage-drive, a court in which a coach could turn, a stableyard and kitchens, servants' quarters and, at the back, a beautiful garden with orange-trees and flower-beds.

The residence she now faced was of comparatively recent construction. Its white, simple façade, with very high windows, wrought-iron balconies, its trim slate roof with rounded dormer windows, were in the fashion of only recent years.

The gate closed again slowly. Angélique lingered on. She noticed that the carved coat-of-arms above the gate seemed to have been broken. It wasn't age or the weather that could thus have effaced the princely arms, but only a workman's deliberate chisel.

"Whose mansion is this?" she asked a florist who had a shop not far away.

"Why, the Prince's of course," said the other, preening herself.

"Why did the Prince remove the coat-of-arms above the gate? It seems a pity, the other sculptures are so beautiful!"

"Oh! that's another story," said the good woman, and her face darkened. "They were the arms of the man who built the mansion. An accursed nobleman. He practised witchcraft and summoned the devil. He was sentenced to death at the stake."

Angélique stood motionless. Then she felt her face slowly drain of blood. So that was why, before this light oak gate brightly gleaming in the sunshine, she had had a feeling of having seen it before. . . .

It was here that she had come when she had first arrived in Paris. This was the gate on which she had seen affixed the seals of the King's justice. . . .

"They say he was a very rich man," the woman continued.

"The King shared out his wealth. His Highness the Prince received the greater part of it, and this mansion along with it. Before moving into it, he had the sorcerer's arms scratched out and holy water sprinkled everywhere. You can imagine . . . he wanted to sleep in peace!"

Angélique thanked the flower-woman and walked away.

Angélique had moved into the Place Royale (or Place des Vosges) a few months after the opening of the chocolate-house. Money was already pouring in. In leaving the rue des Francs-Bourgeois for the centre of the aristocratic quarter, the young woman was mounting a rung in the social ladder.

In the Place Royale gentlemen would fight duels, and beautiful ladies would converse on philosophy and astronomy or compose verses.

Far from the all-pervading smell of cocoa, Angélique felt reborn and opened eyes full of cordiality on this exclusive and so very Parisian society.

The square, set in the frame of its pink houses with their high slate roofs and their shady arcades, which housed novelty shops on the ground floor, offered her a refuge where she could relax from her hard work.

Life here was secluded and precious. Scandals took on a false, theatrical air.

Angélique began to savour the pleasures of conversation, that instrument of culture which for the last half-century had transformed French society. Unfortunately, she was afraid of showing herself awkward. Her mind had for so long been remote from the problems set by an epigram, a madrigal or a sonnet! Moreover, on account of her origins, which were common, or believed to be so, the best *salons* remained closed to her. To conquer them required patience. She dressed richly, but without ever being quite sure that her clothes were fashionable.

When her little boys went for a walk under the trees in the square, people would turn round to look at them, so pretty and well-dressed they were. Florimond and even Cantor now wore real men's suits—in silk, brocade or velvet—with big lace collars, piped stockings, shoes with bows and heels. Plumed hats sat on their pretty curls, and Florimond had a little sword, which delighted him. Under his nervous, fragile appearance, he had a passion for fighting. He would challenge the monkey

Piccolo to a duel, or else the peaceful Cantor, who at the age of four still spoke but little. Had it not been for the intelligence lurking in his lovely green eyes, Angélique would have thought he was a little backward. But he was merely taciturn and saw no need to talk, since Florimond understood him anyway and the servants anticipated his slightest desires.

Angélique had a woman cook and a second footman at the Place Royale. With her coachman, and Flipot, promoted to the post of lackey, Madame Morens could cut quite a respectable figure among her neighbours. Barbe and Javotte wore lace caps, golden crosses, Indian shawls.

But Angélique was quite aware that, in the eyes of the others, she was nevertheless a social upstart. She wanted to rise higher, and the drawing-rooms of the Marais quarter were the very places which enabled ambitious women to move up from the bourgeoisie to the aristocracy, for bourgeois women and noble ladies foregathered here under the ægis of wit.

She began by ingratiating herself with an old spinster who occupied the apartment below hers. This lady had known the heyday of *précieuse* society and its feminine quarrels. She had met the Marquise de Rambouillet, had frequented Mademoiselle de Scudéry's. Her jargon was so affected as to be unintelligible.

Philonide de Parajonc alleged that there were seven different kinds of esteem and divided sighs into five categories. She despised men and detested Molière. Love, in her eyes, was 'the infernal shackle'.

However, she had not always been so disdainful. In her youth, it was whispered, far from contenting herself with the insipid region of Soulful Dalliance, she had not spurned the realm of Coquetry and had often reached its capital, Sensual Rapture. She herself would admit, showing the whites of her eyes: 'Love has most frightfully blighted my heart!'

Angélique attended, with Mademoiselle de Parajonc, the lectures at the Precious Palace. Here she met the flower of honest society, that is to say a great many women of the upper middle class, churchmen, young scholars, provincials.

One day Angélique asked Mademoiselle de Parajonc to accompany her to the Tuileries. The latter was her constant companion. She knew everybody and was able to name each and every one of them for her friend, who was thus becoming acquainted with the new faces at Court. She also served as a foil to Angélique's beauty. She did so quite unconsciously, for the poor Philonide, plastered with white lead up to her eyes, her eyelids ringed with black like an old owl, still thought she was as irresistible as in the days when she made her beaux sigh interminably.

She taught Angélique the right manner of strolling through the Tuileries, miming the necessary gestures with great verve, which made insolent passers-by giggle. But she saw only a homage rendered to her charms.

"In the Tuileries," she was apt to say, "you must saunter nonchalantly in the main avenue. You must chat all the time without saying anything in particular, so as to appear witty. You must laugh without cause, so as to appear gay . . . pull yourself up every now and then to exhibit your bosom . . . open your eyes wide to make them larger, bite your lips to redden them . . . motion with your head to the one, with your fan to the other. . . . Finally, soften up a little, my dear! Trifle elegantly, gesticulate, simper and stress all this with a drooping air. . . ."

It was not really a bad lesson, and Angélique put it into practice with more restraint, and also with more success, than her companion.

The Tuileries, according to Mademoiselle de Parajonc, were 'the lists of high society', and the Cours-la-Reine the 'empire of amorous glances'. One frequented the Tuileries to await the proper hour for the Cours, and one met there again in the evening after the Cours, alternating the drive in the carriage with promenades on foot.

The wooded groves of the park were favourable to poets and lovers. Abbés prepared their sermons there, lawyers their speeches. All persons of rank came there for rendezvous, and one sometimes met the King or the Queen, or Monseigneur the Dauphin with his governess.

Angélique pulled her companion over to the Great Flower-bed, where the high-ranking people could generally be found. The Prince de Condé went there almost every evening. She was disappointed not to find him, flew into a temper, stamped her foot.

"I fain would know why you were so avid to see His Highness," remarked Philonide with astonishment.

258

"I simply had to see him."

"Did you wish to hand him a petition? . . . If so, stop wailing, my dear, for here he comes."

The Prince de Condé had indeed just arrived and was approaching across the wide avenue, surrounded by the gentlemen of his household. Angélique realised that there was no possibility of approaching the Prince. Could she say:

'Monsiegneur, give me back the mansion of the Rue du Beautreillis which belongs to me and which you have wrongfully received from the King's hands'?

Or else:

'Monseigneur, I am the wife of the Comte de Peyrac, whose coat-of-arms you had scratched out and whose house you had exorcised'?

The impulse which had led her to the Tuileries to see the Prince de Condé was infantile and stupid. She was just a newly-rich chocolate-maker. Nobody could possibly present her to the great nobleman, and anyhow, what could she have said to him? . . . She reproached herself vehemently: 'Idiot! If you always behaved so impulsively and unreasonably, your business affairs would be in a nice mess! . . .'

"Come along," she said to the old maid.

And abruptly she turned away from the glittering, gossiping party which was passing nearby.

Despite the radiant evening and the gentle spring sky, Angélique remained sullen during the rest of their walk. Philonide asked her if they should go on to the Cours. She said no. Her carriage was too plain.

An effeminate young dandy approached them:

"Madame," he said to Angélique, "my friends and I have been asking ourselves questions about you. One wagers that you are a proctor's wife, the other that you are a spinster lady and a *précieuse*. Do resolve our dispute."

It could have made her laugh. But she was in a bad temper, and she detested these *petits-maîtres*, painted like dolls, whose affectations included wearing the nail of the little finger longer than the others.

"Why don't you wager that you are a fool?" she retorted. "In that way you'll never lose."

And she left him standing there speechless.

Philonide de Parajonc was shocked.

"Your reply did not lack in wit, but it smacked of the shop-keeper from three miles away. You'll never succeed in the drawing-room if . . ."

"Oh, Philonide!" exclaimed Angélique, stopping suddenly. "Look . . . there!"

"Where?"

"There," repeated Angélique in a voice which had dropped to a whisper.

A few steps from her, framed by the tender green of a shrub, a tall young man was standing, casually propped against the base of a marble statue. He was of outstanding beauty, to which the elegance of his clothes added further perfection. His almond-green velvet suit was overlaid with gold embroideries in a pattern of birds and flowers. It was a little extravagant, but as beautiful as the livery of spring. A white hat adorned with green plumes sat on his flowing, fair wig. Set in the frame of those long curls, his pink-and-white face, softly dabbed with powder, sported a blond moustache finely drawn in a single stroke. His eyes were large, and of a transparent blue which took on a greenish hue in the leafy shade.

The nobleman's features were impassive and his eyes did not blink. Was he dreaming? Meditating? . . . His blue pupils stared vacantly like those of a blind man. In the fixedness of this aimless reverie, they had a snake-like coldness. He did not seem aware of the interest he aroused.

"Well, Angélique," said Mademoiselle de Parajonc sourly, "you've taken leave of your senses, upon my word! This way of staring at a man is dreadfully common."

"What . . . what is his name?"

"It's the Marquis du Plessis-Bellière, of course! What's there so startling about him? He's waiting for his beau, no doubt. I really don't see why you, who don't care for *petits-maîtres*, are standing there as if rooted to the ground."

"Forgive me," stammered Angélique, recovering her wits.

For a second she had become again the wild little girl, sunk in admiration. Philippe! The scornful big cousin. Monteloup, and the smell of the dining-hall where the heat of the the soup drew smoke from the damp tablecloth. Medley of pain and sweetness!

The two ladies strolled past him. He seemed to notice them, stirred, and doffing his hat with a gesture of profound boredom, greeted them.

"He is a gentleman of the King's suite, is he not?" asked Angélique, when they were out of earshot.

"Yes, he went to the wars with His Highness the Prince when the latter was still with the Spaniards. Since then, he has been named Grand Master of the Royal Wolf-hunt. He is so handsome and so fond of war that the King calls him Mars. However, dreadful things are being said about him."

"Dreadful things? . . . Whatever can they be?"

Mademoiselle de Parajonc gave a little resigned snigger.

"There you are, quite shocked to hear aspersions cast on the handsome young lord. But all the women are like you. They run after him and swoon at the sight of his fair hair, his fresh complexion, his elegance. They won't rest till they've slipped into his bed. But then they change their tune. Yes, yes, Armande de Circé and Mademoiselle Jacari have told me in confidence . . . The handsome Philippe seems gentle and polite. He is as absent-minded as an old scholar. But in love, it appears he is an appalling brute: an ostler has more consideration for his wife than *he* has for his mistresses. All the women whom he's taken in his arms detest him. . . ."

Angélique was only half listening. The sight of Philippe, leaning against the marble statue, motionless and almost as unreal as an apparition, would not fade from her mind. He had taken her hand, in the old days, to dance with her. That was in Plessis, in the white château in the great forest of Nieul.

"It seems that he has a most cruel imagination for torturing his mistresses," Philonide continued. "He beat Madame de Circé so horribly for a mere trifle that she practically could not move for a week, which was very embarrassing on account of her husband. And on his campaigns the way he behaves when he's victorious is an outright scandal. His troops are more feared than those of the notorious Jean de Werth. They pursue the women even into the churches and do them violence without a thought. At Norgen he summoned the daughters of the persons of note, half killed them because they offered resistance and, after a night of orgy with his officers, handed them over to the troops. Several of them died as a result, or else went mad. If His Highness the Prince had not intervened on his behalf, Philippe du Plessis would certainly have been sent into disgrace."

"Philonide, you are a jealous old maid!" cried Angélique, gripped by a sudden anger. "This young man is not, can't be, the ogre you describe. You are just wilfully exaggerating all the gossip you have gleaned about him."

Mademoiselle de Parajonc stopped short, choking with indignation.

"I! . . . Gossip! . . . You know how I loathe this sort of thing, all the tittle-tattle of the neighbourhood and everything that smacks of chatty visits to a woman in childbed. I indulging in gossip! . . . When I keep so utterly aloof from all vulgar things! If I talk to you like this, it's because it's *true*!"

"Well, if it is, it's not entirely his fault," Angélique declared. "He's like that because women have hurt him on account of his beauty."

"How . . . how do you know? Are you acquainted with him?"

"N . . . no."

"You are mad, then!" shouted Mademoiselle de Parajonc, flushing crimson with rage. "I'd never have thought you capable of letting a whipper-snapper like that turn your head. Farewell. . . ."

She left her standing there and strode off towards the park gate. Angélique had no alternative but to follow her, for she did not wish to fall out with Mademoiselle de Parajonc, of whom she was fond.

If Angélique and the old blue-stocking had not quarrelled, that day in the Tuileries, on account of Philippe du Plessis-Bellière, they would not have left the park so early. And if they had not left the park at that very moment, they would not have been the victims of a vulgar bet in which the lackeys massed outside the gates had just indulged. Monsieur de Lauzun and Monsieur de Montespan would not have fought a duel for the lovely green eyes of Madame Morens. And Angélique would probably have had to wait for a long while before frequenting again the great ones of this world. Which shows that it is a good thing sometimes to be sharp-tongued and hot-tempered.

Since admittance to the garden was forbidden by a notice on the gate 'to lackeys and the rabble', there always stood, outside the fence, a noisy swarm of footmen, flunkeys and coachmen, who would while away the long hours of waiting with games of cards or ninepins, when they weren't fighting or drinking at the tavern on the corner. That night, the lackeys of the Duc de Lauzun had made a wager. They'd stand a drink to the one

262

among them who would be bold enough to lift up the skirt of the first lady coming out of the Tuileries.

It so happened that the lady was Angélique, who had caught up with Philonide and was endeavouring to calm her.

Before she had had time to foresee the insolent gesture, she found herself gripped by a tall, lanky lout who stank of wine, and her skirts were turned up most impudently. Almost instantly, her hand struck the oaf's face. Mademoiselle de Parajonc uttered parrot-like screams.

A gentleman who was about to mount into his carriage, and who had witnessed the scene, motioned to his men, who, overjoyed at the chance, rushed at Monsieur de Lauzun's footmen. There followed a violent scuffle amid horse-droppings and an interested circle of onlookers. The gentleman's forces carried the day. He himself applauded noisily.

He walked up to Angélique and saluted her.

"Thank you, Monsieur, for your intervention," she said.

She was furious and humiliated, but above all badly scared, for she had been on the verge of chastising the drunkard herself in the well-tried manner of the tavern of 'The Red Mask', seasoning the lesson with some forceful terms drawn straight from Polack's vocabulary. All the care Angélique had taken to become a great lady again would have been instantly set at nought. The next day, the ladies of the Marais would have gloated over the incident.

White with apprehension at this thought, the young woman decided to swoon a little, in the true tradition of good breeding.

"Ah! Monsieur . . . what infamy! It's dreadful! To be thus exposed to the outrage of low reprobates!"

"Calm yourself, Madame," he said, supporting her with a zealous and vigorous arm.

He was a handsome, bright-eyed young man, whose singsong accent was unmistakable. Yet another Gascon, without a shadow of a doubt! He introduced himself:

"Louis Henri de Pardaillan de Gondrin, Sieur de Pardaillan and other places, Marquis de Montespan."

The name was familiar to Angélique. The newcomer belonged to the oldest nobility of the province of Guyenne. She smiled alluringly, and the Marquis, visibly delighted with this encounter, insisted on knowing where and when he might take news of her health. She did not wish to give her name, but answered:

"Come to the Tuileries tomorrow at the same time. I hope that the circumstances will be more favourable and enable us to converse pleasantly."

"Where shall I wait for you?"

"Near the Echo."

It was a promising spot. The Echo was the trysting-place for gallant encounters. Enchanted, the Marquis kissed the hand held out to him.

"Have you a sedan chair? May I take you home?"

"My carriage is not far," Angélique assured him, unwilling to display her modest equipage.

"Till tomorrow, then, mysterious beauty."

This time, he swiftly kissed her cheek, and gaily capered away to his coach.

"You lacked modesty . . ." Mademoiselle de Parajonc began.

But the Duc de Lauzun was just appearing at the park gate. Seeing the state in which his footmen were—one spitting out his teeth, another bleeding from his nose, and all of them torn and grimy—he began to rage in a falsetto voice. When it was explained to him that the mischief had been done by the flunkeys of a noble lord, he shouted:

"Those varlets and their master deserve to be belaboured with sticks. Their sort isn't worthy to be touched with a sword."

The Marquis de Montespan had not yet sat down in his carriage. He leaped down from the step, ran after Lauzun, seized him by the arm, made him wheel round and, after pushing the other's hat down over his eyes, called him a scamp and a lout.

A moment later, the flash of two swords gleamed in the air and the two Gascons were fighting a duel under the eyes of the increasingly interested onlookers.

"Gentlemen, for mercy's sake!" cried Mademoiselle de Parajonc. "Duelling is forbidden. You'll both sleep in the Bastille tonight."

But the two lords took no heed of this sensible forecast and crossed their irons with fervour, while the crowd opposed a a real passive resistance to the squad of Swiss guards who were trying to force their way through to the two duellists.

Happily, the Marquis de Montespan managed to slash Lauzun's thigh. Péguilin stumbled and dropped his sword.

"Come away quick, dear fellow!" cried the Marquis, supporting his opponent. "Let's dodge the Bastille! Help me, ladies!"

The carriage moved off at the very moment when the Swiss guard, amid blows and strokes from their halberds, their neck-ruffs all awry, forged their way through to it.

As the carriage hurtled along the rue Saint-Honoré, Angélique, stanching Péguilin's wound with her sash, found herself piled higgledy-piggledy in the coach with the Marquis de Montespan, Mademoiselle de Parajonc and even the lackey who had provoked the incident and who had been thrown, half stunned, on the floor.

"You'll be sentenced to the stocks and the galleys," Péguilin told him, kicking him in the stomach with his heel. "And I certainly won't pay a single *livre* to buy you off! . . . My dear Pardaillan, thanks to you, my surgeon won't need to bleed me this season."

"You must get a dressing," said the Marquis. "Come to my place. I believe my wife's at home today with her women-friends."

The wife of Monsieur de Montespan was, as Angélique discovered, none other than the beautiful Athénaïs de Mortemart, Hortense's former school friend, with whom she had watched the King's triumphant entry into Paris.

Mademoiselle de Mortemart had married in 1662. She had become even more beautiful. Her rose-like complexion, blue eyes and golden hair, coupled with the famous family wit, made her one of the most widely noticed women at Court. Unfortunately, though both her husband's and her own family were of ancient lineage, they were both similarly impecunious. Harassed by debts and creditors, poor Athénaïs could not show off her beauty in all the glamour it deserved, and she would sometimes have to miss Court balls because she could not afford a new dress.

The apartment where the duellists of the Tuileries, accompanied by Angélique and Mademoiselle de Parajonc, eventually arrived, bore the mark of almost shabby poverty side by side with an almost overwhelming show of elegant wearing apparel.

Sumptuous gowns trailed on the dust-covered furniture. There was no fire despite the still cool season, and Athénaïs, in a taffeta dressing-gown, was fighting like a shrew with a goldsmith's employee who had come to claim a deposit for an order of a gold and silver necklace which the young woman meant to wear for the first time at Versailles the following week.

Monsieur de Montespan immediately took control and kicked the artisan out of the house. Athénaïs protested. She wanted her necklace. There followed an argument, while poor Lauzun's blood kept trickling on to the stone floor. Madame de Montespan became aware of it at last and called her friend, Françoise d'Aubigné, who had come to help her tidy up the apartment, for the maidservants had walked out the day before.

The widow of the poet Scarron promptly appeared, the same as ever, with her shabby dress, her big black eyes and the prim expression on her mouth. Angélique had the impression of having left her at the Temple only yesterday.

'In another moment I'll see Hortense appear,' she thought.

She helped Françoise to carry the Marquis de Lauzun, who had fainted by now, over to a settee.

"I'll fetch some water from the kitchens," said Madame Scarron. "Be good enough to keep the dressing well against the wound . . . Madame."

The imperceptible hesitation showed Angélique that Madam Scarron had recognised her. It did not matter. Madame Scarron was one of those people who themselves have to conceal part of their own existence. In any case, sooner or later, Angélique was determined to confront openly the faces from her past.

In the next room the Montespans continued to squabble.

"However could you fail to recognise her? . . . Why, it's Madame Morens! You're fighting a duel now for a chocolate-shopkeeper!"

"She is adorable . . . and don't forget that she has the reputation of being one of the richest women in Paris. If it's really she, I don't regret my gesture."

"You are revolting!"

"My dear, do you want your necklace, or don't you?"

'All right,' Angélique said to herself, 'I see in what way I shall have to show my gratitude to these people of the great nobility. A sumptuous present, perhaps even a weighty purse, provided it's well coated with discretion and tact.'

The Duc de Lauzun raised his eyelids. His eyes rested dimly on Angélique.

"I am dreaming," he stammered. "Can it be you, my sweet?"

"It can, it is," she said, smiling at him.

"Damn me, I never expected to see you again, Angélique! I often wondered what could have become of you."

"You may have wondered, but admit you didn't try to find out."

"That's true, my sweet. I am a courtier. All courtiers behave rather like cowards towards those who've fallen into disfavour." He scrutinised the young woman's dress and jewels.

"Things seem to have turned out well," he said.

"They had to. My name nowadays is Madame Morens."

"By Jove, I've heard about you! You sell chocolate, don't you?"

"I amuse myself. Some people busy themselves with astronomy or philosophy. For my part, I sell chocolate. What about you, Péguilin? Is your life still as glamorous? Does the King still extend his friendship towards you?"

Péguilin's face darkened and he seemed to forget his curiosity.

"Oh, my dear, my favour is unsteadily poised. The King imagines that I conspired with Vardes in that Spanish letter affair, you know, that letter someone got to the Queen to inform her of her august husband's infidelities with La Vallière. . . . I cannot dispel this suspicion, and His Majesty is shockingly rude to me at times! . . . Thank God, the Grande Mademoiselle is in love with me."

"Mademoiselle de Montpensier?"

"Yes," whispered Péguilin, rolling the white of his eyes. "I even believe she may propose marriage to me."

"Oh! Péguilin!" exclaimed Angélique, bursting out laughing. "You are incredible, incorrigible. You haven't changed a bit!"

"You haven't changed either. And you are as beautiful as a woman come to life again."

"What do you know about the beauty of such women, Péguilin?"

"Why, what the Church tells us! . . . A glorious body! . . . Come over here, my sweetheart, so that I can kiss you."

He took her face into both his hands and pulled her towards him.

"Hell and damnation!" shouted Montespan from the threshold. "It's not enough that I rip your thigh open to stop you from running, you insist on cutting the ground from under my feet in my own house, damned Péguilin! I was a fool not to let you go to the Bastille!"

CHAPTER 76

As a result of this meeting, Angélique frequently saw the Duc de Lauzun and the Marquis de Montespan in the Tuileries and on the Cours-la-Reine. They, in turn, introduced their friends to her. And, gradually, the faces of the past reappeared. One day, as she was driving along the Cours with Péguilin, her carriage passed that of the Grande Mademoiselle, who recognised her. Nothing was said. Was it prudence or indifference? Each of them had so many fish to fry!

After first avoiding her, Athénaïs de Montespan had suddenly taken a fancy to her and asked her to her house. She had noticed that the chocolate-shop keeper was no chatterbox but was admirably adept in rejoinders.

Madame Scarron, whom Angélique saw frequently at the Montespans', introduced her to Ninon de Lenclos.

Angélique was rather proud, too, to figure on the list of persons whom Mademoiselle de Montpensier admitted to the Gardens of the Luxembourg. One day as she arrived there, the caretaker's wife opened the gate for her in the absence of her husband.

Angélique began to stroll along the beautiful walks bordered with willows and clumps of magnolias. After a moment she became aware that the garden, usually full of animation, was almost deserted that day. She saw only two liveried footmen, running as fast as they could and diving into the bushes. And that was all. Intrigued and vaguely perturbed, she continued her lonely stroll.

As she was passing by a small rocky cave, she thought she heard a slight noise and, turning round, perceived a human shape squatting in a shrub. 'It must be some rogue,' she thought, 'one of Wood-Bottom's underlings about to perpetrate some

268

mischief. It would be rather fun to catch him unawares and talk thieves' slang to him, just to see the face he'll make.'

She smiled at the idea. It certainly did not happen every day that a cut-purse on the prowl had the opportunity of finding himself face to face with a great lady who used the unmistakable language of the Tower of Nesle and the Faubourg Saint-Denis. 'And afterwards I'll give him my purse to help him recover his wits, poor fellow!' she thought, delighted at this piece of mischief that would have no witness.

However, as she was stealthily approaching, she saw that the man was richly dressed, although his clothes were mud-soiled. He was on his knees, and propped on his elbows in a peculiar posture. Suddenly he turned his head nervously, as if cocking his ears, and she recognised the Duc d'Enghien, the Prince de Condé's son. She had met him during the promenades in the Tuileries, or on the Cours-la-Reine. He was a very dashing youngster, but said to be intractable in matters of etiquette, and somewhat unrestrained.

Angélique noticed that he was very pale, and wore a wild, frightened expression.

'What's he doing there? Why is he hiding? What's he afraid of?' she wondered, gripped by a vague uneasiness.

After a short hesitation, she withdrew noiselessly, and returned to the broad walks of the garden. She passed the caretaker, who goggled with bewilderment on seeing her.

"Oh, Madame! What are you doing here? Do withdraw quickly!"

"Why? You know quite well that I am on Mademoiselle de Montpensier's list. And, besides, your wife let me in."

The caretaker glanced around with distress. Angélique was always very generous with him.

"May Madame forgive me," he whispered, coming closer, "but my wife doesn't know the secret I shall confide to you: the garden is closed to the public today, for we've been hunting, ever since morning, for His Highness the Duc d'Enghien, who imagines he is a rabbit."

And as the young woman stared at him round-eyed, he touched his forehead with his finger.

"Yes, the poor boy, it comes over him from time to time. Apparently it's a sickness. When he thinks he is a rabbit, or a partridge, he is afraid of getting killed and runs away to hide. We've been looking for him for hours."

"He's in the shrubbery, near the little grotto. I saw him."

"Good God! We must tell His Highness the Prince. Ah! here he is."

A sedan chair was approaching. The Prince de Condé put his head out of the window.

"What are you doing here, Madame?" he asked furiously.

The caretaker hastened to intervene:

"Monsiegneur, Madame has just seen His Lordship near the rockery."

"Ah! good. Open the door for me. Help me to get down, damn it! Don't make so much noise, you'll frighten him. You there, go and fetch his first chamber-valet, and you, go and collect all the men you can find and post them at the gates. . . ."

A few moments later, Angélique heard frantic leaps in the shrubbery, then swift running. The Duc d'Enghien emerged and rushed past at full speed. But two servants in pursuit managed to grab him and hold him back. He was promptly surrounded and restrained. His chamber-valet talked to him gently:

"Nobody'll kill you, Monseigneur . . . Nobody'll lock you up in a cage. . . . You'll be released presently and will be able to run in the fields again."

The Duc d'Enghien was ashen. He did not say a word, but in his eyes there was the pathetic, questioning expression of a hunted animal. His father approached. The young man struggled furiously, although still in silence.

"Take him away," said the Prince de Condé. "Send for his physician and his surgeon. Have him bled, purged and, above all, tied up. I don't feel like playing another game all over again tonight. I'll give a thrashing to whoever lets him escape again."

The group moved away. The Prince came back towards Angélique, who had witnessed this sad scene, profoundly shaken; she looked almost as white as the poor sick man.

Condé posted himself before her and fixed her with a sombre stare.

"Well!" he said, "you saw him? He is grand, isn't he, the descendant of the Condés, the Montmorencys! . . . His great-grandfather had manias, his grandmother was mad. I had to marry the daughter. At the time, she was already beginning to pull her hairs out, one by one, with tweezers. I knew that my progeny would suffer for it, but I had to marry her all the same. It was an order of King Louis XIII. And there you have my son! Sometimes he fancies he's a dog and struggles not to bark before the King. Or else, he thinks he's a bat and is afraid of knocking against the wainscot of his apartment. The other day, he felt he was turning into a plant and his servants had to water him—funny, isn't it? You aren't laughing?"

"Monseigneur . . . how can you believe for a second that I would want to laugh? . . . Of course, you don't know me. . . ."

He cut her short with a sudden smile that brightened his gruff face:

"I do! Indeed! I know you well, Madame Morens. I have seen you at Ninon's and elsewhere. You are as gay as a young girl, beautiful as a courtesan, and you have the soothing heart of a mother. Moreover, I suspect you of being one of the cleverest women in the kingdom. But you don't display the fact, for you are sly and you know that men are afraid of learned ladies."

Angélique smiled in her turn, surprised by this unexpected declaration.

"You flatter me, Monsiegneur . . . and I should be curious to know who gave you this information about me. . . ."

"I don't need any informers," he said, in the brusque, churlish manner of a warrior. "I have observed you. Haven't you noticed that I often looked at you? I believe you are a little afraid of me. And yet, you are not shy. . . ."

Angélique raised her eyes to the victor of Lens and Rocroi. This wasn't the first time that she had thus looked up at him. But the Prince had certainly not the faintest recollection of the little grey quail who had stood up to him and to whom he had said: "I'll wager that when you are a woman men will hang themselves for having met you!"

She had always believed that she harboured a deep grudge against the Prince de Condé, and she had to defend herself against a feeling of sympathy and understanding that rose up between them. Didn't he have them spied upon for years, herself and her husband, by the butler Clément Tonnel? Hadn't he inherited Joffrey de Peyrac's possessions? Angélique had been asking herself for a long time how she might manage to learn exactly what part the Prince de Condé had played in her tragedy. Chance was serving her strangely.

"You haven't answered," said the Prince. "Is it true, then, that I intimidate you?"

"No! But I feel quite unworthy to converse with you, Monseigneur. Your fame . . ."

"Pah! my fame—you are far too young to know anything about it. My weapons are rusty, and if His Majesty does not make up his mind to give a lesson to the rascally Dutch or Englishmen, I may well risk dying in my bed. As for conversing, Ninon has told me a hundred times that words are not bullets that you shoot into your opponent's stomach, and she alleges that I still haven't quite learned the lesson. Ha! Ha!"

He broke into noisy laughter, and casually took her arm.

"Do come. My carriage is waiting outside, but when I walk I'm obliged to lean on a charitable arm. That's what I owe my fame: pains caught in the waterlogged marshes, making my leg drag like an old man's on certain days. Will you keep me company? Your presence seems the only one I could possibly bear after the painful day. Do you know my Hôtel de Beau-treillis?"

Angélique said with a beating heart:

"No, Monsiegneur."

"They say it's one of the prettiest things that old Mansard built. Personally, I don't like being there, but I know that the ladies rave about the beauty of the house. Come and have a look at it."

Although reluctant to admit it, Angélique appreciated the honour of being seated in the carriage of a Prince of the blood whom the passers-by acclaimed in the street.

She was surprised by the attentiveness shown to her by her companion. It was generally said that the Prince de Condé, ever since his friend Marthe du Vigean had entered into the Carmelite order of the Faubourg Saint-Jacques, no longer granted women the consideration which the nobility of France was accustomed to show them. All he asked of them was a purely physical pleasure and, for years now, he had not been known to have anything but passing affairs with women of rather low standing. In the drawing-rooms his rudeness towards the fair sex discouraged the best intentions. This time, however, the Prince seemed to be making an effort to please his companion.

The carriage turned into the courtyard of the Hôtel de Beautreillis.

Angélique mounted the marble terrace. Every detail of this bright and harmonious residence spoke to her of Joffrey de Peyrac. He had wanted its lines to be as supple as vine tendrils on the wrought-iron balconies and balustrades, he had planned those carved gilt wood friezes framing the smooth high planes of marble or mirror, those statues and busts, those stone animals and birds, ubiquitous as the graceful spirits of a happy home.

"You don't say anything?" said the Prince de Condé in surprise, after they had inspected the two storeys of reception rooms. "Generally my visitors emit parrot-like exclamations. Is the house not to your liking? You are supposed to know a good deal about arranging a home."

They were in a small drawing-room, with blue satin hangings embroidered with gold. A wrought-iron screen of exquisite design separated them from the long gallery which overlooked the gardens. At the back of the room the fireplace, flanked by two carved lions, bore a fresh wound on its pediment. Angélique raised her arm and put her hand over it.

"Why has this ornament been broken?" she asked. "It's not the first breakage I've noticed. Why, even at the windows of this drawing-room the pattern has been effaced in some places."

The face of His Lordship clouded over.

"They are the ciphers of the former owner of the house. I had them chipped off. I'll have them repaired some day. Though I'm damned if I know when! . . . I prefer spending my money on the installations of my country house at Chantilly."

Angélique kept her hand over the maimed coat-of-arms.

"Why didn't you leave them as they were?"

"The sight of that man's coat-of-arms gave me a displeasure. He was a cursed man!"

"A cursed man?" she echoed.

"Yes. A nobleman who manufactured gold by means of a secret the devil had imparted to him. He was burned at the stake. And the King made me a present of his possessions. I am not yet quite sure that His Majesty was not seeking to bring me bad luck by his gift."

Angélique had walked slowly over to the window and was looking out.

"Did you know him, Monseigneur?"

"Whom? The damned nobleman? . . . Why no, and thank God for it."

"I think I remember the case," she said, frightened at her own boldness and yet quite composed. "Wasn't he a man from Toulouse, a Monsieur . . . de Peyrac?"

"Yes, indeed," he agreed, with indifference.

"Wasn't there some talk that he had been sentenced above all, because he held some wicked secret about Monsieur Fouquet, who was still so powerful at that time?"

"That's possible. Monsieur Fouquet considered himself the king of France for a long time. He had enough money for that. He made lots of people do all sorts of foolish things. Me, for example. Ha! Ha! Ha! . . . Ah well, all that is over and done with."

Angélique turned round to observe him. He had slumped into an armchair and was tracing the rose pattern of the carpet with the tip of his cane. Though he had smirked bitterly at the memory of the foolish things Monsieur Fouquet had made him do, he had not reacted to the hints concerning Joffrey de Peyrac. The young woman felt certain that he was not the one who had placed the butler Clément Tonnel in her home for years. Why should His Highness now trouble to remember that he had once wanted to poison Mazarin and that he had sold himself to Fouquet? He was quite busy enough trying to regain the favour of the still distrustful young King.

"I was in Flanders at the time of Peyrac's trial," he resumed. "I did not follow the case. Never mind! I got the house and I confess I don't much enjoy it. The sorcerer never lived here, apparently. And yet I can't help finding something sad and sinister about these walls. It's like the décor set up for a scene that was never played. . . . The dainty objects assembled in it are waiting for a host who is not myself. I've kept on an old ostler who belonged to the Comte de Peyrac's staff of servants. He claims he sees his ghost on certain nights. . . . It's possible. I sometimes breathe a presence here which repels me and drives me away. I spend as little time as possible here. Do you also have this unpleasant impression?"

"No, on the contrary," she murmured.

Her gaze roved around. 'Here I am at home,' she thought. 'I and my children are the hosts these walls are waiting for.'

"So you like the house?"

"I love it. It's admirable. Oh! I'd like to live here!" she cried, clasping her hands over her heart with unexpected passion.

"You could live here if you wanted to," said the Prince.

She spun round towards him. He fastened his still magnificent and imperious look upon her, that look of which Monsieur Bossuet would eloquently say some day: 'This Prince . . . who bore victory in his eyes. . . .'

"Live in it?" repeated Angélique. "In what capacity, Monseigneur?"

He smiled again and got up abruptly to go over to her.

"There! I am forty-four years old, I am no longer young, but I am not yet old. I sometimes have pains in my knees, that's a fact, but the rest is still sound. I talk to you straight from the shoulder. I believe I make a tolerable lover. I don't think you'll be shocked by this declaration. I don't know where you come from, but something tells me that you must have heard worse things in your life and, anyway, I'm not trying to catch you off your guard. I never beat about the bush with women; I think it's pointless to hem and haw when there's always the same question at the end: 'Do you want to, or don't you? . . .' No, don't answer yet. I want you to know just what the few advantages are which I can offer you. You'll have a pension—yes, I know, you are very rich. Well, listen! *I'll give you Beautreillis House*, since you like it. I'll look after your sons and will recommend them for a good education. I also know that you are a widow and rather jealous of your reputation for chastity. It's true that this is a precious asset, but . . . consider that I am not asking you to lose your reputation for some low rogue. And since you mentioned my fame, allow me to point out that——"

He hesitated with a genuine and rather touching modesty.

"—that it is not dishonourable to be the mistress of the great Condé. That's the way it is in our society. I'll present you everywhere. . . . Why this sceptical and just a trifle disdainful smile, Madame?"

"Because," said Angélique, smiling, "I was remembering

a ditty which old Hurlurot, an old mountebank, sings at street corners:

> *Les princes sont d'étranges gens.*
> *Heureux qui ne les connaît guère;*
> *Plus heureux qui n'en a que faire. . . ."*[1]

"A plague on your insolence!" he shouted with feigned fury. He took her by the waist and pulled her towards him:

"That's what I like about you, my dear," he said in a restrained voice. "For I've noticed that in your profession as a woman you have the warrior's reckless boldness. You attack at the right moment, you turn the opponent's weakness to account with Machiavellian skill and you deal him terrible blows. But you do not withdraw fast enough to your positions. I am holding you now . . . ! How fresh and firm you are! You have a sound, reassuring little body . . . ! Ah! I'd so much like you to listen to me not as a Prince, but as I am, a poor, rather unhappy man. You are so different from the cold-hearted coquettes!"

He leaned his cheek against Angélique's hair.

"There is in your golden hair one grey strand that moves me. It seems that, under your air of youth and gaiety, you have the experience which great griefs bestow. Am I wrong?"

"No, Monseigneur," Angélique replied obediently.

She was thinking that if someone had told her that very morning that before the night was out she would be in the arms of the Prince de Condé and would be leaning her head submissively against that august shoulder, she would have protested that life could never be so mad. But her life had never been simple, and she was beginning to get used to the surprises sprung on her by fate.

"Since my youth," he continued, "I have never loved but a single woman. I was not always faithful to her, but I loved her alone. She was beautiful, gentle, and the companion of my soul. The intrigues and conspiracies which ceaselessly cropped up to part us eventually tired her. Since she took the veil, what is there left for me? I've known only two loves in all my life: her and war. My beloved has retired to a convent, and that rascal Mazarin signed the Peace of the Pyrénées. I am nothing more than a representative dummy who pays court to

---

[1] Princes are odd folk.
Lucky are those who don't know them;
Luckier still those who don't need them. . . .

the young King in the hope of obtaining—goodness knows when—some military governorship and perhaps a command if he'd chance to have the good idea of demanding the Queen's dowry from the Flemings. There is talk of it. . . . But let's not go into that—I don't want to bore you. Seeing you has kindled in me a flame which I thought was dead. The death of the heart is the worst thing. . . . I would like to keep you near me. . . ."

Angélique had gently disengaged herself while he was speaking; she stepped back a little.

"Monseigneur . . ."

"It's yes, isn't it?" he said anxiously. "Oh! I beg of you . . . What is holding you back?"

He bit his lips.

"Lord! You are formidable. No matter! I desire you just as you are."

He could not understand the dilemma he was putting her in. What would she have answered, had he made his proposition to her in some other place? She did not know.

But here, in this house where she found herself for the first time, she was surrounded by ghosts. Next to the Prince de Condé, risen from the past, with his slightly old-fashioned air, there stood the luminous, hard outline of Philippe in his pale satins and, behind them, a masked wraith, clothed in black velvet and silver, with a single blood-red ruby on his finger, the cursed nobleman who had been her master and her only love.

Among all of them, whom life or death had set free, she alone remained a captive of the old tragedy.

"What's the matter?" asked the Prince. "Why are there tears in your eyes? Have I hurt you in any way? Do stay here, where you seem to like it. Let me love you. I'll be discreet. . . ."

She shook her head slowly:

"No, *it's impossible*, Monseigneur."

CHAPTER 77

THIS WAS a red-letter day.

For on this very evening the famous *hoca* game took place between Madame Morens and the Prince de Condé, which was to set the fashionable set buzzing, scandalise the strait-laced, delight the libertines and amuse the whole of Paris.

277

The party started as usual at the hour when the candles were brought in. According to the varying luck of the players, it could last for three or four hours. Afterwards there would be a light supper. Then everybody would go home.

The game of *hoca* would start with an unlimited number of gamblers. That evening, some fifteen players started out. The stakes were high. The first rounds quickly eliminated half the participants. The pace of the game slowed down.

Suddenly Angélique, who had been absent-minded and thinking of Hortense, noticed with astonishment that she was recklessly engaged in a very close fight with His Highness the Prince, the Marquis de Thianges and President Jomerson. She it was who, for some time now, had been 'leading' the game. The little Duc de Richemont was marking her tablets and, glancing at them, she saw that she had won a small fortune.

"You are in luck tonight, Madame," the Marquis de Thianges said to her, pulling a wry face. "You've been holding the bank for almost an hour and you don't seem ready to let go of it yet."

"I've never seen a player hold the bank for so long!" the little Duc cried, very excited. "Don't forget, Madame, that if you lose it you will have to pay each of these gentlemen the same amount that you have won so far. There's still time to stop. It's your right."

Monsieur Jomerson began to shout that onlookers had no right to intervene and that, if this continued, he would have the room cleared. People hastened to soothe him and to point out that he wasn't in the law courts but at Mademoiselle de Lenclos's. Everyone was waiting for Angélique's decision.

"I continue," she said.

And she dealt the cards. The judge breathed. He had lost a lot and was hoping that a stroke of luck would, in the very next second, repay him a hundredfold for his recklessness. No one had ever seen a player hold the bank as long as this lady. If Madame Morens held on to it, she was doomed to lose, and so much the better for the others. Wasn't it just like a woman to hang on so grimly! Luckily, she had no husband to render accounts to.

Thereupon, President Jomerson had to show his hand, which was lamentable, and got out of the game most crest-fallen.

A circle formed around Angélique, and people who had been about to leave could not make up their minds to tear themselves away, but remained standing on one foot, craning their necks.

During several rounds the players were equal in points. In that case, the stake bid went to Angélique, but no player was eliminated. Then Monsieur de Thianges lost and left the table, wiping his brow. It had been a rough evening! What was his wife going to say when she learned that they'd have to pay two years of their income to Madame Morens, the chocolate-maker? Provided, of course, that she won. If she didn't, she would have to pay the Prince de Condé double the amount she had won. It made one dizzy just to think of it! The woman was mad! She was heading straight for her downfall. At the point she had reached, not even the craziest gambler would be foolhardy enough to continue.

"Do stop, my love!" implored the little Duc into Angélique's ear. "You can't possibly win again."

Angélique held her hand over the pack of cards. It was a smooth, hard little brick which burned her palm.

She looked with fixed attention at the Prince de Condé. Yet the game did not depend on him alone, but on *fate*.

Fate was standing before her. It had assumed the face of the Prince de Condé, his fiery eyes, his eagle nose, his white, carnivorous teeth which were bared in a smile. And what he was holding in his hands were not cards any more, but a small casket in which gleamed a green poison phial.

All around him there was only darkness and silence.

Then the silence broke like glass shattered by Angélique's voice:

"I continue."

Once again, the hands were at '*égalité*'. Villarceaux leaned out of the window. He was calling to the passers-by, shouting that they must come up, that there'd never been such a sensational game since the one when his grandsire had staked his wife and his regiment against King Henri IV at the Louvre.

The drawing-room was packed. The footmen themselves had climbed on to the chairs to follow the battle from afar. The candles were smoking. Nobody troubled to trim them.

The heat was stifling.

"I continue," Angélique repeated.

"*Égalité*."

"Three more ties and it'll be 'the choice of stakes'."

"The supreme throw in *hoca* . . . a throw that is only seen once every ten years!"

"Once in twenty, dear fellow."

"Once in a generation."

"Remember the financier Tortemer who demanded Montmorency's coat-of-arms."

"Who in turn demanded Tortemer's entire fleet."

"And Tortemer lost. . . ."

"Do you continue, Madame?"

"I continue."

The hubbub almost knocked the table over and half crushed the two gamblers on their cards.

"Hell and damnation!" swore the Prince, groping for his stick. "I swear I'll batter you all if you don't let us breathe. What the devil! Move aside. . . ."

Perspiration was running from Angélique's brow. Heat was its sole cause. She felt no anxiety. She was not thinking of her sons, nor of all the efforts she had made and which she was on the point of destroying.

Indeed, it all seemed perfectly logical to her. For too many years she had been fighting against *fate* in the fashion of a plodding mole. And now at last she had come face to face with it, on its own ground, in its folly. She was going to grip it by the throat and knife it. She, too, was mad, dangerous and unconscious, like *fate* itself. They were on equal terms!

"*Égalité.*"

There was a commotion, then shouts.

"Choice of stakes! Choice of stakes!"

Angélique waited for the hubbub to subside a little before asking, with the voice of a demure schoolgirl, what exactly this final throw of *hoca* consisted of.

They all began to talk at once. Then the Chevalier de Méré sat down near the players and explained the matter to them in a trembling voice.

During this last hand the players started from scratch. All preceding debts and gains were wiped out. Each player chose the stakes, that is to say not what he offered, but what he laid claim to. And that must be something enormous. Examples were quoted: the financier Tortemer, in the last century, had thus laid claim to a Montmorency's titles of nobility, and Villarceaux's grandfather had agreed, if he lost, to yield his wife and his regiment to his opponent.

"Can I still withdraw?" asked Angélique.

"That's your absolute right, Madame."

She remained motionless, with a dreamy gaze. One could have heard a pin drop. For several hours Angélique had 'held the bank'. Was luck going to abandon her at this last bid?

Her eyes seemed to awaken and began to blaze with a fierce intensity. However, she smiled.

"I continue."

The Chevalier de Méré swallowed and said:

"For 'choice of stakes' the rules prescribe the following phrase: 'Match accepted. If I win I demand——!'"

Angélique nodded her head obediently and, still smiling, repeated:

"Match accepted, Monseigneur. If I win, I demand of you your Hôtel de Beautreillis."

Madame Lamoignon uttered an exclamation, which her husband promptly stifled with a furious hand. All eyes were turned towards the Prince, who wore his look of blazing anger. But he was a straight, unswerving player.

He smiled and lifted his haughty brow:

"Match accepted, Madame. If I win, you will be my mistress."

All the heads, in a single movement, veered towards Angélique this time. She was still smiling. The lights played on her half open lips. The dampness which oozed on the surface of her golden skin made it gleam, lustrous like petals under the dew of dawn. The fatigue which tinted her eyelids blue gave her a strange expression of sensuality and abandon.

The men who were present quivered. The silence became heavy and charged.

The Chevalier de Méré spke in an undertone:

"The choice is still yours, Madame. If you refuse: match drawn, and one goes back to the previous set. If you accept: match agreed."

Angélique's hand took up the cards.

"Match agreed, Monseigneur."

She had nothing but knaves, queens and low cards, her worst hand since the beginning of the game. However, after a few exchanges, she managed to compose a hand of some small value. Two solutions remained open to her: show her hand at once and run the risk that the Prince de Condé's present hand was stronger than hers, or else try to compose a more important hand, with the help of the 'lottery'. In that case, the Prince, perhaps not too well supplied himself, could improve his game and possibly throw a hand of kings and aces before her.

She hesitated, then showed her cards.

A cannon shot could not have more effectively transfixed the audience.

The Prince, with his eyes on her cards, did not stir.

Abruptly he rose, spread out his cards, then bowed deeply: "The Hôtel de Beautreillis is yours, Madame."

CHAPTER 78

SHE COULD not believe her eyes. A turn of a card, and the most incredible, the most absurd luck had restored the Hôtel de Beautreillis to her!

Holding her two little boys by the hand, she ran through the sumptuous residence. She did not dare tell them:

'This belonged to your father.'

But she kept telling them:

"This is yours! Yours!"

She examined every marvel in detail: the gay decoration of goddesses, children and leaf-work, the wrought-iron balustrades, the wood panelling in the style of the day, which replaced the old-fashioned heavy tapestries. In the half light of the staircases and corridors there glittered a profusion of gold and garlands of flowers whose tiny twinkle was broken here and there by the sparkling arm of a statue holding a torch.

The Prince de Condé had not furnished this house, for which he had little liking. He had removed a few pieces of furniture. Those that remained he had left to Angélique with the generosity of a great lord. A good loser, he had withdrawn after handing over the stake of their game. Perhaps he was more wounded than he cared to admit by the young woman's complete detachment from him. She had eyes only for the Hôtel de Beautreillis, and he wondered with sombre melancholy whether the friendship he thought he had sometimes read in the eyes of his charming conqueror had not been just a scheming stratagem after all.

Moreover, the Prince was a little apprehensive lest the

rumour of that sensational game reach the ears of His Majesty. The latter was not much in favour of resounding eccentricities. His Highness decided to retire to Chantilly.

Angélique remained alone with her glorious dream. With an unadulterated pleasure she started to decorate her house with all the latest novelties. Cabinet-makers, goldsmiths and upholsterers were summoned. She ordered Monsieur Boulle to make her furniture of translucent wood, inlaid with ivory, tortoise shell and gilt bronze. Her carved bed, the chairs and walls of her bedroom were covered with a white-green satin with a big golden flower design. In her boudoir a fine blue enamel adorned the table, the highboy and the wooden seats. The floors of both these rooms were of inlaid wood which was so aromatic that its scent penetrated the clothes of those who walked upon it.

She called Gontran in to paint the ceiling of the big salon. She bought a thousand objects, knick-knacks from China, paintings, linen, gold and crystal-plate. The cabinet which also served her as a writing-desk was considered a rare piece of the Italian school and was almost the only antique piece of furniture in the house. It was of ebony, studded with pink and cherry-red rubies, garnets and amethysts.

In her fever of expenditure, she also purchased a small white palfrey for Florimond, so that he might gallop through the avenues of the park, which she had adorned with tubs of orange-trees. Cantor received two stern but gentle mastiffs whom he could harness to a small gilded wood dog-cart in which he could ride.

She herself followed the season's fashion by buying herself one of those long-haired little lap-dogs which were just then all the rage. She called it Chrysanthemum. Florimond and Cantor, who had a taste for big, fierce animals, openly despised this tousled miniature.

Finally, to celebrate the house-warming, she decided to give a great supper followed by a ball. This fête was to consecrate the new status of Madame Morens, no longer a chocolate-merchant of the Faubourg Saint-Honoré, but now one of the ladies of quality of the Marais.

The ball given by Madame Morens at her Hôtel de Beau-treillis was a great success.

The highest-ranking people in Paris appeared. Madame Morens danced with Philippe du Plessis-Bellière, dazzling in a suit of periwinkle-blue satin. Angélique's dress, of royal blue velvet, braided with gold, matched her partner's outfit perfectly. They were the most magnificent couple at the whole gathering. Angélique had the surprise of seeing the cold face stirred by a smile as he led her, with her hand held high, for a *branle* across the great hall.

"Today you are no longer the Baroness of the Doleful Dress," he said.

She treasured those words in her heart, with the jealous feeling one has for a precious, infinitely rare gift. The secret of her origins made them accomplices. He was remembering the grey little quail whose hand had trembled in that of the handsome cousin.

'What a fool I was!' she said to herself with a smile.

When the house was fully furnished, Angélique had a fit of depression. She was overwhelmed by the solitude of her princely home. The Hôtel de Beautreillis meant too much to her. This abode, which Joffrey had never lived in and which yet seemed impregnated with memories, struck her as having aged with a long-lasting grief.

'The memories of what should have been,' she thought.

Sitting, in the mild spring nights, before the fire or at the casements, she watched the hours pass. Her customary interests forsook her. She was the prey of an ailment she could not understand. For her young body was lonely, while her mind and her heart succumbed to a ghostly presence. She would suddenly get up and, holding a candle, go to the doorstep and wait, in the darkness of the passage, for she knew not what. . . .

Was someone coming? . . . No! All was silent. The children were sleeping in their rooms under the care of devoted servants. She had restored to them their father's house.

One night Angélique was lying in her magnificent bed. She felt cold. She touched her smooth, firm flesh and caressed it with a kind of melancholy. No man alive could have sated her longing. She was alone for life!

It was then that, from the depth of the night, there rose a song, a celestial, exquisite song, like that of angels as they float over the countryside on Christmas Eve.

Angélique at first thought it was a hallucination. But as she approached the corridor, she could distinctly make out a child's voice singing.

Taking a candlestick, she directed her steps towards the nursery. She gently lifted the door-curtain and stopped, charmed by the picture revealed to her eyes.

A silver-gilt night-lamp softly lit the alcove in which was the bed of the two little boys. Standing in the big bed, Cantor in his white shift, with his two plump little hands folded over his stomach and with upraised eyes, was singing like a little cherub of Paradise. His voice was of extraordinary purity, but his childish lisp stumbled over the words most affectingly:

> *"C'est le Zour de la Noël*
> *Que Zésus est né.*
> *Il est né dans une étable,*
> *Dessus la paille;*
> *Il est né dans un coin,*
> *Dessus le foin."* [1]

Florimond, with his elbows propped on his pillow, was listening to him with evident delight.

A slight noise pulled Angélique out of her contemplation. She saw Barbe at her side, wiping tears from her eyes.

"Madame did not know that our treasure had such a beautiful voice?" the maid whispered. "I wanted it to be a surprise for Madame. He is shy. He only wants to sing for Florimond."

Once again, joy took the place of pain in Angélique's heart.

The soul of the troubadours had passed into Cantor. He was singing. Joffrey de Peyrac was not dead, since he lived on in his two sons. One looked like him, the other had his voice. . . .

Very late one evening, as Angélique was strewing sand on a letter to her dear friend Ninon de Lenclos, a footman came to announce that a tonsured cleric was asking for her urgently. In the entrance the young woman found an abbé, who told her that her brother, Father de Sancé, wished to see her.

"At once?"

"At once, Madame!"

---

[1] It's on Christmas Day that Jesus was born. He was born in a stable, on top of the straw; He was born in a corner, on top of the hay.

Angélique went upstairs for a cloak and a mask. A strange hour for the reunion of a Jesuit with his sister, who was also the widow of a sorcerer burned on the Place de Grève!

The abbé said it was not far to go. After only a few steps, the young woman found herself before a private dwelling-house, a small former hôtel of the Middle Ages, which was adjacent to the new Collegiate House of the Jesuits. In the vestibule Angélique's guide vanished like a black phantom. She walked up the stairs, her eyes raised towards the upper landing where a long silhouette leaned over the banister, holding a candlestick.

"Is that you, my sister?"

"It's I, Raymond."

"Come up, please."

She followed him without asking any questions. He showed her into a stone cell which was poorly lit by an oil lamp. Deep in the alcove Angélique distinguished a pale, delicate face—a woman's or a child's—with closed eyes.

"She is ill. She will die perhaps," said the Jesuit.

"Who is she?"

"Marie-Agnès, our sister."

After a moment's silence, he added:

"She's come to take refuge with me. I made her lie down, but in view of the nature of her sickness, I needed the help and advice of a woman. I thought of you."

"What's wrong with her?"

"She's losing blood profusely. I believe she must have provoked a miscarriage."

Angélique scrutinised her young sister. The hæmorrhage did not seem violent, but slow and continuous.

"We must stop it as quickly as possible, otherwise she'll die."

"I thought of sending for a physician, but——"

"A physician! . . . All he'd do is bleed her, which would be the end of her."

"Unfortunately, I can't call in a midwife, who would probably pry and gossip. Our rules are both very free and very strict. I shall not receive any reprimand for having succoured my sister in secret. But I must avoid all scandal. It's difficult for me to keep her here in this house, which is the annexe of a great seminary, you understand. . . ."

"As soon as we have stopped the bleeding, I'll have her

transported to my house. Meanwhile, we must send for Big Matthieu."

A quarter of an hour later, Flipot was scampering towards the Pont-Neuf, whistling now and then to make himself known to marauders. Angélique knew that Big Matthieu had an almost miraculous remedy to stop bleeding. On occasions, when it was specially requested, he also had a way of making himself unobtrusive. . . .

He arrived at once and attended to the young patient with the energy and skill of long experience, while soliloquising as was his habit:

"Ah! little lady, why didn't you use the electuary of chastity which Big Matthieu sells on the Pont-Neuf? It is made of camphor, liquorice, vine-seed and waterlily seeds. Take two drams of it morning and evening, followed by a glass of whey in which you've dipped a piece of red-hot iron. . . . Believe me, little lady, there's nothing better to suppress Venus's excessive ardours, which are paid for so dearly. . . ."

But poor Marie-Agnès was quite unable to hear these belated recommendations. With her diaphanous cheeks, mauve-hued eyelids and the thin, drawn face amid the copious black hair, she looked like a sweet, lifeless wax figure.

At last Angélique noticed that the hæmorrhage seemed to be stopping; a pink glow was returning to her young sister's cheeks. Big Matthieu went away, leaving a herb tea with Angélique which the patient was to drink every hour 'to replace the blood she had lost'. He advised waiting a few hours before moving her.

When he had gone, Angélique sat down near a small table, from which a black crucifix on its pedestal threw a gigantic shadow on the wall. A few moments later, Raymond returned and sat down at the other side of the table.

"I believe that at daybreak we shall be able to have her moved to my place," said Angélique, "but it's advisable to wait a little until she has recovered some strength."

"We'll wait," Raymond agreed.

He inclined his profile, which was perhaps a little less lean than it used to be, in an attitude of meditation. His straight black hair fell on the white neckband of his cassock. His tonsure had grown a little wider under the attack of an incipient baldness, but he had scarcely changed.

"Raymond, how did you know that I was at the Hôtel de Beautreillis, living there under the name of Madame Morens?"

The Jesuit made a vague gesture with his beautiful white hand.

"It was easy for me to make inquiries, to recognise you. I admire you, Angélique. The dreadful case whose victim you have been is now a thing of the remote past."

"Not so very remote," she said bitterly, "since I still cannot show myself in full daylight. Many lords of less noble birth than I look down upon me as an enriched chocolate-house keeper, and I shall never be able to return to Court, to go to Versailles."

He cast a penetrating glance at her.

"Why don't you marry a great name? You don't lack admirers, and your wealth, if not your beauty, can tempt more than one nobleman. You will thus acquire a new name and rank."

Angélique thought suddenly of Philippe, and she felt herself blushing at this new idea. Marry him? The Marquis du Plessis-Bellière? . . .

"Raymond, why didn't I think of that before?"

"Perhaps because you have not yet realised that you are a widow and free," he replied firmly. "You now have all the means to accede honourably to a high rank. It's a position which is not without advantages, and I can help you with all the influence I command."

"Thank you, Raymond. That would be wonderful," she said dreamily. "I have come such a long way, you can't imagine. Of all the family, I am the one who fell lowest, and yet one cannot say that any one of us has known a very brilliant lot. Why have we turned out so badly?"

"I thank you for the 'we'," he said with a brief smile.

"Oh! becoming a Jesuit is also a way of turning out badly. Remember, our father was not delighted. He would have much preferred to see you in charge of a good, sound church living. Josselin has disappeared in the Americas. Denis, the only soldier of the family, has the reputation of being a hothead and a bad loser, which is worse. Gontran? Let's not talk of him. He has lowered himself for the pleasure of daubing canvas like an artisan. Albert is a page to the Maréchal de Rochant. He is the Knight's paramour, unless he is reserved

for the dumpy charms of Madame la Maréchale. And Marie-
Agnès . . ."

She stopped, listened to the almost imperceptible breathing
coming from the alcove, and went on in a lower voice:

"At Court, I do believe she had a go at everybody. Has anyone an idea as to who was the father of this child?"

"I don't think she has herself," said the Jesuit somewhat
crudely. "But what I would like to see you clear up, above all,
is whether this is a miscarriage or a clandestine birth. I
shudder at the thought that she may have left a small living
creature in the hands of that Catherine Monvoisin."

"Did she go to see La Voisin?"

"I think so. She mumbled her name."

"Who doesn't go to see her?" said Angélique with a shrug.
"Recently the Duc de Vendôme went to see her, disguised as
a Savoyard, in order to extract some revelations from this
woman about the treasure Monsieur de Turenne is alleged to
have hidden. And Monsieur, the King's brother, made her
come to Saint-Cloud to show him the devil. I don't know if she
succeeded, but he paid her as if he'd seen him. Soothsayer,
abortionist, poison-dealer, she is a woman of many parts. . . ."

Raymond listened to this gossip without a smile. He closed
his eyes and sighed deeply.

"Angélique, my sister, I am horrified," he said slowly.
"The century in which we live witnesses such infamous morals,
such abominable crimes that future eras will shudder at it. In
this one year, several hundred women have accused themselves
in my confessional of having rid themselves of the fruit of their
womb. That is nothing: it's the normal consequence of licentiousness and adultery. But close on half my penitents confess
to having poisoned one of their family, to having sought to
bring about by demoniac practices the disappearance of someone who stood in their way. Are we, then, still barbarians?
Have the heresies, in shaking the barriers of the Faith, revealed to us the abyss of our nature? There is a terrible dis-
harmony between the laws and peoples' inclinations. It is the
Church's duty to show the way again through this disorder. . . ."

Angélique listened with surprise to the confidences of the
great Jesuit.

"Why do you speak *to me* of all this, Raymond? For all you
know, I may be one of those women who . . ."

The eyes of the priest returned to her. He seemed to be examining her, then shook his head.

"You, you are like a diamond," he said, "a noble stone, hard and unyielding . . . but simple and transparent. I do not know what sins you may have committed in the course of the years during which you disappeared, but I am convinced that if you committed them, then it was mostly because you could not do otherwise. You are like the real poor, my sister Angélique, you sin without knowing it, unlike the rich and the mighty. . . ."

A naïve gratitude filled Angélique's heart on hearing these surprising words, in which she discerned almost a call of Grace and the expression of a pardon come from Heaven.

The night was peaceful. A smell of incense hovered in the cell, and the shadow of the cross which watched over the bedside of their sister in danger of death seemed to Angélique gentle and reassuring for the first time in many years.

With a spontaneous movement she slid down to her knees on the stone floor.

"Raymond, will you hear my confession?"

Marie-Agnès's convalescence proceeded satisfactorily at the Hôtel de Beautreillis. The young girl, however, remained ailing and in low spirits. She seemed to have forgotten her crystalline laughter which had enchanted the Court, and displayed only the demanding and impulsive side of her nature. In the beginning, she evinced no gratitude whatsoever for Angélique's kindness. But as her sister regained her strength, Angélique availed herself of the first opportunity to box her ears soundly. Thereafter Marie-Agnès declared that Angélique was the only woman with whom she could ever get on. With coaxing grace she would nestle close to her sister on winter evenings when they lingered by the fireside, playing a mandolin or doing some embroidery. They would exchange their impressions of the persons they both knew, and as each had a sharp tongue and a quick wit they sometimes laughed uproariously at their sallies.

Once recovered, Marie-Agnès seemed to have no intention of leaving 'her friend Madame Morens'. Nobody knew that they were close relatives. That amused them. The Queen inquired after the health of her lady-in-waiting. Marie Agnès sent word that she was well, but would enter a nunnery. The jesting remark was more serious than it looked. Marie-Agnès obstinately refused to see anyone, and plunged into the Epistles of Saint Paul and went with Angélique to Mass.

Angélique was very glad that she had had the courage to confess to Raymond. This enabled her to appear before the Lord's altar without mental reservations or false shame, and to play her part of a lady of the Marais to perfection. She sank with satisfaction into the atmosphere of the long services redolent with incense and vibrant with the preacher's resounding voice and the sonorous organ music.

It was most soothing thus to have time to pray and think of her soul.

The rumour of their conversation brought a flurry of indignant gentlemen to the Hôtel de Beautreillis. Whether admirers of Angélique or ex-lovers of Marie-Agnès, they all protested.

"What is this we hear? You are doing penance? You are retiring to a nunnery?"

Marie-Agnès met all questions with the mask of a disdainful little sphinx. Most of the time, she preferred not to show herself, or else ostentatiously opened a prayer-book. Angélique for her part, forcefully denied the rumour. The moment seemed to her inopportune. Thus, when Madame Scarron had taken her to her confessor, the honest Abbé Godin, Angélique balked at the mere mention of a hair-shirt. At the very moment when she was busily making plans to marry Philippe, she was not going to spoil her skin and the alluring curves of her beautiful body by bristling girdles and other objects of penance.

She would need all her allurements and more to vanquish the indifference of this strange young man who, with his fair hair and light satins, seemed cast and clothed in ice.

Yet he was a fairly assiduous visitor at the Hôtel de Beautreillis. He would arrive with a nonchalant air and talk little. As Angélique gazed at him in his disdainful beauty, she would recapture the somewhat humble and admiring sensation of bygone days, when she was a little girl over-awed by her tall, elegant cousin. So much so that, in her recollection, this unpleasant memory acquired a sensuous thrill. She remembered Philippe's white hands on her thighs, the scratch caused by his rings. . . . Now that she saw him so cold and aloof, she would sometimes feel regret for that contact and for her own flight. Philippe was certainly unaware that she was the woman he had attacked that night at the inn of 'The Red Mask'.

Whenever his clear eyes dropped on Angélique, she had the depressing feeling that he had never noticed her beauty. He never paid her a compliment, not even the tritest one. He was not very amiable, and the children, far from being charmed by his dash, were afraid of him.

"You have a way of gazing at the handsome Plessis that alarms me," Marie-Agnès said to her elder sister one evening. "Don't tell me, Angélique, that you, the most sensible woman I know, let yourself be ensnared by the charm of that——"

She seemed to be searching for a crushing epithet, failed to find it, and replaced it with a pout of disgust.

"What have you against him?" asked Angélique, astonished.

"What have I against him? Well, just this: that he is so handsome, so attractive, and doesn't even know how to take a woman in his arms. For you'll admit it matters, the way a man takes a woman in his arms? . . ."

"Marie-Agnès, this is a very frivolous subject of conversation for a young person who intends to enter a nunnery!"

"Precisely. Let's make hay while the sun shines. For my part, I first judge a man by the way he embraces me. The gesture of an imperious yet gentle arm, which makes me feel that I cannot struggle out of it and which yet leaves me free. Ah! what a pleasure to be a woman and so frail, at that moment!"

Her finely-chiselled face, with its eyes of a cruel kitten, softened in a dreamy ecstasy, and Angélique smiled at seeing her with the fleeting mask of sensuous pleasure which she showed only to men. Then the girl's brows contracted.

"I must admit that very few men have this talent. But at least they all try to do their best. Whereas Philippe doesn't even try. He knows only one kind of behaviour with women: he throws them down and rapes them. He must have learned love on the battlefields. Ninon herself wasn't able to do anything with him. He probably keeps his pretty graces for his lovers! . . . All the women detest him in proportion to their disappointment."

Angélique, leaning over the fire, on which she was roasting

chestnuts, was annoyed at the anger which her sister's words produced in her.

She had made up her mind to marry Philippe du Plessis. It was the best solution, one that would arrange everything and put the final touch to her ascent and her rehabilitation. But she would have liked to have had some illusions about the man whom she had chosen for her second husband. She would have liked to find him lovable in order to have the right to love him.

In a spurt of sincerity towards herself, she ran to Ninon the next day and broached the subject.

"What do you think of Philippe du Plessis?"

The courtesan pondered, one finger against her cheek.

"I believe that, when one knows him well, one perceives that he is much less nice than he appears. But when one knows him better, one perceives that he is much nicer than he appears."

"I don't follow you, Ninon."

"I mean that he has none of the qualities which his beauty promises, not even the inclination to make himself loved. On the other hand, if you dig deep enough, he inspires esteem because he represents a rare specimen of an almost extinct race: he is the nobleman *par excellence*. He is in agony over questions of etiquette, he is afraid of having a mud-stain on his silk stockings. But he is not afraid of death. And when he dies, he'll be as lonely as a wolf and won't ask for help from any-body. He belongs only to the King and to himself."

"I did not expect such greatness in him!"

"But then you don't see his pettiness either, my dear! The littleness of a true nobleman is congenital. His coat-of-arms has hidden the rest of humanity from him for centuries. Why must one always believe that virtue and its opposite cannot live cheek by jowl within the same person? A nobleman is both great and petty."

"And what does he think of women?"

"Philippe? . . . My dear, you come and tell me when you've found out."

"Apparently he is a terrible brute with them?"

"So they say. . . ."

"Ninon, you aren't going to tell me that he hasn't slept with you."

"Alas, my dear, that's just what I *am* going to tell you. I must admit that all my talents have failed with him."

"Ninon, you frighten me!"

"To tell the truth, this hard-eyed Adonis did rather tempt me. He was said to be ill-bred in matters of love, but I am not averse to a certain clumsy ardour and like to tame it. So I arranged to lure him into my alcove. . . ."

"And then?"

"Then, nothing. I would have had more luck with a snow-man picked up in the yard. He finally confessed to me that I did not inspire him in any way, because he felt friendship towards me. I believe he needs hatred and violence to put him in the right mood."

"He is mad!"

"Maybe . . . no, I'd say he's merely behind the times. He should have been born fifty years sooner. When I see him, he moves me strangely, for he reminds me of my youth."

"Your youth, Ninon? . . ." said Angélique, looking at the courtesan's delicate, unwrinkled complexion. "But you are younger than I am!"

"No, my sweet. People sometimes say, to console certain women: 'The body ages, but the soul remains young.' With me, it's just the opposite: my body remains young—and the gods be thanked for it!—but my soul has aged all the same. The days of my youth were during the close of the last reign and at the beginning of the present one. Men were different then. There was fighting everywhere: Huguenots, Swedes, the insurgents of Monsieur Gaston d'Orléans. Young men knew how to fight but not how to love. They were big savages in lace collars. . . . As for Philippe—do you know whom he reminds me of? Of Cinq-Mars, who was the favourite of Louis XIII. Poor Cinq-Mars! He had fallen in love with Marion Delorme. But the King was jealous. And Cardinal Richelieu had little trouble in precipitating his downfall. Cinq-Mars laid his beautiful fair head on the block. There were many tragic fates in those days!"

"Ninon, don't talk to me like a grandmother. It doesn't suit you in the least."

"But I am obliged to adopt a grandmother's tone to scold you a little, Angélique. For I am much afraid that you are straying from your path. . . . Angélique, my pretty child, you who have known a great love, don't tell me that you've fallen

294

headlong in love with Philippe. He is too far from you. He would disappoint you even more than he does other women."

Angélique blushed, and the corners of her mouth trembled like those of a child.

"Why do you say that I've known a great love?"

"Because it can be seen in your eyes. They are so rare, women who bear deep in their eyes this sad and wonderful trace. Yes, I know—it's over for you now. In what way? . . . Never mind. Perhaps you found out that he was married, perhaps he deceived you, perhaps he is dead. . . ."

"He is dead, Ninon!"

"It's better so. Your great wound is free of poison. But——"

Angélique straightened her back proudly.

"Let's talk no more of it, Ninon, please! I want to marry Philippe. I must marry Philippe. You cannot understand why. I don't love him, it's true, but he attracts me. He always has. And I've always thought that he'd be mine some day. Don't say any more. . . ."

Returning home, Angélique found the same enigmatic Philippe in her drawing-room. He was a frequent caller, but her plans made no progress.

Angélique got to the point of asking herself if he did not come to see Marie-Agnès; however, when her young sister had retired to the Carmelites of the Faubourg Saint-Jacques to prepare her Easter, he continued to be a regular visitor. She heard one day that he had boasted of drinking the best rosolio in Paris at her house. Perhaps he came merely to savour this exquisite cordial which she herself prepared with quantities of fennel, aniseed, coriander, camomile and sugar macerated in brandy.

Angélique was proud of her domestic talent, and she saw no reason to disdain any bait. But the thought wounded her pride. Didn't either her beauty or her conversation hold any attraction for Philippe?

With the coming of the first days of spring, she felt desperate, all the more so as a drastic Lenten fast had weakened her. She had secretly cherished the idea of marrying Philippe with too much enthusiasm to have the courage to give it up. For, once set up as the Marquise du Plessis, she would be presented at Court, she would find again her native soil and her family, and would reign over the beautiful white château which had delighted her youth.

Her nerves frayed by these alternatives of hope and discouragement, she was dying to consult La Voisin to have a confirmation of her future. An opportunity was supplied by Madame Scarron, who called on her one afternoon.

"Angélique, I've come to fetch you, for you simply must accompany me. That madcap Athénaïs has got it into her head to ask advice about I don't know what of some diabolical soothsayer, a woman called Catherine Monvoisin. It seems to me that the presence of two devout women will be more than needed to pray and fight against the evil spell that may be cast on this reckless girl."

"You are perfectly right, Françoise," Angélique hastened to agree.

Flanked by her two guardian angels, Athénaïs de Montespan, bristling with impatience and not at all frightened, entered the witch's lair. It was a fine house in the Faubourg du Temple, the newly-rich sorceress having moved from the sinister hovel where, for a long time, the dwarf Barcarole had ushered in her furtive visitors. Nowadays people called on her almost overtly.

Generally she received her clients on a kind of throne, draped in a cloak embroidered with golden bees, but on that particular day Catherine Monvoisin, whose unpleasant habits had not been changed by contact with high society, was dead-drunk.

No sooner had they stepped over the threshold of the parlour into which they were shown than the three women realised that nothing could be got out of the fortune-teller.

After gazing at them with dim eyes for a long while, the witch descended from her dais, reeling unsteadily, and dashing up to the horrified Françoise Scarron she seized her hand.

"You now," she said, "now you have a most uncommon destiny. I see the Ocean, and then the Night, and then the Sun above all. Night, that's poverty. We know what that's like! There's nothing blacker! Just like the Night! But the Sun, that's the King. There, my dear, the King will love you, and he'll even marry you."

"But you are mistaken!" cried Athénaïs furiously. "I'm the

one who've come to see you to ask whether the King will love me. You are all mixed up."

"Don't get annoyed, little lady," the other protested in a thick voice. "I am not drunk enough to confuse the destinies of two persons. To each his own, isn't that right? Give me your hand. The Sun is in yours too. And then, there is Luck. Yes, the King will love you, too. But he won't marry you."

"A plague upon the fuddled hag!" muttered Athénaïs, drawing her hand away, enraged.

But La Voisin was determined to give each her full measure. She peremptorily took hold of Angélique's hand, rolled her eyes, nodded her head.

"A fabulous destiny! Night, but also Fire, a Fire that dominates all."

"I would like to know if I shall marry a Marquis."

"I can't tell you if he's a Marquis, but I see two marriages. There, those two small strokes. And then six children. . . ."

"Merciful Lord! . . ."

"And also . . . love affairs!—one, two, three, four, five. . . ."

"Don't bother," protested Angélique, trying to withdraw her hand.

"No, wait! . . . The Fire is what's so surprising. It burns right across your whole life . . . to the very end. It blazes so fiercely that it hides the Sun. The King will love you, but you won't love him on account of that Fire. . . ."

In the carriage that was taking them back, Athénaïs raged.

"That woman isn't worth the tiniest *sou* of all the money people give her. I've never heard such a collection of rubbish. The King will love you! . . . the King will love you! . . . She says the same thing to everybody!"

Angélique learned the news from Mademoiselle de Parajonc. She was not expecting it and took a certain amount of time to unravel the truth from the old blue-stocking's impossible jargon. The latter called upon her towards supper-time, emerging from the foggy night like a gloomy owl, rumpled with a variety of ribbons, her eyes fixed and watchful. Angélique offered her some griddle-cakes by the fireside. Philonide talked at length about their neighbour, Madame de Gauffray, who had just 'felt the after-effects of permitted love', meaning that after ten months of marriage she had given birth to a little boy. Then she expatiated on her trouble with her 'dear ailing ones'; Angélique thought she was referring to her aged parents, but in fact she was referring to her own feet, which suffered from corns. Finally, after much splitting of hairs and dissecting of sentiments and declaring, after watching the rain lash against the window-panes for a while: "The third element is falling", Philonide, full of glee at announcing a piece of news, decided to express herself like common mortals:

"Do you know that Madame de Lamoignon is going to marry off her daughter?"

"She does well! The girl isn't pretty but she has money enough to make a brilliant match."

"You are most perceptive, as usual, my dear. Actually it's only the dowry of that mousy little thing that could possibly tempt such a handsome gentleman as Philippe du Plessis."

"Philippe?"

"You've heard no rumour of it?" inquired Philonide, blinking her watchful eyes.

Angélique had recovered herself. She said with a shrug:

"Perhaps I have . . . but I didn't give it any credence. Philippe du Plessis cannot lower himself by marrying the daughter of a judge who, though occupying a high position, is of common extraction."

The old maid sneered.

"A peasant on my estates often used to say: 'Money is found only on the ground and you must stoop to pick it up.' It's common knowledge that young du Plessis is always in financial straits. He gambles heavily at Versailles and he spent a fortune on equipment for his last campaign; he had a train of ten mules trailing behind him, carrying his gold plate and goodness knows what else. The silk of his tent was so richly embroidered that the Spaniards spotted it from their trenches and used it as a target. . . . I do grant you, though, that this insensitive charmer is furiously handsome. . . ."

Angélique let her go on soliloquising. After her first feeling of incredulity, she now felt discouraged. The last threshold to cross in order to bask at last in the light of the Sun King—the marriage with Philippe—was crumbling. For that matter, she had always known that it would be too difficult and that she would not have strength enough. She was worn out, used up. . . . She was but a chocolate-manufacturer and would not be able to maintain herself much longer on the level of the nobility, which would never welcome her. She was being received, but not welcomed. . . . Versailles! . . . Versailles! The glamour of the Court, the radiance of the Sun King! Philippe! Beautiful, unattainable god Mars! . . . She would drop back to the level of a *petite bourgeoise*. And her children would never be gentlemen. . . .

Absorbed in her thoughts, she did not realise that time was passing. The fire was dying in the hearth, the candle smoked.

Angélique heard Philonide summon sharply Flipot, who was standing watch near the door:

"Idler, remove the excess of this glimmerer."

As Flipot stood open-mouthed, Angélique translated wearily:

"Lackey, trim the candle."

Philonide de Parajonc got up, satisfied:

"My dear, you seem pensive. I leave you to your muses. . . ."

CHAPTER 79

THAT NIGHT, Angélique could not sleep. In the morning she attended Mass. On her way back she was very calm. She had come to no decision, however, and when in the afternoon the hour of the promenade arrived and she stepped into her carriage, she did not yet know what she was going to do.

But she had taken special care with her toilet.

Smoothing her silks and taffetas, she scolded herself, all alone in her coach. Why was she wearing today her new dress with three alternate skirts—chestnut brown, autumn leaves, and tender green? A gossamer-fine gold embroidery, set off by pearls, covered, as if with a glittering network of twigs, the top-skirt, dress-mantle and bodice. The lace on the collar and cuffs, tied with green, reproduced the pattern of the embroidery. Angélique had had the lace specially made for her in the workshops of Alençon, according to a design by Monsieur de Moyne, the decorator of the royal households. Angélique had initially reserved this outfit, at once sumptuous and austere, for the gatherings of great ladies such as those given by Madame d'Albret, where conversation tried to keep clear of frivolities. Angélique knew that her dress was wonderfully becoming to her complexion and to her eyes though it aged her a little.

But why had she put it on to go for a promenade on the Cours? Was she hoping to dazzle the impervious Philippe, or to inspire confidence by the severity of her attire? . . . She fanned herself nervously to cool the waves of heat that mounted to her cheeks.

Chrysanthemum puckered her moist little muzzle and cast a baffled glance at her mistress.

"I think I'm going to make a fool of myself," the young woman said to her, sadly. "But I cannot give him up. No, really, I can't."

Then, to the little dog's great surprise, she closed her eyes and let herself drop against the back of the coach as if she had lost her strength.

On reaching the approaches to the Tuileries, Angélique revived abruptly. With sparkling eyes she picked up the tooled little mirror that hung from her belt and surveyed her make-up. Black eyelids, red lips. That was all she permitted herself. She made no endeavour to whiten her complexion, having finally realised that her warm-tinted skin attracted more compliments than all the fashionable experiments in white plaster. Her teeth, carefully rubbed with genista-blossom powder and rinsed with burnt wine, had a moist sparkle.

She smiled at herself.

She took Chrysanthemum under her arm and, holding her dress-mantle up with one hand, passed through the gate of the Tuileries. For a second she told herself that if Philippe wasn't there she'd give up the fight. But he was there. She saw him near the Big Flowerbed, with the Prince de Condé, who was holding forth in his favourite spot where he liked to display himself to the curious.

Angélique stepped boldly towards the group. She knew suddenly that since fate had led Philippe to the Tuileries, she would accomplish what she had set out to do.

The afternoon was mild and fresh. A brief downpour, a short while ago, had darkened the gravel and polished the first leaves on the trees.

Angélique passed, nodding and smiling. She told herself with annoyance that her dress clashed horribly with the suit Philippe was wearing. He, who was always dressed in pale colours, was sporting an extraordinary peacock-blue coat with buttonholes thick with gold embroideries and with no interstices. Ever in the vanguard of fashion, he had already adopted the new fashion of full skirting, which the sword pushed up at the back.

His cuffs were beautiful, but the 'canons' were practically non-existent, and his trunk-hose tightly fitted his knees. Those who still wore a rhinegrave blushed on meeting him. Handsome scarlet stockings with gold corners matched the red heels of his diamond-buckled leather shoes. Under his arm Philippe carried a small beaver hat, so fine-haired that it looked like old polished silver. His plumes were sky-blue. With his blond wig cascading over his shoulders, Philippe du Plessis-Bellière was like a beautiful bird rearing up on his spurs.

Angélique cast her eyes around for the figure of the Lamoignon girl, but her pitiful rival was not there. With a sigh of relief, she walked briskly up to the Prince de Condé, who made a show of lavishing upon her, whenever they met, a disappointed and resigned affection.

"Well, then, my lady-love!" he sighed, rubbing his long nose against Angélique's forehead. "Cruel love, will you do us the honour of sharing our carriage for a drive along the Cours?"

Angélique uttered a little cry. Then she feigned casting an embarrassed glance at Philippe and murmured:

"May Your Highness pardon me, but Monsieur du Plessis has already invited me for the promenade."

"A pox on those feathered young cockerels!" growled the Prince. "Hey! Marquis, will you be presumptuous enough to retain for long one of the most beautiful ladies in the capital for your private and exclusive use?"

"May God preserve me, Monseigneur," replied the young man, who, obviously, had not overheard the dialogue and did not know which lady was referred to.

"Very well! You make take her away. I grant her to you. But in future deign to come down from your cloud in time to reflect that you are not the only cock of the walk and that others too, are entitled to the most sparkling smile in Paris."

"I am taking good note, Monseigneur," the courtier assured him, sweeping the sand with his azure plume.

Angélique, after a deep curtsy to the company, placed her little hand in Philippe's and led him away. Poor Philippe! Why did people seem to fear him? He seemed so disarming, on the contrary, with his haughty absent-mindedness.

She dropped her eyes and watched, with throbbing heart,

Philippe's sure and magnificently poised step crush the wet gravel under his red heels. No nobleman could place his foot as he did, nobody had as beautifully shaped legs. 'Not even the King . . .' thought the young woman. But in order to judge accurately she would have to see the King a little closer, and this required going to Versailles. *She would go to Versailles!* Just like this, with her hand in Philippe's, she would walk up the royal gallery. A crossfire of eyes at Court would pick out every detail of her marvellous clothes. She would stop at a few steps' distance from the King—'Madame la Marquise du Plessis-Bellière——'

Her fingers clenched a little. Philippe then said with sullen surprise:

"I still don't understand why His Highness imposed your presence upon me. . . ."

"Because he thought it would please you. You know that he is even fonder of you than of the Duc. You are the son of his warrior's disposition."

She added, casting a coaxing glance at him:

"Does my presence irk you to such a degree? Were you expecting someone else?"

"No! But I had no intention of going to the Cours tonight."

She did not dare to ask why. There might be no particular reason. With Philippe, it was often like that. His decisions had no serious significance, but nobody dared to question him.

On the Cours there were few strollers. A smell of fresh wood and mushrooms pervaded the air under the shady dome of its tall trees.

As she stepped into Philippe's carriage, Angélique noticed the horsecloth with its silver fringes that almost swept the ground. Where had he found the money for this latest elegance? As far as she knew, he was already deep in debt. Was this the result of Judge Lamoignon's generosity towards his future son-in-law?

Never had Angélique found Philippe's silence so hard to bear. Impatiently she feigned an interest in Chrysanthemum's capers or in the carriages they passed. Several times she was about to open her mouth, but the young man's imperturbable profile discouraged her. His eyes gazing into space, he was slowly moving his cheeks as he sucked a fennel lozenge. Angélique said to herself that she would make him give up this habit once they were married. When one has such an ethereal beauty, one has not the right to indulge in anything that makes one look like a ruminant.

It was getting darker now, for the trees were becoming thicker. The coachman made a lackey inquire whether he was to turn round or go on through the Bois de Boulogne.

"Go on," ordered Angélique, without waiting for Philippe's assent.

And, having broken the silence at last, she went on brightly:

"Do you know what nonsense people are talking, Philippe? It appears that you are going to marry the Lamoignon girl."

He inclined his handsome, fair head.

"That nonsense is correct, my dear."

"But——" Angélique took a breath and plunged on:

"But that isn't possible! You, the arbiter of elegance, aren't going to tell me that you find some charm in that poor little grasshopper?"

"I have no opinion whatsoever about her charms."

"Whatever attracts you in her, then?"

"Her dowry."

So Mademoiselle de Parajonc had not lied. Angélique stifled a sigh of relief. If it was a question of money, everything could be all right. But she tried to give her face a pained expression:

"Oh! Philippe! I didn't think you were so materialistic."

"Materialistic?" he repeated, raising his eyebrows.

"I mean, so attached to earthly matters."

"What else do you expect me to be attached to? My father didn't intend me for Holy Orders."

"Without being a churchman, one can consider marriage otherwise than as a money matter!"

"What else is it?"

"Well!... a matter of love."

"Oh! if that's what's worrying you, my dear, I can assure you that I am perfectly determined to give this little grasshopper a whole series of children."

"No!" Angélique shouted with rage.

"She'll get her money's worth."

"No!" said Angélique again, stamping her foot.

Philippe turned an amazed face towards her.

"You don't want me to give my wife children?"

"That's not the question, Philippe. I don't want her to be your wife, that's all."

303

"And why shouldn't she be?"

Angélique gave a sigh of exasperation.

"Oh! Philippe, you who have frequented Ninon's salon, I cannot understand how you could have failed to acquire the least gift for conversation. With your 'whys' and your stunned expression you make people feel that they are utterly stupid."

"Perhaps they are," he said with a half-smile.

On account of that smile Angélique, who felt like striking him, was filled with an absurd tenderness. He was smiling. . . . Why did he smile so rarely? She had the impression that only she would ever be able to understand him and to make him smile in this way.

"A fool," said some people. "A brute," said others. And Ninon de Lenclos: "When one knows him well, one perceives that he is much less nice than he appears, but when one knows him better, one perceives that he is much nicer than he appears. . . . He is a nobleman. . . . He belongs only to the King and to himself. . . ."

'And he belongs to me, too,' thought Angélique fiercely.

She was raging. How on earth could she pull this boy out of his indifference? The smell of powder? All right, he'd have war, since he wanted it. Nervously she pushed away Chrysanthemum, who was nibbling at the tassels of her cloak, then made an effort to overcome her irritation and said in a light-hearted tone:

"If it's just a matter of restoring your fortune, Philippe, why don't you marry me? I have lots of money, and money that doesn't risk being lost as a result of a poor harvest. I have good, sound business affairs which will go on increasing."

"Marry you?" he repeated.

His amazement was genuine. He burst out laughing unpleasantly.

"I? Marry a chocolate-maker?" he said with supreme scorn.

Angélique flushed violently. This damned Philippe would always have a gift for crushing her with shame and anger. She said, with blazing eyes:

"One might think that I am suggesting mingling common stock with blood royal! Do not forget that my name is Angélique de Ridoué de Sancé de Monteloup. My blood is as pure as yours, Cousin, and it is more ancient, for my family descends from the first Capets, whereas you, on the male side, can only pride yourself on some bastard of Henri II's."

He gazed at her unblinkingly for a long while; a sudden interest seemed to appear in his pale eyes.

"You once said something like that to me before. It was at Monteloup, in that crumbling fortress of yours. An ill-kempt little horror in tatters was waiting for me at the foot of the stairs to point out to me that her blood was more ancient than mine. Oh, it was really very funny and ridiculous."

Angélique saw herself again in the icy corridor of Monteloup, her eyes raised to Philippe. She remembered how cold her hands had been, how hot her head, and how painful her stomach as she watched him coming down the big stone staircase. Her whole young body, labouring with the mystery of puberty, had quivered at the apparition of the beautiful youth. She had fainted. When she had regained consciousness, in the big bed in her room, her mother had explained to her that she was no longer a little girl and that a new phenomenon had taken place in her.

That Philippe should have been involved in those first manifestations of her life as a woman stirred her even after all those years. Yes, it was ridiculous, as he said. But it was not without sweetness.

She looked at him uncertainly and made an effort to smile. Just as on that evening long ago, she felt ready to tremble before him. She murmured in a low, imploring voice:

"Philippe, marry me. You'll have all the money you want. I am of noble blood. People will soon forget my trade. Anyhow, many gentlemen nowadays don't consider it beneath them to engage in business. Monsieur Colbert told me . . ."

She broke off. He was not listening. Perhaps he was thinking of something else . . . or of nothing. If he had asked her: 'Why do you want to marry me?', she would have shouted: 'Because I love you!' For she knew at that moment that she loved him with the same nostalgic, naïve love which had shone over her childhood. But he did not speak. So she went on, clumsily, filled with despair:

"Understand me . . . I want to find my class again, have a name, a great name . . . be presented at Court . . . at Versailles. . . ."

That was not the way she should have talked to him. Immediately she regretted her confession, hoped he had not heard it. But he muttered with a narrow smile:

"One can surely consider marriage otherwise than as a money matter!"

Then, in the same tone of voice in which he would have pushed away a hand tendering a box of sweetmeats to him:

"No, my dear, really not. . . ."

She understood that his decision was irrevocable. She had lost.

After a few moments, Philippe pointed out to her that she had not answered Mademoiselle de Montpensier's greeting.

Angélique noticed that the carriage had returned towards the avenues of the Cours-la-Reine, which was now full of animation. She began to respond mechanically to the greetings addressed to her. It seemed to her that the sun had gone out and that life tasted of ashes. She was distraught at the thought that Philippe was sitting next to her and that she found herself thus disarmed. Wasn't there anything she could do? Her arguments, her passion, slid off him as off a smooth, frozen carapace. You cannot compel a man to marry you when he neither loves nor desires you and when his self-interest can be served as well by some other solution. Fear alone might perhaps constrain him. But what fear could knit the brow of this god Mars?

"There is Madame de Montespan," Philippe went on. "She is with her sister, the abbess, and Madame de Thianges. They really are radiant creatures."

"I thought Madame de Montespan was in the Roussillon. She had begged her husband to take her along so as to escape from her creditors."

"If I can judge by the state of her carriage, the creditors let themselves be mollified. Did you notice how beautiful the velvet was? But why black? It's a sinister colour."

"The Montespans are still in half mourning for their mother."

"Less than half. Madame de Montespan danced at Versailles last night. It is the first time we have had a little fun since the death of the Queen Mother. The King invited Madame de Montespan to dance."

Angélique made an effort to inquire whether this meant that Mademoiselle de La Vallière's fall from favour was approaching. She found it difficult to keep up this mundane conversation. She did not care a rap whether Monsieur de Montespan was cuckolded and whether her intrepid friend became the King's mistress.

"His Highness the Prince is waving to you," said Philippe a little later.

With a movement of her fan, Angélique answered the cane-twirling which the Prince de Condé addressed to her from his carriage window.

"You are indeed the only woman to whom Monseigneur still shows some gallantry," declared the Marquis with a little sneer, whether mocking or admiring it was hard to say. "Ever since the death of his sweet friend, Mademoiselle du Vigean, he swore he would never again ask women for anything but carnal pleasures. He himself made me this confidence. For my part, I wonder what on earth he could have asked of them before."

Then, with a polite yawn:

"There's only one thing he still desires: to be given a command. Ever since he learned that there are thoughts of a campaign in the air, he hasn't missed the King's levée a single day, and he settles his debts with gold pistoles."

"What heroism!" Angélique sneered, finally exasperated by Philippe's weary, precious tone. "Just how far will this perfect courtier crawl in his endeavour to return to favour? . . . When one thinks there was a time when he tried to poison the King and his brother!"

"What are you saying, Madame?" Philippe protested indignantly. "He himself does not deny that he was in rebellion against Monsieur de Mazarin. His hatred carried him further than he intended. But the idea of making an attempt on the King's life could never have even occurred to him. Isn't that just like women's irresponsible talk!"

"Oh, don't feign innocence, Philippe. You know as well as I do that it is true, since the plot was hatched in your own castle."

There was a pause, and Angélique realised that she had hit her target.

"You are mad!" said Philippe in a hushed voice.

Angélique turned towards him. Had she found so soon the way to his fear, his only fear? . . .

She saw him turn pale, his eyes watching her with an expression that was at least attentive. She said in a low voice:

"I was there. I heard them. I saw them. The Prince de

Condé, the monk Exili, the Duchesse de Beaufort, your father, and several others who are still alive and who at present busily bow and scrape at Versailles. I heard them sell themselves to Monsieur Fouquet."

"That's a lie!"

Half closing her eyes, she recited:

"I, Louis II, Prince de Condé, give my word and assurance to Monseigneur Fouquet never to pledge my loyalty to any other person but to him, to place at his disposal my strongholds, fortifications and other such whenever . . ."

"Be silent!" he shouted, horrified.

"Given in Plessis-Bellière, the 20th of September 1649."

Jubilantly, she saw him grow ever paler:

"Little fool," he said, shrugging his shoulders with contempt. "Why do you dig up these old stories? Bygones are bygones. The King himself would decline to give them credence."

"The King has never had the documents in his hands. He never really knew the extent of the treachery of the great lords."

She broke off to greet the carriage of Madame d'Albret, then continued very gently:

"Five years haven't passed, Philippe, since Monsieur Fouquet was sentenced. . . ."

"Well then? What are you driving at?"

"At this: that the King won't, for a long time yet, be able to regard with affection the names of such persons as were linked with Monsieur Fouquet."

"He won't know them. The documents were destroyed."

"Not all of them."

The young man drew closer to her on the velvet seat. She had dreamed of such a move for a kiss of love, but this was obviously not the time for gallantry. He gripped her wrist and crushed it in his slim hand, whose knuckles went white. Angélique bit her lip with pain, but her pleasure was stronger. She infinitely preferred to see him thus, violent and rough, than aloof, slippery, impervious to attack in the shell of his disdain.

Under his light makeup, the face of the Marquis du Plessis was livid. He tightened his hold on her wrist.

"The poison casket . . ." he hissed. "So it was you who took it!"

"Yes, it was me."

308

"Little slut! I was always sure you knew something. My father didn't believe it. The disappearance of that casket tormented him to his deathbed. And it was you! And you still have that casket?"

"I still have it."

He began to swear between his teeth. Angélique thought it was wonderful to see those lovely fresh lips let forth such a string of oaths.

"Let me go," she said, "you are hurting me."

He slowly drew away, but with a flash in his eyes.

"I know," said Angélique, "that you would like to hurt me even more. Hurt me until I close my mouth for ever. But you would gain nothing by it, Philippe. On the very day of my death my testament is to be handed to the King, who will find in it all the necessary revelations and an indication of the hiding-place where the documents can be found."

With a wry grimace, she removed from her wrist the gold chain whose links Philippe's fingers had driven into her flesh.

"You are a brute, Philippe," she said lightly.

Then she pretended to look out of the carriage window. She was quite calm.

Outside, the setting sun no longer trailed its golden hues across the trees. The carriage had turned back towards the Bois de Boulogne. It was still light, but night would soon be falling.

Angélique felt frozen with dampness. With a shiver, she turned again towards Philippe. He was as white and motionless as a statue, but she noticed that his fair moustache was wet with perspiration.

"I love the Prince," he said, "and my father was an honest man. You can't do a thing like that. . . . How much money do you want in exchange for those documents? I'll borrow if necessary."

"I don't want money."

"What do you want, then?"

"I told you a moment ago, Philippe. I want you to marry me."

"Never!" he said, recoiling.

Did she disgust him to that point? And yet there had been more than just worldly small-talk between them. Had he not sought her company? Ninon herself had remarked upon it.

They remained silent. Only when the carriage had drawn up before the Hôtel de Beautreillis did Angélique realise that she was back in Paris. It was quite dark now. The young woman could no longer see Philippe's face. It was better that way.

She was bold enough to question him in a caustic tone of voice:

"Well, Marquis? How far have you got in your meditations?"

He stirred and seemed to wake from a bad dream.

"It's agreed, Madame, I shall marry you! Have the goodness to present yourself tomorrow night at my house in the rue Saint-Antoine. You will discuss the terms of the contract with my steward."

Angélique did not hold out her hand. She knew he would refuse it.

She declined the light repast which the chamber-valet presented to her and, contrary to her habits, did not go upstairs to the nursery, but made straightway for the familiar refuge of her Chinese study.

"Leave me," she said to Javotte, who appeared, to help her undress.

When she was alone, she blew out the candles, for she was afraid of seeing her face reflected in the mirror. She remained motionless for a long time, standing in the dark window recess. Through the darkness the scent of fresh flowers was wafted to her from the lovely garden.

Was the black ghost of the Great Lame Man lying in wait for her?

She refused to turn round, to look into herself. 'You left me alone! So what could I do?' she cried to the ghost of her love. She told herself that she would soon be the Marquise du Plessis-Bellière, but there was no joy in her triumph. She only felt broken, shattered.

'What you have done is ignoble, abominable! . . .'

Tears streamed down her cheeks, and with her brow leaning against the windowpane on which a sacrilegious hand had erased the coat-of-arms of the Comte de Peyrac, she wept with little gasps, swearing to herself that these tears of weakness would be the last she'd ever shed.

CHAPTER 80

WHEN MADAME MORENS presented herself at the house in the rue Saint-Antoine the following evening, she had recovered a little of her self-esteem. She was resolved not to let belated scruples jeopardise the consequences of a deed that had been so hard to accomplish. 'The wine is drawn, it must be drunk,' as Maître Bourjus would have said.

So, holding her head high, she walked into a large drawing-room which was lit only by the fire in the hearth. There was no one in the room. She had time to remove her cloak and her mask, and to hold her fingers out to the flames. Although not allowing herself to show any apprehension, she felt that her hands were cold and her heart was beating fast.

A few moments later, a door curtain was raised and an old man, modestly dressed in black, came up to her and bowed deeply. Angélique had not for a moment imagined that the Plessis-Bellières's steward would still be Monsieur Molines. As she recognised him, she uttered a cry of surprise and spontaneously gripped his two hands.

"Monsieur Molines! . . . Is it possible? What a . . . oh, how glad I am to see you again."

"You do me much honour, Madame," he replied, bowing again. "Will you please be seated in this armchair."

He himself sat down near the hearth, in front of a small table on which writing-tablets, an ink-stand and a cup with sand had been placed.

While he was sharpening a pen, Angélique scrutinised him, still amazed by this apparition. He had grown older, but his features remained firm and his eyes sharp and inquisitive. His hair, worn under a black cloth cap, had turned completely white. Angélique could not help visualising at his side the robust figure of her father, who had so often sat down by the fireside of the Huguenot steward to discuss and prepare the future of his nestful of offspring.

"Can you give me news of my father, Monsieur Molines?"

The steward blew away the parings of his goose quill.

"His lordship the Baron is in good health, Madame."

"And the mules?"

"Those of the last season are coming on well. I believe this little business is giving his lordship satisfaction."

Angélique sat at Molines's side, just as she used to when she was a pure young girl, a little intransigent but very upright. Molines had been the one who had arranged her marriage with the Comte de Peyrac. And now she saw him reappear, but this time on behalf of Philippe. Like a spider patiently weaving its web, Molines had always been mixed up in the fabric of her life. It was reassuring to find him again. Was it not a sign that the present was linked again with the past? The peace of her birthplace, the strength drawn from the depths of her family heritage, but also the worries of child-hood, the poor Baron's efforts to set up his progeny, steward Molines's disquieting generosities. . . .

"Do you remember?" she asked dreamily. "You were there, on the night of my wedding at Monteloup. I bore you such a grudge. And yet I have been wonderfully happy, thanks to you."

The old man glanced at her above his big tortoise-shell-rimmed spectacles.

"Are we here to indulge in moving considerations about your first marriage or to discuss the agreement concerning your second one?"

Angélique's cheeks went crimson.

"You are hard, Molines."

"You too are hard, Madame, if I judge by the means you employed to persuade my young master to marry you."

Angélique took a deep breath, but her eyes did not flinch. She felt the time was no more when, first as an intimidated child, then as a poor young girl, she had looked with fear at the almighty steward Molines who held her family's fate in his hands. She was a business woman, whom Monsieur Colbert did not disdain talking to. Her lucid arguments dumbfounded Pennautier, the banker.

"Molines, you once said to me: 'If one wants to reach a goal, one must be prepared to make some sacrifices'. In this case, I am sacrificing something that is rather precious to me: my self-respect. . . . But no matter! I have a goal to reach."

A thin smile drew the old man's stern lips apart.

"If my humble approval can be of any comfort to you, Madame, I give it to you."

It was Angélique's turn to smile. She would always come to an understanding with Molines. This certainty gave her the courage to face discussing the contract.

"Madame," he went on, "let's be precise. The Marquis gave me to understand that grave things are at stake. That's why I shall expound to you the few conditions to which you will have to subscribe. You will then name your conditions. I shall then draw up the contract and read it out before the two parties. First of all, Madame, you undertake to swear on the crucifix that you know the hiding-place of a certain casket, of which his lordship desires to obtain possession. Only after this oath has been taken will the document have any validity."

"I am ready to do so," Angélique affirmed, holding out her hand.

"In a few moments, Monsieur de Plessis will present himself with his chaplain. Meanwhile, let us clarify the position. Being convinced that Madame Morens is the owner of a secret which interests him to a high degree, his lordship the Marquis du Plessis-Bellière agrees to marry Madame Morens, née Angélique de Sancé de Monteloup, against the following considerations: upon the marriage being performed, that is to say immediately after the nuptial blessing, you promise to part with the said casket in the presence of two witnesses, who will probably be the chaplain who will have blessed the marriage and myself, your humble servant. Furthermore, his lordship demands that he be able freely to dispose of your fortune."

"Oh! Just a moment!" Angélique said quickly. "The Marquis will have at his disposal all the money he wants and I am prepared to fix the amount of the allowance I shall pay him annually. But I shall be the sole owner and manager of my assets. I refuse to grant him any share whatsoever in the management of my affairs, for I have no intention, after working so hard, to find myself reduced to beggary. I know the spendthrift genius of those great lords!"

Molines crossed out a few lines and wrote others above them. He then asked Angélique to give him as detailed a statement as possible of the various business affairs she was engaged in. Rather proudly, she informed the steward of her affairs, glad to be able to hold her own in an argument with the old fox and to mention the important personages with whom he could check her statements. This precaution did not shock the young woman, for she had learned, in fighting her way through the intricate maze of finance and commerce, that words are good only in so far as they are supported by verifiable facts. She noticed a glint of admiration in his eyes when she explained to him her position and how she had attained it.

"Admit that I have not done too badly, Monsieur Molines," she concluded.

He nodded his head.

"You are not without merit. I admit that your affairs do not seem to me unskilful. It all depends, of course, on how much you had at your disposal at the outset."

Angélique gave a brief, bitter laugh.

"At the outset? . . . I had *nothing*, Molines, less than nothing. The poverty in which we lived at Monteloup was as nothing compared to that which I knew after the death of Monsieur de Peyrac."

At the mention of that name, they fell silent for a long while. As the fire was going down, Angélique took a log from the wood-box standing near the hearth and put it on the andirons.

"I'll have to talk to you of your mine at Argentière," said Molines at last, in the same equable tone. "It has greatly helped to support your family these last years, but it is only right that, from now on, you should be able, you and your children, to derive a benefit from this output."

"So the mine wasn't impounded and handed over to others, like all the other estates of the Comte de Peyrac?"

"It escaped the greed of the royal inspectors. At the time, it had represented your dowry. Its legal ownership remained somewhat ambiguous. . . ."

"Like all the things you take a hand in, Maître Molines," said Angélique, laughing. "You have a genius for serving several masters."

"Certainly not!" protested the steward. "I have not several masters, Madame. I have several business affairs."

"I grasp the subtle difference, Maître Molines. So let's talk of the business of du Plessis-Bellière the younger. I sign the undertakings I am asked for concerning the casket. I am prepared to examine the necessary amount for his lordship's allowance. In consideration of these advantages, I demand the marriage and to be recognised as the Marquise and sovereign of the estates and titles that appertain to my husband. I also demand to be presented to his relatives and friends as his legitimate wife. I further demand that my two sons find welcome and protection in their stepfather's house. In conclusion, I wish to be informed of the value of the assets he owns."

"Humph! . . . I am afraid you won't find much to comfort you there, Madame. I won't conceal the fact that my young master is deep in debt. Apart from this town house, he owns two castles, one in Touraine which has come down to him from his mother, the other in Poitou. But the estates of both castles are mortgaged."

"Can you possibly have mismanaged your master's affairs, Monsieur Molines?"

"Alas, Madame! Monsieur Colbert himself, who works fifteen hours a day, cannot do anything against the King's wastefulness, which puts all his Minister's calculations at nought. Similarly, the Marquis squanders his revenues, already much decreased by his father's sumptuous style of living, in campaigns of war or Court frivolities. The King has several times made him a present of official appointments of substance which could have produced financial profit. But he hastened to sell them again to pay a gambling debt or to buy a carriage. No, Madame, the du Plessis-Bellière business is not an interesting one for me. I attend to it out of . . . sentimental habit. Allow me to draw up your propositions, Madame."

For a few moments, all that could be heard in the room was the scratching of his pen.

'When I am married,' Angélique reflected, 'Molines will become my manager. How odd! I had never thought of that. He'll certainly try to poke his long fingers into my affairs. I'll have to look out. But, in a way, that'll be fine. I'll have an excellent adviser in him.'

"May I take the liberty to suggest a supplementary clause?" asked Molines, raising his head.

"To my advantage, or to your master's?"

"To yours."

"I thought you were representing the interests of Monsieur du Plessis?"

The old man smiled without answering, and removed his glasses. Then he leaned against the back of his armchair and fixed Angélique with that lively, piercing gaze which he had fastened on her ten years ago when he said: "I think I know you, Angélique, and I shall talk to you differently than to your father. . . .

315

"I think," he said, "that your marrying my master is a very good thing. I did not believe I'd ever see you again. But you are here, in defiance of all probability, and Monsieur du Plessis finds himself under obligation to marry you. Do me the justice to admit, Madame, that I have had nothing to do with the circumstances that have brought about this union. But now it's a question of that union being a success: and this in my master's interests, in yours and, in fact, in mine, for the master's happiness ensures that of the servants."

"I most certainly agree, Molines. So what is this new clause?"

"That you should exact the consummation of the marriage."

"The consummation of the marriage?" repeated Angélique, opening her eyes wide, like a schoolgirl fresh from the convent.

"Why, eh, Madame . . . I hoped you'd gather my meaning."

"Yes . . . I do," stammered Angélique, recovering her wits. "But you've surprised me. It's obvious that in marrying Monsieur du Plessis . . ."

"It's not obvious at all, Madame. In marrying you, Monsieur du Plessis does not make a love match. I might even say he makes a forced marriage. Would it be a great surprise to you if I told you that the feelings you inspire in Monsieur du Plessis, far from resembling love, rather approach a feeling of anger and even of rage?"

"I can imagine," Angelique murmured, shrugging her shoulders in a way that she hoped was casual.

But at the same time she was filled with pain. She cried vehemently:

"What then? . . . Why should I care whether he loves me or not! All I'm asking is his name, his rank. I don't care about the rest. He can despise me and go to bed with farm wenches if he wants to. I won't run after him!"

"You'd be wrong, Madame. I believe you don't know the man you are about to marry very well. Your position, for the time being, is very strong, that's why you think he is weak. But afterwards, you will have to dominate him in some way or other. Otherwise . . ."

"Otherwise? . . ."

"You'll be *horribly unhappy*."

The young woman's face hardened, and she said through clenched teeth:

"I have already been horribly unhappy, Molines. I have no intention of starting all over again."

"That's why I am suggesting a means of defending yourself. Listen to me, Angélique, I am old enough to talk to you plainly. After your marriage, you will have no more power over Philippe du Plessis. The money, the casket, all will be his. Appeals to his heart have no effect on him. You must therefore dominate him by the senses."

"That's a dangerous power, Monsieur Molines, and a very vulnerable one."

"It is a power. It will be for you to render it invulnerable."

Angélique was deeply troubled. She did not dream of being shocked by this advice from the lips of an austere Huguenot. Molines's entire personality was pervaded by a crafty shrewdness which had never taken principles into account but only the fluctuations of human nature in the service of material ends. Molines was sure to be right once again. In a flash, Angélique remembered those fits of fear which Philippe had inspired in her, and that feeling of helplessness in face of his indifference, his frozen calm. She knew that, deep within herself, she had already counted on the wedding night to enslave him. After all, when a woman holds a man in her arms, she is very powerful. There is always a moment when the man's self-defence yields before the lure of sensual rapture. A clever woman knows how to turn that moment to advantage. Later the man will return to this source of pleasure, even despite himself. Angélique knew that, once Philippe's magnificent body was joined to hers, once that fresh, resilient mouth would drop like a fruit on hers, she herself would become the most responsive and skilful mistress. In the anonymous struggle of love, they would develop an understanding which Philippe would perhaps pretend to forget once morning had come, but which would link them more surely to one another than the most fiery declarations.

Her somewhat vacant gaze returned to Molines. He must have followed the thread of her thoughts on her face, for he gave a little ironic smile and said:

"I also think you are beautiful enough to stand a chance of winning. But to win the match requires . . . first having a chance to play it. Which does not mean, incidentally, that you'll necessarily win the first round."

"What do you mean?"

317

"My master does not like women. He's had affairs, of course, but women are a bitter, nauseating fruit for him."

"And yet he's credited with resounding love affairs. And those famous orgies during his foreign campaigns, at Norgen . . ."

"Those are the reflexes of a soldier intoxicated by war. He takes women in the way he sets fire to a house or runs his sword through a child's belly . . . to do evil."

"Molines, you are saying frightening things!"

"I don't want to frighten you, but only to warn you. You are of a noble but healthy and rustic family. You seem to know nothing of the kind of education to which a young gentleman is subjected, one whose parents are rich and fashionable. From the days of his childhood, he is the plaything of maidservants and lackeys, then of noblemen with whom he is placed as a page. In the Italian practices he is taught——"

"Oh! Be silent. All this is most unpleasant," muttered Angélique, gazing away into the fire with embarrassment.

Molines did not persist, and put his glasses on again.

"Am I to add that clause?"

"Add anything you like, Molines. I——"

She broke off as she heard the door open. In the semi-darkness of the drawing-room, the outline of Philippe, clothed in light satins, first appeared like a snowy statue, then gradually became more distinct. White and fair, covered with gold, the young man seemed about to leave for a ball. He greeted Angélique with indifferent arrogance.

"How far have you got, Molines, with your negotiations?"

"Madame Morens is perfectly willing to give the proposed undertakings."

"You are ready to swear on the crucifix that you *really* know the hiding-place of the casket?"

"I can swear it," said Angélique.

"In that case, you may approach, Monsieur Carette. . . ."

A chaplain, whose lean, black figure had remained invisible behind his master's, now stepped forward. He was holding a crucifix, on which Angélique swore that she knew the hiding-place of the casket and that she bound herself to hand it to Monsieur du Plessis after their marriage. Then Molines announced the amount of the allowance which Angélique would later grant her husband. It was a handsome figure. Angélique pulled a little grimace, but did not wince: if her business

318

affairs continued to be sound and flourishing, she would have no difficulty in carrying out her undertakings. On the other hand, once she was the Marquise du Plessis, she would see to it that Philippe's two estates would yield the maximum profit.

Philippe raised no objections. He affected an air of profound boredom.

"Very well, Molines," he said, concealing a yawn. "Try to settle this unpleasant affair as quickly as possible."

The steward coughed and rubbed his hands with embarrassment.

"There is one more clause, Your Lordship, which Madame Morens, here present, has asked me to include in the contract. It's this: the financial conditions will take effect only if the marriage is consummated."

It seemed to take Philippe a few moments to understand, then his face flushed crimson.

"Oh, really!" he said, "oh, really! . . ."

He seemed at such a loss for words that Angélique had that strange feeling of pity and tenderness for him which he sometimes inspired in her.

"That is the last straw!" he breathed at last. "Immodesty joined to impudence!"

He was now white with rage.

"And can you tell me, Molines, how I am to prove to the world that I have honoured the couch of this person? By damaging the maidenhood of a harlot who has already two children and who has dragged herself through the beds of all the musketeers and financiers of the kingdom? . . . By presenting myself before a court of law like that fool Langey who had to try to prove his virility in the presence of ten witnesses?[1] Has Madame Morens notified the witnesses who are to attend the ceremony?"

Molines made a pacifying gesture with both hands.

"I cannot see, Your Lordship, why this clause should put you in such a state. In fact, the clause is, if I may be allowed to say so, as . . . interesting for you as it is for your future spouse. Consider that if, in a fit of ill-temper or out of an understandable grievance, you were to neglect your conjugal duties, Madame Morens would be entitled to claim, in a few months' time, the annulment of the marriage and drag you into

[1] An allusion to a divorce-court action of the period.

a ridiculous and costly lawsuit. I am a member of the Reformed religion, but I think I know that the non-consummation of a marriage is one of the causes of annulment recognised by the Church. Is that not so, Monsieur le Curé?"

"Quite so, Monsieur Molines, the Christian and Catholic marriage has but a single aim: procreation."

"So there!" the steward said softly. Angélique, who knew him well, was the only one who detected his irony. "As for proof of your good intentions," he went on with a slyly ingratiating manner, "I think the best proof will be for your wife to present you quickly with an heir."

Philippe turned towards Angélique, who, during this conversation, had tried to remain impassive. However, when he looked at her, she could not help raising her eyes towards him. The hard expression on the beautiful face caused her an involuntary shiver, which was not one of pleasure.

"All right, it's agreed," Philippe said slowly, while a cruel smile stretched his lips. "We shall do the necessary, Molines, we shall do the necessary. . . ."

At the outset, Philippe had told her that the wedding would take place at Plessis. He did not care to surround the ceremony with any pomp. This suited Angélique perfectly, for it enabled her to retrieve the famous casket without having to take any steps that might have attracted attention. At times she felt a sudden cold sweat at the thought that the casket might perhaps no longer be in the same spot, in the sham turret of the château. Someone might have discovered it. But the thing was unlikely. Who would have thought of crawling along an eave hardly wide enough for a child for the purpose of peeping inside such an insignificant-looking little turret? She also knew that during the past years the Château du Plessis had not been rebuilt in any way. There was every chance, therefore, that she could retrieve the stake of her triumph. At the very hour of her wedding she would be able to hand it to Philippe.

The preparations for the departure for Poitou were frantic. Florimond and Cantor would be taken along, as well as the whole household: Barbe, Flipot, the dogs, the monkey and the parrots. Philippe's suite would follow separately.

Philippe himself affected an air of aloofness from all this to-do. He continued to rush to all the fêtes and Court receptions.

When anybody alluded to his impending marriage, he would raise his eyebrows with an air of astonishment, and then exclaim in a disdainful, supercilious tone: "Why, yes! Indeed!"

During the past week Angélique had not seen him once. In brief notes, transmitted by Molines, he dictated his orders to her. She was to leave on such and such a date. He would meet her on such and such a day. He would arrive with the abbé and Molines. The wedding would take place at once.

Angélique obeyed like a docile wife. She'd see later about making this greenhorn change his tone. After all, she was bringing him a fortune and she had not broken his heart by separating him from that Lamoignon girl. She would make him see that, even though she had been obliged to act somewhat brutally, this business none the less suited the interests of both of them and that his continued sulking was ridiculous.

At once relieved and disappointed at not seeing him, Angélique tried hard not to think too much of her 'fiancé'. The 'Philippe problem' was a thorn-prick amidst her happiness, and when she thought of it, she realised that she was afraid. So it was better not to think of it.

In less than three days the carriages covered the distance between Paris and Poitiers. The roads were quite bad, hollowed out by the spring rains, but there were no accidents, except for a broken axle just outside Poitiers. The travellers stayed in the city for twenty-four hours. Two days later, in the morning, Angélique began to recognise her whereabouts. They were not far from Monteloup. She had to make an effort not to run straight home, but the children were tired and dirty. They had slept the night before in a filthy inn, infested with fleas and rats. To find the least comfort, they had to reach Plessis.

With one arm around the shoulders of her two little boys, Angélique breathed with delight the pure air of the flowering countryside. She wondered how she could have lived for so many years in a city like Paris. She gave shouts of joy and named the hamlets they were passing through, each of which recalled to her mind some incident from her childhood. For days, she had been giving her sons detailed descriptions of Monteloup and the wonderful games one could play there. Florimond and Cantor knew all about the underground passage which used to serve her as a witch's cave, and about the loft with its enchanted nooks and crannies.

At last Plessis loomed up in the distance, white and mysterious on the edge of its pool. To Angélique, who had meanwhile known the sumptuous abodes and palaces of Paris, it seemed smaller than the image engraved in her memory. A few servants presented themselves. Despite the abandon in which the lords of Plessis had left their distant country château, it was, thanks to Molines's care, in a good state of repair. A courier, dispatched a week before, had had the windows opened, and the fresh smell of wax polish vied with the mustiness lurking in the tapestries. But Angélique did not experience the pleasure she had counted on. Her sensations seemed dulled. What she needed, perhaps, was to burst into tears or begin to dance, and shout, and kiss Florimond and Cantor. Unable to indulge in any such frenzy, she felt as if her heart were dead. Unable to bear the excessive emotion of this return, she was so overwhelmed that she failed to have any reaction whatever.

She inquired about the quarters where her children could rest, attended to their settling-in herself and left them only after having seen them washed and clothed in clean, quilted jackets and seated before a light meal of milk and cakes.

Then she asked to be shown to the room in the north wing which she had ordered to be prepared for her, the room of the Prince de Condé.

She had still to accept Javotte's services and to reply to the greetings of the two footmen who were bringing tubs of boiling water into the adjacent bathroom. Absent-mindedly, she replied to their poor French in their dialect. They gaped with surprise on hearing this great lady from Paris, whose clothes must have seemed to them extravagant, express herself in their tongue as if she had learned it in her cradle.

"But I have!" Angélique told them, laughing. "Don't you recognise me? I am Angélique de Sancé. And you, Guillot, I remember that you are from the village of Maubuis, near Monteloup."

The man called Guillot, with whom she had formerly gone on blackberry- and sour-cherry-picking sprees on lovely summer days, gave an ecstatic smile.

"So it's you, Madame, who married our master?"

"It is indeed."

"Well, that will give great pleasure all round. We were rather wondering about who was the new mistress."

So the village people hadn't even been informed. Or rather they had been misinformed, for they thought she was already married.

"Pity you didn't wait till you got here," Guillot continued, nodding his hairy head. "There'd have been such a fine wedding!"

Angélique dared not give Philippe the lie by telling this clumsy oaf Guillot that the wedding would indeed be held at Plessis and that she, for her part, was looking forward to celebrations which would enable her to meet the whole countryside again.

"There'll be feasts all the same," she promised.

Then she rather hurried Javotte in undressing her. When the little lady's-maid had retired, Angélique, wrapped in her silken dressing-gown, went to stand in the middle of the room.

The setting had not changed in over ten years. But Angélique no longer saw it with the dazzled eyes of a little girl. She thought the heavy, blackwood furniture of Dutch style and the massive four-poster frightfully old-fashioned.

The young woman walked over to the window and opened it. She stood appalled when she perceived how narrow the sill was on which she had once climbed so nimbly.

'I have become too fat, I'll never be able to crawl to the turret,' she thought with distress.

Generally, people raved of her slender figure. . . . Angélique that evening realised with bitterness the relentless march of time. Not only was she no longer light enough, but she lacked the agility and simply ran the risk of breaking her neck. Finally she made up her mind to call Javotte back.

"Javotte, my child, you are slim, small and as supple as a reed. Try to climb on to this sill and get to that corner turret. And try not to fall!"

"Yes, Madame," answered Javotte, who would have squeezed through the eye of a needle to please her mistress.

Leaning out of the window, Angélique anxiously followed the girl's progress along the eaves-gutter.

"Look inside the turret. Do you see something there?"

"I see something dark, a box," Javotte promptly replied.

Angélique closed her eyes and had to lean against the casement.

"That's right. Take it and bring it back to me carefully."

A few moments later, Angélique held in her hands the casket

of the monk Exili. A layer of earth caked by the dampness covered it. But it was of sandalwood, and neither animals nor mould had been able to invade it.

"Go now," said Angélique to Javotte in a toneless voice. "And don't talk to anyone of what you've just done. If you hold your tongue, I'll give you a bonnet and a new dress."

"Oh, Madame! Who do you think I'd talk to?" Javotte protested. "I don't even understand the language of these people."

Angélique cleaned the casket. She had some difficulty in working the rusty spring-lock. At last the lid sprang open, and on the bed of leaves appeared the emerald-hued poison phial. After gazing at it, she closed the casket again. Where was she going to hide it pending Philippe's arrival and the moment of handing it to him in exchange for the wedding-ring? She slipped it into the writing-desk from which she had removed it so irresponsibly fifteen years before. 'If only I'd known!' she said to herself.

When the key to the desk was well concealed inside her bodice, she looked around with despair. This place had caused her nothing but grief. On account of the petty theft she had committed, Joffrey, her only love, had been condemned, and their life destroyed! . . .

She forced herself to lie down. But as soon as the chirruping of young voices on the lawns had told her that her children were up, she went down to them and, together with Barbe, Javotte, and Flipot, bundled them into an old cart, which she drove herself. And they were all gaily off to Monteloup.

The sun was setting and shedding saffron beams on the wide green fields where the mules were grazing. The draining of the moors had transformed the landscape. The realm of the waterways under their verdant arches seemed to have shrunk back farther to the west.

But as they passed over the drawbridge, where the turkeys were preening themselves as in the old days, Angélique could see that the castle of her childhood had not changed. The Baron de Sancé, despite the relative affluence he now enjoyed, had not made all the repairs that the decrepit old building needed. The dungeon, and the ramparts with their battlements, were still crumbling under their coat of ivy, and the main entrance still passed through the kitchen.

They found the old Baron beside Fantine, who was peeling onions. The nurse was still as tall and lively as ever, but she had lost her teeth, and her snow-white hair made her face look as brown as that of a Moorish woman.

Was it a delusion? It seemed to Angélique as if there was something a little constrained in the joy with which her father and the old woman welcomed her. They had grieved for her, no doubt, but the fabric of life had gone on weaving without her, and now room had to be made for her afresh.

The presence of Florimond and Cantor dispelled the awkwardness. The nurse wept as she clasped 'those beautiful darlings' against her heart. Three minutes had not passed before the children had red cheeks from her kisses, and their hands full of apples and nuts. Cantor, who had climbed on to the table, was singing his entire repertoire.

"Does the little old lady of Monteloup, the ghost, still walk?" asked Angélique.

"I haven't seen her for a long time," said the nurse, shaking her head. "Ever since Jean-Marie, the last of the family, went away to college, she has not appeared again. I always thought she was looking for a child. . . ."

In the dark hall Aunt Jeanne still reigned in front of her tapestry-loom, like a fat, black spider in the centre of her web.

"She can't hear any more and her brain is unhinged," the Baron explained.

However, after staring at Angélique, the old woman asked in a croaking voice:

"Has the Lame Man come back, too? I thought he'd been burned?"

That was the only allusion anyone made at Monteloup to Angélique's first marriage. They seemed to prefer to leave that part of her life in shadow. For that matter, the old Baron did not seem to be asking himself many questions. As his children went away, got married, came back or didn't, he got them a little mixed up in his mind. He talked a lot of Denis, the officer, and of Jean-Marie, the last-born. He did not give any thought to Hortense and manifestly had no idea what had become of Gontran. As a matter of fact, his chief topic of conversation was still his mules.

When Angélique had been all through the castle, she felt more cheerful. Monteloup had stayed as it was. Everything there was still a little melancholy, a little shabby, but so cordial!

She exulted to see her children settle down in the kitchen just as if they had been born there amid the steam of cabbage soup and Fantine's tales. They begged to be allowed to stay for supper and to sleep there. But Angélique took them back to Plessis, for she feared Philippe's arrival and wanted to be there to receive him.

Next day, as no courier had yet come to announce him, she returned alone to her father's. She walked all over the estate with him, and he showed her all his new arrangements.

It was a lovely, fragrant afternoon. Angélique felt like singing. When they had finished their stroll, the Baron suddenly stopped and began to look at his daughter attentively. Then he gave a sigh.

"So you've come back, Angélique?" he said.

He put his hand on the young woman's shoulder and repeated over and over again, with eyes wet with tears:

"Angélique, my daughter Angélique! . . ."

She answered, deeply moved:

"I have come back, Father, and we'll be able to see each other often. You know that there's going to be my wedding with Philippe du Plessis-Bellière, for which you have sent me your consent."

"But I thought the wedding had already taken place?" he said, astonished.

Angélique compressed her lips and said nothing further. What were Philippe's intentions in making the village people and even her own family believe that the marriage had been celebrated in Paris? . . .

CHAPTER 81

ON THE way back to Plessis she felt perturbed, and her heart beat faster when she recognised the Marquis's carriage in the courtyard.

The lackeys told her that their master had arrived over two hours ago. She hurried towards the château. As she was mounting the stairs, she heard children screaming.

'Yet another tantrum from Florimond or Cantor,' she said to herself, annoyed. 'The country air is making them unmanageable.'

It was important that their future stepfather should not

come to look upon them as insufferable creatures. She rushed towards the nursery to restore order with some severity. She recognised Cantor's voice. He was yelling in a tone of unspeakable terror and fierce barking mingled with his screams.

Angélique opened the door and stood petrified.

In front of the fireplace, in which a big fire was blazing, Florimond and Cantor, huddling against each other, were held at bay by three huge wolfhounds, black as the devil, who were barking ferociously and tugging at their leather leashes, which were held in the hand of the Marquis du Plessis. The latter seemed to be much amused by the children's fright. On the stone floor, in a pool of blood, Angélique recognised the corpse of Parthos, one of the little boys' own mastiffs, who must have been savaged when trying to defend them.

Cantor was yelling, his round face bathed with tears. But Florimond's white face wore an extraordinary expression of courage. He had drawn his little sword and, pointing it towards the animals, was trying to protect his brother.

Angélique had no time to utter an exclamation. A reflex made her seize a heavy wooden stool, and this she flung at the dogs, which yelped and recoiled with moans of pain.

She clasped Florimond and Cantor in her arms. They clung to her. Cantor immediately fell silent.

"Philippe," she said, panting, "you mustn't frighten the children in this way. . . . They might have fallen into the fire. . . . Look, Cantor has burned his hand. . . ."

The young man turned his eyes, hard and limpid as frost, upon her.

"Your sons are as craven as females," he said in a thick voice.

His complexion was darker than usual, and he was tottering slightly.

At that moment Barbe appeared. Out of breath, she was holding a hand over her breast to contain her beating heart. Her eyes passed with an expression of horror from Philippe to Angélique, then stopped at the sight of the dead dog.

"May Madame excuse me," she said. "I went to fetch milk from the pantry for the children's supper. I left them in Flipot's care. I didn't imagine . . ."

"It's nothing serious, Barbe," said Angélique. "The children aren't used to seeing such fierce hounds. They'll have to get used to them if they want to hunt the stag and the wild boar like true gentlemen."

The future gentlemen cast an unenthusiastic glance at the three hounds.

"You are little sillies," she said to them, in a gently scolding tone.

Standing with his legs apart, Philippe, in a bronze velvet travelling costume, was looking at the group of mother and children. Suddenly he cracked his whip over the dogs, pulled them back and left the room.

Barbe hurried to close the door.

"Flipot came to fetch me," she whispered. "The Marquis had chased him out of the room. You'll never get the idea out of my head that he wanted the children to be devoured alive by his dogs. . . ."

"Don't talk rubbish, Barbe," Angélique stopped her curtly. "The Marquis isn't used to children; he wanted to play . . ."

"Yes, yes! The games of princes! We know how far they can go. I know a little fellow who paid dearly for it. . . ."

Angélique shivered at this reminder of Linot. Had not the blond Philippe, with his nonchalant bearing, been among the tormentors of the little cake-seller? Had he not, to say the least, remained indifferent to his entreaties? . . .

Seeing the children were calm again, she went into her apartment. She sat down before her dressing-table to re-arrange her curls.

What was the meaning of what had just happened? Should the incident be taken seriously? Philippe was drunk, that was plain as daylight. Once sober, he would apologise for having caused such a hubbub. . . .

But one of Marie-Agnés's words rose to Angélique's lips: "A brute!"

. . . A cunning, covert, cruel brute. . . . "When he wants to avenge himself on a woman, he stops at nothing."

'Still, he wouldn't go so far as to attack my children,' Angélique thought to herself, throwing down her comb and rising with agitation.

At that very moment the door of the room was flung open. Angélique saw Philippe on the doorstep. He fixed a heavy look upon her.

"Have you the poison casket?"

"I shall hand it to you on our wedding-day, Philippe, as was agreed in our contract."

328

"We are getting married tonight."

"In that case I'll hand it to you tonight," she replied, trying not to show her dismay.

She smiled and held her hand out to him.

"We haven't greeted each other yet. . . ."

"I see no need for it," he replied, and slammed the door behind him.

Angélique bit her lips. Decidedly, the master she had chosen would not prove easy to mollify. Molines's advice came back to her mind: 'Try to subjugate him by the senses.' But for the first time she began to have doubts about her victory. She felt powerless before this frozen man. She had never sensed any desire aroused in him when he was in her presence. She herself, contracted by anguish, no longer felt any attraction towards him.

'He said we would get married tonight. He doesn't know what he's saying. My father hasn't even been advised. . . .'

She was at this stage in her thought, when there was a timid knock on the door. Angélique went to open the door and discovered her sons, still pathetically holding each other tightly. But this time Florimond's protection extended also to the monkey Piccolo, whom he held perched on one arm.

"Maman," he said in a trembling but firm little voice, "we want to go to our grandfather. Here, we are afraid."

"Afraid is a word which a boy who wears a sword mustn't pronounce," said Angélique sternly.

"Monsieur du Plessis has already killed Parthos. Maybe he'll kill Piccolo next."

Cantor began to weep with stifled little sobs. Cantor, the quiet Cantor, upset! This was more than Angélique could bear. It was useless to discuss whether it was silly or not: her children were afraid. And she had sworn to herself that they would never again know fear.

"All right, you will leave with Barbe for Monteloup at once. Only promise me to be good."

"Grandfather promised me he'd let me ride a mule," said Cantor, already comforted.

"Pah! He'll give *me* a horse!" affirmed Florimond.

Less than an hour later, Angélique packed them into the light cart with their servants and wardrobe. There were beds enough at Monteloup to put them up with their suite. The servants themselves seemed glad to be leaving. Philippe's arrival had brought a breathless atmosphere to the white château. The handsome young man, who played the rôle of grace incarnate at the Court of the Sun King, thrust a despot's fist into his lonely domain.

Barbe murmured:

"Madame, we can't leave you here, all alone with this . . . this man."

"What man?" Angélique asked haughtily.

She added:

"Barbe, an easy life has made you forget certain episodes of our common past. Remember that I know how to defend myself."

And she kissed the maid on her round cheeks, for she felt her own heart trembling.

When the jingling of the little equipage had died down in the blue dusk, Angélique walked slowly back towards the château. She was relieved to know that the children would be under Monteloup's protective wing. But the Château du Plessis only seemed more deserted, and almost hostile despite its charming look of a Renaissance trinket.

In the vestibule a lackey bowed to the young woman and informed her that supper was served. She went into the dining-room, where the table was laid. Almost immediately Philippe appeared and, wordlessly, sat down at the table. Angélique took a seat at the opposite end. They were alone, served by two lackeys. A kitchen boy brought the dishes in.

The flames of three torches were reflected in the pieces of precious silverware. Throughout the meal the only sounds were the rattle of spoons and the tinkling of glasses, above which rose the strident call of the crickets on the lawn. Through the open french window could be seen the misty darkness descending upon the countryside.

Angélique ate with a hearty appetite, in obedience to the peculiar promptings of her nature. She noticed that Philippe was drinking a lot but that, far from making him more expansive, the drink only further increased his coldness.

When he rose after refusing the dessert, she had no alternative but to follow him into the adjacent drawing-room. She found Molines and the chaplain there, as well as a very old peasant woman who, as Angélique learned later, had been Philippe's nurse.

"Is everything ready, Chaplain?" asked the young man, emerging from his silence.

"Yes, Your Lordship."

"Let's go to the chapel, then."

Angélique shivered. The wedding, *her* wedding with Philippe, was surely not going to take place under such sinister circumstances?

She protested.

"You don't mean to say that all is ready for our wedding and that it will be celebrated at once?"

"I do mean to say just that, Madame," replied Philippe, with a jeer. "We signed the contract in Paris. So much for the world. The chaplain here will bless us and we'll exchange the rings. So much for God. No other preparations seem necessary to me."

The young woman looked hesitantly at the witnesses to this scene. They were lit by a single torch, held by the old woman. Outside, it was completely dark. The servants had withdrawn. Had it not been for Molines, the hard, grasping Molines, who nevertheless loved Angélique better than his own daughter, Angélique would have feared that she had fallen into an ambush.

Her eyes sought the steward's glance. But the old man dropped his eyes with the particular obsequiousness which he always affected before the lords of Plessis.

Then she resigned herself to her fate.

In the chapel, lit by two thick tapers of yellow wax, a dazed peasant boy, dressed in a choirboy's chasuble, brought the holy water.

Angélique and Philippe knelt on two prayer-stools. The chaplain took his stand in front of them, recited the prayers and customary phrases in a mumbling voice.

"Philippe du Plessis-Bellière, do you consent to take Angélique de Sancé de Monteloup for your lawfully wedded wife?"

"I do."

"Angélique de Sancé de Monteloup, do you consent to take Philippe du Plessis-Bellière for your lawfully wedded husband?"

She said "I do" and held her hand out to Philippe so that he could place the ring on her finger. There flashed through her the memory of the same gesture, performed years ago in the cathedral of Toulouse.

That day, she had been no less trembling, and the hand that had taken hers had pressed it gently as if to reassure her. In her bewilderment, she had not grasped the meaning of that unobtrusive pressure. Now this detail came back to her and tore her heart like a dagger-thrust, as she saw Philippe, half-besotted, blinded by the fumes of wine, vainly groping to slip the ring on her finger. At last he succeeded. It was finished.

They left the chapel.

"Your turn, Madame," said Philippe, looking at her with his insufferable frozen smile.

She understood and asked the group to follow her to her room.

There she took the casket out of the writing-desk, opened it and handed it to her husband. The candlelight played on the flask.

"It is the lost casket indeed," said Philippe after a moment's silence. "Everything is all right, gentlemen."

The chaplain and the steward signed a document whereby they confirmed that they had witnessed the handing over of the casket by Madame du Plessis-Bellière, in accordance with the terms of the marriage contract. Then they bowed once more before the couple and withdrew with small, shuffling steps, preceded by the old woman who was lighting their way.

The panic that gripped Angélique was not only ludicrous, but baseless. Of course, it is never pleasant to have to confront a man's furious rancour. Still, there were ways and means perhaps of reaching an understanding between Philippe and herself, of signing a truce. . . .

She darted a furtive glance at him. Whenever her eyes dwelt on him, in the perfection of his beauty, she felt reassured. He was bending over the redoubtable casket a profile of medal-like purity. His long, thick eyelashes threw a shadow over his cheeks. But he was more flushed than usual, and the strong smell of wine he exhaled was most unpleasant.

Seeing him raise the poison phial with an unsteady hand, Angélique said quickly:

"Careful, Philippe! The monk Exili claimed that a single drop of this poison was enough to cause permanent disfigurement."

"Really?"

He raised his eyes towards her and a wicked glint flashed through his pupils. His hand weighed the phial. In a flash, Angélique realised that he felt tempted to fling it at her face. Though horror-stricken, she did not wince and continued to look at him with a calm and bold expression. He gave a kind of sneer, then put the phial down, shut the casket and put it under his arm. Without a word, he seized Angélique's wrist and dragged her out of the room.

The château was silent and dark, but the moon, which had just risen, cast the reflection of the high windows on to the stone floor.

Philippe's hand held the young woman's frail wrist so tightly that she felt the throbbing of her pulse. But she preferred that. In his château, Philippe took on a consistency which he lacked at Court. That was probably just how he was at war, dropping the cloak of the handsome, dreamy courtier, to reveal his true personality, that of a noble, precise, almost barbarous warrior.

They walked down the stairs, passed through the vestibule and went out into the park. A silvery mist hovered over the pool. On the small marble landing-stage, Philippe pushed Angélique towards a small boat.

"Get in!" he said curtly.

He in turn sat down in the boat and carefully placed the casket on one of the benches. Angélique heard the rope slip, then the skiff slowly glided away from the bank. Philippe had taken one of the oars. He was rowing the boat towards the middle of the pool. The moonlight gleamed on the folds of his white satin costume, on the golden curls of his wig. The frogs had fallen silent. The only sound was made by the sides of the boat rustling against the tight leaves of the water lilies.

When they reached the black, limpid stretch of water in the centre of the pool, Philippe stopped the boat. He looked around attentively. The land seemed far away and the white château, between the two dark cliffs of the park, looked like an apparition. Silently, the Marquis du Plessis lifted in his hands the casket whose disappearance had daunted the days and nights of his family. Resolutely he flung it into the water. The object sank and the ripples that marked the place of its fall faded quickly.

Philippe look at Angélique. She trembled. He changed his place and sat down next to her. This gesture, which at this hour and in this fairy-like setting might have been that of a lover, paralysed her with fear.

Slowly, with that gracefulness which marked all his movements, he raised both his hands and placed them on the young woman's throat.

"And now, I'm going to strangle you, my beauty," he said in an undertone. "You'll go and join your damned little casket at the bottom of the pool!"

She forced herself not to move. He was drunk or mad. In any case, he was capable of killing her. Wasn't she at his mercy? She could neither shout nor defend herself. With an imperceptible movement, she leaned her head against Philippe's shoulder. On her brow she felt the touch of a cheek that had not been shaved since the morning, a moving, masculine cheek. Everything went blank. . . . The moon travelled in the sky, the casket rested at the bottom of the water, the open fields sighed, the last act of the tragedy was being performed. Was it not right that Angélique de Sancé should die thus, by the hand of that young god whose name was Philippe du Plessis?

Suddenly, her breath returned and the grip that was throttling her loosened. She saw Philippe, with clenched teeth, his face convulsed with rage.

"Hell and damnation!" he swore, "will nothing make you lower this damned, proud little head of yours? Will nothing make you scream or beg? . . . Have patience, you'll come to it!"

He flung her back brutally and took the oars again.

As soon as she had set foot on firm ground, Angélique resisted the urge to flee as fast as she could. She no longer knew what she ought to do. Her thoughts were confused.

Philippe watched her with brooding attentiveness in his eyes. This woman was not of a common kind. No tears, no shouts; she did not even tremble. She was still defying him, yet he was the offended one. She had forced his hand, humiliated him as no man can bear to be without wishing the other's death. A gentleman can answer for such a slight with his sword, a knave with his stick. But a woman? . . . What

334

amends could one demand of these slippery, spineless, hypocritical creatures, whose touch was like that of venomous beasts, and who entangled you so cunningly in their words that you found yourself gulled . . . and in the wrong, to boot?

He gripped her arm with the gesture of a wicked jailer and led her back to the château.

As they were mounting the great staircase, she saw him reach out for the long dog-whip that was fastened to the wall.

"Philippe," she said, "let's part here. You are drunk, I believe. Why quarrel any more? Tomorrow . . ."

"Oh no!" he said sarcastically. "Am I not under obligation to fulfil my conjugal duty? But, before that, I want to chastise you a little to make you lose your taste for blackmail. Do not forget, Madame, that I am your master and that I have every power over you."

She wanted to escape, but he held her back and lashed her, as he would have lashed a recalcitrant hound. Angélique gave a scream more of indignation than of pain.

"Philippe, you are mad!"

"You will ask my pardon!" he said, through clenched teeth. "You'll ask my pardon for what you have done!"

"No!"

He pushed her into the room, closed the door behind them and began to strike her with his whip. He knew how to handle it. His office of Master of the Wolf-Hunt was not undeserved.

Angélique had put her arms before her face to protect herself. She recoiled to the wall and turned round with an instinctive gesture. Each stroke made her quiver and she bit her lip so as not to utter a groan. However, she suddenly cried out:

"Enough, Philippe, enough! . . . I ask your pardon."

As he stopped, surprised by his easy victory, she repeated:

"I do ask your pardon. . . . It's true, I've behaved badly towards you."

Irresolutely, he stood motionless. She was still flouting him, balking his rage with a deceptive humility. Cringing bitches, all of them! Overweening in victory, crouching under the lash! But in Angélique's voice there had been something sincere which troubled him. Could it be that she was not like the others, and that the memory engraved in his mind of the the little 'Baroness of the Doleful Dress' was not just a mere semblance?

In the semi-darkness, where the light of the moon contended

with the glow of the torches, the sight of those bruised, white shoulders, that fragile neck, that forehead buried against the wall like that of a penitent child, aroused in him a violent but unfamiliar desire, such as no woman had ever aroused in him. It was not just blind and bestial lust. There was about it a somewhat mysterious, almost sweet and gentle allure.

Short of breath, he flung his whip away, then tossed off his doublet and wig.

Angélique saw him with alarm suddenly half undressed and disarmed, straight as an archangel in the darkness, with his short fair hair, his lace shirt open over his smooth, white chest, his arms flung out in an undecided gesture.

He came towards her, seized her and clumsily buried his mouth in the burning hollow of her throat, on the very spot which still hurt Angélique as a result of his attack in the boat. Now it was her turn to feel bitterly furious. Moreover, though she was upright enough to admit her wrongs, she was too proud to be put, by the treatment just inflicted upon her, into an amorous mood.

She jerked away from the hands of her new husband:

"Oh no! None of that!"

Hearing this cry, Philippe went mad again. He stepped back, raised his fist and struck Angélique full in the face.

She reeled; then, gripping with both hands the lapels of his shirt, she sent him crashing against the wall. For a second he remained dazed. In self-defence she had used the very motions of a tavern wench accustomed to dealing with drunks.

He had never seen a lady of quality defend herself in this way. It struck him as both very funny and exasperating. Did she imagine he was going to give in? . . .

He ground his teeth, then suddenly bounded forward with crafty suppleness, seized her by the neck and savagely knocked her head against the wall.

Under the shock, Angélique half lost consciousness and slid to the ground. She struggled in order not to faint. A certainty had just come over her: at 'The Red Mask' it was Philippe— she was sure of it now—who had stunned her before the others had grabbed her in order to rape her.

The weight of his body flattened her against the icy stone floor. She felt like the prey of a frenzied wild beast, a beast who, after releasing her, was battering her relentlessly, savage-

336

ly. An inhuman pain shot through her back. . . . No woman could suffer this and not die. . . . He was going to maim her, destroy her! . . .

At last, unable to stand it, she uttered a heart-rending scream.

"Mercy, Philippe, mercy! . . ."

He answered with a muffled, triumphant growl. At last she had screamed. At last he found again the only form of love that could content him, the devilish glee of pressing against him a prey taut with pain, a fear-maddened beseeching prey. His lust, heightened by hatred, made him tense as an iron rod. He crushed her with all his might.

When he released her at last, she was almost unconscious.

He gazed at her, sprawling at his feet.

She was not groaning any more, but was dimly trying to recover consciousness. She stirred a little on the floor, like a lovely, wounded bird.

Angélique opened her eyes. He touched her with the tip of his foot and said with a sneer:

"Well, are you satisfied? Goodnight, Madame la Marquise du Plessis."

She heard him move away, knocking against the furniture. Then he left the room.

For a long time she remained lying on the ground, despite the cold which bit into her bare flesh.

She felt wounded to the marrow, and her throat contracted in a childish desire to weep. Despite herself, the memory of her first wedding, under the sky of Toulouse, came back to haunt her. She saw herself lying inert, light-headed and heavy-limbed from a fatigue she had known for the first time. Over her bed leaned the figure of the great Joffrey de Peyrac.

"Poor little hurt thing!" he had said.

But his voice rang with no pity. And suddenly he had begun to laugh, the triumphant, exultant laugh of the man who was the first to set his seal on the flesh of a beloved companion.

'That's why I love him, too!' she had thought at the time. 'Because he is Man incarnate. What does his ravaged face matter! He has the strength and the intelligence, the virility, the subtle intransigence of conquerors—and simplicity, in

337

short all that goes to make a Man, the first of all beings, the master of creation. . . .'

And that was the man she had lost, lost now for the second time! For she dimly felt that Joffrey de Peyrac's spirit was repudiating her. Had she not just been unfaithful to him?

She began to think of death, of the little pool under the water lilies. Then she remembered what Desgrez had said to her:

"Avoid stirring up the ashes that were scattered to the four winds . . . for whenever you think of them, you'll feel a longing for death . . . and I shan't always be there. . . ."

So, on account of Desgrez, on account of her friend the policeman, the Marquise of the Angels once again brushed aside the temptation of despair. She did not want to disappoint Desgrez.

Getting up, she dragged herself to the door, pushed the bolts home, then slumped down in a heap on the bed. It was better not to think too much. Besides, hadn't Molines warned her: "It may be that you'll lose the first round. . . ."

Fever throbbed in her temples, and she did not know how to soothe the burning aches in her body.

In the moonlight there appeared the light phantom of the Gutter-Poet with his pointed hat and his pale hair. She called to him. But he was already fading away. She thought she heard Sorbonne bark and Desgrez's step receding in the distance. . . .

Desgrez, the Gutter-Poet—she mixed them up a little in her mind, the hunter and the hunted; both were the sons of Paris; both were wags and cynics, who studded their low slang with Latin. But however much she clamoured for their presence, they were fading, losing all reality. They no longer were part of her life. A page had turned. She was parted from them for good.

Angélique woke with a start.

She listened. The silence of the forest of Nieul surrounded the white castle. In one of the rooms the handsome torturer must be snoring, dazed with wine. An owl hooted, and its muted call brought with it all the poetry of the night and the woods.

The young woman felt a great calm. She turned over on her pillow and resolutely tried to sleep.

.She had lost the first round, but all the same she *was* the Marquise du Plessis-Bellière.

The morning, however, brought her a fresh disappointment. As she was coming downstairs, having attended to her toilet herself in order to avoid Javotte's inquisitiveness, and after smearing her face with ceruse white and powder in order to conceal the more obvious bruises, she learned that her husband had returned to Paris at dawn. Or rather to Versailles, where the Court was foregathered for the last festivities before the summer campaigns.

Angélique's blood boiled. Did Philippe imagine that his wife would consent to being buried in the provinces while fêtes were in progress at Versailles? . . .

Four hours later, a carriage drawn by six galloping horses hurtled along the bumpy roads of Poitou.

Angélique, stiff and aching but with adamant will-power, was returning to Paris, too. Not daring to face Molines's sharp-eyed glances, she had left him a note in which she commended her children to his care. With Barbe, the nurse, her grandfather and the steward, Florimond and Cantor would have all their hearts' desires. She could set out with her mind at rest.

In Paris she asked Ninon de Lenclos to lodge her. Ninon for the last three months had been faithful to the love she felt for the Duc de Gassempierre. The Duc having gone to Court for a week, Angélique found the seclusion she desired at her friend's house. She spent forty-eight hours lying in Ninon's bed, with a pultice of Peruvian balsam on her face, two alum compresses on her eyelids, her body rubbed with oils and various creams.

She had ascribed the blame for the numerous cuts and bruises which marred her face and shoulders to an unfortunate accident to her coach. The courtesan's tact was such that Angélique herself never knew whether or not she had believed her.

Ninon spoke to her in very natural terms of Philippe, of whom she had caught a glimpse on his return, on his way to Versailles. A most delightful programme of entertainments had been planned for the Court season: ring-tilting, ballets, comedies, fireworks and other most amusing inventions. The city rang with the chatter of those who had been invited and with the teeth-gnashings of those who had not.

Sitting at Angélique's bedside Ninon talked endlessly so that her patient might not feel tempted to speak, for she needed complete quiet in order to restore her lily-and-rose complexion. Ninon said that she had no regrets at not knowing Versailles, where her reputation barred her admittance. Her domain was elsewhere, in this little mansion in the Marais district, where she was truly a queen and not a follower. She was quite content to know that, when talking of one or another incident in the alcoves or at Court, the King would sometimes ask: "And what does the lovely Ninon say about it?"

"When you are being fêted at Versailles, will you forget me, my dear?" she asked.

Angélique, under her poultices, shook her head.

CHAPTER 82

ON THE twenty-first of June 1666, the Marquise du Plessis-Bellière set out for Versailles. She had no invitation, but, to make up for it, she was endowed with a boldness second to none.

Her carriage, lined with green velvet inside and out, with gold braids and fringes, the body and wheels gilded all over, was drawn by two big, dappled horses.

Angélique was wearing a sage-green brocade dress with a big silver flower-design and, by way of jewellery, a magnificent necklace of several rows of pearls.

Her hair, dressed by Binet, was also adorned with pearls and with two immaculate dainty feathers like a film of snow. Her face, very carefully made-up but without exaggeration, no longer showed a trace of the violence she had been subjected to a few days before. All that remained was a blue mark on her temple, which Ninon had concealed with a heart-shaped taffeta patch. With another, smaller beauty spot at the corner of her lip, Angélique looked perfect.

She put on her Vendôme gloves, opened her hand-painted fan and, leaning out of the carriage window, cried:

"To Versailles, coachman!"

Anxiety and joy made her so nervous that she had taken Javotte with her so as to be able to chat during the journey.

"We are going to Versailles, Javotte!" she kept repeating to the young girl, who sat facing her in a muslin bonnet and an embroidered apron.

"Oh! I've been here before, Madame. With the galley of Saint-Cloud, on a Sunday . . . to see the King at supper."

"That's not the same thing, Javotte. You cannot understand."

The journey seemed interminable to her. The road was bad, deeply rutted by the procession of two thousand wagons which passed over it every day in both directions, transporting stones and plaster for the building of the palace.

"We shouldn't have taken this road, Madame," Javotte was saying, "but gone by way of Saint-Cloud."

"No, that would have taken too long."

Every few moments, Angélique put her head out of the window at the risk of destroying Binet's artistic construction and getting herself splashed with mud.

"Hurry, coachman, for heaven's sake! Your horses are like snails."

But she already saw looming on the horizon a high, rosy cliff flashing with sparks and which seemed to glisten with all the sunbeams of the spring morning.

"What is that, coachman?"

"That is Versailles, Madame."

A line of newly-planted trees shaded the far end of the avenue. At the approaches to the first gate, Angélique's carriage had to stop to give way to an equipage which was arriving at breakneck speed from the Saint-Cloud road. The red coach, drawn by six bays, was escorted by horsemen. It was said that it was the Petit Monsieur. The carriage of Madame followed with six white horses.

Angélique ordered her carriage to drive in after them. She no longer believed in unlucky encounters, in evil spells. She was walking on air, enjoying a kind of immunity. A certainty, stronger than all fears, assured her that her hour of triumph was near.

She waited, however, until the hubbub caused by the arrival of those two great personages had subsided a little. Then she alighted from the carriage and proceeded towards the marble courtyard.

Flipot, in the du Plessis household livery—blue and jonquil —held the train of her mantle.

"Don't wipe your nose on your sleeve," she told him. "Don't forget that we are at Versailles."

"Yes, Marquise," sighed the former ragamuffin from the Court of Miracles, as he looked all around him, gaping with admiration.

Versailles had not yet the crushing majesty which was conferred on it by the two white wings added on by Mansard towards the end of the reign of Louis XIV. It was a fairyland palace, rising on a slender knoll with its gay pink and poppy-red architecture, its wrought-iron balconies, its high, bright chimneys. The pinnacles, ridge ornaments, leads and chimney-pots of its roofs were entirely gilded with gold-foil, and sparkled like the jewels that adorn a precious casket. The new slate, according to whether its angles reflected light or shade, had a black velvety depth or the sparkle of silver, and the sharp outlines of the roofs seemed to melt into the azure of the sky.

There was a great bustle all around the château, for the multi-coloured liveries of the footmen and lackeys mingled with the dark smocks of the workmen who were coming and going with their wheelbarrows and tools. The singing noise of chisels hammering on stone answered the drums and fifes of a company of musketeers who were parading in the centre of the great court.

Angélique saw no familiar faces as she gazed around her. Finally she walked into the château through a door in the left wing, where there seemed to be much coming and going. A vast coloured marble staircase led her into a large room crammed with a throng of rather plainly-dressed people who looked at her with astonishment. She made inquiries and was told that she was in the Guards' room. Every Monday, petitioners came here to hand in their requests or seek a reply to their preceding ones. At the back of the room, above the fireplace, a gold and silver-gilt ship represented the person of the King, but it was hoped that His Majesty would make a personal appearance, as he sometimes did.

Angélique, with her plumes and her page, felt out of place among these old troopers, these widows and orphans. She was about to withdraw when she noticed Madame Scarron. She flung her arms around her neck, delighted at last to meet a familiar face.

"I am looking for the Court," she said, "my husband must be at the King's levée and I want to join him."

Madame Scarron, more impoverished and unassuming than ever, seemed ill-chosen at first sight to inform her of the courtiers' whereabouts. But, after haunting for so long the royal anterooms in her quest for a pension, the young woman was actually better acquainted with the detailed time-table of the Court than the Court gazetteer Loret himself, whose task it was to record their doings hour by hour.

Very obligingly, Madame Scarron led Angélique to another door, which opened on to a kind of vast balcony, beyond which the gardens could be glimpsed.

"I believe the King's levée is over," she said. "He has just gone into his cabinet, where he will converse for a few moments with the Princesses of the blood. Afterwards he will go down into the gardens, unless he comes here first. In any case, the best course for you to take is to follow this open gallery. At the very end, on your right, you will find the anteroom which leads into the King's cabinet. Everybody will be there at this hour. You will find your husband without difficulty."

Angélique darted a glance at the long balcony, where she saw only some Swiss guards.

"I am dying of fear," she said. "Won't you come with me?"

"Oh! my dear, how could I?" Françoise stammered aghast, glancing with embarrassment at her shabby outfit.

Only then did Angélique realise the contrast between their dresses.

"Why are you here as a petitioner? Have you still got money worries?"

"More than ever, alas! The Queen Mother's death resulted in my pension being suppressed. I've come in the hope of getting it restored. Monsieur d'Albert has promised me his support."

"I do hope you'll succeed. I am so very sorry. . . ."

Madame Scarron smiled very sweetly and stroked her cheek.

"You mustn't be. It would be a pity. You look so happy! Besides, you deserve your happiness, my dear. I am delighted to see you looking so beautiful. The King is very sensitive to beauty. I have no doubt that he will be charmed by you."

'I am beginning to have my doubts,' thought Angélique, whose heart started to beat a wild tattoo. The magnificent setting of Versailles spurred her to carry her boldness to its limit. She was mad, of course. But never mind! She was not going to act like the runner who breaks down a few yards from his goal. . . .

Smiling at Madame Scarron, she plunged into the gallery, walking so fast that Flipot panted behind her. When she had got half way, a group appeared at the other end. Even at that distance, Angélique had no trouble in distinguishing, walking in the centre of the courtiers, the majestic figure of the King.

His stature heightened by his red heels and his abundant wig, Louis XIV stood out from the others by his admirable bearing. Moreover, none knew better than he how to use those tall canes for which he had set the fashion, and which had hitherto been reserved for the old and disabled. He turned these canes into instruments of self-assurance, of beautiful postures and even, in his own case, of allurement.

So he advanced, leaning on his ebony cane with its gold pommel, exchanging playful words with the two Princesses who were at his sides: Henriette of England and the young Duchesse d'Enghien. Today the official favourite, Louise de La Vallière, did not take part in the promenade. The poor girl was becoming less and less decorative. On these beautiful mornings Versailles, bursting with all its splendours, seemed to stress the pallor and emaciation of Mademoiselle de La Vallière. It was as well that she stayed in her retreat, where the King would presently go to see her and inquire after her health.

The morning was really lovely and Versailles marvellous. But wasn't that the goddess of spring herself who was coming towards the sovereign in the shape of an unknown woman? . . . The sunshine spread a halo around her, and her jewels were dripping down to her waist like pearls of dew. . . .

Angélique had realised immediately that if she turned back now, she would cover herself with ridicule. So she continued to advance, but ever more slowly, with that strange sensation of helplessness and fatality which one sometimes has in a dream. In the surrounding haze she no longer saw anyone but the King. She looked at him fixedly, as if drawn by a magnet.

Had she wanted to drop her eyes, she could not have done it. She was now as close to him as she had once been in the gloomy room at the Louvre when she had faced up to him, and everything went blank for her except that terrible memory.

She was not even conscious of the spectacle she offered, alone in the middle of this sun-bathed gallery in her magnificent attire and her radiant, full-blown beauty.

Louis XIV had stopped, and so had the courtiers behind him. Lauzun, who had recognised Angélique, bit his lips and concealed himself behind the others, jubilantly. They were about to witness something surprising!

Very courteously, the King doffed his hat trimmed with fiery plumes. He was easily moved by the beauty of women, and the calm boldness with which this one was gazing at him with her emerald eyes, far from displeasing him, completely charmed him. Who was she? . . . How had he failed to notice her before? . . .

Meanwhile, obeying an unconscious reflex, Angélique dropped a deep curtsy. Now, half kneeling, she would have wished never to rise again. She straightened up, however, her eyes irresistibly drawn to the King's face. Despite herself, she was gazing at him provocatively.

The King was astounded. There was something unusual in the attitude of this strange woman and also in the surprised silence of the courtiers. He glanced around him, his brow slightly knit.

Angélique thought she was going to swoon. Her hands began to tremble in the folds of her dress. She was drained of all strength, she was lost.

It was then that someone's fingers took hers, gripped them so hard she could have screamed, and Philippe's voice said very calmly:

"Sire, may Your Majesty grant me the honour of presenting to him my wife, the Marquise du Plessis-Bellière."

"Your wife, Marquis?" said the King. "This is surprising news. I heard some mention of the matter, but was expecting that you would come to inform me of it yourself."

"Sire, it had not seemed necessary to me to inform Your Majesty of such a trifle."

"A trifle? A marriage! Take care, Marquis, lest Monsieur Bossuet hear you! . . . And these ladies! By Saint Louis, even after all the time I've known you, I still wonder at times what stuff you are made of. Do you know that your discretion towards me amounts almost to insolence? . . ."

"Sire, I am distressed that Your Majesty should thus interpret my silence. It was such an unimportant matter!"

"Be silent, sir. Your lack of feeling is beyond limit, and I shall not permit you to indulge in such vile speech before this charming person, your wife. Upon my word, you are just a hard-bitten soldier. Madame, what do you think of your husband?"

"I shall try to make do with him, Sire," answered Angélique, who had recovered during this dialogue.

The King smiled.

"You are a sensible woman. And a most beautiful one, moreover. The two don't always keep company! Marquis, I forgive you on account of your excellent choice . . . and her lovely eyes. Green eyes . . . a rare colour which I have not often had an opportunity to admire. Women with green eyes are . . ."

He broke off, mused for a moment, while attentively scanning Angélique's face. Then his smile faded, and the monarch's whole figure seemed to become transfixed as if struck by lightning. Before the eyes of the courtiers, first perplexed then frightened, Louis XIV was growing pale. The phenomenon could not escape anyone, for the King had a ruddy complexion and his surgeon frequently had to bleed him. Now, however, within a few seconds, he became as white as his shirt-ruffle, although not a feature stirred in his face.

Angélique, distraught, looked at him again and defiantly, despite herself, as guilty children sometimes look at the person who will mete out punishment to them.

"Are you not a native of the south, Madame?" the King asked abruptly. "From Toulouse?"

"No, Sire, my wife is a native of Poitou," Philippe said promptly. "Her father is the Baron de Sancé de Monteloup, whose estates are in the neighbourhood of Niort."

"Oh! Sire, to confuse a Poitevine with a southern lady!" exclaimed Athénaïs de Montespan, bursting into her lovely laughter. "You, Sire! . . ."

The beautiful Athénaïs already felt firmly enough in favour not to shrink from an audacious remark of this kind. It helped to dispel the embarrassment. The King recovered his natural colour. Always in control of himself, he cast an amused glance at Athénaïs.

"It is true that the ladies of Poitou have very great charm," he sighed. "But take care, Madame, lest Monsieur de Montespan be obliged to compare himself with all the Gascons of Versailles. They might wish to avenge the insult to their women."

"Is it an insult, Sire? If so, it is quite unintentional. I only meant that though the charms of both races are alike in quality, they are not likely to be confused. May Your Majesty pardon my humble remark."

The smile in the big blue eyes was nothing less than contrite, but it was certainly irresistible.

"I have known Madame du Plessis for many years," Madame de Montespan continued. "We were brought up together. Her family is related to mine. . . ."

Angélique promised herself never to forget her debt to Madame de Montespan. Whatever the motives which actuated the beautiful Athénaïs, she had none the less saved her friend.

The King bowed again, with an appeased smile, before Angélique du Plessis.

"Very well! . . . Versailles is happy to receive you, Madame. Be welcome."

In a lower tone, he added:

"We are glad to see you again."

Angélique then understood that he had recognised her, but that he was accepting her and wanted to blot out the past.

For the last time, the fire of a stake seemed to flare up between them. Prostrated in a deep curtsy, the young woman felt a flood of tears swelling her eyelids.

Thank heaven, the King had resumed his walk. She was able to rise, furtively wipe her eyes and cast a somewhat constrained glance in Philippe's direction.

"How can I thank you, Philippe? . . ."

"Thank me!" he gnashed under his breath, his jaw tense with anger. "Why, I was defending my name from ridicule and disgrace! . . . You are my wife, hang it! I beg you to remember it henceforward. . . . To arrive at Versailles in this manner! Without an invitation! Without being presented! . . . And you were staring at the King with such insolence! . . . Will nothing ever crush your infernal cheek! I should have killed you the other night."

"Oh, please, Philippe, don't spoil this lovely day!"

In the wake of the other courtiers, they had arrived in the gardens. The blue shimmer of the sky merging with that of the playing fountains, the sparkle of the sunshine gleaming on the smooth surface of the great ponds of the first terrace, dazzled Angélique.

She thought she was walking in the midst of a paradise where all was light and orderly as in the Elysian Fields.

From the top of the steps shaped like a rounded pyramid which towered over a pond, she could see the pattern of the rows of tall trees surrounded by a garland of white marble statues. The flowerbeds scattered their scintillating carpets over the park all the way to the horizon.

With her hands clasped before her lips in a gesture of childish fervour, Angélique remained motionless, gripped with an ecstasy in which the enthusiasm of her dreams mingled with genuine admiration.

A light breeze stirred the white feathers of her coiffure against her brow.

At the bottom of the flight of stairs, the King's carriage had come to a halt. But just as he was about to step into it, he turned back and mounted the steps again. Angélique suddenly found him at her side. He was alone beside her, for, with an imperceptible gesture, he had motioned his entourage to keep at a distance.

"You are admiring Versailles, Madame?" he asked.

Angélique dropped a curtsy and replied very gracefully:

"Sire, I thank Your Majesty for having placed so much beauty before the eyes of your subjects. History will owe you a debt of gratitude."

Louis XIV remained silent for a moment.

"You are happy?" he asked at last.

Angélique turned her eyes away and, in the sun and the breeze, she suddenly felt younger, just like a young girl who had known no grief or anguish.

"How can one fail to be happy at Versailles?" she murmured.

"Don't weep any more, then," said the King. "And give me the pleasure of accompanying me on my promenade. I want to show you the park."

Angélique put her hand into that of Louis XIV. With him she descended the steps of the pond of Latone; the courtiers bowed as they passed.

When she had sat down next to Athénaïs de Montespan, facing the two Princesses and His Majesty, she caught a glimpse of her husband's face.

Philippe was looking at her with an enigmatic expression which was not lacking in interest. Was he beginning to realise that he had married a real phenomenon?

Angélique could have floated, she felt so light. The future, to her eyes, was as blue as the horizon. She was saying to herself that her sons would never again know poverty. They would be brought up at the Academy of Mont-Parnasse and would become gentlemen. Angélique herself would be one of the most fêted women at Court.

And, since the King had expressed this wish, she would try to erase from her heart all traces of bitterness. Deep in her heart, Angélique knew that the flame of the love which had consumed her, that dreadful flame which had also consumed her love, would never die out. It would last all her life. The woman Voisin had said so.

But fate, which is not unjust, wanted Angélique to rest for a while on the enchanted knoll, in order to gather fresh strength in the intoxication of her success and the triumph of her beauty.

Later, she would return to the path of her adventurous life. But today she no longer had any fears. *She was at Versailles!*

Angélique

'The intrepid, passionate and always
enchanting heroine of the most
fantastically successful series of historical
romances ever written.'
DAILY HERALD

These novels by SERGEANNE GOLON
comprise a tremendous saga of
17th-century France, tracing Angélique's
career from childhood through a series of
strange marriages and amorous adventures,
perils and excitements, unequalled in the
field of historical fiction. Translated into
most European languages, a sensational
runaway success in France, Angélique is
one of the world's most fabulous best-sellers.

The most ravishing — and surely the most
ravished — heroine of all time.

Winner of the Prix Goncourt

MAURICE DRUON

THE IRON KING 5/-

Set against the exciting but cruel fourteenth
century, here are the last few months of the
tremendous reign of Philip IV, the tyrant who
was also known as Philip the Fair.

Here too is the tragic story of Philip's two
adulterous daughters ; the war waged against
the chivalrous institution of the Knights
Templar ; the sadism and obsessions which
ruled this ruthless monarch.

'Dramatic, highly coloured, barbaric,
sensual, teeming with life' *Times Literary Supplement*

THE STRANGLED QUEEN 3/6

Louis X, fourteenth-century King of
France, was puny, pusillanimous, semi-
impotent, vacillating between self-pity
and vainglory.

He imprisoned his wife for adultery.
But without a Pope, the marriage
could not be annulled. Louis was
prepared to go to any lengths to
get his way and a new wife—
even murder . . .

'A scrupulous regard for historical
fact fired by a lively imagination
makes a fine novel' *Evening Standard*

A series of historical novels in the lusty, turbulent tradition of *Angélique*

JULIETTE BENZONI

One Love is Enough 5/-

Set in fifteenth-century France against the horrors of the Hundred Years War, the squalid Cour de Miracles in Paris, and the magnificent Burgundy Court, this novel tells of Catherine Legoix. She was a lovely and desirable woman, virgin wife of the Court Treasurer, unwilling mistress of a Duke, and in love with a man she could not hold...

Catherine 6/-

In this turbulent sequel, Catherine follows her lover all over France, encountering adventure, brutality and the lust of greedy men.

PIERRE SABBAGH and ANTOINE GRAZIANI

Fanina 5/-

She was chosen to become a vestal virgin. Should she break her vows of chastity, she faced being buried alive. But when she met a blue-eyed young man from Gaul, she found her life and her values changing. Set in Ancient Rome during the reign of the wicked Emperor Tiberius, this book lays bare the corruption, cruelty and superstition of a bygone age.